A TICKET TO OBLIVION

By Edward Marston

THE BRACEWELL MYSTERIES

The Queen's Head • The Merry Devils • The Trip to Jerusalem
The Nine Giants • The Mad Courtesan • The Silent Woman
The Roaring Boy • The Laughing Hangman • The Fair Maid of Bohemia
The Wanton Angel • The Devil's Apprentice • The Bawdy Basket
The Vagabond Clown • The Counterfeit Crank
The Malevolent Comedy • The Princess of Denmark

THE RAILWAY DETECTIVE SERIES

The Railway Detective • The Excursion Train
The Railway Viaduct • The Iron Horse
Murder on the Brighton Express • The Silver Locomotive Mystery
Railway to the Grave • Blood on the Line
The Stationmaster's Farewell • Peril on the Royal Train
A Ticket to Oblivion

Inspector Colbeck's Casebook:
Thirteen Tales from the Railway Detective

The Railway Detective Omnibus:
The Railway Detective, The Excursion Train, The Railway Viaduct

THE CAPTAIN RAWSON SERIES

Soldier of Fortune • Drums of War • Fire and Sword
Under Siege • A Very Murdering Battle

THE RESTORATION SERIES

The King's Evil • The Amorous Nightingale • The Repentant Rake
The Frost Fair • The Parliament House • The Painted Lady

THE HOME FRONT DETECTIVE SERIES

A Bespoke Murder • Instrument of Slaughter
Five Dead Canaries

A TICKET TO OBLIVION

EDWARD MARSTON

Allison & Busby Limited
12 Fitzroy Mews
London W1T 6DW
www.allisonandbusby.com

First published in Great Britain by Allison & Busby in 2014.

A CIP catalogue record for this book is available from
the British Library.

First Edition

ISBN 978-0-7490-1427-8

Typeset in 12.25/16.5 pt Adobe Garamond Pro by
Allison & Busby Ltd.

The paper used for this Allison & Busby publication
has been produced from trees that have been legally sourced
from well-managed and credibly certified forests.

Printed and bound by
CPI Group (UK) Ltd, Croydon, CR0 4YY

To
John Swift QC
friend and former Rail Regulator
with whom I enjoyed many happy times and
wonderful arguments at the Oxford college
featured in this novel

CHAPTER ONE

Summer, 1858

As the landau rolled on through the Worcestershire countryside, the passengers were unusually quiet. Vernon Tolley was surprised. When the coachman had driven them to the railway station before, there'd been continuous conversation. The piercing voice of Lady Burnhope had always risen effortlessly above the clip-clop of the horses and the scrunching of the wheels on the hard track. Without her characteristic bray to listen to, there'd be no gossip for Tolley to share with the other servants when he got back to Burnhope Manor. Though he strained his ears, he could pick up nothing from those behind him. Because it was the first time she'd made this journey without her mother, he'd expected Imogen Burnhope to be excitedly talkative. The trip to Oxford was in the nature of an adventure for her yet it produced no cheerful banter between Imogen and her maid. She and Rhoda Wills were apparently content to do little more than exchange smiles, converse with gestures and enjoy the beauty of the landscape.

Imogen was a striking young woman of twenty with a shapely figure, a natural elegance and a face of such exaggerated loveliness that it turned the heads of men and women alike. Even when partially hidden beneath a poke bonnet trimmed with flowers, her features were arresting. Rhoda, by contrast, cut a more homely figure, pleasantly plain and with a body that could best be described as endearingly plump. Ten years older than her companion, she was as much a trusted friend as a servant. When they were alone together in the back of the landau, the barriers between them were removed in a way that the haughty Lady Burnhope would never have tolerated.

It was only when Shrub Hill station came into sight that Imogen spoke aloud.

'We've got here!' she said with relief. 'I had this dreadful feeling that Mother would change her mind at the last moment and either come with us or insist that we abandoned the visit altogether.'

'Lady Burnhope is in no fit state to travel,' Rhoda reminded her. 'You heard what the doctor advised. She's to have complete rest.'

'Mother would have preferred it if I'd stayed to look after her.'

'She has servants to do that – not to mention Sir Marcus.'

Imogen stifled a bitter laugh. 'Father is hopeless at looking after anyone,' she said. 'Whenever I was ill as a child, he never came anywhere near me. He's wedded to politics. The only thing that concerns him is his next speech to Parliament.' The town clock chimed and she brightened instantly. 'That's eleven o'clock. We got here in perfect time.'

'You can always rely on Vernon. He never lets us down.'

Tolley savoured the compliment. Socially and otherwise, the tall, graceful Imogen was totally beyond his reach and the most that he could do was to steal an admiring glance at her. Rhoda, however, was a very different matter. He found her appealing, warm-hearted and delightfully companionable. More to the point, she came from the same stock as himself. A few years older than her, Tolley had nurtured hopes for some time. Rhoda had kept him politely at arm's length until now but he was prepared to wait.

When he brought the landau to a halt outside the station, he beckoned a porter over and indicated the luggage. While the man began to unload it, Tolley jumped down onto the pavement so that he could open the carriage door, flip down the step and help the passengers to alight. He felt only the lightest of touches as Imogen held his hand but, when it was her turn, Rhoda gave his fingers a squeeze of gratitude reinforced with a smile. He would have fond memories of both on the drive back home.

Opened in 1850, Shrub Hill still had an air of novelty about it for Imogen and Rhoda. Regular travellers in Worcester might take their station for granted but that was not the case with the two women. The only time they ever got to see the compact shape of Shrub Hill was on their twice-yearly visits to Oxford. For the most part, their lives were circumscribed by the limits of the Burnhope estate and, generous as those limits undoubtedly were, they could nevertheless resemble the confines of a wooded prison. As they adjourned to the comfort and privacy of the waiting room, Imogen and Rhoda both experienced a sense of release. They were free.

Under the direction of Tolley, the porter positioned

himself at a point on the platform where the first-class carriages would stop. Though it stretched for less than ninety miles between its termini, the Oxford, Worcester and Wolverhampton Railway had, in its relatively short existence, been a boon to those within reach of one of its many stations and halts. In this instance, however, it was only serving the three major communities. Having set off from the industrial haze of Wolverhampton, the express train was due to make a single stop at Shrub Hill before powering on to Oxford General station. It was late but punctuality had never been the company's strongpoint. In fact, the OWWR had been plagued by problems since its inception and a woeful timekeeping record was only one of them. As soon as he heard the train's clamorous approach, Tolley strode quickly across to the waiting room to alert Imogen and Rhoda. They were on their feet at once and followed him down the platform to where their luggage stood. The porter tipped his hat to them.

The train steadily lost speed as it clanked into the station. Imogen was thrilled to see the name on the locomotive's boiler – *Will Shakspere*. In the past, she'd been lucky enough to see some of Shakespeare's plays performed and had studied others when educated by a governess with literary inclinations. There was also a more personal reason why Shakespeare had a special place in her heart. A locomotive that bore a variant of his name was a good omen. She couldn't wait to get aboard.

The porter had intended to ingratiate himself by opening the door of an empty compartment for them but Tolley reserved that task for himself, darting forward the moment that the train came to a halt. Before Imogen stepped aboard, she asked for the valise to be put inside the compartment. The porter was told to put the heavier luggage on the roof. Tolley took the liberty of putting an arm around Rhoda's waist as he eased her into the carriage and he was rewarded with a second smile. Having secured the luggage on the rack above, the porter joined him and beamed when Imogen reached out to press a coin into his hand. A second coin was given to Tolley who touched his forelock in acknowledgement. Imogen resumed her seat, leaving the porter to close the door and gaze in wonderment at her through the window.

'She gets prettier every time I sees her,' he observed with a sigh.

'Yes,' said Tolley, eyes fixed on Rhoda, 'that she does.'

There was a slamming of doors, a cacophony of hissing steam, belching smoke, raised voices and rattling carriages, then *Will Shakspere* headed off on the fifty-seven mile run to Oxford. Vernon Tolley stood there until the train vanished from sight, his mind filled with promising thoughts of Rhoda Wills. Desire stirred in his breast. He vowed that she would one day be his. As he sauntered back to his carriage, he was quite unaware of the significant part he'd just played in her life.

Cassandra Vaughan was impatient at the best of times and the delay made her even tetchier. Standing on the platform at Oxford General station, she peered angrily down the line as if demanding that the train appear. Cassandra was a middle-aged woman of middle height and a spreading girth that was cleverly concealed by her dressmaker. Handsome in repose, she looked quite forbidding when roused. Her daughter, Emma, stood meekly beside her. She was a slim, self-effacing young woman with something of her mother's features but none of her outspokenness.

'This is disgraceful!' said Cassandra, irritably.

'Yes, Mother.'

'Why can't the trains run on time?'

'It's only twenty minutes late,' her daughter pointed out.

'It's nearer half an hour, Emma. I shall write another letter.'

'Yes, Mother.'

'What's the point of building a railway when it constantly lets one down?'

Emma knew better than to argue with her mother. She was just as disappointed with the long wait but she did not vent her spleen on the railway company. Her abiding concern was for her cousin, Imogen, who would probably be fretting in a stuffy carriage. While her mother thought only of herself, the considerate Emma was hoping that Imogen would not be too discomfited. She loved her cousin dearly and had spent weeks looking forward to the visit. The fact that Lady Burnhope would not be coming to Oxford meant that Imogen and Emma would be able to spend more time alone together, liberated from the surveillance of the older woman. It served to sharpen Emma's anticipatory pleasure.

'Where the devil is it?' snapped Cassandra.

'I don't know, Mother.'

'It's supposed to be an express train, for heaven's sake! They'd have got here sooner had they walked. Oh, this is intolerable,' she went on, clicking her tongue then looking around for someone to blame. 'Where's the stationmaster? Why doesn't the fellow *do* something?'

'It's not his fault,' said Emma.

'Well, someone should be held responsible.'

'The train will be here soon.'

Cassandra stamped a foot. 'Stop saying that, Emma! It's driving me insane.'

'I'm sorry, Mother.'

'And don't keep apologising all the time.'

Before her anger could spill over into a full-blown rage, Cassandra heard a noise that made her start. The distant thunder of the train was accompanied by clouds of smoke curling up over the trees. *Will Shakspere* finally came into view, puffing bravely as it rattled along. There was a collective sigh of relief from the crowd on the platform. Several people had gathered there, either to welcome passengers who got off the train or to climb aboard for the return journey. Cassandra summoned a porter with a regal wave. Emma was elated, standing on her toes and ready to wave the moment she clapped eyes on her cousin. Her mother couldn't resist the temptation to complain to the driver and fireman as they rolled past on the footplate but her words were lost in the pandemonium.

Carriage after carriage went past but Emma could see neither Imogen nor her maid. When the train juddered to a halt, she jerked her head to and fro so that she could cover both ends of the platform. Wanting to embrace her cousin by way of a greeting, she searched the sea of faces emerging from the carriages. Cassandra was equally alert, eager to welcome her niece before going off to confront the driver of the locomotive. In fact, she did neither. Though she and her daughter waited for some time, there was no sign of the visitors from Burnhope Manor. The platform was thronged for a couple of minutes, then people gradually dispersed or boarded the train. Cassandra and Emma were left alone to walk the length of the platform so that they could look into every carriage. The fruitless search left them utterly dismayed.

'They would surely have travelled first class,' decided Cassandra.

'Yet they didn't get out of any carriage, first or otherwise.'

'Where on earth can Imogen be?'

'Perhaps they missed the train, Mother,' Emma surmised.

'Don't be ridiculous. Your aunt would have taken great care that they got to the station in time. They must have been on board.'

'Then where are they?'

Her mother was vengeful. 'I don't know,' she said, taking a last look up and down the train, 'but someone will suffer for this. I simply won't stand for it!'

CHAPTER TWO

When he entered his office at Scotland Yard, the first thing that Robert Colbeck did was to doff his top hat and stand in front of the mirror so that he could check his appearance. He used a hand to smooth down his hair then he adjusted his cravat and brushed some specks of dust from the shoulder of his frock coat. Satisfied that he looked at his best, he became aware of the faintest aroma of cigar smoke. It meant that Tallis had been in the room and he would only have come there if he wanted to see the inspector as a matter of urgency. Colbeck didn't keep him waiting any longer. Marching off, he knocked on the superintendent's door and entered the room in answer to a gruff invitation. Edward Tallis was seated at his desk, poring over a map. As he looked up, there was an accusatory note in his voice.

'So – you finally got here, did you?'

'Yes, sir,' replied Colbeck.

'Where, in the name of all that's holy, have you *been*?'

'I had a prior commitment, Superintendent.'

'Nothing takes precedence over your work here.'

'It was my work at Scotland Yard that led to the arrest and conviction of Amos Redwood,' explained Colbeck. 'He preyed on unaccompanied young women on the South Eastern Railway until we caught him. I was in court all morning, giving evidence at his trial. You should have remembered that, sir.'

Tallis was nettled. 'Don't tell me what I should have remembered. It was your duty to remind me that you were unavailable this morning. You failed to do so.'

Colbeck deflected the criticism with an appeasing smile. Because of the unresolved tension between them, Tallis was always ready to pick a fight with him. While he admired the inspector's unrivalled skills as a detective, he resented the fame and approbation that they brought him, contrasting, as they did, with the censure that Tallis routinely encountered from a hostile press. Colbeck had learnt to avoid conflict with his superior by pretending to take the blame.

'The fault was, indeed, mine, sir,' he conceded, shutting the door and crossing to look down at the map. 'I see that you are studying some of the most beautiful counties in England. Does this mean that you are searching for somewhere to spend a well-earned holiday?'

'Holiday?' repeated the other, testily. 'Don't talk nonsense. With all the heavy responsibilities I bear, I never have time for a holiday.'

'Yet you obviously need one, Superintendent.'

'What are you talking about?'

'You push yourself too hard, sir. Nobody can work continuously throughout the year, as you strive to do. Your health and judgement are bound to suffer.'

'There's nothing wrong with my health or my judgement,' said Tallis, stung by the comment. 'Do I look unhealthy to you?'

'No, no – of course not, sir,' said Colbeck, tactfully.

In fact, the superintendent did look more than usually careworn. He was a big, solid man with iron-grey hair and a neat moustache. The pouches under his eyes had darkened and his normal straight-backed posture had acquired a pronounced droop.

'Nevertheless,' added Colbeck, 'a week or even a fortnight in some rural retreat would be the making of you.' Hearing a warning growl in the other man's throat, he quickly changed the subject. 'You have a new case for me, sir?'

'It's one that needs immediate attention.'

'I'm all ears.'

'It concerns the disappearance of Sir Marcus Burnhope's daughter.'

'That name sounds familiar.'

'And so it should. If you perused the newspapers as thoroughly as I do, you'd know that Sir Marcus is a member of the Cabinet. He is President of the Board of Control.'

'Forgive my correcting you,' said Colbeck, smoothly, 'but there's something that you missed in your thorough perusal of the press. That particular Cabinet post will soon be abolished. Sir Marcus will instead become Secretary of State for India.' He raised a teasing eyebrow. 'Since your army career took you to the subcontinent, I'm surprised that you didn't pick up that important detail.'

'That's neither here nor there,' said Tallis, blustering. 'The point is that Sir Marcus is a man of immense influence. There's a crisis in his family. We must solve it and do so with speed.'

'How much information do we have?'

'There's precious little, I fear.'

'Did you receive a telegraph?'

'I've had three so far,' said Tallis, lifting the map so that he could pick them up. 'They'll tell you enough to send you off to Worcestershire. Take the map as well. I've marked the approximate location of Burnhope Manor.'

While Tallis folded up the ordnance survey map, Colbeck read the telegraphs handed to him. They were terse and peremptory.

'There's no actual proof that a crime was committed,' he argued.

'Use your eyes, man – his daughter has been abducted.'

'With respect, sir, you're making a hasty assumption.'

'How else can you explain it?' challenged Tallis. 'Sir Marcus's daughter gets onto a train yet fails to reach the destination. What do you think happened?'

'There are a number of possibilities,' said Colbeck, taking the map from him. 'I'll be interested to find out which is the correct one.'

Tallis was on his feet. 'Bear in mind what I told you. Sir Marcus wields great power. If we fail, he's in a position to inflict untold damage on our reputation. Handle him with extreme care.'

'I will, sir,' said Colbeck, opening the door. 'I'd never willingly offend the future Secretary of State for India.'

He sailed out and left Tallis throbbing with anger.

Sir Marcus Burnhope walked endlessly up and down the room like a caged animal looking for a means of escape. In his case, he was held behind bars of the mind and they induced a mingled sense of rage, fear and impotence. Habituated to authority, he was for once in a situation that he could not control. It was a highly uncomfortable place to be. He was so preoccupied that he didn't even hear the door of the library open. It was only when he turned to walk in the opposite direction that he saw his wife holding on to the frame for support. He rushed towards her.

'You shouldn't be here, Paulina,' he said, slipping an arm around her. 'You're supposed to rest.'

'How can I rest at a time like this?' she asked, hopelessly.

'Go back to bed and leave everything to me.'

'I'm not going until I know the truth. Don't try to fob me off, Marcus. I'm not so ill that I can't cope with unpleasant facts.' Her eyelids narrowed. 'It's Imogen, isn't it?' He shook his head. 'Don't lie to me. She's my daughter as well. Now help me across to that chair and tell me what's going on.'

Sir Marcus was a tall, lean man in his fifties with an air of distinction about him and a luxurious grey moustache that blended with his long, curling hair. Only a few years younger, his wife was a stately woman with the classical beauty that her daughter had inherited. It looked slightly ravished at the moment but had not been obliterated by the wasting disease that was lapping at her.

After helping her across the room, Sir Marcus lowered her into an armchair and remained standing. Not wishing to alarm her, he chose his words with care.

'There was a problem with the train,' he began.

Paulina tensed. 'There hasn't been an accident, has there?'

'No, no – nothing like that.'

'What happened?'

'Imogen caught the train at Shrub Hill with Rhoda Wills.'

'And . . . ?' When he turned away, her tone hardened. 'I'm staying until I hear exactly what occurred,' she said stoutly. 'Who was the man who came here at a gallop earlier on? I caught a glimpse of him through the bedroom window. He was in uniform.'

Sir Marcus moistened his lips. 'It was a policeman,' he said at length.

'Dear God!' she exclaimed. 'Is our daughter in trouble with the law?'

'Keep calm,' he advised. 'The doctor said that you were not to get excited.'

'I'm not excited, Marcus. I'm just burning with frustration because you won't tell me what I'm entitled to hear. It's cruel of you. I have a right to know.'

Producing a handkerchief, she dabbed at the tears that started to flow. Her husband realised that he couldn't hide the full facts from her any longer. Going down on one knee, he put a consoling hand on her shoulder and soothed her as best he could. When she stopped crying, he dragged an upright chair across so that he could sit beside her. She looked imploringly up at him.

He cleared his throat before speaking in a low voice.

'Imogen caught the train – there's no doubt about that. When it arrived in Oxford, neither she nor Rhoda got off it. Your sister looked into every single carriage. They were not there.'

Paulina was trembling. 'Wherever can they be?'

'That's what I intend to find out,' he said, firmly. 'We have Cassandra to thank for taking prompt action. She was so convinced that Imogen would have caught the train that she made the stationmaster send a railway policeman on the return journey to Shrub Hill in order to make enquiries.'

He hesitated for a few seconds. 'Go on, go on – don't stop.'

'The two of them did catch the train. The policeman spoke to a porter who put their luggage on board. He knew Imogen by sight. Hearing that, the policeman did what Cassandra had ordered him to do. He hired a horse and brought word here as fast as he could. The man is to be commended – and so, of course, is your sister.'

'But wait a moment,' she said, raising a palm. 'I thought that the train didn't stop anywhere between Worcester and Oxford.'

'It didn't. The driver confirmed that.'

'So how did Imogen get off it?'

He shrugged. 'I wish I knew, my dear.'

Paulina's mind was aflame. Her imagination conjured up all sorts of horrors. On the one occasion that her mother didn't travel to Oxford with her, Imogen had vanished into thin air. It was therefore her mother's fault. Racked by guilt, she began to quiver with apprehension.

'She must have been attacked,' she wailed. 'Someone got into the carriage and assaulted both Imogen and Rhoda before throwing them out of the train.'

'That's nonsense,' he said. 'Tolley obeyed my orders to the letter. He put them into an empty first-class compartment and waited until the train had departed.'

'Then Imogen must have fallen out accidentally.'

'Paulina—'

'That's what must have happened, Marcus. Perhaps

the door wasn't closed properly. When she got up to see to it, the door suddenly opened and Imogen somehow fell through onto the track.'

'Stop torturing yourself with fevered speculation.'

'It could easily have happened. I've read about incidents like that.'

'There's someone you're forgetting,' he told her, squeezing both of her hands, 'and that's Rhoda. If there had been a problem with the door, Rhoda would certainly have dealt with it. She'd never let Imogen struggle with something like that. And – even supposing that our daughter *did* somehow fall out – her maid would still have been in the carriage to report what happened.' He leant forward to kiss her on the temple. 'It would have been far better if I'd kept you in the dark until this mystery has been solved.'

'But I *had* to know,' she insisted. 'After all, I'm the culprit.'

'Don't be absurd.'

'It was my decision to let her go alone. I should have made her wait until I was fit enough to accompany her. I should have cancelled the trip to Oxford.'

'But that would have been a terrible disappointment to all concerned. You know how much Imogen enjoys seeing her cousins and vice versa. It would have been wrong to call off the visit.'

'But it would have saved our daughter's life!'

'There's no need to be so melodramatic.'

'She's dead, Marcus. I sense it.'

'And I have an equally strong feeling that Imogen is still alive,' he said with far more confidence than he actually possessed.

'Then where on earth can she be?' she cried.

'I've engaged the services of the one man who can find her for us.'

'And who is that?'

'His name is Inspector Colbeck. He's being sent here from Scotland Yard.'

'Do you really think that he can help us?'

'I'm certain of it,' he said, sitting up. 'Because of his unblemished record of success, Colbeck is known as the Railway Detective. Earlier this year, he saved the royal family from being blown up on a train taking them to Balmoral.'

'Goodness!'

'Can you think of a better recommendation than that?'

Detective Sergeant Victor Leeming was a realist. He knew that his luck could not last indefinitely. It had given him precious, uninterrupted weeks when he was able to spend every night at home with his wife and two children. Since their investigations had been confined to London, he and Colbeck could go everywhere on foot or by cab. It was a far cry from the cases that had taken them to places like Wales, Scotland and France, separating him from his family in the process. Leeming had revelled in the joy of being back on the territory he knew best. His good fortune had now come to an abrupt halt. Instead of walking through familiar streets in the capital, he was forced to use a mode of travel that he detested. The sergeant found trains noisy, smelly, uncomfortable and potentially dangerous. What made his reluctant journeys even more trying was the fact that Colbeck was always singing the praises of a railway network that had spread all over the country. To him it was a cause for celebration; to Leeming it was a source of unrelieved anguish.

They were an incongruous pair. Colbeck, the dandy of Scotland Yard, was impeccably dressed and sporting a dazzling new waistcoat. He was tall, sinewy and debonair. Leeming, by contrast, looked more like a fairground ruffian than someone involved in law enforcement. He was shorter, stockier, less well proportioned and had a face that was almost intriguingly ugly. While the inspector exuded refinement, the sergeant was unapologetically down to earth. Though his apparel was vaguely similar to that of his companion, it was baggy and crumpled. His top hat had lost much of its sheen. Anyone seeing them for the first time would have identified Colbeck as a member of the gentry with a bodyguard in tow.

The inspector watched the fields of crops and green pastures scudding past.

'We'd never have been able to get there so quickly by stagecoach,' he said, turning to his friend. 'Trains have revolutionised the way that we work.'

'Not for the better,' said Leeming, sourly. 'All that trains have done is to give villains new ways to commit crimes. They've blown them up, robbed them, damaged them, assaulted women on them and done all manner of dreadful things. Stagecoaches were far safer and much more reliable.' He folded his arms. 'That's my opinion, anyway.'

'I respect it, Victor.'

Leeming bristled. 'Are you mocking me, sir?'

'I'd never do that.'

Colbeck was sincere. He was too fond of his sergeant to deliberately upset him by poking fun at him. The two detectives were seated alone in a compartment of a jolting train taking them to Worcester. Having set out from London, their first port of call had been Oxford where they'd interviewed both the stationmaster and the porter who'd stood beside Cassandra Vaughan and her daughter awaiting what turned out to be phantom passengers. Neither man could offer any convincing explanation of how the two ladies had disappeared in transit. Unlike the train from London, the one on the OWWR was slow, jerky and inclined to stop at almost every station it came to. As they began to lose speed yet again, Leeming stared hopefully through the window.

'Have we got there at last?' he asked.

'No,' replied Colbeck, consulting the open copy of *Bradshaw* in his lap. 'This will be Moreton-in-Marsh. The station was opened in 1853.'

'I can live quite happily without that information, sir.'

'Knowledge is power, Victor.'

'I'll take your word for it,' grumbled Leeming.

'Travel is an education in itself.'

'That's the main reason I prefer to stay in London.'

'Doesn't this investigation appeal to you in any way?'

'Not when it involves spending hours on the railway.'

'A real challenge confronts us,' said Colbeck, enthusiastically, 'and it's one that's brimming with interest. In the course of a non-stop train journey of just under sixty miles, two young women disappear as if in a puff of smoke. Surely that fact excites your curiosity?

Leeming grimaced. 'To be honest, sir, it doesn't.'

'Why not, may I ask?'

'It's because we both know how this investigation will end.'

'Do we?' Colbeck was surprised. 'Please enlighten me.'

'Those women must have left the train while it was travelling at speed,' said Leeming. 'It's only a matter of time before their dead bodies are found in the bushes somewhere along the line.'

'Are you suggesting that they had a bizarre suicide pact?'

'No, sir – I believe that they fell out by accident.'

'In that case, the entire train must have been occupied by blind passengers. Evidently, they were also deaf. As the two women tumbled out of their carriage, nobody managed to see them or hear their terrified screams. And then there's the guard,' added Colbeck. 'He's paid to keep his eyes peeled for anything untoward.' He pursed his lips. 'I'm sorry, Victor. Your theory doesn't hold water.'

Leeming was hurt. 'What do *you* think happened?'

'I prefer to keep an open mind. Strange things happen on the OWWR. It's no wonder my father-in-law calls it the Old Worse and Worse. But then, of course, he's biased. Until he retired, he drove locomotives for the LNWR and looks with disdain on rival companies. In his view,' Colbeck went on, 'the OWWR had a fatal defect.'

'What was that, sir?'

'In its early stages, Brunel was heavily involved.'

'Mr Andrews has no time for Brunel, does he?'

'Let's just say that he's yet to recognise Brunel's undoubted genius. I suspect that you'd agree with him on that score, Victor.'

'People who build railways have ruined this country,' asserted Leeming.

'I see them as far-sighted men who are pioneers of progress. The day will come when their achievement is fully appreciated. Admittedly,' said Colbeck, 'the development of the railway system has attracted its fair share of rogues, men like George Hudson who sought to exploit it for his own ends and who was involved in all manner of financial malpractice. It remains to be seen if Sir Marcus Burnhope views railways as a priceless national asset or merely as a source of personal income.'

'Why do you say that, sir?'

'Read these telegraphs, Victor,' said the other, extracting them from an inside pocket. Leeming took them and studied each one. 'What do you notice about them?'

'They tell us very little about his missing daughter,' noted Leeming.

'But they reveal something important about Sir Marcus himself.'

'Do they?'

'He's very frugal with words until we reach his name. Then he feels obliged – in all three cases – to state that he's on the board of directors of the OWWR.' Colbeck gave a questioning smile. 'What sort of man does that?'

CHAPTER THREE

Dominic Vaughan had been wrong about the Beckford sisters. Of the two, he'd found Cassandra infinitely more patient, intelligent yet submissive and therefore far more suitable as the wife of a husband drawn to the groves of academe. It was not that he thought Paulina unattractive. On the contrary, he willingly conceded that, in purely physical terms, she was unequalled but it was a glaring beauty that unnerved instead of enticed him. Paulina also had a patrician air that was much more at home in Burnhope Manor than in the cloistered world of the Oxford college where Vaughan had been a fellow at the time. While one sister would surely have rejected his proposal of marriage, the other had accepted it with muted pleasure and been – in the early years – exactly the sort of spouse he'd envisaged as his preferred partner in life.

Motherhood had wrought a profound change in both sisters. The arrival of Imogen, an only child, turned the serene Paulina into a nervous, ever-watchful chaperone, determined to protect her daughter from what she perceived as the rampant wickedness of the outside world. Cassandra, too, had undergone a kind of metamorphosis. Having given birth to three children, she'd become more strident, more assertive and less ready to accept her husband's decisions without first questioning them. Since he hated confrontation of any kind, Vaughan had given ground to her time and again. Even though he now enjoyed the elevated status of being Master of University – the oldest college endowment in Oxford – he lacked authority on the domestic front. Cassandra was always prone to challenge his judgement and advance her own plausible alternatives to his plans. Everyone at the college was aware of the marital imbalance in the Master's Lodging. It had led to waspish comments from his detractors in the Senior Common Room.

'Don't just sit there, Dominic,' she complained. 'Do something.'

'What am I supposed to do, my love?'

'Anything is better than hiding away in your study.'

'I need to check these accounts from the bursar.'

'Heavens!' she exclaimed. 'Must the safety of our niece take second place to the erratic mathematics of the bursar? Don't you *care* about Imogen?'

'I care a great deal, Cassandra,' he said, rising from his desk, 'and I've already been to the chapel to pray for her deliverance. But, in practical terms, all that was needful has already been done by your good self. You promptly set the wheels of the investigation in motion and I applaud you for that.'

'Somebody had to do so,' she snorted.

'Are you insinuating that I would have failed to do likewise?'

'Frankly, I am.'

'That's unjust of you.'

'Is it? You couldn't even be bothered to meet Imogen at the station.'

'You and Emma formed a perfectly adequate welcoming party.'

'Your presence would have given it more body and you'd have been able to remonstrate with the stationmaster and the driver of the locomotive. In your absence, I had to tackle them both.'

'I don't see that either of them could be blamed,' he said, reasonably. 'If you set on them, they have my sympathy. You can be unnecessarily sharp at times, my dear. I've mentioned it to you before.'

'You're doing it again!' she protested. 'You're worrying about two mere railway employees instead of about your niece. What if she's been killed or kidnapped? What if Imogen has been *ravished*? Supposing,' she continued, voice soaring a whole octave, 'that it had been Emma who boarded that train then disappeared? Wouldn't *that* have engaged your attention?'

'You know quite well that it would, Cassandra. You chastise me unfairly. I have the greatest concern for Imogen – and for her maid, of course. It's a shared plight and we must remember that. But having no idea what happened to them, I'm determined not to fall prey to the wild imaginings that you have just listed. Let me finish,' he went on quickly as she was about to speak. 'All that we can realistically do is to watch, pray and rely on the goodness of our Creator. The situation may look baffling but there may well be a perfectly logical explanation.'

'That is patently untrue.'

'We must never surrender to despair.'

She rolled her eyes. 'Your words push me perilously close to it.'

'That's unkind and unwarranted, Cassandra.'

She had the grace to look shamefaced and even mouthed an apology. Anger then gave way to a moment of weakness and she allowed him to embrace her in his usual clumsy way. For all his faults – she'd enumerated them many times – she knew that she'd married a good, honest, conscientious Christian gentleman, wedded to scholarship and devoted to his family. When she pulled away and looked up at him, her ire had cooled.

'What will Marcus do?' she asked, softly.

'I should imagine that he'll take care to say nothing to alarm your sister when she is unwell. Secondly, he'll curse the railway company and wish that he never got involved with the enterprise. The OWWR has presented him with an unbroken series of shocks and disappointments, the culmination of which is that it now appears to have mislaid his daughter.'

'It's done more than simply mislay her, Dominic. They should be prosecuted.'

'We must first establish what offence – if any – they committed. But,' he went on, 'to return to your original question about what action he'll take, Marcus will do what he always does in a crisis. He'll find the ideal person to pour oil on what are extremely troubled waters.'

Unlike the cab driver who drove them to Burnhope Manor, Colbeck refused to be cowed by the presence of aristocracy.

It was an article of faith with him that a police investigation merited the utmost respect. When the driver unthinkingly took his passengers to the servants' entrance, therefore, Colbeck insisted that they went instead to the front door. It gave the detectives an opportunity to appraise the house. Built towards the close of Elizabeth's reign, it had been designed by someone who was enthralled by the sumptuous Hardwick Hall in Derbyshire. Indeed, the manor was conceived as a smaller version of it with the same bold lines as Hardwick and the same stunning expanse of glass. There were so many windows in the front elevation that the whole edifice seemed to glisten in the afternoon sunshine.

Victor Leeming looked up at it in dismay. After the ordeal of rail travel, he'd enjoyed the comparative luxury of a horse-drawn vehicle and it had helped him to relax. The sight of Burnhope Manor made every muscle tense instantly. Colbeck, on the other hand, was not intimidated. When they stood outside the front door, he pulled on the bell rope with conviction. The butler soon answered the summons, looking askance at Colbeck but reserving his most disapproving glance for Leeming. On learning who the visitors were, he conducted them along a corridor lined with gilt-framed portraits, then took them into the library. Left alone, they looked around the long, well-proportioned room with its leather-bound tomes stacked neatly on oak shelves covering three walls. A large globe stood in a corner.

Colbeck's primary interest was in the books and he took a quick inventory of their titles. Leeming, however, was transfixed by the full-length portrait of Sir Marcus Burnhope that hung above the magnificent marble fireplace. One admonitory finger in the air, he looked as if he were addressing a large audience and the fierce glint in his eye made Leeming flinch slightly. Sir Marcus exuded a sense of wealth, breeding and power. The real-life version was even more daunting.

'Ah, there you are at last!' he said, sweeping into the room like a gust of wind. 'What on earth kept you?'

'Part of the blame must lie with the railway company on whose board you happen to sit, Sir Marcus,' said Colbeck, evenly. 'The journey from Oxford to Worcester was punctuated by an inordinate number of stops.'

He introduced himself and the sergeant. Sir Marcus deigned to exchange a handshake with Colbeck. To his relief, Leeming escaped with a perfunctory nod from him. The detectives were offered seats but their host remained on his feet so that he could strut and dominate. He gave them all the information he had, then he demanded immediate action.

'Some has already been taken, Sir Marcus,' said Colbeck. 'We've questioned the stationmaster and a porter at Oxford station and spoken to the man who loaded your daughter's luggage at Shrub Hill station. What we need now is more detail than you were able to include in your telegraphs.'

'What sort of detail?'

'Why was your daughter going to Oxford? Had she made the same journey many times before? How long did she expect to be away? What might she be doing during her stay?'

Sir Marcus answered the questions with suppressed irritation. Since he was unsure how long Imogen and her maid would remain in Oxford, it was clear that he'd taken little interest in the arrangements. He explained that his wife was indisposed and thus unable, for the very first time, to accompany their daughter. Catching Leeming's eye, Colbeck saw that he'd registered that important fact. When he finished, Sir Marcus struck a pose with his hands on his hips.

'Well?' he asked. 'Is there anything else you wish to know, Inspector?'

'I did wonder why you felt it necessary to describe your relationship with the OWWR in your telegraphs.'

'I wanted you to know that I don't only speak as a concerned parent. I felt that my presence on the board would secure the attention of the Railway Detective and not,' he added with a scornful look at Leeming, 'of some blundering nonentity.'

'My achievements, such as they are,' said Colbeck, modestly, 'would have been impossible without the help and expertise of the sergeant. Essentially, we operate as a team, deserving equal credit.' Leeming shot him a grateful smile. 'We have two requests, Sir Marcus. The first is that we'd like to interview the coachman who drove your daughter and her maid to the station.'

Sir Marcus was dismissive. 'That won't be necessary,' he said. 'I've already spoken to Tolley. You won't learn anything from him that I haven't already told you.'

'Nevertheless, we would like to meet the fellow. We're likely to ask him questions that might never have occurred to you.'

'What sort of questions?' asked the other, suspiciously.

'If you wish to know that,' said Colbeck, 'you're welcome to be present.'

There was a considered pause. 'Very well,' said Sir

Marcus, grudgingly. 'You can speak to Tolley, if you must. But you said that you had *two* requests.'

'The second is of a more delicate nature, Sir Marcus.'

'Go on.'

'Well,' said Colbeck, 'I wondered if we might be permitted to take a look at your daughter's bedchamber.'

'Indeed, you may not!' exploded Sir Marcus. 'I find the very notion both impertinent and distasteful. My daughter disappeared on a railway line, Inspector. You'll not find her hiding upstairs in a wardrobe.'

'If my suggestion was offensive, I apologise.'

'It was offensive and wholly improper.'

'Then I ask you to forgive me,' said Colbeck, getting to his feet and signalling that Leeming should do likewise. 'You have a beautiful library, Sir Marcus. I see that you're an admirer of Shakespeare's sonnets.'

'I never have time to read poetry,' snarled Sir Marcus with something akin to disgust. 'Whatever gave you the idea that I did?'

'That chair by the window is placed to catch the best of the light. I assumed that it's your chosen place for reading. On the table beside it is a copy of the sonnets.'

'Well, I certainly didn't put it there – and neither did my wife. Lady Burnhope has even less interest in poetry than I. Really, Inspector,' he chided, 'I wish you'd ignore our reading habits and concentrate on finding our daughter.'

'We'll speak to the coachman at once,' said Colbeck.

Sir Marcus tugged at a bell pull. 'One of my servants will take you to him.'

'Thank you, Sir Marcus – and thank you for putting your trust in us. I have no doubt that we'll find out exactly what happened to your daughter and her maid. Oh,' he added, meeting the other's glare, 'there is one last question.'

'What is it?'

'Would you describe your daughter as happy?'

'Damn you, man!' bellowed Sir Marcus. 'Of course she's happy. Imogen has everything that she could ask out of life. Apart from anything else, she's due to get married soon. It's a positive love match. Our daughter has never been happier.'

Edward Tallis had had a particularly busy day, attending a lengthy meeting with the commissioner, deploying his detectives on new cases, sifting through interim reports on existing investigations, berating anyone within reach and trying to ensure that Scotland Yard avoided making the sorts of mistakes that newspapers loved to seize on and mock. Satire could be a cruel weapon and Tallis had felt its searing thrust far too often. After hours of constant activity, he retired to his office and rewarded himself with a cigar, puffing on it with satisfaction and filling the room with a haze of smoke. His pleasure was short-lived. Knuckles rapped on his door, then it opened to admit a tall, dark-haired, fleshy man in his thirties with a prominent nose and a jutting chin. His manner was brusque.

'Superintendent Tallis?' he asked.

'Yes,' replied the other, stubbing out his cigar.

'I am Clive Tunnadine. I wish to know what you are doing in relation to the disappearance of the dear lady to whom I am betrothed. I speak of the daughter of Sir Marcus Burnhope. How many men have you engaged in the search and what results have they so far reported?'

Tallis was on his feet at once. 'Excuse me, sir,' he said, stoutly, 'but you have no right to force your way into my office and make demands.'

Tunnadine inflated his chest. 'Do you know who I am?'

'I do – you're a person who should learn to control his vile temper.'

'I'm an elected Member of Parliament, serving in Her Majesty's Government.'

'You'd oblige me by moderating your voice,' said Tallis, pointedly. 'You're not addressing a public meeting. If you would care to take a seat, I'll endeavour to offer you an explanation. If, however, you try to browbeat me any more, I'll have you removed from the premises – by force, if need be.'

Tunnadine was on the point of a volcanic eruption and the molten words trembled on his tongue. What held him back was the superintendent's firm stance and unyielding stare. It had terrified soldiers of lower rank during his army days and it was enough to warn Tunnadine that he'd met his match. The visitor curled his lip, waited a full minute, then sat reluctantly down. Walking around him, Tallis closed the door then returned to his own chair behind the desk.

'First of all,' he began, 'let me offer you my sympathy. It must have come as a great shock to you.'

'It did, Superintendent. Word arrived by courier sent from Worcestershire. I became aware of it when I returned home less than fifteen minutes ago. Sir Marcus informs me that he sent telegraphs to Scotland Yard.'

'There were three of them in all, sir.'

Tallis told him that he was treating the case as a matter of priority and that the detectives would probably have already reached Burnhope Manor. Tunnadine listened with a mingled rage and impatience. Whenever he tried to speak, however, he was interrupted by Tallis, determined to keep the upper hand. Though arrogant and high-handed himself, he hated those traits in others and saw both in his visitor. When the superintendent finally relented, Tunnadine pounced on him.

'You dispatched only *two* detectives?' he asked, aghast.

'They are highly experienced, sir.'

'Scores of men will be needed to comb the area between Shrub Hill and Oxford. How can two individuals cover an area that vast?'

'Any search of the line would be undertaken by railway policemen. They do not answer to me. Since he is on the board of the railway company, I've no doubt that Sir Marcus will already have cracked the whip and instigated a methodical search. What my detectives will be doing,' said Tallis, 'is to gather evidence painstakingly before reaching a conclusion.'

'What more evidence is there?' said Tunnadine, slapping a knee. 'Two people board a train then vanish before it reaches its destination.'

'It's not as simple as that, sir.'

'They must somehow have fallen out of the train.'

'That's only supposition.'

'Can you suggest an alternative explanation?'

'I can think of a few,' Tallis told him, 'but then I'm rather more acquainted than you with seemingly impenetrable mysteries. Your concern is understandable and may – to a limited extent – excuse the way that you barged unannounced into my office. I would advise you to keep calm and have confidence in Inspector Colbeck.'

'Has he ever handled a case like this before?'

'No, I don't believe that he has, sir.'

'Then he is just groping in the dark,' said Tunnadine, hotly.

Tallis smiled. 'I can see that you've never met the inspector.'

'I insist on doing so at the earliest possible time.'

'That can be arranged.'

'What are his movements?'

'When he's finished at Burnhope Manor, he intends to visit Oxford to meet the family with whom the two ladies were intending to stay.'

'What use is that?' asked Tunnadine. 'Imogen never even reached them. They can tell him absolutely nothing of value.'

'You underestimate Inspector Colbeck,' said Tallis, speaking about him with a fleeting affection. 'He is a master of the unorthodox. His methods may at times seem odd – not to say perverse – but I can assure you that they invariably bear fruit.'

When the detectives found him, Vernon Tolley was polishing the landau in a desultory way. His mind was clearly on other things and it didn't take them long to find out what they were. Because he'd driven Imogen and her maid to the station, he felt obscurely to blame for the tragedy and knew that Sir Marcus took the same view. If the missing passengers were not found alive and well, Tolley expected to be dismissed summarily. What really concerned him, however, was the fate of Rhoda Wills. When Colbeck asked him to describe the appearance and character of the two women, he spoke with undisguised fondness of Imogen's maid. He was too loyal to be drawn into any criticism of Sir Marcus and his wife, though he did admit that the latter kept their daughter under constant surveillance.

'Let's go back to the start,' suggested Colbeck. 'When the two ladies left the house, were both parents there to see them off?'

'Oh, no,' said Tolley, wiping the back of a hand across his mouth. 'Lady Burnhope was too ill to come out so she waved them off from an upstairs window.'

'Which one?' asked Leeming. 'There must be twenty or more to choose from.'

'People in the village call this the Glass House.'

'What about Sir Marcus?' wondered Colbeck. 'Did he wave them off?'

'He was busy somewhere inside the house.'

'Was that typical of him? Does Sir Marcus always show such little interest in his daughter's movements?'

'He's a very important man, Inspector.'

'It would only have taken a matter of minutes,' observed Leeming.

'This was the first time his daughter had travelled to Oxford without her mother,' said Colbeck. 'That made the visit rather special.'

'It did, Inspector,' agreed Tolley. 'It was unusual not to have Lady Burnhope holding forth in the carriage. I could see that Rhoda – Miss Wills, that is – was very pleased that they were alone.'

'What else was unusual, Mr Tolley?'

The coachman shook his head. 'Nothing,' he said.

'There must have been *something*,' pressed Colbeck. 'Think hard.'

'The tiniest detail may be of interest to us,' said Leeming. 'Tell us about any variation from the norm.'

Tolley frowned. 'Well, there was the money,' he recalled. 'When Sir Marcus and Lady Burnhope travel by train, they never give money to me or to the porter who stows their luggage aboard. Their daughter was different. Both of us got a sovereign for our pains. Imagine that – a whole sovereign apiece' His face clouded. 'I'd sooner lose the money and have the two of them safely back here again.'

'I'm sure that you would,' said Colbeck, touched by his distress. 'Is there anything else you can tell us, Mr Tolley? What made this journey a little different?'

Tolley removed his hat to scratch his head. He had been over the events of the morning countless times in his head and thought that he had a complete picture of what had happened. It took a long time before one more detail popped out.

'There was the valise,' he remembered.

'What about it?' asked Colbeck.

'Well, it's rather large and heavy. Whenever they've travelled with it before, it was always loaded onto the roof of the carriage with the other luggage. For some reason, it travelled inside with them this time.' His eyes widened hopefully. 'Is that the kind of thing you mean, Inspector?'

Colbeck was grinning. 'It is, indeed,' he said.

'Will it help you to find them?'

'Let me put it this way, Mr Tolley. You may take heart. I have a strange feeling that your job will be safe, after all.'

CHAPTER FOUR

Bent on pursuing his political career, Sir Marcus Burnhope had left the upbringing of their daughter almost wholly to his wife. He put in a token appearance at crucial moments in Imogen's young life but otherwise saw very little of her. To atone for his frequent absences, he gave her a generous allowance and plied her with gifts. Paulina, too, had been neglected in favour of parliamentary affairs and he was very conscious of that as he climbed the staircase to her bedchamber. It had taken Imogen's dire predicament to remind him of his many shortcomings as a husband and father. For once in his life, the future Secretary of State for India was compelled to put the family first. It was a novel experience and deeply unsettling as a consequence.

'How did you find her?' he asked the doctor.

'Lady Burnhope is still very agitated,' replied the other.

'I tried to conceal the news from her but she insisted on hearing it.'

'She talked of nothing else.'

'Is there some way to calm her down?'

'I've given her a sedative, Sir Marcus. She'll soon be asleep.'

'Thank you. Call again tomorrow. You may well be needed'

They'd met on the landing. Doctor Ferris was a white-haired old man with sharp instincts acquired over many years of sitting at the bedsides of the sick and dying. Though softly spoken and deferential, he made it clear that his patient was to be given the medication prescribed.

'I've left my instructions on the bedside table,' he said.

'They'll be obeyed to the letter.'

'In that case, Sir Marcus, I'll take my leave.' The doctor looked over his shoulder. 'If you wish to speak to Lady Burnhope, I suggest that you do so very soon. She's already drowsy.'

While the doctor padded off down the staircase, Sir Marcus knocked gently on the door of his wife's bedchamber then let himself in. Paulina was propped up on some pillows, mind in turmoil. When she saw her husband enter, she reached out a desperate hand. He moved across to hold it between both palms.

'How do you feel, my dear?' he asked with awkward tenderness.

'Is there any news?' she gasped.

'Not as yet, I fear.'

'It's been hours and hours. Will our torment never end?'

'Fretting about it will not help, Paulina.'

'But I'm bound to fret. Any mother would do so in the circumstances – and any father as well. Don't *you* fret, Marcus?'

'I am naturally anxious,' he told her, 'but I'm schooling myself to remain calm and to allow for a modicum of optimism.'

'Optimism?' she echoed in surprise. 'I see no cause for that.'

'Hope is a better medicine than despondency.'

But his wife was well beyond the reach of hope, still less of optimism. From the moment she learnt of her daughter's disappearance, she'd been plunged into an unrelieved misery. To her rheumy eyes, the situation was impossibly bleak.

'She's gone, Marcus. We have to accept it – Imogen has gone.'

'I refuse even to countenance the thought,' he said, decisively.

'She was our one and only child – truly, a gift from God. Need I remind you of the difficulties attending her birth?'

'This is no time to dwell on such matters, my dear.'

'But the memories come flooding back to me.'

They were not memories that he chose to share. Complications arising from Imogen's birth had meant that she would have no siblings. It was a bitter blow to a man who'd longed for a son to follow in his footsteps and preserve the traditions of the Burnhope dynasty. Imogen might have her mother's exquisite beauty but she could never inherit her father's baronetcy, join him as a Member of Parliament or take part in the manly country pursuits he enjoyed during occasional moments of leisure. A son would have been bursting with ambition to make his mark and achieve something of note; his daughter's talents lay chiefly in being decorative.

Paulina was on the point of dozing off when she shook herself awake again.

'What about poor Clive?' she asked. 'Have you told him?'

'I sent a letter by courier.'

'He'll be desolate.'

'Clive will do what I have done, my dear,' said Sir Marcus, pompously. 'He'll substitute action for anguish. Instead of wallowing in despair, he'll want to join the search for Imogen. Clive Tunnadine is a splendid fellow – that's why I chose him as our prospective son-in-law.'

She heaved a sigh. 'We've lost a daughter and he's lost a wife.' As her eyelids began to flutter, a thought made her fight off sleep. 'You mentioned a detective to me. Has he arrived yet?'

'Inspector Colbeck has come and gone,' he said, shielding from her his disappointment with the visit. 'He and his sergeant gathered information here before taking the train back to Oxford. For some reason, Colbeck felt that it would be valuable to speak to your sister and her husband.' He gritted his teeth. 'We can only pray that the so-called Railway Detective knows what he's doing.'

When they reached the railway station in Worcester, the detectives were met by a happy coincidence. Not only could they catch an express train to Oxford, the locomotive that pulled it was *Will Shakspere*. According to the porter who'd put their luggage on the train, it was the self-same one that had taken Imogen and her maid off on their travels. Colbeck and Leeming were thus able to recreate their journey, very confident that they wouldn't disappear into a void as the women had apparently done. The hectic dash to Shrub Hill in the cab had left little opportunity for reflection on what they'd so far discovered. In the privacy of a railway compartment, they were able to compare notes properly.

'What did you make of Sir Marcus?' asked Colbeck.

'People like that always frighten me, sir.'

'I don't see why they should. You're never frightened when you take on a ruffian armed with a cudgel or arrest an obstreperous drunk. When it comes to a brawl, you're the most fearless person I've ever met.'

'Sir Marcus is rich, he's titled, he's important. I'm none of those things.'

'You're rich in the things that matter, Victor. As for a title, "detective sergeant" is something of which to be proud when attached to your name. Then we come to importance,' said Colbeck. 'Answer me this. When someone's daughter vanishes from the face of the earth, which is more important – her father or the man who helps to find her?'

'I never thought of it that way,' admitted Leeming with a chuckle. 'Sir Marcus *needs* us. He may look down on us but we are the ones leading the chase.'

'What did you learn at Burnhope Manor?'

'I learnt that I don't belong there, sir. I felt like an intruder. I was also in awe of that portrait of him over the fireplace. It made him look so . . . majestic.'

'It flattered his vanity,' said Colbeck, 'which is why he paid the artist a large amount of money to give prominence to his better features while, at the same time, concealing the less appealing ones – and there were several of those. What struck me,' he continued, 'was how little he knew of his daughter's life and movements. Evidently, she's led an isolated existence under the aegis of Lady Burnhope.'

'Why did you ask to see her bedchamber?'

'I wanted some idea of what she'd taken on the trip.'

'Your request really upset Sir Marcus.'

'I was prepared for such a reaction. It's a great pity. We could have learnt a lot from seeing what apparel she'd taken, but my principal interest was in her jewellery. Had she simply been going to stay at an Oxford college for a relatively short time, she wouldn't have needed to take it. Academic institutions give a young lady little scope for display. If,' Colbeck went on, 'she nevertheless *did* take her most precious possessions, then a whole new line of enquiry opens up.'

'Does it?' Leeming was bewildered. 'I fail to see it, sir.'

'Remember what the coachman told us. He and the porter were each given a handsome tip. What does that tell you?'

'The young lady was uncommonly kind-hearted.'

'I prefer to think that she was excessively grateful.'

'Yet all that they did was to put her on a train.'

'Without realising it,' said Colbeck, thinking it through, 'they might have been doing a lot more than that. This was the first time that Lady Burnside's daughter was travelling unsupervised. Imagine the sense of independence she must have felt.' He looked across at the sergeant. 'What else did the coachman tell us?'

'He told us that he was sweet on Rhoda Wills. Not that he said it in so many words,' Leeming recalled, 'but I could read that fond smile of his. He was far less upset about the disappearance of Sir Marcus's daughter than he was of her maid.'

'He gave us a vital clue, Victor.'

'Did he?'

'Think hard.'

Face puckered in concentration, Leeming went through the meeting with Vernon Tolley in his mind. A smile slowly spread across his face and he snapped his fingers.

'It was that valise,' he said. 'It went inside the carriage instead of on top of it.'

'And why do you think that was?'

'It contained something needed on the journey.'

'Well done!'

Leeming's smile froze. 'But that still doesn't explain how they disappeared.'

'Perhaps they didn't,' said Colbeck.

'Then where did they go?'

'They stayed exactly where they were, Victor.' He laughed at the sergeant's expression of complete bafflement. 'They got on the train at Worcester and left it at its terminus in Oxford.'

'Then why didn't Mrs Vaughan and her daughter see them?'

'It's because – and this is merely guesswork on my part – they didn't recognise Sir Marcus's daughter and her maid.'

'That's impossible. They knew both of them well.'

'Mrs Vaughan and her daughter were expecting two women to get off the train. It was a crowded platform, remember. They wouldn't have looked twice if a man and a woman had alighted together – or if two men stepped out of a carriage.'

Leeming snapped his fingers. 'It's that valise again!'

'Suppose that it contained a means of disguise.'

'They'd have plenty of time to change on their way to

Oxford and they could easily have lost themselves in the crowd when they got there. I think you've hit on the solution, sir.' The excitement drained out of Leeming's voice. 'There's just one thing,' he said, dully. 'I can't think of a single reason why Sir Marcus's daughter should want to sneak past her aunt and her cousin. She enjoyed her visits to Oxford. The coachman confirmed that. Why deceive her relatives in that way?'

'Imogen Burnhope was seizing her one chance of escape.'

'Why should she want to escape from a life of such privilege?'

'I'm not certain, Victor, but it may be related to that book of Shakespeare sonnets in the library. *She* was the person who'd been reading them, not her parents. Poetry would seem to be signally absent from the Burnhope marriage.'

'I've never read any sonnets,' confessed Leeming. 'In fact, I don't even know what a sonnet is. What's so special about them?'

'The overriding theme of Shakespeare's sonnets is love.'

'Then someone about to get married would be likely to read them.'

'Only if she was pleased with the wedding plans,' said Colbeck, 'and I fancy that she may have had reservations.'

'Yet her father insisted that she'd never been happier.'

'That only means that the marriage had *his* blessing. His daughter would have had no freedom of choice in the matter. I doubt very much if her happiness was even considered. It was just assumed by her father. We heard how beautiful Imogen Burnhope was. She must have had many admirers. Being trapped on the estate for most of the time, she'd have been unable to enjoy their admiration unless . . .' Colbeck hunched his shoulders. '. . . unless she found a way to circumvent her mother's control of her life. If that were the case, she'd be in a position to make her own choice.'

Leeming goggled. 'You think that the young lady is on the run?'

'Yes, Victor, I do. I wouldn't dare mention it to her family or to her relatives but her behaviour smacks of calculation. Her reading of the sonnets suggests that Imogen Burnhope is in love but it may not be with the man she is destined to marry.'

'Yet she accepted his proposal.'

'So it seems.'

'She can't renounce that.'

'It's highly unusual, I grant you. It would take a great deal of courage for her to make such a momentous decision but love can embolden even the meekest of individuals. The truth will only emerge when we meet the man to whom she is betrothed. Is she running *to* him?' asked Colbeck, stroking his chin meditatively, 'or running *away* from him?'

Clive Tunnadine was an unwelcome visitor to Oxford. He stormed into University College and ordered the head porter to take him at once to the Master's Lodging. He was received politely by Dominic Vaughan and offered refreshment that he spurned rudely as if he'd just been invited to drink poison. Before he could explain why he'd descended on the college in such an ill-tempered way, Tunnadine was interrupted by the arrival of Cassandra and obliged to go through ritual greetings. Her presence made him moderate his tone somewhat.

'I saw you through the window,' she said, 'and guessed why you must have come. It's this terrible business about Imogen. We are quite distraught.'

'We are also mystified,' said her husband. 'The OWWR is capable of some catastrophic errors but it has, to my mind, never before contrived to lose two of its passengers in transit. Sir Marcus will take the company to task.'

'The fault may not lie at their door, Mr Vaughan.'

'Where else, I pray?'

Tunnadine looked from one to the other. He'd met them only twice before at social gatherings and formed a clear view of the couple. Vaughan struck him as a refugee from a real life in which he was too timid to thrive, preferring instead to inhabit the alternative universe of scholarship with its mild intellectual joys and its monastic affinities. Cassandra, however, was too forceful and opinionated to blend easily into the surroundings. While her husband may have withdrawn from the workaday world, she still kept one foot in it and felt able to pass judgement on major events of the day in a way that Tunnadine found annoying and unbecoming in a woman. It was something he was determined to prevent Imogen Burnhope from ever doing when she eventually became his wife.

For their part, Dominic and Cassandra Vaughan accepted him at face value because he was about to join the family. Vaughan had a natural respect for any member of the government and his wife could see that – though wholly lacking in charm or good looks – Tunnadine would be a vigorous husband in every sense. Her view of him was about to be changed.

'It pains me to say this,' he said with blatant dishonesty, 'but I'm led to think that you, Mrs Vaughan, may have been at fault.'

Cassandra blenched. 'How dare you even suggest it!'

'Imogen *did* get off that train but you must have missed her in the crowd.'

'That's an appalling allegation.'

'And it's one that I refute,' said Vaughan, coming to her aid. 'My wife is exceptionally sharp-eyed. There is no way that she – or Emma, for that matter – would have failed to see a face that is so lovingly familiar.'

'I believe that Mrs Vaughan may have been cleverly distracted,' argued Tunnadine. 'It was all part of a game. Let me finish,' he added, quelling them with a wave of his arm. 'On the train from London, I've had ample time to explore the possibilities and I've come to one conclusion. This family is to blame.'

'That's a monstrous accusation!' cried Cassandra.

'I demand that you withdraw it,' said Vaughan, confronting him. 'Even if my wife and daughter *did* miss them in the crowd, it would not account for their total disappearance. Imogen and her maid would simply have caught a cab and come straight here to the college. Your claim is baseless, sir.'

'I think not,' asserted Tunnadine.

'I'm afraid that I must ask you to leave this college.'

'I'll not go until this matter is finally sorted out.'

'My wife and daughter are wholly innocent of your charge.'

'That may be so.'

'It is so!' shouted Cassandra. 'I demand an apology.'

Vaughan drew himself up to his full height. 'Well, Mr Tunnadine?

'There is someone you are conveniently overlooking,' said their visitor. 'Perhaps I was too hasty in apportioning blame. Your wife and daughter may, after all, bear no direct responsibility. Both were unwitting victims. They were duped by someone who'd take delight in such an exercise.'

'To what exercise are you referring, may I ask?'

'I speak of the disgraceful prank that has caused us so much pain.'

'I'm not aware of any prank

Tunnadine's eyes blazed. 'Need I speak his abominable name?'

There was a long, eventful silence. Vaughan's jaw dropped and Cassandra's cheeks turned crimson. Their visitor's accusation no longer seemed so far-fetched. He had reached a conclusion that neither of them had even considered. Husband and wife were so troubled by mutual embarrassment that they dared not look at each other.

'I see that you've understood me at last,' said Tunnadine.

Colbeck and Leeming were part of a sizeable number of passengers who left the train at Oxford General station. They were in the same position as the missing women would have been, two bodies on a platform awash with people waiting to welcome friends, well-wishers bidding farewell to travellers and eager porters going about their business. In such a melee, they both realised, it would not have been difficult to slip out of the station unnoticed. That fact lent credence to Colbeck's theory that the women had indeed reached Oxford.

When they hired a cab to take them into the town, Leeming was restive.

'Do we really need to speak to Mrs Vaughan and her daughter?'

'What does the superintendent always say?'

The sergeant grimaced. 'Leave no stone unturned.'

'That's why we're here, Victor – to turn over some stones.'

'Is that the only reason, sir?'

Colbeck smiled. 'No,' he admitted, 'it isn't. The plain truth is that I couldn't resist the temptation to come back to a place where I spent such happy times as an undergraduate. Not that I'm here to rekindle old memories,' he promised. 'We have a lot of work to do and that has priority.'

Leeming's education had been short and unremarkable. People from his humble background could never aspire to study at a place like Oxford. Intellectually, he and Colbeck were poles apart and he was grateful that the inspector never drew attention to the fact. Colbeck had come into the Metropolitan Police after working as a barrister, taking, in the eyes of his colleagues, a foolish fall of status as well as a substantial cut in income. Leeming, meanwhile, had been a uniformed constable on the beat in one of the most dangerous districts of London, gaining a reputation for bravery and tenacity. Fate had eventually brought them together and the two men respected each other so much that the profound differences between them became an irrelevance.

Suddenly, those differences began to surface. Colbeck was back in a famous university where he was completely at ease. Leeming was already fidgeting. He felt like a stranger in a foreign land, having to rely on his companion to act as interpreter. Colbeck sensed his discomfort.

'Don't worry, Victor,' he said, reassuringly. 'The place won't be overrun by undergraduates. They disappear in the summer and leave Oxford to the townspeople. You probably won't even glimpse a gown or a mortarboard.'

'Is that what you had to wear, sir?'

'Forget about me. Just think about Mrs Vaughan and her daughter.'

'I'll feel like an interloper in that college.'

'But you'll behave like the good detective that you are. You'll watch, listen and absorb every detail that may be of use to us. Sir Marcus was economical with facts about his daughter, perhaps because he saw so little of her. Mrs Vaughan, I hope, will be more helpful. From what we've heard about her, she sounds as if she's very forthright.'

Leeming shifted in his seat. He was as uneasy in the presence of forthright women as he was when confronted by members of the peerage. Adding to his discomfort was the scene that was conjured up slowly in front of him. It was a forbidding panorama. Oxford was an amiable jumble of spires, domes, towers, churches, colleges, civic buildings, shops and houses, all of them seemingly wreathed in a kind of medieval grandeur that gave them a sheen of nobility. Colbeck nudged him in the ribs and indicated an ancient structure to the right.

'Is that a castle?' asked Leeming.

'It used to be,' said Colbeck. 'It's been converted into a prison.' He saw his companion relax at once. 'I thought that fact would please you, Victor. Don't be overwhelmed by Oxford. There's nothing sacred about it. St Aldate's is as squalid and insanitary as Seven Dials. Like every other town, it has its fair share of villains and ne'er-do-wells. I venture to suggest that we'll meet one or two of them in due course.'

The Master of University College was slight of build with shoulders rounded by decades of study. When roused, however, he belied his appearance. Stunned at first by Tunnadine's blunt accusation, he soon showed his resilience. His wife also recovered her composure with speed. She let him issue the first denial.

'You are woefully mistaken, sir,' said Vaughan, stepping towards their visitor. 'I should have thought that a man of your intelligence had better things to do on a train journey than to invent such arrant poppycock.'

'Hear, hear!' said Cassandra on the sidelines.

'Having unfairly traduced my wife and my daughter, you have the audacity to bear your fangs at my younger son. I can say categorically that George would never lower himself to the antics you allege.'

Tunnadine sniffed. 'Then you clearly do not know him as well as you should.'

'Who knows a child better than his parents?' demanded Cassandra.

'George is no longer a child – though he still has the childish inclinations that guided me to my conclusion. Your niece and her maid did not disappear on that train. They were smuggled past you at the railway station as part of a jape conceived by your madcap son.'

She flicked a hand. 'George is above such nonsense.'

'He wasn't above stealing the chaplain's dog and hiding the animal in a broom cupboard,' said Tunnadine. 'Nor could he resist the urge to purloin the false teeth belonging to one of the emeritus fellows. Then, of course, there was the time when he was so inebriated that he climbed onto the roof of the chapel and began to shed his clothing.' He shared a crooked smile between them. 'Must I go on?'

'George has let his high spirits get the better of him at

times,' conceded Vaughan, 'but that's all in the past. He's outgrown such behaviour and adopted a more responsible attitude to life.'

'That's not what Imogen told me. When she listed his escapades, she said she was bracing herself for another of George's japes when she arrived here. Neither she nor I anticipated that it would involve kidnap. Much as she loves her cousin,' said Tunnadine, 'she does feel that she's a target for his amusement. George needs putting firmly in his place and I intend to do exactly that.'

'You've no call to interfere in our family matters,' warned Cassandra.

'I have a right to protect my future wife from being the butt of a joke.'

'George would never go to the lengths that you claim.'

'Apart from anything else,' said Vaughan, 'he's not even in Oxford. He's moved to London to pursue his career as an artist.'

'What's to stop him sneaking back without telling you?'

'He wouldn't do that.'

'According to Imogen, he's done it more than once. George told her that he's a free spirit, subject to nobody's control. He needs to be smacked down,' growled Tunnadine. 'I'll put a stop to these confounded tricks of his.'

'You're barking up the wrong tree, sir,' said Vaughan.

'Yes,' said Cassandra with well-bred venom. 'You've already hurled false accusations at me, our daughter and our younger son. Why does Percy, our elder son, escape your censure? Or are you going to charge him with a crime as well?'

Tunnadine was adamant. 'George is the culprit here. I'll

wait until he tires of his silly game and releases Imogen.'

'You'll be wasting your time,' declared Vaughan. 'George is in London and no silly game exists. On the train journey back to London, I'd advise you to think of a more convincing explanation of the agonising situation that confronts us.'

'I shall be staying in Oxford overnight.'

Cassandra was blunt. 'We'll not be able to offer you hospitality.'

'There'll be a room at Brasenose for me. I've done so much on behalf of my alma mater that I may come and go there as I wish. And before you try to send me on my way,' he went on as Vaughan opened the door wide to usher him out, 'I must tell you that I intend to remain until I've met the two detectives on their way here.'

Vaughan blinked. 'I know of no detectives.'

'They were engaged by Sir Marcus who sent telegraphs to Scotland Yard. We don't need the celebrated Inspector Colbeck. His presence here has been rendered superfluous,' said Tunnadine, complacently. 'I've already solved the riddle of Imogen's disappearance.'

Two figures suddenly materialised in the open doorway.

'I'll be most interested to hear how you did it, sir,' said Colbeck.

CHAPTER FIVE

Vernon Tolley did not know whether to be reassured or unsettled by the visit of the two detectives. Colbeck and Leeming had struck him as shrewd and approachable. They'd asked searching questions yet treated him with respect as they did so instead of adopting the condescending tone more usual among his social superiors. Their meeting with Tolley had given him more than a glimmer of hope. At the same time, he reflected, the very fact that they'd been summoned from Scotland Yard showed the gravity of the situation. They'd arrived at the house several hours after the fateful departure of the two women from Shrub Hill station. The trail would thus have gone very cold. It meant that Tolley's hope was tempered with anxiety. No matter how clever or confident the detectives were, they would start their investigation at a severe disadvantage. They could well fail. The thought that he might never know what had happened to his beloved Rhoda Wills made him shudder.

He was coming out of the stables when a woman waddled towards him.

'What are you doing out here, Vernon?' she asked with concern.

'The horses had to be fed.'

'You always put them first. A coachman needs to be fed as well, you know. Come along inside and see what I saved for you.'

'I'd rather stay out here, Win.'

'Aren't you hungry?'

'I've too much on my mind to worry about food.'

'I'm the same,' she said, changing tack and investing her voice with a sense of foreboding. 'This is a sad day for us all and no mistake. It's tragic, that's what it is. Sir Marcus and his wife have seen their only child snatched cruelly away from them. This house will be in mourning for a long time.'

He was curt. 'Don't try to bury them before they're even dead.'

'I'm only saying what everybody else is thinking.'

'Well, *I'm* not thinking it,' he warned. 'There's still cause for hope.'

'I know, I know and I'm glad.' She smiled sweetly. 'I only came to see you because I'm worried about you.'

Win Eagleton was the cook, a plump woman in her late thirties with a vulgar appeal that was offset by a gushing manner and by her habit of producing a broad grin that revealed huge gaps left by missing teeth. The coachman might have set his heart on marrying Rhoda Wills but the cook – even though given no encouragement – had long harboured designs on Tolley. With her rival apparently out of the way, Win thought she could begin to circle her prey.

'Are you sure you're not hungry?' she said, brushing his arm with podgy fingers. 'You've had a long and troubling day, Vernon. You need food inside you.'

'I couldn't touch a thing.'

'You know how much you like my pies.'

'Thank you, all the same, but I have no appetite.'

'It's always a pleasure to cook for you, Vernon.' She moved closer to him. 'But you're right, of course,' she went on, face solemn. 'At a time like this, we shouldn't be thinking about our bellies. Our minds and our prayers should be fixed on them. Whatever could have happened on that train?'

'I wish I knew, Win. They were safe and sound when I waved them off.'

'And were they alone in the compartment?'

'I made certain of it.'

'That was wise,' she said. 'You do hear terrible stories of nasty men who take liberties if they catch a woman alone on a train. I know that I wouldn't dare to travel by myself. You can't be too careful.'

'Nothing like that happened,' he declared. 'I'm sure of it.'

'So am I, Vernon. I told them that the rumour was nonsense.'

He turned to her. 'What rumour?'

'Oh, I don't even want to repeat it. I shouldn't have mentioned it except that they were all talking about it in the kitchen. It would only upset you,' she told him. 'It's far better that you don't even hear it.'

'Don't keep anything from me, Win,' he insisted. 'What's this about a rumour? If it's more than idle gossip, I want to know what it is.'

Having got his attention at last, she wanted to flash a broad grin to signal her triumph but overcame the urge to do so and furrowed her brow instead.

'It's about the Mickleton Tunnel,' she said, confidingly. 'It's always caused trouble. Well, it's not so many years ago that we had that riot there with thousands of people fighting a battle. And there have been other problems since. Someone started a fire in there. Two people committed suicide together by standing on the track. Last year, they found another dead body in there, curled up against a wall. Some folk believe that the tunnel is cursed. That's the rumour, Vernon. They say that, when the train slowed in the dark of the tunnel, someone might have been able to climb into their carriage and commit whatever crime he did. I don't believe it myself,' she said quickly, 'but that's what I heard. If anything really dreadful happened on that journey to Oxford, it would have taken place in the Mickleton Tunnel.'

Vernon Tolley swallowed hard and his gloom deepened.

After a flurry of introductions, Dominic Vaughan tried to dispel the tension in the room by producing a decanter of the college sherry and pouring a glass for all five of them. Everyone sat down. The person most grateful for the drink was Victor Leeming, perched on the edge of a chair and feeling so alienated in the strange environment that his throat had gone dry and his body numb. The sherry at least brought him back to life again. Colbeck complimented the Master on the quality of his sherry then invited Tunnadine to explain how he'd achieved the miracle of unravelling the mystery. The politician was disdainful, mocking the efforts of the detectives and boasting that he'd succeeded where they had floundered. Ignoring the sergeant as if he were not even there, his words were aimed solely at Colbeck. When he sat back at the end of his recitation, Tunnadine looked as if he expected a round of applause.

Colbeck sipped some more sherry then shook his head in disagreement.

'It's an interesting theory, Mr Tunnadine, but it's fatally flawed.'

'I know what George Vaughan is capable of, Inspector.'

'That may well be so, sir. Throughout its long and illustrious history, this university has been enlivened by undergraduate jests. When I was a student here myself,' said Colbeck, deliberately letting him know his academic credentials, 'I saw countless examples of what one might call youthful exuberance. One of my own contemporaries, for instance, thought it would be a splendid joke if he clambered up on the roof of the Sheldonian Theatre with a live sheep tied around his shoulders. Why do it? The answer is simple – he wanted to cause a stir.'

'What has that got to do with George Vaughan?'

'He and my old college friend are two of a kind, Mr Tunnadine. Both like to shock people with their bravado. But a shock, by definition, is a temporary event. Once accomplished, its effect soon wears off. If, as you argue, the Master's son is responsible for what you refer to as devilry, why has he let it drag on for such a long time? The joke had worn thin several hours ago.'

'That's precisely what *I* told him,' said Vaughan.

'George would never make us all suffer like this,' added Cassandra. 'He's grown up in the last year. He's finally seen the error of his ways.'

'Once a joker, always a joker,' argued Tunnadine. 'I've met him. He can't stop himself from being the family clown.'

'Clowns perform in search of immediate applause, sir,' said Colbeck. 'They never extend their act *ad nauseam* until it causes pain and anguish. I'm sorry, Mr Tunnadine, but your so-called solution is utterly worthless.'

'I couldn't have put it better myself,' agreed Cassandra.

'Nor could I,' said Vaughan. 'You cast unjustified slurs on the honour of our younger son, Mr Tunnadine. I'd say that an apology was in order.'

'None is deserved and none will be given,' said Tunnadine, stonily.

'Inspector Colbeck has exposed your theory for the gibberish that it is.'

Looking from one face to another, Tunnadine saw that he was outnumbered. Since nobody took his explanation seriously, he began to have his first niggling doubts about it. Too wily to admit defeat, he tried to turn the tables on Colbeck.

'What progress have *you* made, Inspector?' he demanded.

'We're still harvesting information, sir.'

'You must have reached a conclusion.'

'I never do that on insufficient evidence,' said Colbeck.

'So, in effect, your investigation has yielded nothing of consequence.'

'I wouldn't put it like that, Mr Tunnadine.'

'Then how would you put it?' pressed the other.

'Possibilities are beginning to emerge.'

'I'm not interested in possibilities,' said Tunnadine with vehemence. 'The dear lady I intend to marry may be in some kind of danger. She must be found quickly and returned safely to me. The culprit -- and I still name him as George Vaughan -- must be subjected to the full rigour of the law.' After draining his glass, he rose to his feet, set the glass on the desk, then plucked a card from his waistcoat pocket. 'This is where I may be reached in London,' he said, thrusting the card at Colbeck. 'I'll be spending the night at Brasenose before returning there.'

'As you wish, sir,' said Colbeck, getting up to see him off.

'Good day to you all!'

After snatching up his hat, Clive Tunnadine let himself out and slammed the door behind him to indicate his displeasure. Colbeck resumed his seat.

'We can now begin to have a less fraught discussion,' he observed.

'I'm sorry that you came when you did, gentlemen,' said Vaughan. 'He was in a foul mood when he barged in here. We've only met Mr Tunnadine twice before and he doesn't improve on acquaintance.'

'He was obnoxious,' said Cassandra. 'I loathe the fellow.'

'What he said about our younger son was quite scandalous.'

'We must make allowances for his natural apprehension,' said Colbeck, easily. 'Anyone told that his future bride has just disappeared is bound to be at the mercy of wild fantasies. Mr Tunnadine was casting around for someone to blame and he happened to alight on your younger son.'

'George can be a clown at times but he's not *that* irresponsible.'

'At heart,' said Cassandra, fondly, 'he's the soul of kindness.'

'Leaving him aside for the moment,' said Colbeck, 'let's turn to the moment when the train from Worcester actually arrived at the station here. What did you and your daughter see, Mrs Vaughan?'

'Everything but what we wanted to see – namely, Imogen and her maid.'

'Could you be more specific?'

'I don't follow.'

'Well, when Sergeant Leeming and I arrived at the station earlier, we were part of a swirling crowd, yet we could pick out some of its constituent members.'

'Yes,' said Leeming, taking his cue. 'There was a priest, an old lady with a walking stick, another with a small dog under each arm, a group of giggling young girls and an elderly gentleman with a monocle. Then there was a—'

'Thank you, Sergeant,' said Colbeck, cutting him off. 'The point has been made, I fancy. Even though we were not looking for those individuals, they impinged on our consciousness. Did something similar happen to you, Mrs Vaughan?'

'Why, yes – as a matter of fact, it did.'

'Please go on.'

'I remember the woman with her arm in a sling and a man with a violin case. Emma will certainly recall the four children who got off the train with their parents because one of the boys bumped into her. Both of us spotted the soldier, of course.'

Colbeck's ears pricked up. 'What soldier was that?'

'He was waiting on the platform with us, Inspector. He was tall and rather resplendent. When the train pulled in, he welcomed another soldier who had bandaging over one eye. The wounded man was travelling with a woman. I only caught a fleeting glimpse of them because I was too busy keeping my eyes peeled for Imogen.' Cassandra was taken aback. 'Why are you smiling like that, Inspector?' she asked. 'Have I said something amusing?'

'No, Mrs Vaughan,' he replied, 'quite the contrary.'

'Please explain yourself.'

'You said exactly what I was hoping you'd say.' Colbeck turned to her husband. 'Would it be possible to speak to your daughter?'

'Is that necessary?' wondered Vaughan. 'Emma can give you no information that my wife has not already vouchsafed.'

'Nevertheless, we'd appreciate a word with her.'

'In that case, I'll send for her at once.'

'To be honest,' said Colbeck as the Master got to his feet, 'we'd prefer to speak to your daughter alone, if at all possible.'

'Emma would prefer that I was there,' said Cassandra, puzzled by the request.

'We must comply with the inspector's wishes, my love,' advised Vaughan.

'I'm her mother, Dominic. I have a right.'

'If you wish to enforce it,' said Colbeck, pleasantly, 'then, of course, you're most welcome to join us. But consider this, Mrs Vaughan. Your daughter and her cousin are of a similar age. When left alone together, they would be likely to share confidences. They would exchange the kind of harmless little secrets that would not come to the ears of their parents.'

'The inspector is correct,' decreed Vaughan, overriding

his wife's wishes for once. 'He and the sergeant must speak to Emma alone. Were you there, my love, our daughter might unwittingly hold back things that are germane to the investigation. She must be allowed the freedom to express herself.'

Cassandra's protest was quelled by a decisive gesture from her husband.

'Follow me, gentlemen,' invited Vaughan, moving to the door.

'Thank you for your cooperation,' said Colbeck, rising to his feet.

'I'll want to know *everything* that Emma tells you,' said Cassandra.

'Nothing will be kept back from you, Mrs Vaughan.'

But even as he spoke the words, Colbeck suspected that there might well be certain things that the daughter might not wish her mother to know and he was more than ready to conceal them if they would save Emma Vaughan from embarrassment.

On receipt of the news of the disappearance of his daughter, Sir Marcus Burnhope had reacted with speed and determination. He'd ridden at a gallop to Shrub Hill station and used its telegraph system to fire off messages hither and thither. Not only had he alerted Scotland Yard to the crisis, he made sure that senior figures working for the Oxford, Worcester and Wolverhampton Railway were aware of it as well. At his behest, teams were sent out from intermediate stations between Shrub Hill and the intended destination of Imogen and her maid. There were well over twenty possible stops on the line, many of them little more than a halt in the middle of open countryside. Such places lacked the manpower to join in the hunt. While some stretches of the line were searched, therefore, long tracts of it were untouched. To those trudging along the line, the hunt seemed a forlorn exercise.

'We're wasting our time,' grumbled the policeman.

'Aye, Tom, I know.'

'We can never look behind every bush.'

'It's what Sir Marcus ordered.'

'Then let *him* join in the search. It's his daughter, after all.'

'They say she's a real beauty.'

'Oh, she is. I've seen her. She doesn't take after her father, I'll tell you that. Sir Marcus is an ugly old bugger.'

Instead of walking along the track, the railway policeman wanted to be at home with his wife. His companion was an off-duty stationmaster, ordered to spend his evening joining in the hunt for the missing women. Like the policeman, he was weary and disenchanted. He used a stick to push back some shrubs.

'There's nobody here, Tom. How much longer must we do this?'

'We go on until it gets too dark to see.'

The stationmaster looked slyly upwards. 'I'd say it was pretty dark already.'

In fact, there was still plenty of light in the sky but there was nobody about to contradict him. The two men traded a conspiratorial grin. If they abandoned what they saw as an aimless plod, nobody would be any the wiser. They were just about to give up and retrace their steps when the policeman caught sight of something in the long grass some forty yards or so ahead of them. He nudged his companion and pointed. The stationmaster saw it as well. It was the long, trailing hair of a woman. Convinced that they'd found one of the missing passengers, after all, they shook off their fatigue and ran towards her, their boots clacking on the hard wooden sleepers. The noise had an instant effect. A scantily clad woman suddenly came to life and sat up with the young man hiding in the grass beside her. When they saw the policeman's uniform, they didn't stand on ceremony. They snatched up their discarded clothing and fled the scene. The two men stopped to catch their breath.

'Poor devil!' said the stationmaster with a laugh. 'We spoilt his fun.'

'It's a pity. She was a nice-looking girl with a lovely arse on her.'

'Do you think we should report it?'

'No, I think we should go home and forget all about it.'

'What about Sir Marcus's daughter?'

'Let someone else find her.'

As they walked along the track in the opposite direction, they heard a train approaching in the distance. They jumped quickly aside and watched it come into view, hurtling towards them, then racing past so fast that they were forced back by the rush of air. They waited until its deafening tumult had faded.

'I tell you one thing,' said the policeman. 'If Sir Marcus's daughter jumped off the train at that speed, she'd be as dead as a door-nail.'

Emma Vaughan had been moping in her room for hours, praying fervently for the safety of her cousin and reliving the horror of realising that she had simply vanished. When her father introduced her to the detectives, she was at first alarmed, thinking that their arrival meant that a heinous crime had been committed. It took Colbeck some time to calm her down and to offer a measure of reassurance. At the Master's suggestion, they adjourned to the drawing room with his daughter. Emma was uneasy at being left alone with them and she found Leeming's features disquieting. Colbeck's charm and sensitivity slowly won her over.

'You're very fond of your cousin, are you not?' he asked.

'I love Imogen. She's my best friend.'

'How often do you see her?'

'It was not nearly enough,' she replied. 'Imogen only came here twice a year but I stayed at Burnhope Manor three or four times.'

'Which place did you prefer?'

'Oh, it was much nicer when she came here. We could talk properly.'

'Couldn't you do that at her house?'

'Not really, Inspector,' she said. 'Lady Burnhope always seemed to be there. I love my aunt, naturally, but I did get the feeling of being watched all the time. Imogen was forever apologising for it.'

'Did she resent being under her mother's watchful eye?'

'Yes, she did.'

'I can see why she looked forward to coming here where she had a little more freedom. Tell me,' Colbeck went on, 'about the arrival of the train from Worcester. You and your mother were waiting on the station, weren't you?'

'That's right. I was so excited when it came in and so

heartbroken when Imogen wasn't on it. I was certain that she must have caught the train.'

'Who got off it?'

'Lots of people – every single carriage had been occupied.'

'Mrs Vaughan mentioned a soldier,' recalled Leeming.

'Yes, I saw him as well. He had a bandage over one eye. Before I could take a proper look at him, I was bumped into by a little boy who leapt out of a carriage. Mother chided him for being so careless. But I do remember the soldier on the train,' she said, 'and the one who greeted him on the station.'

'You've met Mr Tunnadine, I take it,' said Colbeck.

'We've seen him a couple of times.'

'And was he in company with your cousin?'

'Yes,' said Emma with a smile. 'They made such a handsome pair. Clive Tunnadine was entranced by Imogen and she was enchanted by him. She told me that he swept her off her feet.'

'She was happy with the match, then?'

'Who wouldn't be happy with a man like that? He's very wealthy and comes from a good family. My uncle says that he has a brilliant career in politics ahead of him. Imogen was taken completely by surprise when he proposed. He gave her the most gorgeous engagement ring,' she said, enviously. 'Imogen couldn't stop smiling when she showed it off to me.'

The information made Colbeck look at Tunnadine afresh. He and Leeming had found the man both arrogant and somewhat rebarbative. Clearly, he had a different effect on young women. He encouraged Emma to say more about his relationship with her cousin then he turned his attention elsewhere.

'You have a brother called George, I hear.'

'George is my younger brother. The elder is Percy. They couldn't be more unlike each other,' she said with an affectionate smile. 'George is an artist, living in London while Percy is a curate in Gloucestershire. Father loves poetry, you see. That's how he came to choose their names.'

Leeming was dumbfounded but Colbeck was quick to understand.

'Could Percy be named after a certain Percy Bysshe Shelley, by any chance?'

'Yes, Inspector, he was.'

'Shelley was an undergraduate at this college, wasn't he? It's odd that a curate like your brother should bear his name. My memory is that Shelley was sent down for writing a pamphlet called *The Necessity of Atheism*.'

'You're very well informed.'

'I, too, admire his poetry, Miss Vaughan.'

'Father speaks very highly of it. In fact, he believes that we should have some kind of memorial dedicated to him. Unfortunately, the fellows won't hear of it. They think that Shelley brought discredit on the college.'

'Who is your other brother named after?' asked Leeming.

'It is another favourite poet of my father's – Lord Byron.'

'Even *I* have heard of him.'

'It sounds as if it might have been a more appropriate christening,' said Colbeck. 'Lord Byron was famed for his wildness and it seems that your younger brother is not without a reckless streak in his nature.'

She laughed. 'George is a loveable madman.'

'Mr Tunnadine believes that he is behind your cousin's

disappearance. He claims that your younger brother kidnapped her and spirited her away.'

'That's absurd!' she cried.

'George has been the family clown, by all accounts.'

'I freely admit it, Inspector, but that doesn't mean he'd do anything to hurt Imogen – or to upset us, for that matter.'

'What if he wanted to upset Mr Tunnadine?'

'It doesn't sound as if he and your brother would see eye to eye,' said Leeming. 'How did they get on, Miss Vaughan?'

'George only met Clive once,' she replied, 'and there was some friction between them, I must confess.'

'Then your brother had a motive to strike back at Mr Tunnadine.'

'He'd never do anything to spoil Imogen's happiness.'

'What about his own happiness?' asked Colbeck. 'We gather that your cousin was famed for her beauty. It can't have gone unnoticed by your brother. Perhaps he was nursing hopes on his own behalf.'

'You obviously don't know my brother. George loved Imogen as a friend and as a cousin. It never went beyond that. The sort of young women to whom he was attracted were always . . .' Emma left the words unspoken. 'Let's just say that they were of a wholly different character to Imogen. George likes to describe himself as a free spirit. He seeks female company of a like persuasion.'

'Thank you for eliminating that theory once and for all, Miss Vaughan,' said Colbeck. 'When I first heard Mr Tunnadine voice it, I thought it lacked credibility. Your brother is exonerated. He has no reason at all to abduct his cousin. However,' he added, looking at the sergeant, 'it won't do any harm for you to meet the gentleman, Victor. I'm sure that he'd like to be made aware of the predicament in which his cousin finds herself and – based on his knowledge of her – he may be able to offer a suggestion as to what might have happened to her.'

'I'll give you George's address,' volunteered Emma. 'He ought to be told about this terrible situation. Underneath all that wildness, he's a very caring person.'

'Then he'll want his cousin found.'

'And so will Percy. He should be told as well. In fact, Percy should be the first to hear about Imogen's disappearance.'

'Why is that?'

'Well,' she explained, 'it's something of an open secret. Percy would never admit it, of course, but I'm his sister and I can read his mind. George will tease Imogen and laugh at her expense but Percy wouldn't dream of doing that. In his own quiet way,' she said, 'my elder brother has been in love with her for years.'

CHAPTER SIX

Caleb Andrews was never satisfied. When he was working as an engine driver, he was always complaining about the long hours, the attendant dangers of hurtling around the country at speed and the inevitable grime he picked up in the course of a normal day. Now that he'd finally retired, he moaned about having nothing to do and nowhere to go. Eager to leave the London and North West Railway after a lifetime's service, he was equally eager to be back on the footplate. Ideally, he'd have liked a halfway stage between work and retirement but the LNWR didn't employ part-time drivers or cater for the individual demands of someone as capricious as Andrews. When he called on his daughter that evening, he brought his usual list of grievances. Madeleine gave him no chance to unpack his heart.

'I'm afraid that Robert won't be joining us,' she explained.

'Why is that, Maddy?'

'He's involved in a case that's taken him to Worcestershire.

The note he sent mentioned two passengers who'd disappeared on a train journey to Oxford.'

'That's hardly surprising, is it?' he said, contemptuously. 'They must have been travelling on the OWWR and it has no right to call itself a railway company. It's a disaster. The person I blame is Brunel. He was the chief engineer when the project was first started. No wonder they had problems.'

'Robert thinks that Mr Brunel is in a class of his own.'

'Yes – it's a class of fools and village idiots. The man is a menace.'

Madeleine Colbeck had achieved her aim of deflecting him away from his regular litany of woes but she had to endure a diatribe against Brunel instead. It went on for a few minutes. Since her husband was unlikely to return that day, she was glad of some company and had long ago learnt to tolerate her father's impassioned lectures on anything and everything concerning the railway system. He was like a cantankerous old locomotive, pulling into a station and filling it with an ear-splitting hiss of steam. The noise slowly subsided and Andrews' rage cooled.

'Don't ask me for details,' she said, 'for I have none.'

'You don't need any, Maddy. I can tell you what happened. If two people vanished on the Old Worse and Worse, it means that they were so horrified by the way that the train shook and rattled that they jumped off in a bid for safety.' He wagged a finger. 'You need to make your will before you travel on that line.'

Madeleine laughed. 'You will exaggerate.'

'I know what I know.'

Andrews was a short, wiry man of peppery disposition.

Approaching sixty, he was showing signs of age, his back bent, his hair thinning and his fringe beard in the process of turning from grey to white. Madeleine, by contrast, was looking younger than ever as if marriage to the Railway Detective had rejuvenated her. She was an alert, attractive, buxom woman in her twenties with endearing dimples in both cheeks that reminded Andrews so much of his late wife at times that he had to look away. Madeleine had first met Colbeck as a result of the daring robbery of a train that her father had been driving. Andrews had been badly injured during the incident but had made a full recovery and was eternally grateful to Colbeck for catching those behind the robbery.

'I wish that your mother could see you now,' he said. 'She wouldn't believe the way you've settled into this lovely big house. It's a far cry from our little cottage in Camden Town, yet you seem completely at home here.'

'I don't always feel it,' she admitted. 'It took me ages to get used to the idea of having servants at my beck and call.'

'I don't see why, Maddy. You had me at your beck and call for years.'

She stiffened. 'That's not how I remember it, Father. I was the one who looked after *you*.'

'Don't quibble.'

'Then don't tell lies.'

'The important thing is that you're happy.' He gave her a shrewd look. 'You are, aren't you?'

'I couldn't be happier,' she replied, beaming. 'I have everything I want.'

'Make sure that it stays that way. If you're not properly looked after, I'll need to have a stern word with my son-in-law.'

'That won't be necessary. Robert is a wonderful husband.'

Madeleine still couldn't believe her good fortune in meeting and marrying Colbeck. At a stroke, she'd acquired a new social status, moved into a fine house in John Islip Street and been given the best possible facilities to pursue her career as an artist. Thanks to her husband's encouragement, she'd reached a stage where her paintings of locomotives were commanding a good price. Inevitably, her father appointed himself as her technical advisor.

'Another thing to remember about Brunel,' he said, getting his second wind, 'is the way he started a riot on the Old Worse and Worse. Have I ever told you what happened at the Mickleton Tunnel?'

'Yes, Father, you have.'

'It was a disgrace. Brunel should have been imprisoned for what he did.'

Madeleine sighed. 'You've said so many times.'

'I've kept the cuttings from the newspapers.'

'I've seen them, Father.'

'He took the law into his own hands,' he went on, 'and recruited an army of drunken navvies to take on the contractors responsible for building the tunnel. The police were called out and the Riot Act was read twice by magistrates, but did that stop Isambard Kingdom Brunel? Oh, no – he came back in the dark with his navvies, all of them armed with pickaxes, shovels and goodness-knows-what. There was a fierce battle. Brunel seemed to think he was the blooming Duke of Wellington, leading the charge at Waterloo. When the troops were called in from Coventry, they were too late to prevent bloodshed and broken bones. I tell you this,

Maddy,' he concluded with a favourite phrase of his, 'the Mickleton Tunnel is a monument to Brunel's stupidity.'

When they reached the tunnel, they were about to plunge into complete darkness. They'd come prepared. The two men were off-duty porters from Moreton-in-Marsh station and – when Sir Marcus Burnhope raised the alarm – they'd volunteered to join in the search. Travelling north-west, they went past Blockley and Chipping Campden to be confronted by the gaping hole that was the Mickleton Tunnel. Having lit their lantern, they entered with trepidation into a pitch-black, brick-lined tube some 887 yards in length. They were not afraid of being caught in there when a train shot through the tunnel because they'd taken the precaution of checking the timetable beforehand. What they feared were rats and other lurking creatures that might attack them. They'd also heard stories of tramps sleeping in the tunnel from time to time and of desperate criminals on the run who used it as a temporary refuge.

To bolster their confidence, they walked shoulder to shoulder. Peter Dale, the chubby man holding the lantern, let it swing to and fro so that its glare lit up both sides of the tunnel. They moved furtively into the gloom. After fifty yards or more, there was a rustling noise then a rat dashed past them, brushing against the trouser leg of the other man. He lost his nerve at once.

'We'll find nothing here,' he said, shivering. 'Let's go back.'

'We haven't searched it properly yet,' said Dale, lifting the lantern higher. 'Sir Marcus Burnhope has promised a reward for anyone who finds his daughter. We may have a chance to claim it.'

'There's nobody in here, Peter.'

'We need to be sure of that.'

As Dale walked cautiously on, his companion stayed reluctantly beside him. The thought of being bitten by some sharp-toothed denizen of the darkness made him flinch and he fought hard to control the queasiness in the pit of his stomach. They were halfway along the tunnel when the lantern's beam revealed something that brought them to an abrupt halt.

'Do you see what I see?' asked Dale.

'Hold the lantern higher, Peter. I can't make out what it is.'

Dale took a tentative step forward so that the glow from his lantern illumined the object clearly. When he saw what it was, he grinned.

'Now that could be interesting,' he said.

It was late evening when Victor Leeming finally reached Scotland Yard but he knew that the superintendent would still be there. The indefatigable Tallis often worked on into the night yet still contrived to look alert and attentive in the morning. At the moment, the sergeant was neither of those things. As he delivered his report, his voice was weary and he came perilously close to yawning. Tallis was not impressed.

'I expected something more tangible out of this investigation,' he said.

'It will take time, sir.'

'We don't *have* time. A young woman's life is at stake here. I've got Sir Marcus hounding me with telegraphs and

I had Mr Tunnadine in here, demanding that I commit more resources to the case.'

Leeming was rueful. 'Mr Tunnadine is fond of making demands.'

'Well, I'll not allow him to hold the whip hand over me,' said Tallis with a grim smile. 'On the other hand, I was hoping that your enquiries would yield me something with which I could appease both him and Sir Marcus.'

'Tell them that the young lady is still alive – and so is her maid.'

'How do you know that?'

'Frankly,' said Leeming, 'I don't but the inspector is certain of it. He has a sixth sense in situations like this.'

'I dispute that. The famed intuition of his is a myth.'

'It's never let him down before, sir.'

'That's a moot point, Sergeant.'

Leeming glanced hopefully at the door. 'May I go home now, please?'

'No, you may not. Your report left out far too much. For instance, I still haven't established why Colbeck is pursuing his particular line of enquiry.'

'He believes that the answer to the conundrum lies within the family.'

'I remain unconvinced of that.' He jabbed a finger at Leeming. 'And don't you dare tell me that we have another example of the inspector's sixth sense. It sounds like a wild guess to me, unsubstantiated by any firm evidence.'

'It's all we have to go on at this stage, Superintendent.'

Tallis glowered at him. 'Is Colbeck seriously suggesting that someone *within* the family actually connived at this disappearance?'

'No, sir,' replied Leeming, careful not to disclose the full details of the inspector's theory. 'He just feels that he needs to know more about how the family members behave towards each other before he can reach a considered decision.'

'So what does he propose to do?'

'He's staying the night in Oxford so that he can travel to a village in Gloucestershire called North Cerney.'

'Why the devil does he want to go there?'

'Sir Marcus's nephew is the curate at the local church.'

'Hell and damnation!' exclaimed Tallis, aghast at the news. 'Is Colbeck so desperate that he's turning to the church for help? Are you telling me that this sixth sense of his is no more than a resort to prayer? A detective is supposed to detect – not go down on his knees before an altar. What does he hope to find in Gloucestershire?'

'You'll have to ask him, sir.'

'I'm asking *you*, man!'

'The inspector feels that it's important to do so.'

'Well, I feel it important to rearrange Colbeck's priorities for him. His first duty is to gather relevant facts, not to go gallivanting around the countryside. When I assigned this case to him,' said Tallis, bitterly, 'I did so because of his past successes with crimes relating to the railways. Sadly, this investigation has exposed the limits of his capabilities. It's also proved the uselessness of his sixth sense and the deficiencies of some of the other five. He needs to be reprimanded for his shortcomings.'

'I disagree, sir.'

Tallis rounded on him. 'Did I ask you to speak?'

'The inspector *has* made some progress.'

'Hold your tongue!' snarled the superintendent.

'You've nothing worth saying at the best of times and your misguided loyalty to Colbeck is infuriating. You may take a message to him from me.'

'Yes, sir, I will.'

'Shut up, man – just *listen*!' Leeming recoiled from the rebuke as if struck by a blow. 'Warn him,' continued the other, quivering with fury. 'Warn him that, if he doesn't achieve results very soon, *I* will take over the investigation myself. We cannot afford to antagonise Sir Marcus. He has friends in the highest places. If we upset him, we will pay a heavy price.' Standing up, he towered over Leeming. 'What will *you* be doing tomorrow?'

'The inspector has asked me to speak to another member of the Vaughan family, sir. His name is George Vaughan.' Leeming attempted a disarming smile that somehow ended up as a crude leer. 'He's named after Lord Byron.'

'I don't care if he's named after the Queen of Sheba. Who is he?'

'He's the younger son of the Master of that college we went to and he lives here in London.'

'What possible connection can this fellow have to the disappearance of two women?'

'That's what I have to find out, sir.'

'A visit to this George Vaughan is a needless distraction.'

'He interests the inspector. He's an artist, of sorts.'

'An *artist*!' The superintendent gave a wild laugh. 'This gets worse and worse. We need someone who can *find* Sir Marcus's daughter, not an artist who can paint her portrait. As for Lord Byron . . . the man was a talented poet with disturbing emotional inclinations.' He snapped his fingers. 'Where did you say that Colbeck was going?'

'He wants to speak to a curate in North Cerney.'

'And whom will he consult after that?' asked Tallis with blistering sarcasm. 'Will he seek guidance from the Archbishop of Canterbury? Or is he minded to talk things over with the Man in the Moon?'

Leeming was glad to escape alive.

Having spent the night at University College as a guest, Colbeck left early and headed for the railway station. He was sorry that he'd had to decline the Master's invitation to tour the building. He liked Dominic Vaughan and admired everything he saw of the college but leisure time did not exist in an investigation. He needed to press on. A train took him over halfway to his destination, then he alighted, hired a trap and drove in the direction of Cirencester. Highly conscious of Oxford's antiquity while he was there, he was now reaching even further back into history because he was travelling on the Fosse Way, the great thoroughfare built by the Romans to connect Exeter with Lincoln. Long stretches of it were as straight as an arrow.

After resting and watering his horse at a wayside inn, he set off again through pleasant countryside and weighed up all the information he'd so far accumulated. In meeting the irascible Clive Tunnadine, his belief that Imogen Burnhope might not be wholly committed to the notion of marrying him had been strengthened. Tunnadine might be an effective politician but he was not an appealing bridegroom. Markedly older than Imogen, he was harsh and peremptory, talking about her as if she were a valuable property that had gone astray rather than as the woman he loved enough to want as his wife. Colbeck could imagine only too well how he'd feel if Madeleine ever went missing. Unlike Tunnadine, he'd be at the mercy of swirling emotions, not venting his anger on someone who was trying to find her. To his credit, Sir Marcus Burnhope had shown genuine fondness for his daughter. There was no corresponding affection in Imogen's future husband. The love match proclaimed by her father no longer existed.

If she and her maid had been smuggled off the train at Oxford, then the women would have needed both a disguise and an accomplice. Since she was the tall, lithe young woman of report, Imogen might be able to pass for a soldier, especially if her face was partly hidden by a bandage. Rhoda Wills would have been invisible on the wounded soldier's arm. They could have been whisked away by a waiting accomplice with military connections and the two red uniforms would have melted into the crowd, unseen by Cassandra and Emma Vaughan. The deception had been an undoubted success. But what had happened then? Where had the women been taken and how would they survive now that they'd apparently severed their links with the Burnhope family? Only something – or someone – of irresistible desirability could provoke the Honourable Imogen Burnhope into taking the momentous step of turning her back on her family to seek a life elsewhere. Colbeck hoped that Percy Vaughan would be able to shed light on the mystery.

North Cerney was little more than a straggle of houses and a cluster of farms. Bathed in sunshine, All Saints Church was perched on a hillside overlooking the village and was one of the most picturesque buildings in the whole of the Churn valley. At first glance, Colbeck judged it to have an ideal location and he appreciated its abundant charm. Closer inspection revealed the medieval structure to be slightly disproportionate. Cruciform in shape, it had a saddle-backed west tower of Norman origin. Transepts had been added at a later date but the different architectural elements combined to give the church an almost tangled appearance. Tethering his horse at the gate, Colbeck went up the winding path in the churchyard to the sound of buzzing bees. Birds on the slate-covered roof added their individual songs to the chorus. Discordant notes were occasionally provided by the sheep grazing between the headstones. It was a place of rural enchantment and Colbeck could understand why Percy Vaughan had chosen it.

Carved into the wall where the chancel met the southern transept was a manticore, a beast with human head, the arms and body of a lion and a scorpion's sting in its tail. It seemed an unlikely decoration to find on the exterior of a church. Colbeck was still trying to work out why it had been put there when he heard a voice behind him.

'Can I help you, sir?' asked Percy Vaughan.

'Good day to you,' said Colbeck, turning round to see the curate walking towards him. 'I suspect that you may well be the person I came to see.'

After introducing himself, he explained why he'd come. The curate was both shocked and wounded. He was a lanky, rather sallow man in his mid twenties with a scholarly intensity. He peered at Colbeck through narrowed lids as if scrutinising a problematical passage of Scripture.

'Imogen has *disappeared*?'

'I fear so,' said Colbeck. 'I've yet to decide if she was

abducted or if the young lady disappeared of her own volition.'

'Why, pray, should she do that?'

'I was hoping that you might be able to provide an answer.'

'I'm afraid that I can't.'

'Mr Tunnadine thought it might be some jape devised by your brother.'

'No,' said the curate, forcefully. 'Even George wouldn't stoop that low. He loves Imogen – we all do. He'd never do anything to frighten her like that. Tunnadine is quite wrong.'

'Have you met the gentleman?'

'Indeed, I have, Inspector.'

'Did he strike you as a fit husband for your cousin?'

'It's not for me to pronounce upon that. He was Imogen's choice.'

'I fancy that Sir Marcus might have brought his influence to bear.'

'Well,' said the other, guardedly, 'that's inevitable, I fear. He's always taken the major decisions at Burnhope Manor. And if *he* hasn't done so, then my aunt has been a willing deputy.'

'In other words,' said Colbeck, watching him carefully, 'their daughter had no control over her life. Do you think she found that irksome?'

Percy Vaughan made no reply. His sister had told Colbeck that her elder brother was in love with Imogen but the curate did not wear his heart on his sleeve. From his blank expression, it was impossible to tell what he might be thinking. There was a lengthy pause. To break the silence, Colbeck nodded towards the church.

'I was just admiring your manticore,' he said.

'I'm impressed that you know what it is, Inspector. Very few people do. It's supposed to hail from Abyssinia. We have a second one at the foot of the tower. They add something to the church. Some believe that they were put there to ward off evil spirits.'

'Or to ward off questions from Scotland Yard detectives,' suggested Colbeck, with a mischievous gleam. 'Your father told me that you were keen to come to North Cerney. It has a link to his college, I gather.'

'It's true,' said the curate, showing some animation at last. 'The college bought the advowson in 1753. It cost an immense amount of money. At the time, of course, theology was the main subject of study at the college. I'm by no means the first person to move from there to North Cerney.'

'But you're only a curate here.'

'The rector will retire in due course and I will take his place. At the moment, I have a small cottage in the village. I look forward to moving closer to the church.' He glanced covetously at the nearby rectory. 'As it is, the rector spends a lot of time elsewhere. I have to take most of the services.'

'That seems a trifle unfair.'

'One has to earn one's spurs, Inspector.'

'That's a curious phrase for a man of God to use.'

'I don't see why. When I visit my parishioners, I spend a lot of time in the saddle. Some of them live in outlying farms and hamlets.'

Colbeck looked across at the rectory. It was a long, low, capacious house with a thatched roof and an ample garden in full flower. At times when he'd contemplated ending his life in a rural retreat, the rectory – in size, shape and position – was exactly the image that had come into his mind.

'It will be a fine place to live,' he observed. 'The rectory will make an ideal family house. I envy you. Tell me,' he went on, probing gently, 'has your cousin ever visited you here?'

'Unfortunately,' said the curate, sadly, 'she has not. However,' he added with the first hint of a smile, 'when I was ordained as a deacon in Gloucester Cathedral, both Imogen and Lady Burnhope attended the service. I was touched by their support.'

'No doubt your own family was there as well.'

'My parents came and so did my sister, Emma, but it was too much to ask of my brother. George is something of an apostate. My own view is that it's more of a posture than anything else. He keeps rather unsavoury company in London and has to treat religion scornfully to stay in with his cronies.'

'Is he a good artist?'

'He has a talent, assuredly, but I'm not certain that he knows how best to develop it. Artists are peculiar individuals.'

'I know,' said Colbeck, fondly. 'I live with one. Though the kind of paintings that my wife produces are, I suspect, far distant from anything your brother might choose to put on canvas.'

A sudden look of panic came into the curate's eye. He grabbed Colbeck's arm.

'You will find Imogen, won't you?' he asked.

'Without question, I will – and I expect her to be unharmed.'

'That's a relief,' said the other, leaving go of him. 'But you won't find her in North Cerney. That much is certain. What exactly prompted this visit?'

'I was interested to hear your opinion of the young lady and of the man to whom she is betrothed. Anything you can tell me about her life at Burnhope Manor would be of use. I'm sorry that you feel unable to talk about it.'

Percy Vaughan studied him for a long time before finally speaking.

'I will answer your questions, Inspector,' he promised, 'but I have a more urgent summons. Forgive me while I go into the church to pray for Imogen and her maid. The Almighty must be enlisted in the search for her.'

'I'll gladly join you,' said Colbeck, following him towards the door. 'And afterwards, I trust, you'll talk more freely.'

'I give you my word.'

'Thank you.'

They walked on together. The curate stopped him at the door.

'Do you have any clues at all as to the reason for her disappearance?'

'We have a number of clues,' said Colbeck, 'and others will certainly turn up.'

Sir Marcus Burnhope held it in his hands and examined it from all angles. When he put it back on the table, he walked around it in a circle and kept his eyes fixed on it. Eventually, there was a tap on the door and the butler ushered in Vernon Tolley. After nodding obsequiously, the coachman approached his master.

'You sent for me, Sir Marcus?'

'Yes,' replied the other. 'Something was found yesterday evening in the Mickleton tunnel.' He pointed to the table. 'I've never set eyes on it before so it can't belong to my daughter. What about you, Tolley?'

The coachman recognised the hat at once and leapt forward to snatch it up. He stroked it lovingly and even held it to his cheek for a second. Aware that he was being watched, he carefully replaced the hat upon the table.

'It belongs to Rhoda Wills, Sir Marcus,' he explained.

'Are you quite certain of that?'

'Oh, yes,' said Tolley. 'I'd know it anywhere.'

CHAPTER SEVEN

A night in the bosom of his family had left Victor Leeming feeling restored and refreshed. On the previous day, he'd quailed in the presence of aristocracy, felt the weight of his ignorance in an Oxford college and experienced sheer terror when subjected to the full force of Edward Tallis's ire. As he left the house to continue the investigation, therefore, he braced himself. From all that he'd heard about it, the artistic community lived by strange and often scandalous rules. The only artist he knew was Madeleine Colbeck but she was an exception to the rule, pursuing her career in the privacy and comfort of her home and leading a blameless existence. That, he suspected, was not the case with George Vaughan. He would be going into enemy territory once more.

His first problem was to find the artist. The address they'd been given by Emma Vaughan turned out to be that of a house that her brother had vacated weeks earlier. Leeming was given a forwarding address but, when he got there, he learnt that George Vaughan had moved on from that place as well and stayed odd nights with a succession of friends. It was not until late morning that Leeming finally ran him to earth. The artist occupied the attic of a crumbling old house in Chelsea. When the sergeant was admitted to the room, he was startled to find a beautiful young woman posing naked on a chair. Unabashed at his entrance, she gave him a roguish smile. He was too embarrassed even to look at her.

George Vaughan laughed. 'Don't mind Dolly,' he said. 'She's my model.'

'That may be so, sir, but I find the young lady . . . distracting.'

'Most men would love to see me like this,' she boasted.

'And so they shall,' said the artist, indicating his easel. 'When my painting is finished, you'll be the toast of London.' He smiled at Leeming. 'You, sir, are in the privileged position of being able to make a first offer for the portrait. Wouldn't you like to have Dolly hanging on the wall of your bedroom?'

Leeming gurgled.

'I want to be on display in a grand house,' she said, standing on her toes and spreading her arms wide. 'What about that uncle of yours, George? You're always saying how wealthy he must be. Is Sir Marcus a man with a taste for art?'

'No, my angel, my uncle is a born philistine.'

'Sir Marcus has other matters on his mind at the moment,' Leeming blurted out. 'His daughter has disappeared.'

The artist gaped. 'Can you be serious, sir?'

'My name is Sergeant Leeming and I'm a detective from Scotland Yard, engaged in the search for your cousin. May I speak to you in private, please?'

'Yes, yes, of course.'

He gestured to his model. Gathering up a robe, Dolly pulled it around her shoulders and swept past Leeming, giggling at his discomfort. When she'd left the room, he took a quick look around the attic. It was large, low-ceilinged and cheerless, having no carpet or curtains and only a few sticks of furniture. At one end of the room was a large bed with rumpled sheets. Half-finished paintings stood against the walls. Artist's materials were scattered everywhere.

'What's this about Imogen?' asked George Vaughan.

'We're very concerned about her whereabouts, sir.'

'Tell me all, man.'

While Leeming gave him the details of the case, George Vaughan was both attentive and alarmed. He was tall, angular and smelt of oil paint. There was a faint resemblance to his father but his face was largely hidden beneath a straggly beard and by the mop of hair that cascaded down to his shoulders. He wore a loose-fitting shirt opened to expose some of his chest and a pair of incongruous red breeches with silver buttons down the sides. His feet were bare. When he'd heard the full story, he was shaking with exasperation.

'I'll kill the villain who did this to her!' he vowed.

'Mr Tunnadine felt that *you* might be the villain in question, sir.'

'What!'

'It seems that you have a reputation for playing practical jokes.'

'I'd never go to those lengths,' said the other, hotly. 'That's a wicked allegation to make against me, but it's typical of Tunnadine.'

'You've met him, I believe.'

'I saw enough of him to take a rooted dislike. Imogen is a delightful person. She has every virtue that a young woman should possess. It's cruel to sacrifice her to an ogre like Clive Tunnadine. Men like him don't love and cherish their wives. They simply acquire them for the purposes of adornment.'

'You seem to have upset the gentleman, sir. He spoke of you unkindly.'

The artist laughed. 'That was because I provoked his jealousy. When I met him with my cousin, I swooped on Imogen and embraced her warmly, pleading that she should have married me instead. Tunnadine was outraged.' He became serious. 'Do you have any idea where she might be?'

'Inspector Colbeck, who leads the investigation, is convinced that she's still alive and unharmed.'

'In short, she's run away from Tunnadine!' George Vaughan clapped his hands. 'Well done, Imogen! I'd do the same in your position. Wherever you are, you can rely on my love and support.'

'Don't get carried away, Mr Vaughan,' warned Leeming. 'Bear in mind that we are still at the stage of conjecture. It could equally well be the case that the young lady and her maid have been abducted.'

'Perish the thought!'

'How much did you see of her?'

'Not nearly enough, Sergeant,' said the other, sorrowfully. 'Imogen only came to Oxford twice a year. I went on occasional visits with my family, of course, and always relished her company. She's a wonderful person, fun-loving and full of spirit. It's such a shame that she was cooped up in Burnhope Manor all the time.'

'Did she resent that?'

'She did more than resent it – she plotted her escape.'

Leeming's eyebrows shot up. 'Could you repeat that, please?'

'Imogen dreamt of freedom, Sergeant. Who would not do so in those circumstances? But I never thought that she would actually pluck up the courage to act. In fact, I put her to the test last year,' said the artist with a nostalgic smile. 'I contrived to be alone with her when she stayed in Oxford. I offered to carry her off so that she could experience a taste of freedom at last. Naturally, it was all in fun but Imogen was not amused by the idea. She was too concerned about what she stood to lose than by what she might gain. There'd have been dreadful repercussions. I know what you're thinking,' he added, as suspicion came into Leeming's eyes. 'You're thinking that Tunnadine may not have been so wide of the mark when he accused me of kidnapping my cousin on that train. But this would have been no jape. It would have been an honest attempt to let Imogen flap her wings and fly for once.'

'Yet you say that she spurned the idea.'

'Her parents exert too strong a hold, Sergeant. That was the trouble.'

'I don't understand, Mr Vaughan.'

'Well,' said the other, airily, 'to atone for a single day of freedom, she'd have had to endure even tighter control over her movements. That would be an unfair punishment but it was bound to follow. Imogen thanked me but rejected my offer. In retrospect, it might have been just as well. An artist's studio is not the ideal place in which to hide. Someone like Dolly is at home here; my cousin, alas, would be almost as uneasy as you are in the libertarian world that I inhabit.'

'It's not for me, sir, I know that.'

'We obey no rules, Sergeant. We simply follow our instincts.'

'I spend most of my time arresting people who follow their instincts, Mr Vaughan. Criminals break laws because it's second nature to do so.'

'There's nothing criminal about creative art,' declared the other. 'We fill the world with beauty and excite the mind. Well, look at my latest work,' he went on, taking the portrait from the easel and holding it under his visitor's nose. 'Is that not something to gladden the heart of any red-blooded man?'

Dolly looked up from the canvas with her chin tilted high. One whole arm was missing but the rest of her body was there in all of its alluring glory. Notwithstanding his embarrassment, Leeming had to admit that it was work of some quality. Radical changes had occurred. A squalid attic had been transformed into a palace, the chair became a throne and the model had a regal presence. Dolly was now a princess. The brushwork was uneven but the overall effect was nevertheless stunning. The sergeant had to make a conscious effort to turn away.

'Do you have any idea where your cousin might be?' he asked.

'You're the detective.'

'Inspector Colbeck feels that this whole episode has been triggered by something from within the family.'

'It has,' said the artist, replacing the portrait on the easel. 'Imogen has fled from tyrannical parents who keep her locked to a ball and chain. As to where she might have gone—' George Vaughan stopped as a new possibility presented itself. 'Why, yes,' he cried, 'it *could* be a family matter, after all. Lovely as she might be, Imogen was always too pure and unworldly for me. I prefer someone like Dolly Wrenson, an uninhibited woman with real fire and passion. But there is someone in the family who revered Imogen as a saint. That's the person you want, Sergeant. Speak to my brother, Percy. He's been longing for Imogen to marry him one day.'

After kneeling in prayer at the high altar, Colbeck and Percy Vaughan rose to their feet. Though relatively small, the church had an abundance of interesting features and the curate enjoyed pointing them out. Colbeck's attention was drawn to the finely carved corbels in the perpendicular roof, the heads on the north side being identified as William Whitchurch, a former rector, Henry VI, the reigning monarch when the roof was built, and the Duke of Buckingham, the contemporaneous landowner and lord of the manor. The pulpit dated from the late fifteenth century, its bowl carved from one piece of stone. Like many other things in the church, the lectern came from the Continent, the top being of Flemish brass and the steel pedestal hailing from Spain. The seventeenth-century reading desk was made out of an old box pew. The most unusual item was a barrel organ, reached by a quaint little staircase and able to play a couple of dozen tunes to the congregation.

Interested as Colbeck was, he felt that his guide was deliberately keeping him there because he was reluctant to talk about his family. The church was Percy Vaughan's domain. Inside it, he felt safe, in charge, at peace. When they came back out into the churchyard, however, he was tense and anxious.

'You promised me that you'd talk more openly after we prayed,' Colbeck reminded him. 'Your church is a delight but I didn't come all this way simply to admire it.'

'I'm grateful that you *did* come, Inspector. I'd hate to have been left unaware of dear Imogen's plight.' The curate moistened his lips before continuing. 'If you've spoken to my sister, she might well have told you that I was very fond of my cousin. So was my brother, for that matter, but George's yearning is for ladies of a less virtuous kind. When I took him to task on the subject, he simply laughed at me.' He pulled a face. 'I suppose that every family must have its black sheep.'

'In your case, the family also has a good shepherd.'

'I took holy orders out of inner conviction,' said Percy Vaughan, 'but there was a degree of penance involved.'

'I can't imagine that you were in need of repentance.'

'My mind was not as settled as it now is, Inspector. It was once occupied by a vision of life with Imogen, a hopeless vision because my feelings were not requited and because her parents had higher ambitions than to see their daughter married to a humble curate. But strong emotions can overpower us,' he continued, 'and I was in their grip for a long while.'

'Your sister indicated something of the kind, sir.'

'Poor Emma never understood what I was *really* feeling and I was unable to confide in her lest she should tell Imogen in an unguarded moment. That would have been humiliating.' He looked at Colbeck. 'You said that you were married?'

'I am and happily so.'

'Then you were able to follow your heart and choose freely.'

'It was so in both our cases.'

'You were fortunate – I am not.' He let out a groan of pain. 'Imogen is lost to me forever.'

'She will be found,' affirmed Colbeck. 'Of that I have no doubt.'

'Then you must have received a different answer when you knelt at the altar,' said the curate, solemnly, 'for all I heard was silence. Whenever I've prayed in the past, there was always a sign – however slight – that God was listening. He may not have been able to grant me my wishes but at least God was aware of them and that in itself was a consolation. Today in church, I prayed in earnest for Imogen and her maid to be returned to us without delay.' Percy Vaughan looked bereft. 'I got no answer, no hint even that my words had been heard. Do you know what that means? It's too late, Inspector. They are beyond saving.' He bit his lip. 'Imogen and her maid must be dead.'

'How are you feeling now, Paulina?'

'I feel very frail and very confused.'

'There's no colour in your cheeks.'

'The doctor says that all I can do is rest.'

'Well,' said Cassandra, 'at least do so where you can breathe in fresh air. It's far too stuffy in here.' Crossing the bedchamber, she flung open a window. 'That's better. It will do you good to be fanned by a light breeze.'

'Thank you for coming, sister. I do appreciate it.'

'There was no point in staying in Oxford. Dominic is

preoccupied with college matters and Emma has a fit of weeping whenever she thinks of her cousin. I left both of them to their own devices. My place is here. I'd like to think that Marcus has been looking after you,' she added, tartly, 'but that's too much to expect.'

'He's done his best.'

'It's not good enough, Paulina, and never has been.'

Cassandra Vaughan had never been in awe of her brother-in-law. While others admired Sir Marcus as a man of distinction, she saw his deficiencies as a husband and had the courage to tackle him about them. Her comments were invariably brushed aside with a lordly wave of the hand but that didn't stop her continuing to speak up on behalf of her sister. Paulina was clearly ailing and there was a marked deterioration in her condition since Cassandra's last visit to Burnhope Manor.

'When did the doctor last call, Paulina?'

'He came first thing this morning.'

'I'd like to speak to him.'

'He said that he'd try to come again tomorrow.'

'If he doesn't,' said Cassandra, 'I shall go looking for him. Having brought three children up, I'm used to dealing with the medical profession. So many of its members try to fob you off with glib diagnoses – I know how to get the truth out of a doctor. It's something your husband should have done.'

'Don't blame Marcus. This dire news about Imogen has hit him hard.'

'What about you? You're her mother. It's hit you even harder because Marcus is in better health to withstand the blow. Have there been any developments?'

'Two detectives came but I was not allowed to see them.'

'It was your right to do so, Paulina.'

'I lacked the strength to enforce that right.'

'Well, I can tell you that Inspector Colbeck visited us as well. We were struck by his acumen and by his confidence. Mr Tunnadine happened to be there at the time, making a nuisance of himself.'

Paulina sat up anxiously. 'How is dear Clive?'

'You'd not have spoken of him so solicitously had you been there. He was both offensive and insulting. I'd not let a bully like that marry *my* daughter,' said Cassandra. 'I was grateful when Inspector Colbeck put him in his place.'

'Was the inspector able to raise your hopes?'

'Yes, he was – to some extent.'

'It's so maddening to be stuck up here in bed,' whined Paulina. 'Nobody tells me a thing. I'm left here alone with my fears.'

'That will change now that I'm here.'

'What are you going to do, Cassandra?'

'I'm going to adopt the policy I use with Dominic,' said the other. 'I'm going to state my demands to your husband and keep repeating them until he succumbs. *Something* must have happened since yesterday.'

'I daresay that it has.'

'Then we're entitled to hear about it.'

'Please don't upset Marcus. He's feeling very sensitive at the moment.'

'He's not as sensitive as I felt when I stood on that station yesterday and realised that Imogen was not on the train. It was mortifying. That's why I took steps to confirm that she'd left Worcester at the time agreed. Imogen definitely got on that train to Oxford.'

'No, Cassandra,' said her sister, mournfully. 'She had a ticket to oblivion.'

'That's nonsense!' protested Cassandra, 'and if you'd met Inspector Colbeck, you'd have banished such thoughts.' She pulled the bed sheet over Paulina's arms. 'Try to get some rest while I have a frank talk with my brother-in-law.'

Before Paulina could stop her, she bustled out of the room and went along the landing before descending the stairs with purposeful steps. When the butler came into the hall, she summoned him over to her.

'I wish to see Sir Marcus,' she said.

'That won't be possible, I fear,' he replied.

'I'll *make* it possible. He won't be allowed to hide from me. Where is he?'

'Sir Marcus left some time ago, Mrs Vaughan.'

Cassandra was deflated. 'Where did he go?'

'He went to London as a matter of urgency.'

'Did he say why?'

'No,' returned the butler, 'he merely said that he had to get to Scotland Yard.'

As soon as he reached London, Colbeck took a cab to his house to acquaint his wife with what had happened while he was away. Madeleine was fascinated by the case and wished that he had time to give her the full details but she knew that he had to report to the superintendent.

'Father kept me company yesterday evening,' she said.

'What did he have to say?'

'Nothing to the credit of the OWWR – he derided it.'

'Some of his derision was merited,' said Colbeck, kissing her before putting on his top hat. 'I'll tell you more anon.'

'When shall I expect you?'

'It's impossible to say.'

She opened the front door and waved him off. In less than a minute, he'd hailed a cab and climbed inside. Madeleine retreated into the house with a smile of resignation, accepting that there would be some investigations when fleeting moments with him were all that she could enjoy.

Colbeck, meanwhile, was sitting in the cab and rehearsing what he was going to say to Tallis. Since the whereabouts of the two women remained unknown, he knew that he was in for severe criticism from his superior but hoped that he could convince him of the theory that had now hardened into fact in his mind. The cab dropped him off at the Lamb and Flag, the public house close to Scotland Yard. He'd arranged to meet Leeming there so that they could trade information before they were pounced on by Edward Tallis. The sergeant was in a corner, nursing a tankard of beer. He leapt up at the sight of Colbeck.

'Thank heaven you're back!' he said, laughing in gratitude. 'I'd hate to face him alone again. The superintendent roasted me on a spit yesterday evening.'

'Leave him to me, Victor.'

'He's all yours, sir.'

Colbeck bought himself a drink then joined him at his table.

'I want to hear what you discovered when you spoke to George Vaughan.'

Leeming winced. 'I discovered more than I wanted to, sir.'

'That sounds ominous'

'An artist's life would not suit me, sir.'

'It's not so daunting, Victor. Ask my wife and she will tell you that it's a rewarding occupation. Madeleine revels in it.'

'That's because she paints locomotives, sir. Mrs Colbeck doesn't share a room with any of them. Mr Vaughan lives with his model in an attic and she's . . . unclothed when he works on his portrait of her.'

'There's a long and noble tradition of nude portraiture,' said Colbeck. 'Look at the sculpture of the Greeks and the Romans. The human body is celebrated in all its glory.'

'If it was made out of marble, *I* might celebrate it. In this case, however, the body was made out of flesh and blood and it was right there in front of me. The young woman had no shame. She actually smiled at me.' Colbeck laughed. 'It's no joke, sir. I daren't tell my wife about it.'

'Why not? I'm sure that Estelle would be pleased to know that her husband could not be led astray by a naked woman. But do go on,' urged Colbeck. 'Tell me exactly what happened.'

Leeming gave an account of his meeting with George Vaughan, trying his best to keep disapproval out of his voice. He described the artist's reaction to the news about his cousin and mentioned his attempt to spirit her away on his own accord. Colbeck was not surprised to hear how constrained Imogen felt at Burnhope Manor, believing that it was a critical factor in her disappearance. He was interested to hear that the artist had told the sergeant to look closely at Percy Vaughan.

'What sort of person was he?' asked Leeming.

'He and his brother are opposites, by the sound of it,' said Colbeck. 'One is an artist who follows his Muse while the other is committed to God. Each has found his natural habitat. Percy Vaughan is a serious, reserved, somewhat enigmatic young man. He's a true Christian but not wholly immune to the desires and passions that animate most people. George Vaughan seems to have had a warm friendship with his cousin but it was his brother who cared for her the most. Not to put too fine a point on it, he's pining for her.'

They discussed the case in detail until they'd finished their drinks, then they crossed the road and entered Scotland Yard. Leeming was delighted when Colbeck went off to confront Tallis on his own. The superintendent was waiting for him. The moment that Colbeck came through the door, Tallis was on his feet with his teeth bared like a guard dog growling at an intruder.

'Well,' he began, 'what have you to say to me?'

'The sergeant and I have looked more deeply into the state of relations within the family and we've come to the conclusion that the missing women were complicit in their own disappearance.'

'Talk sense, man.'

'Imogen Burnhope and her maid were running away.'

'Ah, I see,' said Tallis, mordantly, 'we are back in that fairyland known as your sixth sense, are we?'

'We are reading the facts as they're presented to us, sir.'

'Then you are reading them incorrectly.'

'Do you have a different version of events to offer, Superintendent?'

'I don't – but Sir Marcus Burnhope does.'

'Has he sent another telegraph?'

'No,' said Tallis, 'he took the trouble to come here in person. To put it mildly, he was not happy with your handling of the case. He felt that you and Leeming were not only dragging your feet but looking in the wrong direction altogether.'

'The evidence points to the fact that his daughter wanted to escape from her family and lead a new life elsewhere.'

'Balderdash!'

'Sir Marcus, I regret to say, is part of the reason that she fled.'

'And what part did the maid, Rhoda Wills, play in this fantasy?'

'She was also ready to leave Burnhope Manor forever.'

Tallis picked up the hat that stood on his desk behind a pile of documents.

'Do you know what this is, Colbeck?' he said. 'It's a hat belonging to the aforesaid maid. It was found yesterday evening in the Mickleton tunnel. If this Rhoda Wills was running away, don't you think she'd have needed some headgear? Sir Marcus brought it here and it's not the only thing that disproves your fanciful theory. Earlier today, this was delivered to Burnhope Manor.'

Putting the hat aside, he snatched up a letter and brandished it in the air.

'What is it, sir?' asked Colbeck, taking it from him.

'It's a ransom demand,' said Tallis. 'Unless the money is paid, Sir Marcus will never see his daughter alive again. It could not be more explicit.'

Colbeck read the letter with a blend of interest and profound discomfort. His theory about a flight to freedom had been completely exploded. Imogen Burnhope had been kidnapped and her life was in danger.

'Sir Marcus is at his club,' explained Tallis, 'awaiting our advice.'

'I'll go to him at once, sir.'

'We'll go together.'

'There's no need, Superintendent.'

'Yes, there is. You've bungled this investigation, Colbeck. You've bungled it badly. From now on, I'm taking charge of it.'

Colbeck was dismayed. He would not only be admonished by Sir Marcus, he'd have to work henceforth with the heavy burden of Tallis on his back. It would make a satisfactory outcome far more difficult to achieve. Handing back the ransom demand, he manufactured a submissive smile and spoke with apparent sincerity.

'It will be a pleasure to serve beside you, sir,' he said.

CHAPTER EIGHT

In spite of all the years he'd spent at the college, Dominic Vaughan still found its architecture inspiring, its history uplifting and its atmosphere conducive to study and contemplation. As he walked briskly across the Radcliffe Quadrangle that afternoon, however, he was in no mood to admire the beauty of its Dutch gables or to reflect on the beneficence of John Radcliffe after whom it was named. The small statue of the former royal physician that stood over the gate tower went for once unnoticed. While detectives were searching for his niece and her maid, the Master of University College was engaged in a frantic hunt for his own daughter. Without warning, Emma had unaccountably vanished. Ordinarily, Vaughan would have left the task of finding her to his wife but Cassandra had gone off to Burnhope Manor, so the task fell to him. He was on his second circuit of the college. As he came into the main quadrangle, he stopped and looked around, wondering if there was anywhere he'd missed in his earlier search.

Emma was such a dutiful girl that she always told her parents if she was venturing outside the college. In view of what had happened to her cousin, she was now too nervous even to walk up the High Street alone. It meant that she had to be in the college somewhere. Turning left, her father approached the south range with its looming facade of chapel and hall. There was no reason why Emma should have entered the hall but he nevertheless went inside to make sure that she was not there, even peering under the long oak tables. Framed portraits of former college luminaries looked down unhelpfully from the panelled walls. When he left, he went straight across to the chapel, opening the heavy door to reveal an interior that was shadowed without ever being gloomy. As before, Vaughan could see no sign of his daughter. He walked halfway down the aisle but the place seemed cold and categorically empty. Turning on his heel, he headed for the door until a noise halted him in his tracks. It sounded like the rustle of a dress.

'Emma!' he called out. 'Are you in here, Emma?'

'Yes,' she replied, faintly.

Then, to his amazement, she sat up in the pew where she'd been asleep.

He hurried towards her. 'What are you doing in here?'

'I came to pray for Imogen – and for Rhoda as well. But I was very tired because I was awake all night wondering what had happened to them. I must have dozed off.' She rubbed her back. 'This pew is very uncomfortable.'

'You frightened the life out of me,' he said, sitting down beside her. 'Your mother made me promise to keep an eye on you but, the first time I looked up from my work, you'd disappeared.'

'I've been here for hours. It's so peaceful in the chapel.'

'You always liked to come in here.'

It was true. Even as a child, Emma had been fascinated by the stained-glass windows, her favourite being the one that told the story of Jonah, with the college flag – a feature absent from the Biblical version – fluttering on the ship from which he was thrown. For her younger brother, however, a visit to the chapel was an imposition and a source of continuous boredom. While George had always found the college chaplain sanctimonious, Percy sought him as a mentor. He was so devoted to his theological studies that his decision to take holy orders was a foregone conclusion.

'I wish that Percy was here,' said Emma.

'Why is that?'

'He always knows the right words to say.'

'Prayer is always valid if it comes from the heart, Emma. It doesn't have to be couched in a special language.'

'Percy is a curate. His prayers are more likely to be heard.'

'I don't think God makes petty distinctions like that.'

She grabbed his arm. 'Are they still alive, Father?' she asked.

'I believe so. More to the point, so does Inspector Colbeck.'

'But it's been well over twenty-four hours now. Where did Imogen and Rhoda spend the night? Who's looking after them? How and what are they eating? Why have we had no word whatsoever from them?'

He shrugged. 'I have no answers to those questions.'

'I've been racking my brains, trying to think of a way to help.'

'You've done all you can do by coming in here, Emma.'

'George will be upset when he hears what's happened,' she said. 'Sergeant Leeming was going to call on him today. I do wish George was here now. He always cheers me up.'

'I wish that he did the same for me,' sighed her father, 'but he tends to bring more chaos than cheer into my world. His escapades are the talk of the Senior Common Room and the rumour that he lives a decadent life in Chelsea has caused justifiable outrage. In a sense,' he admitted, 'I'm glad that he's no longer here to set tongues wagging.'

'But he'd know what to *do*, Father. George was always so practical.'

'Your uncle has already taken the appropriate steps, Emma. He's called in detectives from Scotland Yard. Mr Tunnadine might sneer at them but they imbued me with confidence. I put my trust in Inspector Colbeck.'

They met in a private room at Sir Marcus's club in Pall Mall. Edward Tallis chose the larger of the two unoccupied armchairs, leaving Colbeck to perch on the edge of a much smaller one. Sir Marcus, reclining on a button-backed leather sofa, lifted a questioning eyebrow.

'I've shown the ransom demand to the inspector, Sir Marcus,' said Tallis.

'Yes,' added Colbeck, 'and I believe it to be genuine.'

'How can you be sure?' asked Sir Marcus.

'Only the person who abducted your daughter and her maid would be able to make such specific demands. It's an educated hand. The calligraphy is neat and there are enough details to convince me that the person who wrote that letter is holding the two of them.'

'What should we do, Inspector?'

'Comply with his wishes.'

'But he's asking for a huge sum.'

'Your daughter's life is worth far more than that, Sir Marcus. Besides, you have to signal agreement or we'll never be able to draw him out into the open. Once we do that,' said Colbeck, 'we will have a chance to rescue both ladies and have some idea of who kidnapped them in the first place.'

'Is there any way of getting the money back?'

'I believe so. But we need it to act as a lure. I take it that you can have that amount in cash ready in the time specified?'

'Of course,' said Sir Marcus, indignantly. 'I've already spoken to my banker.'

'Then all we need to do,' said Tallis, taking over, 'is to devise a plan of action. The letter demands that you hand it over in person but that would expose you to unnecessary danger. Since it's unlikely that this anonymous kidnapper has ever set eyes on you, I propose to go in your stead.'

'That would put *you* at risk, sir,' Colbeck pointed out.

Tallis straightened his shoulders. 'I'm an army man. I thrive on risk.'

'You may have done so in your younger days, Superintendent, but you are not as sprightly as you were then. There are three things to remember about the person we are up against. First,' said Colbeck, 'I believe that he is or was a soldier. Second, I am certain that he'll be armed.'

'Let me take issue with you on the first point,' said Sir Marcus. 'How do you know that he is a soldier?'

'A man in uniform was seen waiting on the platform at Oxford when the train arrived. The one convincing explanation for your daughter's disappearance is that he cleverly smuggled her away with her maid before her aunt or her cousin could even see them.'

Colbeck did not disclose his belief that Imogen had been in disguise as a soldier herself because that would have argued collusion on her part, a possibility that would have been fiercely denied by her father. The inspector therefore simply argued that a man with military training would be able to plan and execute a daring kidnap in a public place.

'You said that there were three things,' noted Sir Marcus.

'Yes,' replied Colbeck. 'He is not acting alone. He will certainly have an accomplice – perhaps more than one.'

Tallis was adamant. 'No British soldier would *dare* to behave in the way you indicate. It would be wholly against his moral code.'

'Not if he was a deserter in search of money, sir. Wearing a uniform, as you know only too well, does not confer sainthood on someone. Every army has its share of malcontents.'

'Why has this fellow chosen *me* as a target?' asked Sir Marcus.

'It's because you are rich and famous. Your name is frequently in the newspapers. I seem to recall a sketch of you and your family at a garden party with the Prime Minister. Your wealth and position have attracted someone's interest,' said Colbeck, 'and he has looked for a sign of vulnerability. Unfortunately, it comes in the shape of your beautiful daughter.'

'I'll have this devil flayed alive!'

'He has to be caught first.'

'Then I'll go armed when I hand over the money,' decided Tallis.

'If anyone should go,' asserted Sir Marcus, 'it should be me. I'm Imogen's father and I want to let her kidnapper know what I think of him.'

'Antagonising him would be a great mistake,' reasoned Colbeck. 'Your emotions would get the better of you, Sir Marcus, and what is needed most of all is composure. Our priority is to ensure the safety of the two ladies. Once that's been achieved, we can resort to action. That's why I'm volunteering to act as the go-between tomorrow.'

'But you'd never pass for Sir Marcus,' said Tallis. 'You're too young.'

'I can easily add a couple of decades to my appearance, sir.'

'I am running this investigation, so I am electing myself.'

'Then I have to overrule you,' said Sir Marcus, sternly. 'The inspector is more vigorous than either of us. He should be the person to confront the kidnapper and decide when force can be used.'

'It will only be when the two ladies are released,' Colbeck told him.

'And after my money has been retrieved, I hope.'

'That will be borne in mind, Sir Marcus.'

'I insist on being present at the exchange,' said Tallis, pompously.

'And so you shall be,' agreed Colbeck, 'but we must obey the instructions to the letter. The money is to be handed over at a place that has been carefully chosen. Only one person – Sir Marcus – is to go to the designated meeting place. When I go instead of him, I expect that I will be under surveillance each step of the way. If the kidnapper has the cunning to abduct two ladies in broad daylight, he will also have the sense to bring a telescope. Come to Worcestershire, if you must, Superintendent,' he said, 'but you and Sir Marcus will have to remain out of sight.'

Tallis grumbled but eventually he agreed to the plan.

'What about Mr Tunnadine?' he asked. 'He'll want to be involved.'

'Clive will do as I tell him,' said Sir Marcus.

'Is he aware of the ransom demand?'

'He soon will be. A letter of explanation has been delivered to his house.'

Clive Tunnadine had never been the most considerate lover but he was rougher than usual that evening, arriving in a temper, falling upon her without preliminaries and, it seemed, taking out his anger on her. Lucinda Graham was pummelled, squeezed and bitten so hard that she called out in protest. Tunnadine smothered her cries with a brutal kiss before thrusting, arching and twisting in pleasure. When he'd finished, he rolled off her and lay panting beside her.

'I'll have bruises all over me,' she complained, rubbing an arm.

'They'll soon disappear.'

'If you sink your teeth into me like that, you'll draw blood.'

'I don't see any.'

'Why were you so rough with me?'

'I needed to be,' said Tunnadine as if it were explanation enough.

Lucinda had been his mistress for over a year now and had enjoyed the privileges that came with her position. He'd provided a house and servants for her. A generous allowance meant that she could afford a succession of new dresses and indulge herself in other ways. His visits were intermittent but he often brought lavish gifts for her. All that he'd given her this time were some painful memories. She nestled against him.

For his part, Tunnadine found her both enticing and accommodating. Lucinda was prepared to do everything that he demanded, whether it was to be as submissive as a nun or as vicious as a wild animal. She adapted to his moods more readily than any of his previous mistresses. It was the main reason that she'd lasted much longer than they did. He stroked her hair with an apologetic hand.

'I'm sorry if I hurt you,' he murmured.

'We usually have champagne beforehand.'

'I was in a hurry.'

'You've no need to tell me that.' She stroked his chest with the tips if her fingers. 'Are you displeased with me?'

'No, Lucinda.'

'I felt as if I was being punished.'

'You were not, I assure you.'

'Has something happened to upset you?'

'It's no business of yours.'

'I don't like it when you're unhappy.'

She waited for a reply that never came. Lucinda knew little of his life when he was not with her. The few facts she'd gathered had come from the newspapers. When parliament was in session, his name often cropped up in reports of debates. Though she had a studied indifference to politics, she nevertheless combed the press for any mention of him. It was from an article in a newspaper that she'd discovered he was about to be married. Though she'd never challenged him on the subject, she was increasingly worried about the consequences.

He moved her brusquely aside and got out of the bed.

'I have to go,' he announced.

'But you've always stayed the night before.'

'I'm too busy.'

'I was right, wasn't I?' she said, sitting up. 'Something *has* occurred. That's why you're behaving strangely.'

'It's not your place to make comments like that, Lucinda.'

'Is it something to do with your marriage?'

His eyes blazed. 'Who told you about that?'

'I read it in a newspaper. Your future wife is the daughter of Sir Marcus Burnhope. You might have mentioned it to me.'

'Hold your tongue!' he roared. 'It's no concern of yours. I don't want to hear another word about it. Is that understood?'

'But I'm bound to wonder what will happen to me afterwards.'

'Be quiet, I said!'

When he raised his arm to strike her, she cowered on the bed and pleaded for mercy. Tunnadine turned away from her and grabbed his discarded apparel. He dressed quickly in a bruised silence, then stormed out, leaving her bewildered. The cosy world in which Lucinda Graham lived suddenly seemed to be under threat.

'What did I do wrong?' she asked, plaintively.

The fact that a hat belonging to Rhoda Wills had been found on a railway line had caused great distress to Vernon Tolley. He brooded on it all the way to Shrub Hill station.

Sir Marcus's behaviour troubled him. Without explanation, he demanded to be taken to the station and seemed to be excessively anxious. Clearly, there'd been an unwelcome development. After waiting until Sir Marcus had left on the first stage of his journey to London, the coachman had driven back slowly towards Burnhope Manor, stopping so that he could pause for reflection in a clearing. Heartened by Colbeck's promise that his job would be safe and that the missing women would therefore be found unharmed, he'd then been shown the hat that Rhoda had been wearing on the previous day. It robbed him instantly of his faith in the two detectives. What he'd been offered was false hope. If Rhoda's hat could be thrown from a moving train, she could just as easily be pushed out herself. A search of the line was continuing but limited resources meant that it would be days before the whole fifty-seven miles had been thoroughly explored. Rhoda's dead body – and that of Imogen, perhaps – could be lying at the bottom of an embankment.

Common sense argued that nobody could have got into their compartment while the train was in transit yet the hat, to him, showed at the very least that there'd been some kind of struggle. It was inconceivable that the two women had argued and resorted to violence. When they'd set off, they were both so happy in each other's company. A third person had to be involved and there *was* a way in which he could have entered their compartment. Tolley remembered hearing of a driver who'd been sacked by the OWWR for leaving the footplate of his freight train while it was in motion and climbing back to the brake van so that he could enjoy a drink of beer with the guard. Both men had been dismissed along with the fireman who'd been left in charge of the locomotive. Out of this stray recollection, Tolley concocted a narrative that involved someone who watched the two women getting onto the train at Shrub Hill station, concealed himself under the brake van, then climbed on top of it once the train was haring along. Having made his way along the roofs of the carriages, he lowered himself down, opened the door of the compartment in which the women were travelling and killed them before disposing of the bodies.

It was an absurd idea but, once it had taken hold if his mind, it quickly gained veracity. Instead of walking down the aisle with Rhoda Wills, he'd be attending her funeral. As a consequence of the crime, he would almost certainly lose his position as coachman. The future looked unrelievedly black to Tolley. It was hours before he was able to shake off his despair and return to Burnhope Manor. Having unharnessed, stabled and fed the horses, he wanted some time alone in his room. Win Eagleton had other ideas. She intercepted him on the stairs.

'I hear that Rhoda's hat has been found,' she said, feigning concern.

'Yes, it has.'

'I told you that the Mickleton Tunnel would be involved.'

'It's just a coincidence, Win.'

'If they search it properly, they'll probably find her corpse in there as well.'

'Don't be silly.'

'Dark deeds have taken place, Vernon. I know it.'

'Then you know a lot more than the rest of us,' he said, robustly. 'You must be the only cook in England with second sight. You've probably never even been on that railway. How is it that you can tell exactly what happens on it?'

'I didn't mean to upset you, Vernon.'

'Then leave me alone.'

'There's no need to speak so harshly,' she said, hand on his shoulder. 'I can see that you're upset – we all are. Rhoda was a good friend to me. I'll always remember that. This is a time when we should all pull together for her sake.' She flashed her gap-toothed smile at him. 'Are you hungry?'

'No, I'm not.'

'Would you like me to bring something up to your room?'

'Stay away from me, Win.'

'It's no trouble.'

'Stay away,' he repeated, moving her hand from his shoulder. 'I need to be alone. I'm not hungry and I don't need company. All I want is peace and quiet.' He glared at her. 'Is that too much to ask?'

Climbing up the stairs, he left her with his rhetorical question hanging in the air. Win was not disturbed by his abrupt manner. He was in mourning for Rhoda Wills. Allowances had to be made for that. Tolley would come round in time. All that Win had to do was to be patient and to wait. When she went back to the kitchen, she wore a smile.

'When did this come?'

'It was early in the afternoon.'

'Who delivered it?'

'A boy, apparently – he tossed it into the porch and made off.'

'Did nobody go after him?' asked Tunnadine, angrily.

'It would have been a waste of time, sir,' said Colbeck.

'What makes you say that?'

'The boy is not an accomplice. He's probably just some local lad who was offered a few pence to deliver the ransom note to Burnhope Manor. The kidnapper would never have dared to do it himself. He needed an intermediary.'

'The inspector is right,' confirmed Tallis. 'Forget the boy.'

'But he might have been able to describe the man who employed him to run the errand,' contended Tunnadine. 'He should have been stopped.'

'Nobody knew what he'd just delivered,' explained Colbeck. 'They had no reason to stop him. It might just have been a note from one of the tenant farmers.'

'If that boy *is* the son of one of my tenants,' said Sir Marcus, grinding his teeth, 'I'll have the whole family turned out.'

'That would be cruel and undeserved. Blame the man who sent the message and not the messenger himself. The important point is that your daughter and her maid are being held against their will. We have to rescue them.'

'And kill those responsible!' said Tunnadine, vengefully.

When he'd returned to his home after his visit to Lucinda Graham, he found Sir Marcus's letter waiting for him. It threw him into a rage and sent him hastening to the club in Pall Mall. Sir Marcus was still in the private room with the two detectives. After being shown the ransom demand, Tunnadine was pulsing with fury. He turned on the superintendent.

'I told you before,' he snarled, 'we need more men deployed.'

'What good would that do?' asked Tallis.

'We could surround the area where the money is supposed to be handed over and catch this rogue.'

'With respect, Mr Tunnadine, that would be a foolish thing to attempt.'

'A show of force is required.'

'That's the last thing we must resort to, sir,' said Colbeck. 'We will be seen coming. The moment any of the conditions set down in the demand are not met, you may wave farewell to your bride. We are dealing with a ruthless man. If the two ladies do not bring in the reward he seeks, he'll have no compunction in killing them.'

'Are you able to read his mind, then?' sneered Tunnadine.

'He has not gone to such trouble in order to walk away empty-handed. If his captors can be exchanged for money,' said Colbeck, 'they have value. If we fail to cooperate, they will become a burden to him.'

'We follow *your* advice, Inspector,' decreed Sir Marcus.

'It's what I would have advised,' said Tallis.

'Well, I still think that you're wrong to give in to him like this,' said Tunnadine. 'Think before you act, Sir Marcus. Do you really want to hand over all that money to this despicable villain?'

'Of course I do not,' barked Sir Marcus, 'but the inspector assures me that there's a good chance that we may retrieve it once Imogen and her maid are safe.'

'I don't share your confidence in Inspector Colbeck. All that he has done so far is to "harvest information" and it has got him nowhere.'

'On the contrary,' said Colbeck, 'it was because I took the trouble to gather all the facts before reaching a conclusion, that I was able to dismiss your ludicrous notion that this was a jape invented by George Vaughan. It may interest you to know that Sergeant Leeming has spoken to the young artist and repeated the accusation to him. George Vaughan felt that your claim was nothing short of slanderous.'

'My nephew would never dare to harm his cousin,' said Sir Marcus.

'It was a natural mistake,' argued Tunnadine, trying to shrug it off.

'You are rather prone to making natural mistakes, sir,' said Colbeck.

'I'll take no lectures from you, Inspector.'

'I was not aware that I was giving you any.'

'Let's get back to the ransom demand,' suggested Tallis, conscious that he'd lost control of the discussion. 'We've agreed that the sensible course of action is to obey the kidnapper's demands and to hand the money over, once we've established that the two ladies have been released. Inspector Colbeck will act on behalf of Sir Marcus and actually meet the kidnapper face to face.'

'Why can't I do that?' said Tunnadine, tapping his chest.

'It's because you are too hot-headed, sir.'

'I have a right to take on the role – Colbeck does not. We're talking about my future wife. Who could have a better claim than her future husband?'

'Listen to the superintendent, Clive,' said Sir Marcus. You are not experienced in these matters. A trained detective is. The inspector has spent years dealing with desperate criminals. He will be cool and objective. Your impulsiveness could ruin everything.'

Tunnadine was shocked. 'You wish to hand over this task to a complete stranger, Sir Marcus?'

'Colbeck is the best man in a situation like this,' said Tallis.

'I dispute that, Superintendent.'

'He's highly experienced.'

'I still believe that I have a prior claim,' insisted Tunnadine.

'The decision lies with me,' declared Sir Marcus. 'If I have to choose someone to impersonate me, then I elect the inspector to go in my stead. Superintendent Tallis is too old and you are too excitable. Let's hear no more on the subject,' he went on, stifling Tunnadine's protest with a gesture. 'The matter is closed.'

Colbeck took note of Tunnadine's reaction. Silenced by Sir Marcus, the politician was burning with resentment and smarting from the rebuff. He was not accustomed to having his wishes overridden. Since he'd been quashed in front of the two detectives, he was even more livid. After bidding a token farewell, he marched out of the room with a face like thunder.

Tunnadine was a problem.

CHAPTER NINE

Dolly Wrenson was in a peevish mood. She stared sullenly at the nude portrait of her.

'What about my missing arm?' she asked.

'It will have to wait, alas.'

'You can't just walk away and leave me like that.'

'I'm needed elsewhere, Dolly,' said George Vaughan. 'Besides, you shouldn't really have seen the portrait before it's completed. I always think it bad luck if a model views a painting too soon in the creative process.'

'I look ridiculous without an arm.'

'Think how many Greek and Roman statues lack a limb of one kind or another. It adds character. In some cases, they don't even have a head.'

'I'm not a statue, George,' she said, fiercely. 'I'm a real woman and I want to be *finished*.'

'And so you shall be – when I return from Oxford.'

'But you said you never wanted to go there again.'

'That was before I heard about Imogen's disappearance.'

'Oh, it's *her*, is it?' she said, jealously. 'It's that precious cousin of yours. Because she's more important than me, I'm left in London with a missing arm.'

'Don't be absurd.'

'You love her more than you love me. That's what it amounts to, isn't it?'

'I love her as a cousin. When she's in danger, I'm bound to worry about Imogen.' He glanced across at the bed. 'I love you in a very different way.'

It was not long after dawn and they were in his studio at the top of the house in Chelsea. After a restive night thinking about Imogen, he'd felt the urge to go back to his family. Having left under a cloud, he was not sure what kind of reception he'd get but nevertheless felt impelled to return to Oxford. Dolly looked upon the decision as a betrayal.

'You said that I'd taught you the meaning of freedom,' she recalled.

'And I'm eternally grateful to you, Dolly.'

'So why are you putting *her* before me?'

'That's not what I'm doing. In most things, you'll always come first.'

'Prove it,' she challenged.

'What do you mean?'

'If you really love me, take me to Oxford with you.'

'I can't do that,' he spluttered.

'Exactly – you're ashamed of me, George Vaughan.'

'I'm prouder of you than of anyone else in my life. You've changed the way I look at the world, Dolly. Nobody else could have done that. Living and working with you has made me feel that I'm in paradise.'

'Then stay here and give me a second arm.' She moved in close to embrace him. 'I'll be *extremely* grateful,' she purred. 'You've no idea what treats I'd have in store for you. Why bother about your old life? Put it behind you for good.' She caressed his hair. 'Come to bed with me and talk it over.'

'I'm sorry,' he said, tempted by her blandishments but easing her gently away. 'This is something that I have to do. I'm not leaving you, Dolly. I'll be back before you know that I've gone.'

'And will you tell your family about me?'

'I . . . might do so.'

'Will you say that I mean far more to you than your cousin?'

'No – I'm simply going there to offer support in a fraught situation.'

'In other words,' she said, astringently, 'Dolly Wrenson won't even deserve a mention. She'll cease to exist because she'll be an embarrassment to you. Real freedom consists in being true to yourself, George. It's showing the whole world what you believe in and care about. You can't be a devil-may-care artist in Chelsea and a dutiful son in Oxford at one and the same time. You can't live in sin and pretend to lead a virginal existence. It's sheer hypocrisy.'

'That's enough!' he yelled, banging the table. 'There's a crisis in my family and my place is with them. If you can't appreciate that, then you've lowered yourself in my esteem. You must stop being so infernally selfish, Dolly. Someone else's need is greater than yours. For heaven's sake, learn to accept that.' He picked up a battered valise and headed for the door. 'We'll discuss this in full when I get back.'

Dolly folded her arms. 'How do you know that I'll still be here?'

At a time when his thoughts were concentrated solely on his daughter's safety, what Sir Marcus Burnhope needed least was an attack by his sister-in-law. He'd returned home too late for her to ambush him that night so she bided her time and waited until he descended for breakfast. Before he could even enter the dining room, Cassandra Vaughan popped out from behind a suit of armour in the hall to accost him.

'What's going on, Marcus?' she asked.

'I'm having an early breakfast,' he replied, astonished to see her. 'What are you doing here, Cassandra?'

'I came to look after my sister and to find out the facts. Paulina is in low spirits as it is. Why make her condition worse by concealing the truth from her? Do you wish your wife to expire from neglect and anxiety?'

'Paulina has not been neglected. The doctor calls every day. As for her anxiety, I share it. I wish I was in a position to alleviate it.'

'Something is afoot,' said Cassandra, suspiciously. 'I know it.'

'Then you know more than I do.'

'Why is that disagreeable Mr Tunnadine staying under our roof? I was asleep when you finally returned last night but his booming voice woke me up. I could hear him stamping around down here in the hall.'

'Clive is here as our guest,' said Sir Marcus, wanting to

divulge as little as possible. 'He is, after all, an interested party.'

'What about Imogen's mother? Is not she an interested party? As for her aunt, I am *very* interested and I won't leave your side until you let me in to whatever secret you're hiding. Come on, Marcus. We are adults. Tell us the truth.'

When he'd first met her, Sir Marcus had been fond of Cassandra because she was unfailingly pleasant and comparatively subdued. The emergence of a new sister-in-law, strong-willed and outspoken, had dulled his affection and he'd tried to avoid her on social occasions. He was now in a quandary. Cassandra was too intelligent to be fobbed off with a paltry excuse. As long as she was in the house, she'd stick to him like a burr. If he told her the full truth, on the other hand, the information would be passed on to his wife and he believed that it would cause her even greater alarm than if she were left in ignorance. Uncertain as to what he should do, he opted for a compromise, deciding to release crucial facts while holding back others.

'All that I can tell you is this—' he began.

'I want the truth,' she warned, 'with no prevarication.'

'Imogen and her maid are alive.'

'Thank God for that!'

'Of her whereabouts, however, we have no details.'

'Then how can you say that they're still alive?'

'I've told you all I can, Cassandra,' he lied.

'Have they been kidnapped? Are they being held against their will?'

'You know as much as I do.'

'Someone has been in touch with you, haven't they?'

'When I learn more,' he said, trying to mollify her with a

smile, 'I'll be sure to pass on the news to you and to Paulina.' He moved away. 'Now, if you'll excuse me, I'd like to have some breakfast.'

'You're not getting away as easily as that, Marcus,' she said, tugging at his sleeve. 'I feel as if I'm only hearing a portion of the truth. Is there nothing you can tell me that will help to revive Paulina?'

'There's nothing.'

'I don't believe you.'

'That's your prerogative,' he retorted. 'I'm sorry that our late arrival disturbed you. Since you must be very tired, I suggest that you get some sleep now instead of hounding me like this. I'm hungry,' he went on, detaching her hand from his sleeve. 'Good day to you, Cassandra.'

Before she could stop him, he went into the dining room and closed the door behind him with such finality that even she did not dare to go in pursuit. She'd learnt something of moment. It would have to suffice her for a while.

A welcome night at home had not only cheered Colbeck, it had given him the opportunity to share more details of the case with his wife. Madeleine was no silent helpmeet who simply ran the household in his absence. She was an intelligent woman who'd been involved in the investigative process a number of times. Edward Tallis would have been beside himself if he'd known how many of Colbeck's successes had owed something to the enterprise of his wife. But there was another reason why her husband had consulted her. Madeleine had experience of being abducted. Had she not been rescued by Colbeck from the ship on which she was being held, she would have been taken abroad by two strangers, one of whom had already molested her. It had left an indelible mark on her.

As she helped Colbeck on with his frock coat, she relived the memories.

'What frightened me most,' she said, 'was being completely unaware of what was really going on. And I hated being locked up like a criminal.'

'I'm sorry that you had to go through that ordeal, Madeleine.'

'I survived.'

'It still gives me pangs of guilt,' he said. 'You were kidnapped because of me. When I was on their tail, they needed a hostage and they chose you. I dread to think what might have happened if we hadn't intercepted you in Bristol.'

'I often have shivers about that, Robert,' she admitted. 'The worst moment was when one of them cornered me in a wine cellar and tried to take advantage of me. I managed to smash a wine bottle over his head but, if his friend had not interrupted us, God knows what would have happened to me.' She brightened. 'But there was one consolation.'

'What was that?'

'He told me that I'd been abducted because you were my "ardent admirer". You've no idea how much that phrase rallied me.'

'I was and still am your ardent admirer, Madeleine,' he said, gallantly. 'But you were snatched from your house as a means of keeping me at bay. Sir Marcus's daughter and her maid are being held for ransom.'

'They'll still feel as I did – trapped, helpless and terrified. The one advantage is that there are two of them. They'll be able to draw comfort from each other. I was alone and defenceless.'

He grinned. 'Not entirely defenceless,' he observed. 'You excelled yourself with a bottle of wine in your hands.' He became serious. 'There's another aspect to this case, however. I'm still convinced that the two of them cooperated in a scheme to disappear. That being the case, they may be totally oblivious to the fact that they are victims of kidnappers. Instead of being in a state of terror, they may believe that the fulsome promises made to them will be honoured.'

'What will happen if the ransom is not paid?'

'I've no doubt that the threat made against them will be carried out.'

'So they could be ignorant of the fact that their lives are in danger?'

'It's a possibility that I've chosen not to share with Sir Marcus. He would never accept that his daughter would actually run away from home.' He took out his pocket watch and glanced at it. 'I must rush. Victor and I have a train to catch.'

Transport once again brought misery into Leeming's life. He loathed trains and hated voyages at sea even more. Both had prominence in his nightmares. On balance, however, neither provoked the immediate sense of danger that riding a horse did. As he hauled himself up into the saddle outside Burnhope Manor, he felt as if he was risking life and limb. His mount was far too frisky and bucked mutinously. He and the animal could never be described as sharing a marriage of true minds. In fact, it was clear that the horse – a bay mare, skittish by nature –

had a mind of her own and she'd taken a particular dislike to her rider. Even before they were in motion, Leeming was dividing his time between hanging on for dear life and fervent prayer.

It was afternoon and Vernon Tolley had harnessed the horses and put them between the shafts. Sir Marcus had already climbed into the landau with Clive Tunnadine and Edward Tallis. Though they said nothing to the coachman, their very presence helped to instil hope in Tolley. He believed that they would not all be there unless they were going to retrieve the missing women. His earlier pessimism waned. Rhoda Wills was still alive. It sent the blood coursing through his veins.

While Leeming was still trying in vain to control his mount, Colbeck strolled across to him. The inspector had used cosmetics to put dark shadows under his eyes and he'd added a silver moustache to his face.

'What do you think, Victor?' he asked. 'Do I look old enough?'

'You're not as old as I feel, sir. Sitting up here has added years to my age. This horse is determined to kill me one way or another.'

Colbeck was amused. 'Show her that you're the master.'

'But I'm not – she's in charge.' The horse bucked violently and he was almost thrown from the saddle. 'Do you see what I mean? I'd much rather walk than ride. Why can't I go in the carriage?'

'There's no room, I'm afraid.'

'There would be if we changed places. You're an experienced horseman.'

'I'm also the owner of Burnhope Manor,' teased Colbeck.

'You can't expect a man of my age and distinction to forego the comfort of a carriage.'

'What if I get thrown off?' wailed Leeming.

'You simply get back on again, Victor.'

Crossing to the landau, Colbeck clambered into it and sat beside Tallis. He would have been far happier not to have the superintendent there but had no choice in the matter. Tunnadine was grim and patently aggrieved. Sir Marcus was hunched in his seat, clutching a leather bag protectively in his lap. His curt command made the coachman crack his whip and the horses set off. Leeming followed the carriage on his prancing bay mare. The journey only lasted a couple of miles. Colbeck had some idea of what to expect because he'd studied the ordnance survey map of the area. The site had been well chosen. The kidnapper had insisted that Sir Marcus came alone with the specified amount of money in a bag. When it was counted and deemed correct, his daughter and her maid would be released. The actual point of exchange was at the base of a hill. To reach it, Colbeck – in the guise of the older man – would have to walk two hundred yards or more across a field.

The carriage reached a copse and drew to a halt. Beyond it was open country where it was certain to be seen. Everyone climbed out of the vehicle. Colbeck was momentarily diverted, helping Leeming to dismount. As she was reined in, the bay mare tried to dislodge her rider by rising up on her rear legs. Leeming more or less fell into the inspector's arms. Showing great presence of mind, Tolley leapt from his seat, grabbed the reins and calmed the horse with soft words and gentle caresses on her neck. Tallis was unimpressed by the sergeant's horsemanship.

'You must learn to ride properly, Leeming,' he said, sharply.

'I'd rather not, sir.'

'It could be the saving of you one day.'

'I was born to keep my feet on the ground.'

Colbeck consulted his watch again. 'It's almost time to go.'

'I still think it's *my* right to undertake the exchange,' said Tunnadine, chafing. 'Imogen would expect it of me.'

'This is a task for a professional detective, sir,' said Tallis.

'I endorse that,' added Sir Marcus. 'You'll take no part in this, Clive.'

Tunnadine scowled and retreated to the carriage, lurking beside it. Colbeck had come prepared. During an earlier investigation in Scotland, he'd learnt the value of using a telescope and had brought one with him. With Leeming at his heels, he crept through the trees until he reached the edge of the copse, then used the instrument to survey the land ahead. The hill was visible but he could see nobody on its summit. Handing the telescope to Leeming, he returned to the others.

'I'll need the ransom money now, Sir Marcus,' he said.

Reluctant to part with it, the older man suddenly thrust it into his hands.

'Take great care, Inspector. You are holding a small fortune.'

'I'll exercise every caution,' Colbeck promised.

Tunnadine appraised him. 'Are you armed?'

'No, sir – it would be pointless.'

'In the interests of self-preservation, you should at least have a pistol.'

'The best way to safeguard my life is to carry no weapon,' said Colbeck. 'The kidnapper will not approach me until he's certain that I bear no arms.'

Tolley was thrilled by the confirmation that Rhoda Wills was alive. In return for a large amount of money, she'd be set free. When the others wished the inspector good luck, he joined in. Colbeck thanked them all and moved off.

Breaking cover, he walked for a few minutes before he reached the field designated in the ransom demand. He opened the five-barred gate then closed it behind him, moving slowly to indicate advanced years and bending forward to make it more difficult for his face to be scrutinised through the telescope that he was sure would be trained on him. When he reached the base of the hill, he stopped and waited. There was a long, uneasy silence. Though he could see nobody ahead of him, he knew that someone was there. To his right were acres of farmland, stretching into the distance. To his left was a low hedge that fringed the field on that side. Colbeck had a strong feeling that he was under surveillance from the hill and from behind the hedge. The kidnapper was taking no chances. Apparently, he'd brought an accomplice.

Eventually, he came into view at the top of the hill, one eye peering through a telescope. He was tall, slim, well dressed and had a voice that easily carried across the distance. Colbeck was subjected to a cross-examination.

'Are you Sir Marcus Burnhope?'

'Yes,' replied Colbeck.

'Do you have the money?'

He patted the bag. 'It's here.'

'Is it the full amount?'

'It's as you requested.'

The man laughed harshly. 'It was no request – it was a command.'

'Where are my daughter and her maid?'

'I'll ask the questions, Sir Marcus. Are you armed?'

'No, I am not.'

'How can I be certain of that?'

'I give you my word.'

'Take off your coat,' ordered the other. 'Drop it on the ground.'

Colbeck hesitated. Punctilious about his attire, he didn't want it stained by the grass but he had to obey. Putting the bag down, he removed his coat and laid it carefully on the ground.

'Put your hands in the air and turn around slowly,' said the man on the hilltop.

This time there was no hesitation. Colbeck stretched his arms up high and went in a slow circle. He could almost feel the telescope scanning his body to make sure that no weapon was concealed on it. When he faced the hill again, he picked up the bag and waited. Another figure appeared, an older, stockier man in rougher garb.

'Give the money to my friend,' the first man called out.

'I need to see the ladies first.'

'Do as you're told and I'll honour my side of the bargain.'

Colbeck was resolute. 'Unless I see that they are safe, there'll be no bargain.'

'Are you defying me?' asked the man, angrily.

'I want proof that my daughter is still alive before I hand over a penny.'

'You can take my word for it.'

'I don't trust you,' said Colbeck. 'I don't believe that you have Imogen.'

Picking up his coat, he turned on his heel and deliberately walked away.

'Wait!' shouted the man. 'You shall see her.' He laughed in approval. 'You're not the gullible old fool I took you for. Here she is.'

Colbeck turned round and saw a young woman coming into view in a dress that proclaimed her social position. She was too far away for Colbeck to see her face clearly but she had the tall, lean body described by her father. Colbeck laid his coat back on the ground and waited. The stocky man began to descend the hill.

'Hand the bag to my friend,' instructed the kidnapper. 'He will bring it to me. When I've counted the money and found it correct, the two ladies will be released.'

The older man came slowly down the hill, watched carefully through the telescope by his companion. He was not the only person keeping Colbeck under observation. Over to his left, he felt, someone was hiding behind the hedge to watch the proceedings. Colbeck had to suppress the desire to look in that direction. The man lumbered on towards him. Colbeck could now see that he had the appearance of a farm labourer. He certainly didn't look like someone capable of devising a kidnap plot. The inspector's instinct told him that the man was simply employed to assist in recovering the money and probably had no idea of the full implications of what was taking place. When he reached Colbeck, he had a bewildered air about him. Licking his lips, he shifted his feet then reached out both hands.

'Give him the money!' shouted the man on the hill.

'Let my daughter come closer first,' replied Colbeck.

'I make the demands, Sir Marcus. Hand over the bag.'

'I must be able to see Imogen properly.'

The intermediary was nervous and confused. Not knowing quite what he should do, he tried to wrest the bag from Colbeck's hands but he reckoned without the inspector's strength and persistence. As the two of them struggled, a shot rang out and Colbeck's assailant was hit in the head, causing blood to spurt everywhere, some of it over Colbeck's new waistcoat. The man collapsed to the ground in a heap. The young woman on the hill let out a shriek of horror and ran down the long incline. At the same time, Tunnadine came into view over to the left with a pistol in his hand. He jumped over the hedge and sprinted towards the inspector.

'That was madness, sir!' yelled Colbeck, reprovingly. 'You've killed him.'

'Who cares?' replied Tunnadine with a wild cackle. 'I've rescued Imogen and saved the money. You'd have done neither.' Arms wide open, he ran towards the approaching figure. 'Come to me, Imogen. You're safe now.'

But it was not his future bride who was tearing down the hill towards him. It was a pretty country girl with red cheeks. Ignoring the outstretched arms, she went past him and flung herself at the man on the ground.

'Father!' she cried. 'What have they done to you?'

Colbeck was furious as he walked over to Tunnadine. 'I'll trouble you for that weapon, please, sir.'

'What are you talking about?' snapped Tunnadine.

'You've just committed a murder.'

'Use your eyes, man. I've just rid the world of a kidnapper.'

'This man had no connection with the plot, sir. He and his daughter were suborned.' He extended a hand. 'I'll have that pistol now.'

'Damn you, Inspector! I'm not the criminal. He is – and so is the man at the top of the hill. Instead of bothering me, you should be chasing him.'

'There's no point, sir,' said Colbeck. 'The moment you fired that gun, he would have mounted his horse and ridden away hell for leather. By the time I climb that hill, he'll be a mile or more away. You've ruined everything, Mr Tunnadine. Instead of rescuing Sir Marcus's daughter, you've made it more likely that she'll be killed out of spite.' Tunnadine shook his head, refusing to accept that he'd made a mistake. 'The kindest way to describe your actions is that they were an example of misplaced heroism. I view them as mindless stupidity.'

Colbeck reached forward to snatch the pistol from his hand. Tunnadine made no protest. He gazed down at the dead man and the weeping girl, realising that they were merely pawns used by the real kidnapper. The gunshot had brought the others out of hiding. Leeming was leading the way at a trot, with Tallis and Sir Marcus walking quickly behind him, breathing heavily from their exertions. Tolley came after them, his face a study in fear. Colbeck tried to comfort the girl but she was beyond sympathy. Utterly forlorn, she kept shaking her father as if expecting him to wake up.

'What the devil happened?' demanded Sir Marcus, taking the bag with the money from Colbeck.

'We heard a shot,' said Tallis. He saw the body. 'Who's this?'

'He's a local man paid to act as a go-between,' said Colbeck. 'Unfortunately, Mr Tunnadine decided to kill him.'

'I thought he was the kidnapper,' howled Tunnadine. 'I acted from the best possible motives. I sought to rescue Imogen.' He pointed to the girl. 'I believed that this was her. I've seen that dress before. I know it belongs to Imogen.'

'What about Rhoda Wills?' asked Tolley.

'She's still being held with Sir Marcus's daughter,' explained Colbeck, 'though the two of them may well suffer as a result of Mr Tunnadine's folly.'

'I only did what I felt was right,' said Tunnadine, defensively.

Sir Marcus was seething. 'You blundered, Clive.'

'I saved your money from being handed over, Sir Marcus.'

'What use is the blasted money without my daughter?'

'I'll find her, I promise. I'll bring her back alive.'

Tolley wanted to ask if Rhoda would come back alive as well but it was not his place to do so. His earlier optimism had now darkened considerably. He skulked on the edge of the group and looked up imploringly at the heavens.

Tallis asserted himself. 'What crime has taken place here, Inspector?'

'A murder was committed.'

'Were you injured in any way?'

'Happily, I was not,' said Colbeck, 'but I might easily have been. I was wrestling with the man when the shot was fired. It could well have been me lying there on the ground.'

'When I take aim at something,' boasted Tunnadine, 'I always hit the mark.'

'What you hit was no mark,' protested Leeming. 'It was

a human being. All you've done is to deprive this poor child of a father.'

'I've heard enough,' decided Tallis. 'Sergeant . . .'

'Yes, sir?'

'Arrest Mr Tunnadine. He'll be charged with murder.'

'You can't do that,' bellowed Tunnadine, backing away. 'It was an accident.'

'When you aim at something,' taunted Colbeck, 'you always hit the mark.'

'How was I to know who the fellow was?'

'You'll have plenty of time to reflect upon that while you're held in custody. I fancy that he may choose to resist arrest, Sergeant Leeming. It will be another charge against him. Go on,' urged Colbeck. 'Do your duty.'

Leeming grinned. 'It will be a pleasure, Inspector.'

Reaching under his coat, he produced a pair of handcuffs and moved in.

CHAPTER TEN

Clive Tunnadine was fuming. He would not allow someone from what he considered to be the lower orders even to touch him yet Leeming was threatening to put him under restraint. Pushing the sergeant firmly away, he tried to walk off, head held high in disdain. He did not get far. Leeming was on him at once, grabbing an arm and clipping a handcuff to the wrist before Tunnadine could resist. Securing the other wrist proved slightly more difficult because the prisoner swung round with his fist bunched. Leeming parried the blow then grappled with the politician for a few moments before twisting the man's free hand behind his back and snapping the handcuff in position. Tunnadine went berserk, yelling obscenities and kicking out wildly at his captor.

'Attacking a police officer is a criminal offence, sir,' said Tallis, 'and that foul language should never be used in front of a young female, especially one who's mourning the death of her father.'

The rebuke stopped the outburst of violence but Tunnadine still simmered.

'What shall we do with him, sir?' asked Leeming.

'He must be taken before a magistrate and remanded in custody,' said Tallis.

'You can't arrest *me*,' cried Tunnadine. 'I'm a Member of Parliament.'

'That doesn't entitle you to kill someone,' Colbeck pointed out. 'If the Prime Minister himself had done what you've just done, he'd be treated the same.'

'It was an accident, I tell you. I acted from the best possible motives.'

'That's debatable, Mr Tunnadine. A clever barrister may be able to commute the charge to one of manslaughter but you must face justice.'

'Take him back to the carriage, Sergeant,' ordered Tallis.

Tunnadine turned to Sir Marcus with a pleading note in his voice.

'Are you going to let them do this to me?'

'No,' said the other, putting friendship before justice, 'I'm sure that there's an easier way to settle this. I'm sad for this girl, of course, but the fact remains that she and her father were aiding and abetting a kidnapper. *They* are the criminals here – not Mr Tunnadine.'

'I'm glad that someone realises that,' said Tunnadine.

'He was too headstrong, I grant you, and he may inadvertently have complicated the situation that my daughter is in by his intemperate action. However, he is no killer. Let's be reasonable, gentlemen,' he went on, looking from Tallis to Colbeck. 'In essence, this was a tragic accident. It's the kind of thing that happens sometimes during a shooting party. One of the beaters is killed by a stray shot. It's regrettable, naturally, but not something one should worry about overmuch. The widow – if there is one – is always given compensation.'

'Does that mean that this man's family will be offered reparation?' asked Colbeck, comforting the girl and offering her a handkerchief. 'They're certainly in need of it.'

'The matter will be considered,' said Sir Marcus, huffily.

'But you are holding a large amount of money in your hands.'

'This is the ransom for my daughter and her maid.'

'Besides,' said Leeming, 'it wasn't Sir Marcus who shot him. It was Mr Tunnadine who had the gun. He's the one who should cough up.'

'I can hardly reach for my wallet when I'm handcuffed like this,' said Tunnadine, nastily, 'and, in any case, I refuse to pay anything. I shot a man engaged in a criminal act. Any barrister will be able to get me off scot-free.'

'Don't be too sure of that, sir,' said Colbeck. 'Before I became a detective, I practised at the bar myself. If I was involved in the prosecution, I guarantee that you'd end up with a custodial sentence.'

'Now, now,' said Sir Marcus with a conciliatory smile, 'there's no need for any of this to reach that stage. I appeal to your discretion, Superintendent. Have him released. In my view, he has no case to answer.'

'The law is the law, Sir Marcus,' said Tallis, solemnly.

'See it for what it was, man. A random shot happens to hit a man who, by the look of him, is nothing but a labourer. His life is worthless compared to that of a leading politician like Mr Tunnadine? It's a question of degree.'

'With respect, Sir Marcus,' said Colbeck, one arm around the weeping girl, 'I find that argument both specious and insulting. This man is a murder victim and therefore deserving of our compassion. In my opinion, his death has equal value to that of a ranting politician with an ill temper and a vicious tongue.'

'Take care, Inspector,' warned Tallis, starting to become fearful of the consequences of upsetting Sir Marcus. 'This discussion is becoming too heated.'

'Then release Mr Tunnadine,' suggested Sir Marcus, 'and we can talk this over sensibly.'

'He'll have to give us his word that he won't try to escape.'

'He will do so.'

Sir Marcus nodded at Tunnadine who glowered hard at the detectives.

'You have my word of honour,' he grunted.

Tallis gave a signal and Leeming unlocked the handcuffs and stowed them under his coat. The prisoner rubbed his wrists. With great reluctance, Tunnadine opened his wallet, took out some banknotes and gave them to Colbeck before being led away by Leeming in the direction of the landau. Tolley went with them. Sir Marcus glanced at the girl, choking back her tears as she talked to Colbeck, who made sure that she could no longer see the lifeless body of her father. It was a touching scene. Sympathy aroused, Sir Marcus opened the bag and took out a few banknotes. He thrust them at Colbeck then strode off towards the carriage.

'What will you do, Inspector?' asked Tallis.

'I'll take her back home with her father,' replied Colbeck. 'She told me that they came here by horse and cart. I'll use the cart to transport him. If you can spare the sergeant, I'll be glad of his help.'

'I'll send him back to you.'

'We leave it to you to take Mr Tunnadine before a magistrate.'

'Yes, yes,' said Tallis, irritably, 'I don't need advice about police procedure. Do what you have to do then meet me back at Burnhope Manor.'

'I will, sir.'

About to leave, the superintendent looked at the girl, crying piteously into Colbeck's handkerchief. Moved by her plight, he took out his wallet and extracted some banknotes before giving them to the inspector. He then trudged off towards the carriage. While he was waiting, Colbeck tried to get more information from the girl.

'What's your name?' he asked.

'Mary, sir – I didn't know we was doing wrong.'

'You were cruelly misled, Mary. A man paid your father money, didn't he?'

'That's right, sir.'

'What did he ask you to do?'

'I was to put on this dress,' she said, looking down at it in dismay. 'I've never seen anything as beautiful. It's not the sort of thing the likes of me wears, sir. I was so pleased when he gave it to me. But now . . .' She glanced down at her father. 'I wish we'd never met that man.'

'Can you describe him?'

'He was tall like you and very smart. Oh, and he had a nice voice.'

'What age would he be?'

'He was about the same as you, sir.'

'Did he give you a name?'

'No, sir, he just gave us money and told us what to do.'

'What was he riding?'

'It was a fine horse, sir – a roan, sixteen hands. He was a good horseman.'

'Why do you say that?'

'I've never seen anyone ride that well, sir. My father said he looked as if he'd been born in the saddle.'

The same could not be said of Victor Leeming. Summoned by Colbeck, he took no chances with his mettlesome horse. In the interests of safety, he led her by the reins. After letting himself and the mare into the field, he walked across to them.

'This is Mary,' introduced Colbeck. 'And this,' he said to her, 'is Sergeant Leeming. He'll look after you for a minute.'

'Where are you going, sir?' asked Leeming.

'You'll soon see.'

Taking the reins from Leeming, he put his foot in the stirrup and hauled himself up into the saddle. One dig of the heels sent the bay mare cantering up the hill. Leeming was amazed at the inspector's control of the animal.

'Why didn't she behave like that for *me*?' he complained.

Emma had been so delighted to see her younger brother that she'd clung to him for minutes. It was some time since George Vaughan had been in Oxford and she'd only seen him once during the interim when they met in London at the home of a mutual friend. Pleased with the warmth of his welcome, he did not expect the same response from his father. In the event, it was hours before he even met him. Dominic Vaughan was at a meeting in Corpus Christi College and didn't return until the afternoon. When he came back to the Master's Lodging and saw his son there, he was momentarily aghast.

'What are you doing here, George?' he asked.

'Hello, Father – it's good to see you again.'

'I thought you'd wiped the dust of Oxford from your feet forever.'

'It seems that I haven't done so, after all.'

'Then welcome back,' said Vaughan, shaking his hand. 'It's a pleasure to see you again.' He eyed his son's flamboyant apparel, 'though I wish that you'd been wearing something more in keeping with college attire.'

His son grinned. 'Would you have me in subfusc, then?'

'There'd be no need to go to that extreme.'

'Isn't it wonderful to see him again?' asked Emma. 'It seems that Sergeant Leeming called on George and told him what had happened. George was keen to hear news of Imogen so he came here this morning.'

'I'm just sorry that Mother isn't here as well,' said her brother. 'I'm told that she's gone off to Burnhope Manor.'

'That's right.' Vaughan inspected him from top to toe. 'You look different, George. I can't put a finger on it but . . . you've changed somehow.'

'I don't think so, Father,' said Emma. 'He looks the same as ever to me.'

'That's odd,' teased George Vaughan. '*You* look ten years older than when I last saw you – and you're twice as fat.'

'It's not true!' she protested.

'Of course, it isn't,' said her father, 'but George has to

have his little joke. Could you leave us alone for a while, please, Emma?'

'But I want to stay with George.'

'I won't keep him long, I promise. I just wanted a private word.'

Emma pouted then moved towards the door. She blew her brother a kiss. He pulled a face at her and she laughed as she let herself out. When he turned to his father, he saw a grave expression on his countenance.

'The news about Imogen is very distressing, Father,' he said.

'She is never out of our thoughts.'

'Have there been any developments?'

'There are none that I know of, George.'

'If there is anything I can do, just tell me what it is.'

'First of all, you can sit down.' In response to his father's gesture, he lowered himself into a chair. Vaughan sat opposite and fixed him with a stare. 'Second, I'd be obliged if you could inform me what exactly is going on.'

'I only know what the sergeant told me.'

'I'm not talking about Imogen now. My question relates to you.'

'Oh, I see.'

'You *do* look different. It's a look I've seen on certain undergraduates when they mistake debauchery for education. It signals a decline in moral standards.'

'I'm no longer an undergraduate here, Father,' his son reminded him. 'I'm old enough to follow my own destiny.'

'Yet your destiny still seems to require financial help from me.'

'It's only until I get established as an artist,' argued his son. 'As soon as I do that, I can pay back everything you kindly gave me. Meanwhile, I'm very grateful for your help. It may not be needed for that long.'

Vaughan leant forward. 'I'm very worried, George.'

'If I'm getting too much, reduce the size of the payments.'

'I'm not worried about the amount of money. What concerns me is the use to which it's put.' His voice hardened. 'Let me be candid. I wish to know what exactly I am subsidising.'

'You are helping a young artist to blossom into full flower.'

'Leave metaphors aside and tell me the plain truth.'

'I have a deal of creative talent – you've admitted that yourself – and I am working hard to develop it. I already have one commission and there are two others in the wind. The fees will not be very large at this stage in my career but, in due course, I can assure you that—'

'Forget your creative talent,' interrupted Vaughan. 'I speak of the rumours.'

His son beamed unconcernedly. 'To what rumours do you refer, Father?'

'They are rumours too disturbing to mention to your mother. Their source appears to be Professor Triggs. He, as you know, has a son of your age – one who joined a more respectable profession.'

'Respectability is the death of art.'

'You were seen by the professor's son at a party, entertaining low company.'

'I'm surely permitted to choose my own friends. And if this famous son is so respectable, what was he doing at the sort of party to which I'm invited?'

'His uncle is an art dealer in London.'

'Ah,' said George Vaughan, 'that explains it. We may well have rubbed shoulders at such a gathering. As a breed, I loathe art dealers but they are a necessary evil, so I never miss a chance to cultivate them.'

'It seems that another form of cultivation is taking place.'

'Speak more plainly, Father. Of what am I being accused?'

'Fornication is a sin.'

'Then you've been wise to abstain from it.'

'Do you dare to mock me!' shouted Vaughan, jumping to his feet. 'Remember where you are, sir, and who I am.'

'I tender my sincerest apologies, Father. I did not mean to be flippant.'

'You were crude and I'll not tolerate such behaviour.'

His son was contrite. 'Then I take back what I said unreservedly.'

'When I named you after Lord Byron, I hoped that you'd be inspired by his poetry and not ape some of the alleged excesses of his private life.'

'What alleged excesses? Has Professor Triggs been spreading rumours about Byron as well? How does the good professor find time to write his theological tracts when he's otherwise engaged, listening to silly gossip about artists and poets.'

'Stop it at once!' insisted Vaughan. 'Let's have no more sarcasm.'

'Then let's have no more rumours.'

His father flopped down into his chair. 'What am I to do with you, George?'

'Well, you might start by opening a bottle of the college sherry.'

George Vaughan saw the anger welling up in his father's eyes and he steadied himself to withstand the reprimand that was trembling on the older man's tongue. It was stillborn. Before Vaughan could speak, there was a tap on the door and it opened to reveal his son, Percy. Overcome with relief, he jumped up to embrace him. The greeting between the two brothers was less emotional. They merely exchanged nods of recognition.

'We have terrible news to impart about your cousin,' said Vaughan.

'I've already heard it,' explained his elder son. 'In fact, I may know more than either of you. I took a train from Moreton-in-Marsh and called first at Burnhope Manor. Mother fell upon me. It seems that Imogen is still alive but is being held somewhere against her will. Three detectives came to the house. One of them was Inspector Colbeck.'

Driving a horse and cart was a mode of travel that really suited Victor Leeming. At least, it would have done so had he not been sitting beside a distraught young woman with the corpse of her father lying behind them under some sacking. Robert Colbeck rode alongside them on the bay mare, which was now supremely obedient. Leeming's only interest was in his own horse, a shaggy creature with a dappled coat, moving at a benign trot and answering every twitch of the reins without protest. As the cart trundled on over uneven ground, the sergeant was able to indulge in his fantasy of being a cab driver, an occupation that had always had a great appeal to him. It would keep him in London, rescue him from the dangers concomitant with police work and relieve him of the dread of having to jump on a train, a ship or an unruly bay mare at a moment's notice. When he came out of his reverie, he saw a tiny thatched cottage ahead of him. A middle-aged woman came bustling out to greet them, her face pitted by hard work and disease.

Colbeck reached her first and introduced himself. Though he broke the news as gently as he could, she almost fainted. Mary leapt off the cart and ran to her. They clutched each other in sheer desperation. When she finally adjusted to the shock, the mother walked slowly to the rear of the cart and lifted the sacking, producing a fresh waterfall of tears when she saw the wound. Colbeck and Leeming offered words of condolence that went unheard. Both were saddened by what they saw. Mother and daughter were survivors of a poor family, scratching a living off an inadequate piece of land. With their breadwinner dead, they'd be turned out of their tied cottage without compunction. Their future was daunting.

When the women had calmed down sufficiently, the detectives carried the body into the house and laid it on the table in the scullery. The wife gazed down at the corpse but Mary scampered off upstairs. Colbeck felt it was the moment to offer what he hoped would be a form of balm.

'There'll be compensation for this,' he said, taking out the money. 'It will never atone for what happened, I'm afraid, but it may make things easier for a while.' When he offered the banknotes, she drew back in surprise. 'Please take them. They come with sympathy.'

'I've done nothing to deserve all that, sir,' she said, querulously.

'You deserve that and more,' said Leeming.

'But there's . . . so much.'

Out of compassion, both detectives had made their own contribution. What Colbeck handed over to her was more than her husband could earn in two years. She was pathetically grateful.

'I can't thank you enough, Inspector,' she said, biting back tears.

'I only wish it were more.'

'It were my husband's own fault, really. I told him not to take the money but it was too big a temptation. Then there was Mary, of course. It would have broken her heart if she hadn't been allowed to wear that lovely dress. Anyway, they didn't listen to me – and this is the result!'

'Why did you tell your husband to refuse the money?' asked Colbeck.

'I didn't like the look of him as offered it.'

'Mary said that he was tall, well dressed and had a nice voice.'

'It was too nice a voice,' she said, gruffly, 'and that's what troubled me. He had a smooth tongue on him and no mistake. Also . . .' She shut the door at the bottom of the staircase so that Mary couldn't hear her. 'Also,' she continued, 'I didn't like the way that he looked at my daughter. Mary didn't notice – God bless her – but I did.'

'What exactly do you mean?' wondered Leeming.

'He was ogling her, sir.'

'Didn't your husband object?'

'He was too busy counting the money.'

Colbeck questioned her further but there was nothing

she could tell them about the stranger that her daughter hadn't already divulged. There was a creaking of the floorboards above their heads then feet came down the rickety staircase. Mary entered in a smock. Over her arm was the dress belonging to Imogen Burnhope.

'Do I have to give it back?' she asked, wistfully.

During the drive to Worcester, Edward Tallis became increasingly uncomfortable. His companions exerted joint pressure on him, urging him to forget the whole incident and to drop all charges. While not wishing to offend them, the superintendent kept repeating that a crime had been committed and that punishment was therefore due. Tunnadine's reasoning quickly turned to vituperation and he had to be calmed down by Sir Marcus. The older man tried a different approach.

'Your writ does not run here, Superintendent,' he warned.

'We shall see about that, Sir Marcus.'

'The Detective Department is part of the Metropolitan Police. It is supreme in London but far less so in the provinces.'

'Then why were you so anxious to engage our services?' asked Tallis, pointedly. 'If you believe that power should reside with local constabularies, why didn't you turn to one of them? I'm sure that Worcester has its share of willing Dogberries.'

'I wanted the best detective,' said Sir Marcus, crisply.

'You got him.'

'I'm beginning to doubt that.'

'So am I,' said Tunnadine, acidly.

'Had he been left alone to do his work,' said Tallis, 'I'm certain that Inspector Colbeck would have brought the investigation to a successful conclusion. Thanks to Mr Tunnadine's foolhardy intervention, a man has been shot dead and Sir Marcus's daughter is in greater jeopardy.'

'I was trying to rescue her.'

'Imogen was never there to be rescued,' said Sir Marcus. 'That rogue would have taken my money and given us nothing in return.'

'Colbeck will hunt him down,' Tallis told them. 'Meanwhile, there are criminal charges to face. The law must run its course.'

Before Tunnadine could protest once more, Sir Marcus silenced him with a firm nudge. Tallis could not be bullied or persuaded to change his mind. No more words were exchanged during the rest of the journey. Lost in their private thoughts, the three men simply sat back in the carriage. Vernon Tolley was dejected. Having listened to the arguments bubbling away behind him, the coachman had heard no mention whatsoever of Rhoda Wills and no suggestion that she might still be alive. It alarmed him. In retrospect, he sided with Tallis. The blame for what happened should rest squarely on Tunnadine. He hoped that the politician would be held in custody but that hope was soon dashed.

When they reached the home of Joshua Pearl, the passengers alighted. The magistrate was a fleshy man in his fifties with jowls that wobbled as he spoke. In the presence of Sir Marcus, he was deferential to the point of obsequiousness and he was overly impressed to learn that Tunnadine was a Member of Parliament. Long before Tallis spoke, the outcome of the visit had been decided. The superintendent presented a strong case for the refusal of bail but it was swept aside with a flabby arm. Pearl released the prisoner for a nominal amount. As they left the magistrate's house, Tunnadine grinned in triumph.

'Do pass on the good news to Colbeck,' he said to Tallis, 'and you can tell that grotesque sergeant of yours that I'll be suing him for assault.'

Offered the chance to ride the bay mare again, Leeming declined. He and Colbeck therefore walked back in the direction of Burnhope Manor with the inspector leading the horse by the rein. Both men were saddened by the fate of Mary and her mother and hoped that the compensation would bring them a measure of solace. Colbeck had promised to contact an undertaker in Worcester so that someone could be sent out to take care of the body. As long as it remained in the cottage, it would only deepen their misery.

'It's a pity they couldn't tell us anything useful about that man,' said Leeming.

'But they did, Victor.'

'Really? I heard nothing, sir.'

'Mary told us what a fine horseman he was. She's a country girl, accustomed to seeing riders in the saddle and able to judge the height of a horse at a glance. If this fellow is the former soldier I suspect, then Mary's evidence puts him in a cavalry regiment. It's a clue that may help us to find him.'

'What about the mother?'

'She remarked on his character. He's a ladies' man, no question of that.'

'Soldiers always are,' said Leeming. 'With the exception of Superintendent Tallis, that is,' he added with a mirthless laugh. 'One woman is enough for me. When I met Estelle, it was the most wonderful moment of my life. Since then, I've never looked at another woman.'

'The man we're after behaves differently,' said Colbeck. 'My guess is that he's a predator who's had a number of ladies in his life, dazzled by his redcoat and brass buttons. Imogen Burnhope happens to be the latest one.'

'What will happen to her, sir?'

'I don't rightly know. After the failure of today's exercise, he may choose to cut and run, but I doubt it.'

'The two ladies are assets. He won't toss them away lightly.'

'That's my feeling, Victor. Do you remember the case we had in Wales?'

Leeming groaned. 'I remember it only too well, sir. Someone stole a silver coffee pot in the shape of a locomotive and demanded a lot of money for it. I was unlucky enough to be the person who handed over the ransom.' He removed his hat to rub his scalp. 'I can still feel the blow that knocked me out. The villain took the money. All I got in return was a headache that lasted for a week.'

'What happened then?'

Leeming pondered. 'Ah, I see what you mean,' he said at length. 'There was a second demand and it was for a lot more money.'

'That is what will happen here,' decided Colbeck. 'Our cavalry officer will be back for a larger ransom, to be exchanged under stricter conditions.'

'How will Sir Marcus react to that?'

'He'll pay up. He has to, Victor. It's the only way to get his daughter back.'

'She must be going through the most terrible ordeal, poor woman.'

'I wonder,' said Colbeck. 'Patently she's been duped and is at the mercy of the kidnapper, yet she may not realise it. Imogen Burnhope is defenceless. By making her fall in love with him, he has the tightest possible hold on her.'

The hotel was luxurious and Imogen had everything that she wanted but the delay was irksome. Expecting to be hundreds of miles away by now, she was still in England. Suspicion slowly taking root, Rhoda Wills was restive. Most of the promises made had yet to be honoured and she was wondering if they ever would be. When she tried to confide her worries, however, they were completely ignored by Imogen. Her faith was absolute and she'd hear no criticism of the man she adored. It was only a question of time, she believed, before they sailed away on their adventure.

Imogen was at the window when she saw him come into view, cantering as he entered the courtyard and clattering across the cobbles. He tugged the horse to a halt and leapt from the saddle, leaving the animal to the ostler who came running from the stables. When Imogen moved to the door, Rhoda got there first.

'We have to stay here,' she reminded Imogen.

'But I want to give him a welcome.'

'You heard what he told us. We're not to be seen.'

'I've been locked away in this room for too long, Rhoda.'

'So have I,' said the maid, mournfully, 'but there's no help for it – we're like birds in a cage.'

'No, we're not,' retorted Imogen. 'I won't have you saying things like that. We've *escaped* from a cage and we're free at last. I resent your tone, Rhoda. It's uncalled for. I don't want to hear any more complaints.'

Rhoda bobbed apologetically. 'I'm sorry. I spoke out of turn.'

'Nobody forced you to come with me.'

'I was happy to do so.'

'Try to remember that. You'll thank me one day. In fact—'

She broke off as she heard heavy footsteps approaching in the corridor. When there was a knock on the door, she unlocked it and opened it wide. He gave her a warm smile that instantly wiped away all of her lingering anxieties. Rhoda slipped away to the adjoining room to leave them alone. The man stepped into the room and closed the door behind him. Removing his hat, he tossed it onto a chair.

'Well?' she asked, breathlessly. 'When do we leave?'

'It won't be long now, my darling,' he promised. 'We set sail in a day or two.'

'Is everything in hand?'

'It soon will be.'

'What's holding us up?'

'There are a few minor details to sort out,' he said, kissing her on the forehead and stroking her hair with a covetous hand. 'You're so beautiful, Imogen. I can't wait to make you my wife.' He held her by the shoulders and stood back a little. 'It's not too late to change your mind. You're under no compulsion. If you want to go back to your dreary family, you can walk out of that door right now.' He looked deep into her eyes. 'Remember how badly they treated you and compare it to the way you've been cared for by me. Weigh us both in the balance. Which do you choose – your old life with them or an exciting new one abroad with your husband?'

Imogen laughed and hurled herself unconditionally into his arms.

CHAPTER ELEVEN

When they finally got back to Burnhope Manor, the detectives first went round to the stables. An ostler came to meet them and took the reins of the horse from Colbeck. The bay mare whinnied in farewell as she was led away. Leeming was relieved to part from the animal. Before they could leave the stable yard, the landau returned with Vernon Tolley on the box seat. It described a semicircle then came to a halt beside the well. The coachman jumped down and hurried across to them.

'Might I have a word, good sirs?' he asked.

'Of course you may,' said Colbeck.

'I'm fair frightened to death by what's been going on.'

'So am I,' murmured Leeming, glancing after the bay mare.

'I fear for the lives of the two ladies.'

'That's only to be expected, Mr Tolley,' said Colbeck, 'but I believe that they are still alive. As long as they are unharmed, they can be traded by the kidnapper. He will doubtless try to strike a bargain once more.'

'I couldn't help listening to what was being said when I drove Sir Marcus and the others into Worcester. They seemed to think they'd been hoodwinked.'

'We were,' admitted Colbeck.

'What if the kidnapper tries to hoodwink you again?'

'That's unlikely. We've learnt our lesson – and so has he.'

'The inspector might even have caught him if it hadn't been for Mr Tunnadine thinking that he could do our job for us,' said Leeming, resentfully. 'He deserves to cool his heels behind bars for a long time.'

Tolley's laugh was hollow. 'There's no chance of that, Sergeant.'

'Why not?'

'The magistrate released him on bail.'

Leeming gasped. 'But the man committed a murder.'

'That's not how the magistrate saw it,' said the coachman. 'They were in his house for little more than five minutes. When they came out, Mr Tunnadine had a grin on his face. He was taunting your superintendent.'

'Then he's a braver man than I am,' muttered Leeming.

'Where is Mr Tunnadine now?' asked Colbeck.

'He's catching the next train to London, sir. After I dropped the others off here, I took him to the railway station. He was still smiling to himself.'

'I don't know that *I'd* be smiling if the woman I was intending to marry was being held by a ruthless criminal. Mr Tunnadine seems to be more interested in escaping incarceration than in the fate of his beloved.'

As he thought of Rhoda Wills, the coachman nodded soulfully.

'What will you do now, Inspector?' he asked.

'We'll wait until we are contacted for the second time.'

'I pray that it may be very soon.'

'I fancy that it will be, Mr Tolley. Let me give you a word of warning, however,' Colbeck went on. 'What I've told you is in confidence. I don't want it spread among the servants. Enough rumours are circulating here as it is. Don't add to them. I've only spoken freely to you because I'm aware that you have a special interest in the case.'

'Thank you, sir,' said the other, shaking his hand. 'My lips are sealed.'

'Good man.'

'You'll find Rhoda for me, won't you?'

'I'll do my utmost.'

'I'm sure you will, sir.'

'You'll have to excuse us,' said Colbeck. 'We must send someone into Worcester to instruct an undertaker to go out to the cottage where the body was taken. The sooner it's removed, the better for the wife and daughter.'

He exchanged a nod with the coachman then took his colleague away. Tolley watched them go with fresh hope stirring. As soon as the two men went around the angle of the building, Win Eagleton scuttled out from a door to the kitchen. She tripped across the yard and arrived panting.

'I saw you through the window, Vernon. You talked to those detectives.'

'What of it?'

'Tell me what they said.

'Nothing,' he replied, stonily. 'They said nothing at all.'

* * *

167

None of them could remember the last time they were alone together. Emma Vaughan was the only one who'd been a constant resident at the college. Her younger brother had fled to London in search of fame as an artist and her elder brother had more or less disappeared into the Gloucestershire countryside. It was thrilling to see them both again but distressing to think that it took a crisis in their cousin's life to bring them under the same roof once more. They were in the drawing room. George Vaughan was stretched out languidly on the chaise longue while his brother perched on the edge of an armchair. Emma was on the sofa between them.

'What can we do?' she asked in despair.

'We must pray for their deliverance,' said her elder brother.

'I've already been doing that, Percy.'

'Never underestimate the power of supplication. Later on, we'll all pray together in the college chapel.'

'Don't include me in the service,' said his brother, tossing his hair back. 'I've seen the light and turned my back on religion.'

'That's an appalling thing to say!' chided Emma.

'It's the truth.'

'It's your version of the truth, George,' said Percy Vaughan, 'and it's based on a misapprehension. What you claim to reject is Christianity but all that you've done is to replace it with an alternative religion, one that is founded on vice and cupidity.'

'That's quite right, Percy,' agreed his brother, cheerfully. 'I follow a different god now and he's far less austere than yours. We are opposites, dear brother. You are the

Reverend Vaughan and I am the Irreverent Vaughan.'

'Beware what you say in front of Emma,' warned the curate.

'Oh, I don't believe all this nonsense about his life of wild abandon,' she said with a giggle. 'George is simply trying to shock us.'

'He's certainly shocked our father. His letters to me are full of tales about my dissolute brother. The stories cannot all be invention.'

'*What* stories?' asked Emma. 'I've heard none.'

'It's best that you don't.'

'But I love George. I want to know about his life in London.'

'It's the capital city of corruption.'

'Well,' said his brother, sitting up, 'it certainly has more temptations than a village like North Cerney could ever offer. But let's forget about my supposed descent into unbridled wickedness, shall we?' he continued. 'Imogen should occupy our thoughts now – and that jolly maid of hers. I liked Rhoda. All three of us have spoken to a detective. Let's pool our knowledge and see what we've learnt between us.'

'That's the first sensible thing you've said since I got here,' said the curate, approvingly. 'Let Emma go first.'

'I spoke with Inspector Colbeck and Sergeant Leeming,' she said.

'I only met the sergeant,' explained her younger brother. 'He was an unsightly creature but I took him for an upright fellow.'

'It's reassuring to know that you can still recognise virtue in a human being,' said the curate, tartly. 'Now, don't interrupt our sister.'

Emma recalled the interview with the two detectives, teasing out every detail from her memory with one striking omission. She was too embarrassed to confess that she had told them about Percy Vaughan's love for his cousin. Her younger brother also chose to forget certain things that occurred during Victor Leeming's visit to his studio. Dolly Wrenson was painted discreetly out of the picture. Having listened to his siblings with great interest, the curate talked about Colbeck's visit to the parish church in North Cerney. What he suppressed was the fact that he'd firmly believed Imogen and her maid to be dead. The news about the ransom demand had convinced him that both of them were still alive, albeit in serious danger.

'Inspector Colbeck surprised me,' he confessed. 'I never expected a policeman to be quite so intelligent. In younger days, he was an undergraduate at Pembroke College. Having read law at Oxford, he's now committed to its enforcement.'

'Having read almost nothing here,' interjected his brother, 'I'm committed to a life of pure – or impure – enjoyment.'

'Be serious for once, George,' urged Emma.

'I was never more so.'

Comparing their respective experiences had proved to be a useful exercise. Each one of them had learnt something new about the investigation. As a result, Emma was deeply troubled and her elder brother moved to sit beside her so that he could console her. It was George Vaughan who grasped at a stray memory.

'Wait!' he said, rising to his feet. 'Emma remembers

telling the detectives about a soldier on the platform at Oxford station. That could be significant.'

'I don't see why,' she said. 'I only saw him for a second.'

'Think back. Didn't you and Imogen once have an encounter with a soldier?'

'That was over a year ago, George. In fact, it might have been eighteen months. I don't see that it's at all relevant.'

'It was relevant to our cousin at the time. I recall her telling me about it.'

'What's this about Imogen and a soldier?' asked the curate, anxious to learn any detail about his cousin. 'Why was I not told about it?'

'It wasn't *that* important,' argued Emma.

'I should let the detectives decide that,' said the artist.

'But we never saw that soldier again, George.'

'*You* might not have seen him – what about Imogen?'

Having watched the comings and goings from an upstairs window, Cassandra Vaughan waited until her sister had dozed off again, then descended the stairs at speed, determined to learn exactly what had happened. When she barged into the library, she made no apology for disturbing the four men there. Tallis, Colbeck and Leeming rose politely from their seats but Sir Marcus showed her no such respect. He strode across to her, intent on ushering her out of the room again.

'I'm not a cat, Marcus,' she warned. 'I'll not be shooed away.'

'This is a private conversation, Cassandra. You are interrupting us.'

'I'm staying until someone finally tells me what's going on.'

'I'll be pleased to do so, Mrs Vaughan,' said Colbeck, indicating a seat. 'You haven't met Superintendent Tallis, have you?'

'No, Inspector, I've not had that pleasure,' she said, acknowledging Tallis with a nod before sitting down. He responded with a pale smile. 'Now, who is in charge?'

'I am, Mrs Vaughan,' said Tallis.

'Then tell me where you all charged off to earlier.'

Tallis hesitated and Sir Marcus was a block of granite. Colbeck stepped in.

'The facts are these,' he began. 'A ransom note was received by Sir Marcus. In receipt of a certain amount of money, your niece and her maid were due to be released today. Unfortunately, the kidnapper chose to deceive us. He wanted the ransom without having to surrender his captives.'

'What about the man who tried to take the money from you, Inspector?' asked Leeming. 'Tell Mrs Vaughan what Mr Tunnadine did.'

'Be quiet, man!' hissed Tallis.

'But it's a crucial part of the story.'

Cassandra was curious. 'What's this about Mr Tunnadine?'

'We should never have let him come with us.'

'I'd agree with the sergeant there,' said Colbeck, easily, 'but let's keep Mr Tunnadine out of this for the time being. Mrs Vaughan is now in possession of the salient facts. How much of them she decides to pass on to her sister is for her to decide.'

'Tell her nothing,' ordered Sir Marcus. 'My wife is too ill to cope.'

'Paulina is stronger than you think,' said his sister-in-law.

'I forbid you to pass on this information, Cassandra.'

'She must be told *something*.'

'Then give her a version of the truth,' suggested Colbeck. 'We are convinced that both of them are still alive and we hope – nay, expect – to rescue them very soon. There's no need to go into detail.' He shot a glance at Leeming. 'And there's certainly no need to bring Mr Tunnadine's name in.'

'What will happen next?'

'That's what we were trying to discuss before you forced your way in here,' said Sir Marcus, testily. 'If you'll be so good as to leave us in peace, we can formulate our plans.'

'I would have thought we'd already reached a conclusion,' said Tallis. 'My feeling is that we should follow Inspector Colbeck's advice. I'll return to London with the sergeant who can make contact with Mrs Vaughan's son. Out of courtesy, the young man should be informed of the latest developments. He must be worried stiff.'

Cassandra bristled. 'Why is George being kept informed while I am not? Am I not worthy of the same courtesy, Superintendent?'

'Indeed you are, dear lady.'

'Tell that to my brother-in-law.'

'I believe that Sir Marcus accepts your right to be told.'

'Where will Inspector Colbeck be when you go off?'

'He will remain here until the kidnapper gets in touch again. Sir Marcus has kindly offered him a bed for the night.'

Cassandra was satisfied. Having achieved her objective – partially, at least – she left the room and went back upstairs. Tallis rose to his feet and went out. Sir Marcus made for a decanter of brandy and poured himself a glass. Leeming seized the opportunity of a quiet word with Colbeck.

'Do I have to go back to London, sir?' he asked.

'I thought you'd want to see Estelle and the children.'

'Oh, I do. But I'd hate to travel on the train with the superintendent.'

Colbeck smiled. 'I can arrange a loan of that bay mare, if you prefer.'

'You know what he's like, Inspector.'

'I do, Victor, and I sympathise. Remember that he's still smarting over the release of a man who should have been remanded in custody. Whatever you do,' counselled Colbeck, 'don't mention the name of Mr Tunnadine.'

Lucinda Graham hoped that she would not be seeing him for some time. She still had the bruises from his last visit and wondered why he'd been so unnecessarily rough with her. In the past, she'd been able to flatter and cajole him in order to get what she wanted. Those days were gone, it seemed. Clive Tunnadine's imminent marriage was a watershed. It was no use fooling herself that, after the wedding, they would continue exactly as before. Their relationship would change abruptly. The way she'd been treated on his previous visit was a warning. Lucinda might be able to stay at the house for another month, perhaps more, but she was wise enough to prepare for the inevitable.

To that end, she went from room to room and gathered up all the items she treasured. Jewellery came first, then ornaments and then the gifts that he'd showered upon her in the early stages of their romance. Lucinda put them all together in one chest of drawers, planning to move them out in stages so that he was unaware of their disappearance. She expected no more expensive gifts from Tunnadine. They would be reserved for his wife. Lucinda felt sorry for the woman. She'd be entering a hollow marriage with a man who would never wholly commit himself to a wife. There would always be someone like Lucinda Graham in the shadows.

She was examining a silver locket he'd given her when she heard the key turn in the lock downstairs. Tunnadine had returned. The maid gave him a dutiful welcome but all he did was to stuff his hat into her hands. Pounding up the stairs, he came into the room where Lucinda had just hidden the locket away. Tense and throbbing with anger, he began to take off his clothes. Lucinda immediately did the same thing, afraid to speak or to contradict him in any way. When he was ready, Tunnadine grabbed her remaining underwear and tore it off her. She didn't dare to protest as he lifted her up and threw her onto the bed. There had been times, especially at the start, when he'd taken care to give as well as to take pleasure. He was in no mood to caress and excite her now. Driven by lust, he simply kissed, groped and rolled on top of her until he was ready to thrust deep inside her. She winced at the sudden pain.

It was even more of an ordeal than on his previous visit. All that she could do was to grit her teeth and run her hands up and down his back. The one consolation was that it did not last long. When he reached the height of his pleasure, he let out a cry of satisfaction and pumped away even harder. Lucinda could smell the whisky on his breath. He seemed heavier than ever and she began to feel smothered. All at once, it was over. Tunnadine pulled out of her and sat up on the bed, shaking his head as if trying to clear it. When he realised where he was, he ran an absent-minded hand across her breasts as a vague token of gratitude.

Lucinda was in pain and quietly terrified. She had, in effect, been ravished and there'd been nothing whatsoever that she could do about it. Tunnadine owned her. Having enjoyed all the advantages of being his mistress, she was now suffering the disadvantages. She felt sick, unprotected and violated. Was this how he intended to treat his wife?

It was a disturbing thought.

Tunnadine got up, dressed and left without saying a single word.

A train journey in the company of Edward Tallis could never be a source of enjoyment but it was far less of a trial than Victor Leeming had imagined. On the first stage of their return to London, he listened patiently to the superintendent's lengthy fulminations against the way that Clive Tunnadine had escaped justice. The sergeant was treated to a lecture on the sanctity of the law and made to feel, at one point, that he was the malefactor. Their arrival in Oxford terminated the lecture. It was never continued because Tallis fell asleep almost as soon as the second train was in motion. Leeming was able to review the day's events in comparative safety before he, too, was lulled into a deep slumber. It was only when the train squealed to a halt in Paddington that the two detectives woke up.

Tallis hailed a cab and headed for Scotland Yard. Leeming, meanwhile, was driven at a comforting trot towards John Islip Street so that he could deliver the letter that Colbeck had written to Madeleine. After a few pleasantries with her, Leeming took the cab on to Chelsea. All that he had to do was to tell George Vaughan what had happened in the Worcestershire countryside that day, then he could go home to his family. When he reached the crumbling old house, he was admitted by the landlady and allowed to walk up the interminable stairs to the attic. He knocked on the door of the artist's studio. After a few seconds, it was flung open by Dolly Wrenson. A welcoming smile congealed on her face and disappointment filled her voice.

'I thought it was George, coming back at last.'

'It's only me – Sergeant Leeming.'

'Nothing terrible has happened to George, has it?' she asked, seizing him by the shoulders. 'If he's been in an accident, tell me the truth. I'll go to him instantly.'

'Mr Vaughan has not been hurt in any way. I came here to see him.'

'He went off to Oxford and left me all alone. I've been so lonely, Sergeant.' Her smile slowly came back into view. 'I'm a woman who likes company.'

'Can I leave a message for Mr Vaughan?'

'You can do more than that,' she said, pulling him into the attic and shutting the door behind them. 'I need your opinion and I want you to be honest.' She released her hold. 'By the way, do you have a Christian name?'

'It's Victor – Victor Leeming.'

'Then it looks as if the spoils go to the victor.'

'I don't understand.'

She giggled. 'You will. Come over here.'

Dolly guided him across to the easel and lifted off the tattered sheet from the portrait. Before he could stop himself, Leeming was gazing at her nude body. When he tried to look away, she held his head between her hands and forced him to study the canvas. His cheeks were crimson and his mind in turmoil.

'What do you think, Victor?' she asked.

'You look . . . very nice,' he croaked.

'But I have no arm. George should have given me an arm before he left. It was cruel of him to leave me looking like that. I have lovely arms.' She turned him to face her. 'Don't you think they're beautiful?'

'Yes, yes, I do.'

'But you haven't seen them properly.'

'I'll take your word for it.'

'You can take more than that,' she said, slipping her robe off one shoulder to reveal a naked arm of exquisite loveliness. 'George needs to be punished. Will you help me to punish him, Victor?'

Leeming was nonplussed. Wanting to leave, he somehow felt rooted to the spot. He was hopelessly unequal to the situation. It was odd. When he'd been a uniformed constable on the beat, he'd been offered favours by any number of prostitutes and turned them down without embarrassment. He always felt sorry that they'd been reduced to selling their bodies. Most of the ladies of the night had either been sad young creatures with cosmetics daubed liberally over their pinched faces or raddled older women bearing the telltale marks of their profession. Dolly Wrenson fitted into neither category. She was young, wholesome and very alluring. Leeming was not so much tempted as horrified. Her smile broadened.

'If you're a policeman,' she cooed, 'you must be big and strong. Are you?'

'All I wish to do is to deliver a message,' he said, backing away.

'Tell me afterwards.'

'The two women have been kidnapped. We received a ransom note.'

'You've seen my arms, Victor, now you can feel them wrapped around you.'

He inched towards the door. 'I'm afraid that I have to go.'

'The night is young.'

'Please pass on the message to Mr Vaughan.'

'A gentleman should never reject a lady.'

Leeming was beyond the point of rejection. He was in a complete panic. As Dolly lunged towards him, he evaded her grasp, opened the door and fled down the stairs as if the house was on fire. He didn't stop running until he was three streets away. It was an incident he wouldn't mention to his wife, yet it would lodge in his memory a very long time.

Ordinarily, Sir Marcus Burnhope would never have dreamt of inviting a detective to dine with him but Colbeck was different from the normal run of policemen. He was astute, well educated and clearly dedicated to the task in hand. Cassandra had chosen to dine with her sister, leaving the two men to discuss the case freely. They were still reconstructing the events of the afternoon when wholly unexpected visitors arrived at Burnhope Manor. Believing they might have useful information to impart, Emma and George Vaughan had caught the train to Worcester and hired a cab to bring them to their uncle's house. Sir Marcus was surprised to see them. While giving Emma a cordial greeting, he felt less hospitable when he saw her brother's startling attire and long hair. He caught a decided whiff of dissipation. Colbeck was far more tolerant. Pleased to see Emma, he was delighted to meet the artist about whom Leeming had spoken. By the same token, George Vaughan was glad to meet the inspector.

On hearing that two of her children had arrived, Cassandra came downstairs to embrace her daughter and to scold her son for his disreputable appearance. All five of them adjourned to the drawing room and found a seat.

'Whatever brought you here?' asked Cassandra.

'We have something to tell the inspector,' replied the artist. 'It could have a bearing on the case.'

'On the other hand,' said Emma, 'it might be irrelevant. I have my doubts.'

'I don't.'

'Be quiet, George,' said his mother. 'Let your sister tell her tale.'

Emma looked around the ring of faces and began to lose her confidence. It took some prompting from her mother and some gentle persuasion from Colbeck to get her to speak. She plunged in.

'Some time last year,' she said, 'Aunt Paulina and Imogen came to stay with us in Oxford. I think it was February or March because there was snow on the ground. Imogen and I went for a walk one day in Christ Church Meadow. It was a glorious morning with the sun turning everything bright and shiny.'

'We don't need to hear that,' complained her brother.

'Don't interrupt,' said Cassandra, sharply.

'But Emma needs to get to the point.'

'Let her proceed at her own pace,' said Colbeck. 'There's no hurry.'

'I think that there is,' grumbled Sir Marcus. 'If Emma has any information that will help us in the search for Imogen's kidnapper, I want to hear it now.'

'Then you shall, Uncle,' said Emma, spurred on by the rebuke. 'We were enjoying our walk when this ruffian suddenly leapt out from some bushes to accost us. He demanded money. Imogen was so frightened that she was ready to hand over some coins just to get rid of him. He was a fearsome man, old, dirty, bearded and wearing tattered clothing that looked as if he'd slept in it. Also, he gave off the most noisome stink.'

'Why did you never mention this incident to me?' demanded Cassandra.

'Now who's interrupting?' said her son, smirking.

'We thought it would alarm you, Mother,' explained Emma, 'and it would certainly have upset Aunt Paulina. We were afraid that you'd stop us going out alone together and we didn't want that.'

'It's a fair assumption,' observed Colbeck. 'How did this business end?'

'A soldier came to our rescue, Inspector. He grabbed hold of the man and pitched him back into the bushes. Then he introduced himself and insisted on escorting us back to the safety of the college.'

'What happened then?'

'Nothing,' said Emma. 'We went into the college and never saw him again.'

'*You* never saw him again,' her brother reminded her. 'What about Imogen?'

'I can't believe that she had any further contact with him. If she had, then Imogen would certainly have told me.'

'She'd have told her mother as well,' declared Sir Marcus. 'Our daughter has been brought up properly. She'd never encourage the interest of some stranger she met in a chance encounter, especially if he was a mere soldier. What was his rank?'

'He was a captain, Uncle. The name he gave us was Captain Whiteside.'

'Would you recognise him if you saw him again?' asked Colbeck.

'Oh, yes, Inspector – he was very dashing.'

'But he was not the soldier you saw on the platform at the station?' Emma shook her head. 'What about the second soldier, the one who got off the train.'

'I didn't really take much notice of him.'

'We were too busy looking out for Imogen,' said Cassandra.

Sir Marcus was sceptical. 'None of this sounds remotely germane to the kidnap,' he decided. 'It was all of eighteen months ago and Imogen has probably forgotten all about it.'

'That's what I did,' volunteered Emma. 'Being pounced on by that ruffian was so distressing that I tried hard to put it out of my mind.'

'I was the one who dug it out again,' boasted her brother.

'You should have saved yourself the trouble, George,' said his uncle.

'I'm glad to hear about the incident,' added Cassandra. 'One thinks of Oxford as a seat of learning but we have plenty of vagabonds in our midst as well. You should be more careful where you walk, Emma. Male company is always advisable.'

'I believe that Emma and her cousin were entitled to be on their own,' said the artist. 'The presence of a man – even one as sensitive as me – would only serve to inhibit their conversation. What happened was unfortunate but they survived intact.' He turned to Colbeck. 'I felt that it was important for you to hear about the incident, Inspector,' he went on. 'Were we justified in making the effort to get here?'

'I'm not entirely sure about that, Mr Vaughan,' said Colbeck, 'but I'm grateful that you came and I'm very glad to make your acquaintance.'

Convinced that they had something crucial to report, George Vaughan was downcast. Colbeck's lukewarm response had also upset his sister. Emma was self-conscious about the fact that she'd described an event that she'd have preferred to stay hidden. Not only had it been more or less dismissed as irrelevant, it had given her mother ammunition to use against her. Emma's freedom to come and go from the college would henceforth be supervised more closely.

Colbeck was sorry to upset the two of them. Privately, he was delighted to hear about the encounter and certain that it was directly related to the kidnap. In admitting that, however, he would be alerting Sir Marcus to the possibility that his daughter had had a clandestine friendship with Captain Whiteside. If and when Imogen was released, it would sour relations between father and daughter and Colbeck was very keen to protect her.

'There has to be a connection,' emphasised George Vaughan. 'A soldier came to their rescue and a soldier was seen waiting at Oxford station.'

'There's a regiment stationed near the city,' said Sir Marcus, dismissively. 'It's not surprising that redcoats appear from time to time at the station.'

'Exactly,' said Colbeck, endorsing the remark. 'What we've been told was very interesting but of no practical value. The fact that a soldier greeted the train that day is pure coincidence.'

CHAPTER TWELVE

Since she knew for certain that her husband would not return home that evening, Madeleine Colbeck elected to visit her father. Light had faded from the sky so it was impossible for her to work at her easel and, in any case, she wanted some company. It was several weeks since she'd gone back to the little house in Camden Town and, as the cab drew up outside it, she felt a nostalgic pull. It disappeared the moment that she stepped inside. Now that she lived in a much larger and more comfortable abode, the house in which she'd been born seemed impossibly cramped. As her horizons had broadened, her old home had diminished in size. Yet she'd enjoyed her childhood there and, after the death of her mother, virtually ran the house. Caleb Andrews was very pleased to see her and she, in turn, was glad to find the place looking as neat and tidy as it had been during her time there.

'Where's Robert this evening?' he asked.

'He's spending the night at Burnhope Manor. Victor

Leeming brought me a letter from him. There have been complications.'

'What sort of complications?'

'I don't know, Father, and I wouldn't tell you even if I did.'

'But I might be able to help, Maddy.'

'You can help Robert best by letting him do his job unimpeded.'

'I wouldn't impede him,' he protested. 'I'd just give him the benefit of my superior judgement. Yes,' he continued, quashing her attempt at a reply, 'I know that you think I'm senile enough to be measured for my coffin but there's nothing to compare with experience and I've had plenty of it. Who provided Robert with a vital clue when he was up in Scotland earlier this year?'

'You did very well,' she conceded. 'But this is a different case altogether.'

'If it's connected to the railways, I'm the man they need.'

'Robert is well aware of that,' she said with a smile. 'Every time you set eyes on him, you remind him of the fact.'

'Then why doesn't he call on me?'

'Victor Leeming provides all the assistance he needs, Father. He's a good detective. Robert has taught him everything he knows.'

'I wish he'd teach the sergeant to wear a mask,' said Andrews with a dry laugh. 'That face of his would frighten anybody.'

'Victor has a heart of gold.'

'What use is that when he looks like something out of Regent's Park Zoo?'

'His wife doesn't think so, Father, and neither do his

children. Anyway,' she went on, weighing her words, 'Victor is not ugly – it's just that he's not as handsome as some men. When you get to know him, you forget his appearance.'

'Speak for yourself, Maddy.'

It was always the same. Whenever his son-in-law embarked on a new case, Andrews craved involvement. Because it was invariably denied him, he found something or someone to criticise out of pique. Leeming was the victim this time. Tallis had also been the whipping boy on occasion. Madeleine herself had attracted adverse comment from him though she'd defended herself robustly and forced an apology out of him. Before her father could make further comments about Leeming's face, she diverted him by crossing to the picture that hung over the mantelpiece. It was one of her earliest paintings and she could see the distinct signs of the amateur she'd been at the time. Andrews, however, would hear no disparagement of her work. It occupied a unique position in his memoirs.

'I had a grand time when I drove *Cornwall*,' he said, fondly. 'She was built at Crewe for the LNWR and was a joy to drive.'

'I only wish that my painting had been more accurate.'

'You caught the spirit of the locomotive, Maddy, and that's why I love it. I've spent hours just staring at her. What made her different was the combination of inner plate frames, with the cylinder mounted outside and securely held by a double frame at the front end. We used to have a problem with fractures in the crank axle,' he recalled. '*Cornwall* avoided that because the drive from the cylinders was delivered to the driving wheels by means of connecting rods attached to the crank pins on the wheels.'

'I wasn't able to show technical aspects like that,' she confessed.

'You showed enough for me to recognise a fine locomotive and a wonderful artist. Who'd have thought you could bring her to life like this?'

'I did my best, Father, but I can do much better now. That's why I'm painting her again in a very different setting. I hope you approve.'

'I'm proud of you, Maddy,' he said, giving her a hug, 'and I was proud to drive *Cornwall*. You won't find a locomotive as good as this on the Old Worse and Worse. It's a shambles. I'm amazed that company is still in business if they lose passengers while the train is steaming along. Talking of which,' he continued, 'did Robert's letter say that he hoped to find the missing women?'

'Robert always sounds hopeful. Even in the most difficult investigations, he remains optimistic.'

'So why is he staying at this big house in Worcestershire?'

She clicked her tongue. 'Stop probing. I've told you all I know.'

'Does he just want the pleasure of sleeping in a four-poster bed?'

'Oh, I don't think Robert will get much sleep,' she confided. 'That's one of the things he *did* say in his letter. He has to maintain a vigil all night.'

Colbeck knew that somebody would come. Whenever he was in pursuit of a criminal, he tried to put himself inside that person's mind, considering the available options before choosing the most advantageous. The kidnapper would be annoyed at the failure of his original plan and would want to extort an even larger ransom the next time. He would act quickly because the longer he delayed, the greater the opportunity to track him down and rescue his two captives. At the earlier exchange, the man he'd employed as a go-between had been shot. Careful not to expose another intermediary to danger, he would be more likely to send him under cover of darkness. That was why Colbeck was sitting beside a window on the ground floor of Burnhope Manor. If he could intercept the messenger, he might learn more about the man who'd sent the message. The long wait began.

Though he'd never met the Honourable Imogen Burnhope, he'd built up a composite portrait of her from the comments made by various members of the family. She was young, beautiful but largely ignorant of the ways of the world. Her innocence was her potential weakness. The coachman had given Colbeck a good description of Rhoda Wills. Because of her loyalty to her mistress, her plight was equally dire but it was Imogen's reckless decision that had imperilled them. Colbeck had begun to understand her urge to escape. For all its opulence, Burnhope Manor had a hollow feeling to it. Since her father was away most of the time, Imogen would have been kept under the close supervision of her mother. It must have been oppressive.

Sir Marcus's one major intrusion into his daughter's life was to select a husband for her. That, Colbeck believed, was what might have tipped the balance in favour of flight. While there might have been fleeting delight when the match was made – and when Tunnadine seemed an appealing bridegroom – even someone as naive as Imogen would have soon entertained doubts about him. The unfavourable reaction to him of members of the Vaughan family would have influenced her. In getting married, she must have realised, she would simply be moving from one unhappy situation to another. When an avenue of escape appeared, therefore, she was minded to take it, and her maid had apparently encouraged her to do so. Yet only an offer of overwhelming appeal would have made Imogen shun the countless privileges bestowed upon her by her family.

Colbeck was convinced that the offer had been made by the soldier whom she met in Christ Church Meadow. He was also convinced that the man's appearance at precisely the right moment to rescue the women had not been fortuitous. Stage management had been involved. The ruffian who'd leapt from the bushes had probably been an accomplice of the soldier who beat him off. Imogen and her maid would have been relieved and thankful. On the walk back to the college, Captain Whiteside – if that was his real name – had no doubt further ingratiated himself and set in motion a process that had culminated in the abduction.

Acutely aware that it was all supposition, Colbeck nevertheless believed that there was more than a germ of truth in his theory. He wished that Madeleine had been there to offer her advice. While he felt confident about entering the warped minds of villains, he was less sure-footed when trying to determine how a young woman thought and acted. There were other reasons why he longed to be beside his wife.

When the clock chimed in the hall, he shook off his fatigue. It was three o'clock in the morning and all he could see through the window was a vast expanse of gloom. Yet he kept his eyes peeled and was eventually rewarded. A figure was conjured out of the darkness, approaching the house with furtive steps. Colbeck jumped up from his chair and went into the hall. He reached the front door in time to see a letter being slipped under it. That was all the prompting he required. After pulling back the bolts, he turned the massive key in its lock and opened the door. Alarmed at the unexpected noise, the visitor took to his heels. Colbeck went after him, guided by the noise of his footsteps on the gravel path and judging by their evident speed that the postman was young and fit.

Colbeck was fast but his anonymous quarry was even swifter and he might well have escaped had he not decided to leave the path and plunge into the cover of the trees. Almost as soon as he did so, he tripped over an exposed root and dived headlong to the ground. His cry of surprise told Colbeck exactly where he was. Before he could haul himself up, the man felt the full weight of the inspector on his back.

'Let me go,' he cried.

'We must first have a talk, my friend.'

After lifting him to his feet by his collar, Colbeck introduced himself and elicited the name of Dick Rudder from the messenger. The young man was terrified. He was an apprentice at a flour mill and had been approached by a stranger while drinking at an inn.

'All I had to do was to deliver a letter after dark,' he said.

'Why did you come so late?'

'He paid me well, sir. I spent it on drink and fell asleep.'

'Describe the man to me.'

'He was about my height and I'd put him at thirty or more. And he had a way about him, sir. He made you feel that you were a friend. It was so with me, anyway, and we only talked for five or ten minutes.'

'Was he well spoken and smartly dressed?'

'Yes – that's right, Inspector.'

'What else can you tell me about him?'

'I took him for a soldier.'

'Why do you say that?'

'My uncle was in the army,' replied Rudder. 'He had the same straight back and the same swagger as this man. At least, my uncle did until he got killed in the Crimea. You'd never get me in an army uniform.'

'Tell me exactly what this stranger said to you.'

'Will you let me go then?'

'Yes, Dick – you're not in any trouble.'

Rudder was so pleased that he shook Colbeck's hand as if operating a village pump. He then launched into an account of the conversation he'd had. Sobered by his capture, he recalled almost all the details of his chat. Colbeck now had a much clearer image of the kidnapper. He was grateful to the apprentice.

'How much did he give you, Dick?'

'I got half a sovereign, sir – just for delivering a letter.'

'Then I'll match that amount,' said Colbeck, reaching into his pocket and handing the money over. 'It will help to soothe your bruises. Now, away with you and don't tell a soul about what happened here tonight. Is that a promise?'

Rudder nodded repeatedly then slipped away into the darkness.

Dominic Vaughan sat beside his elder son on a bench in the Master's garden. It was a sunny day but the fine weather did not dispel their mutual sadness. The fate of Imogen and her maid was a weight that pressed down heavily on both of them. The curate was particularly despondent. His father sought to distract him from his grief.

'How are things in North Cerney?' he asked.

'I am very contented, looking after my flock.'

'Have you no greater ambitions, Percy?'

'In time, as you well know, I'll become rector there.'

'I'd hoped that you'd set your sights higher,' said Vaughan. 'There's only so much one can do in a parish church.'

'It suits my temperament, Father. Small and insignificant as it may appear, All Saints has an intriguing history. If you look at the rectors' board, you'll see that the first incumbent was John de Belvale in the year 1269. When I become the next link in that long chain of worship,' said the curate, 'I intend to write a history of the clergy who've served North Cerney over the centuries.'

'Why confine yourself to a church when a cathedral might beckon?'

'I lack the qualities for high office.'

'You are clever enough to acquire them, Percy. Look at me,' said his father. 'When I was an undergraduate, I was so meek that people thought I was waiting to inherit the

193

earth.' His son smiled wanly at the biblical reference. 'But I applied myself and eventually learnt the skills needed to become a fellow. When I rose to be Master, of course, I had to become more adept at political dagger-work and less tolerant of my colleagues' prejudices.'

'My memory is that Mother helped to stiffen your resolve.'

'A good woman is a blessing to any man.' His son lowered his head. 'In time, you will find someone to share your life then you can enjoy the benison that only marriage can bring.'

'I have no plans to take a wife, Father.'

'Neither did I until I met your mother.'

'My case is different,' explained his son, looking at him. 'If I cannot have the wife of my own choosing, I'd prefer to remain celibate.'

Vaughan understood. Though his elder son had tried to keep his love for Imogen a secret, it had become clear to all members of the family. Percy Vaughan's passions ran deep. Losing her to a man like Clive Tunnadine had been a shuddering blow to him but discovering that she'd been abducted was far worse. The curate was suffering agonies.

'May I ask you something?' he said at length.

'You know full well that you may.'

'And will you promise to give me an honest answer?'

'I'd like to think that all my answers are honest,' said Vaughan, seriously.

'Why did you always favour George over me?'

His father was taken aback. 'But I didn't, Percy. I loved you both equally.'

'You may have attempted to do so but he was the one you indulged. I was admired for my discipline and my scholarship but George was the one who could make you laugh, even when his mischievous streak got out of hand. You gave him opportunities, Father,' he complained. 'You gave George licence that was denied me.'

'You didn't *need* licence – he did.'

'After all that's happened, he's still your favourite.'

It was true and Vaughan was ashamed to admit it. George had always been given preferential treatment by both parents. Emma, too, had sought her younger brother's company first. Percy Vaughan had felt isolated and undervalued.

'If I've shown George more kindness,' said the Master, 'then it was a grievous fault and I apologise for it. You've brought nothing but honour to the family name. George, alas, is more likely to besmirch it. A moment ago, you spoke of celibacy as something you'd willingly embrace. It is a concept entirely foreign to your brother.'

'You'll forgive him, whatever he does.'

'He's my son, Percy.'

'So am I.'

There was a noticeable tension in the air. Neither man had meant to talk about their relationship but it had nevertheless happened. As a result, both of them felt raw. Vaughan wrenched the conversation back to the abduction.

'It is such a strain, not knowing what's happening to Imogen and her maid,' he said, sorrowfully. 'I'm on tenterhooks, as indeed you must be. What on earth can we do, Percy?'

'We must continue to pray for both of them,' advised the curate, 'and we must pray for Inspector Colbeck as well. He needs all the help he can get.'

At that moment in time, Colbeck was, in fact, getting help from the head porter of the college. The letter delivered during the night had contained a demand for twice the amount of the original ransom. Sir Marcus Burnhope was given a day and a half to raise the money. Since there was nothing he could usefully do in the Worcestershire countryside, Colbeck had taken the train to Oxford to pursue a line of enquiry there. Samuel Woolcott, the venerable head porter, seemed to blend in perfectly with the ancient stonework all around him. His head was bald but strands of hair grew in profusion all over the lower part of his face like so much ivy. Old age had not dulled his mind or prevented him from carrying out his duties with commendable vigour. He and Colbeck conversed in the Lodge. Woolcott spoke in a local accent that had a soft, bewitching burr.

'When would this be, Inspector?'

'It was probably some eighteen months ago.'

Woolcott chortled. 'Why, that's as recent as yesterday afternoon to me,' he said. 'My memory goes back over six decades. Nobody here can match that, sir.'

'Let's confine ourselves to an afternoon in February or March of last year. Lady Burnhope and her daughter were staying with the Master.'

'You don't need to remind me of that.'

'Why not?'

'It was always an event when that young lady visited. The undergraduates buzzed round her like wasps around a pot of strawberry jam, so they did. I felt sorry for her because all that attention bothered her. The Master's daughter was used to it. The other young lady was not.'

'Cast your mind back to a day when there was snow on the ground and the two of them went out for a walk.'

Woolcott scratched his head. 'There'd have been a few days like that, sir.'

'This one was special. She went out with one companion and came back with two. The ladies were escorted back here by a soldier in the uniform of a captain.'

'You don't need to tell me his rank,' said the old man. 'I'd have recognised it just from looking at him. I've a grandson in the army, you see. He was a wayward lad until he went off to serve Queen and Country but they've beaten good manners into him. Now,' he added, 'you'll be wanting to know if I recall the incident and I do. The captain was very attentive to the ladies.'

The head porter went on to describe the soldier at exhaustive length and every detail corresponded with those already gleaned by Colbeck. By the time Woolcott had finished, the inspector was certain that the hero of Christ Church Meadow was the same man as the one issuing ransom demands.

'He was a cavalry officer,' said Woolcott. 'I know my regiments, sir.'

'What happened when the two ladies walked away?'

Woolcott chortled again. 'He did what all the undergraduates were doing and that was to stare at them and nurse foolish hopes. Once they went through into the Radcliffe Quad, the captain asked me who the prettier one was and how long she'd be in Oxford. I saw no harm in telling him.' His face creased into an apology. 'I'm sorry if I did wrong, Inspector.'

'You weren't to know what he had in mind.'

'I still don't.'

'Did you ever see the fellow again?'

'Oh yes,' replied Woolcott. 'I saw him a few times. He looked very different out of uniform but I knew that it was him. Once I've seen a face, I never forget it. The captain never came to the college, as far as I know, but he was here in Oxford, no question of that.'

'When was the last time? Can you remember?'

'I will if you give me a moment, sir. It was earlier this year on a very cold day. I know that because I had my collar turned up and my hat pulled down. So did the captain,' he said. 'I passed him outside Elliston and Cavell's. That's the big store in the high street.'

'I know it well from my days as an undergraduate, Mr Woolcott.'

'He didn't recognise me but I spotted him at once.'

'Could you put a date on the encounter?'

'I can give you a time, Inspector. It was near enough to noon. As for the date, it must have been late in February. Yes,' he confirmed, 'that would be it for sure. It was rather odd, now that I think of it.'

'In what way was it odd?'

'Well, I hadn't laid eyes on the man for months, then he turns up at the very time that Lady Burnhope was staying here with her daughter. Isn't that peculiar?'

Colbeck made no comment. Everything he'd been told by Woolcott had reinforced his theory about the kidnap. After thanking the head porter, he stepped out of the Lodge at exactly the same time that the Master and his elder son were coming into the Main Quadrangle. They were very surprised to see him. Percy Vaughan was carrying a valise as if about to depart but he was desperate for information before he went. He and his father descended on Colbeck and pressed him for the latest news. They were told about the way that Tunnadine had intervened during the attempted exchange and were disheartened when they heard that the two women had not, in any case, been there.

'He's killed them,' said the curate, forlornly. 'He's only pretending that they're still alive in order to extract money from my uncle. The man is an absolute monster.'

'No, sir,' said Colbeck, 'he's a wily character who is exploiting to the full the advantage he holds. I don't believe that either of the two ladies is dead. They are being held somewhere, though under what conditions, I couldn't hazard a guess.'

'Is there no hope of catching this villain?' asked Vaughan.

'There's every hope. Thanks to the assistance I received from your daughter and from the head porter here, I know who the man is and how he operates. He's no longer a phantom but a hazy photograph inside my head.'

While he told them enough to satisfy their curiosity, Colbeck held back much detail. They were cheered by the progress he'd made, though still very concerned for the safety of the two women. He did his best to reassure them.

'What's the next step, Inspector?' said Vaughan.

'I need to ask you a favour, sir,' replied Colbeck. 'Every

college relies on an army of scouts. They are the unsung heroes of this university.'

'I couldn't agree with you more, Inspector.'

'When Lady Burnhope and her daughter stay here, who looks after them?'

'They travel with their own maids, of course, but I always assign a scout to each of them. He's there to fetch, carry, change the beds and answer any other needs.'

'Whom did you assign to look after your niece?'

'Oh, it was always Arthur Lugstone. He's very reliable.'

'I'd like to meet him as soon as possible.'

'That can be arranged.'

'I've been puzzling over something,' said Percy Vaughan, brow furrowed. 'If Mr Tunnadine shot a man dead in cold blood, why is he not being held in custody?'

'Sir Marcus had too much influence over a local magistrate.'

'Then he's abused that influence.'

'Too true, sir,' said Colbeck. 'Superintendent Tallis will be seeking ways to rectify the situation. As upholders of law and order, we cannot allow anybody to evade justice. Mr Tunnadine will be called to account before long. His status as a Member of Parliament can only offer him a degree of protection. It will be insufficient to save him from prosecution. Oh,' he went on with a half smile, 'there's something else you may care to know about the gentleman.'

'What's that?' asked the curate.

'On the balance of probability, I'd say that it was highly unlikely that Mr Tunnadine will ever marry your cousin, Imogen.'

Percy Vaughan was both startled and elated by the good news. Shedding his inhibitions for once, he put his head back and emitted a laugh of pure joy that echoed around the quadrangle.

Clive Tunnadine was not without his finer feelings. Having used his mistress to allay his frustration, he began to be troubled by remorse. Lucinda Graham had met his needs for over twelve enjoyable months and deserved more than to be treated with such inconsiderate brutality. He needed to make amends. When he returned to the house, therefore, he did so with a basket of flowers and a series of apologies. Having nursed her resentment, Lucinda was inclined to rebuff him but Tunnadine continued to smooth her ruffled feathers and to tell her how much she meant to him. Her anger slowly melted into a vague feeling of pleasure. What eventually won her round was the promise that, after his marriage, he would still retain his intimate relationship with her. Lucinda might be able to stay at the house, after all.

'I'm still very cross with you,' she warned.

'You've every right to be so.'

'It will take more than a basket of flowers to make me forgive you.'

'A fresh supply of flowers will arrive every week,' he promised.

'What would please me more is an explanation. You've dealt with me roughly before but not with the same violence as you did this last time. What did I do to provoke such behaviour? For what offence was I being punished?'

'It was not punishment, Lucinda,' he assured her. 'It was a mistake.'

'You were like a man possessed.'

'I can see that now and I swear that it will never happen again. All that I can tell you is that . . .' he paused as he searched for the words '. . . is that there has been a serious problem in my private life that has yet to be resolved. That's no reason to behave as I did towards you, of course. What I did was reprehensible. Suffice it to say that it belongs in the past. Our future together will be a source of continuous pleasure to both of us.'

'I trust that it will be,' said Lucinda, forcefully. 'I'll not stay to be treated again so harshly. Use me as the loving friend that I am and not as a common trull whose slit can be bought cheaply in the backstreets of Seven Dials.'

Tunnadine admired her show of spirit. It made him enfold her gently in his arms and kiss her full on the lips. Lucinda pulled away.

'Will you spend the night here?' she asked.

'No, Lucinda. I have to go. There's someone I must see.'

She was about to ask if the meeting related to the problem of which he'd spoken but she checked herself. Certain that he'd been referring to his forthcoming marriage, she remembered what had happened when she'd first mentioned the event. It had caused him to stalk out and slam the door on her. Now that they'd been reconciled, she had no wish to upset him again. By way of a farewell, he took a long, luscious kiss from her and left her feeling once more that he really cared for her.

'When will I see you again?'

'It will be as soon as I may arrange it,' he promised.

On that note, he sniffed the flowers then took his leave, closing the door softly behind him. Lucinda glanced at the chest of drawers in which she'd hoarded all her treasures. It might yet be possible to put some of them back on display.

Tunnadine, meanwhile, took a cab back to his house. Dismissing Lucinda from his mind, he concentrated his thoughts on the other woman in his life. He had no illusions about Imogen Burnhope. She could never offer him the delights he found in the arms of his mistress. Imogen would be a highly suitable wife, obedient and undemanding. She would give him an important link to a titled family and, in time, bear his children. Her future, he envisaged, would be one of quiet domesticity, leaving him to roam freely. First, however, she needed to be released from danger and restored to him. It was that consideration that had made him spurn the chance of a night with Lucinda Graham. For the moment, she had to take her turn behind Imogen.

When he reached the house, he paid the cab driver and let himself in. A letter awaited him on the hall table. He snatched it up and tore it open. The words ignited a fire inside his head. Tunnadine reeled from their impact.

CHAPTER THIRTEEN

Edward Tallis was not a man to let the sun go down on his anger. Furious at the way that Tunnadine was still at liberty after shooting someone dead, he'd returned to Scotland Yard to set legal wheels in motion. The following day saw him reading reports of other crimes that his detectives were investigating. Conscientious to a fault, he worked hard to ensure that cases were swiftly resolved so that his men could be redeployed on one of the other crimes that merited the attention of the Detective Department. The telegraph arrived late that morning. Victor Leeming was in the superintendent's office at the time. As he read the short message, Tallis inhaled deeply through his nose.

'It's exactly as Colbeck predicted,' he said, passing it to Leeming. 'A second demand has arrived. The money is to be handed over tomorrow.'

'Then I'd suggest we don't take Mr Tunnadine next time.'

'He won't be allowed anywhere near the kidnapper.'

'The demand is for *twice* as much,' noted Leeming, seeing

the figure. 'I didn't think that anybody had that amount of money tucked away.'

'Sir Marcus inherited both capital and extensive property. That is why his daughter was selected as a target. The kidnapper knew that Sir Marcus would be able to afford the ransom.' He took the telegraph back and read it again. 'We were lucky that this whole business happened between Worcester and Oxford.'

'Why is that, sir?'

'Both of them have telegraph stations. Messages can be sent to London at a fraction of the time it would take a courier to bring them. It's one of the many boons that the railway has brought us.'

'I preferred it the way it was before.'

'You can't stand in the way of progress.'

'It's not progress in my eyes,' said Leeming, grumpily.

'Then you need spectacles, Sergeant. The world is changing fast and we must change with it or the criminal fraternity will outpace us. They've already seized on the potentialities of railways as a source of crime. Look at this very investigation, man, or consider what happened on the Caledonian Railway earlier this year.'

Leeming started. The enforced stay in Scotland was not an enticing memory. Before he could say why, they were interrupted. There was a tap on the door then Colbeck stepped into the room.

'Good day to you both,' he said, genially.

'What kept you in Worcestershire so long?' asked Tallis. 'This telegraph says that a ransom demand was delivered during the night. You could have caught a train shortly after dawn.'

'That's exactly what I did do, Superintendent. It took me to Oxford where I was able to make a number of productive enquiries. I also had the pleasure of meeting the Reverend Percy Vaughan again and of talking to his father. When my work there was done,' admitted Colbeck, 'I did permit myself half an hour to reacquaint myself with a city that is very dear to me.'

'It's a pretty place,' observed Leeming. 'It's got fine old buildings galore.'

'When I require a gazetteer of Oxford' said Tallis with a glare, 'I'll ask for one. As for you, Inspector, let me remind you that you went there to solve a crime, not to indulge in distracting reminiscences.'

'Oh, I was not distracted,' said Colbeck. 'I felt from the start that the city held secrets that I needed to bring into the open and so it proved.'

He gave the account that he'd prepared carefully on the train journey to London. Colbeck told them about the way that he'd intercepted the visitor to Burnhope Manor during the night and how he'd questioned the head porter at University College. Thanks to the Master's help, he'd been able to identify a critical factor in the wooing of Imogen Burnhope.

'His name is Arthur Lugstone,' said Colbeck.

'Who is he?'

'He is a scout at the college, sir – or, at least, he was until the truth came out.'

'What's a scout?' asked Leeming.

'Try listening for once,' said Tallis, sardonically, 'and you may find out.'

'A scout is a manservant,' explained Colbeck.

'Undergraduates enjoy the luxury of having one to look after them. It's one of the university's traditions. Until today, Arthur Lugstone was part of it.'

'Why did you seek this particular fellow out?' asked Tallis.

'According to the Master, he was engaged to take care of guests at the college. Whenever she visited, Sir Marcus's daughter was looked after by him. In other words, he was in the perfect position to carry any messages to her. It was the way that Captain Whiteside kept in touch when she was in the city. Lugstone denied his involvement at first,' said Colbeck, 'but I threatened him with a spell in prison and he crumbled at once. To be fair to him, he had no idea what the letters contained but he's still culpable of aiding what amounts to a conspiracy. The moment that the Master heard what had been happening under his nose, he dismissed Lugstone on the spot.'

'But wait,' said Leeming, 'the young lady only went to Oxford twice a year. Was that enough time for the captain to work on her emotions?'

'They doubtless had another arrangement when she was at Burnhope Manor,' suggested Colbeck. 'Clandestine correspondence would have been smuggled in somehow. The obvious go-between was Rhoda Wills.'

'I think you're right, Inspector. From what the coachman told us, I sensed that the maid was a resourceful woman.'

'It sounds as if she paid for her resourcefulness,' muttered Tallis. 'It helped to lead her mistress into a trap.'

'You say that she received letters while in Oxford,' recalled Leeming. 'Did this scout carry replies back to Captain Whiteside?'

'He did, Sergeant,' said Colbeck, 'and he gave me the address to which he took the missives. That gave me even further insight into the character of this self-styled gallant soldier.'

'You say that with a degree of sarcasm,' remarked Tallis.

'It was intentional, sir. Lugstone gave me the address to which he took any correspondence from the young lady. The house was in Walton Street,' said Colbeck, 'not far from the Clarendon Press. It was owned by a Mrs Greenfield, a widowed lady who took in lodgers. Captain Whiteside stayed there often. Sometimes he brought an army friend, a Sergeant Cullen, with him.'

'It must be his accomplice.'

'He is, Superintendent. Mrs Greenfield had little to say about the sergeant but she spoke well of Captain Whiteside. When he stayed there alone, he always told her about his escapades in the Crimean War. She was enthralled by his tales. Though she didn't confess it in so many words,' Colbeck went on, 'I got the distinct impression that she fell victim to his charms.'

'The blackguard!' exclaimed Tallis. 'While he's paying court to one woman, he's enjoying the favours of another. That's despicable.'

Leeming was even more shocked but it was not the image of the seduced landlady that came into his mind. It was the disturbing sight of Dolly Wrenson's naked body – minus one arm – on canvas in a Chelsea studio. He fought hard to expunge it from his memory.

Colbeck's visit to the house in Walton Street had provided him with far more detail of the kidnapper. Feeling profoundly sorry for the landlady, he said nothing to disillusion her. Mrs Greenfield had been a lonely woman in a house that seemed increasingly empty after the death of her husband. Still in her thirties, she'd felt young enough to contemplate a second marriage and Colbeck was certain that hints of it had been dropped by her favourite lodger as a means of gaining access to her bed.

'In moments alone with the landlady,' said Colbeck, 'the captain would have been off guard. He talked at length about his military career. Those details need to be corroborated.'

'I'll instigate checks in the army records,' said Tallis, picking up the telegraph. 'There's nothing much we can do until the ransom is handed over tomorrow.'

'There's a lot we can do, Superintendent.'

'I fail to see it.'

'The chosen spot for the exchange is in the Oxfordshire countryside. I think that the sergeant and I should reconnoitre it well in advance.'

'Does that mean I have to ride a bay mare again?' moaned Leeming.

'You'll do as you're told,' said Tallis, unsympathetically.

'That animal could have killed me, sir.'

'Don't worry,' soothed Colbeck. 'You won't need to be in the saddle this time. We'll hire a trap at the station and we'll go far and wide. If the captain has shifted the venue to Oxfordshire, the likelihood is that the two ladies are being held somewhere in the county. He'll not wish to travel any distance with them.'

'What can I do in the meantime?' wondered Tallis.

'You face a difficult task, sir.'

'Oh – and what's that?'

'Well,' said Colbeck, 'I've already asked Sir Marcus to

say nothing of the second demand to Mr Tunnadine. He agreed, albeit reluctantly. If the gentleman somehow finds out what's afoot, it could prove disastrous. That's why I'm turning to you, sir. You must stop Mr Tunnadine from ruining everything for a second time.'

When he recovered from the shock of reading the letter, Clive Tunnadine came to see that it presented him with a number of opportunities. The amount of money demanded, while less than the previous ransom, was excessive but he consoled himself with the thought that he would not actually lose it. Cleverly handled, the exchange could work entirely to his benefit. He would make possible Imogen's release, kill or capture her kidnapper and have the deep satisfaction of solving a crime that Inspector Colbeck had been investigating. It was this last element that had immense appeal to his visitor.

'The prospect fills me with pleasure,' said Alban Kee.

'You like the idea, then?'

'It's precisely what I would have recommended, Mr Tunnadine.'

'How well do you know the inspector?'

'I know him far too well.'

'Did you work alongside him at Scotland Yard?'

'Nobody works alongside Colbeck,' said the other. 'You are always beneath him. I occupied the same rank yet had less power when measured against him. He's the commissioner's favourite and that always rankled with me.'

Tunnadine was glad that he'd engaged Alban Kee. Though he now worked as a private detective, Kee had served in the Metropolitan Police before being promoted to the Detective Department. His elevation had taken rather longer to come there because he was overshadowed by other officers, principal among them being Robert Colbeck. It had left him with bitter memories. Kee was a sturdy man of middle height with dark, mobile eyes either side of a bulbous nose that seemed to explode out of his face. His sparse hair was combed forward and slicked down. The moustache was virtually invisible beneath the domineering proboscis. He'd been recommended to Tunnadine by a friend.

'Your reputation goes before you, Mr Kee,' said the politician.

'I work quickly, effectively and discreetly, sir.'

'It's your discretion that I need most. Nothing of our discussion must be leaked to anyone else. Most vital of all, it must not reach the ears of anyone at Scotland Yard – especially those of Inspector Colbeck.'

'I'll be as silent as the grave, Mr Tunnadine.'

'What do you think of that letter?'

'It's obviously genuine,' said Kee, passing it back to him, 'because you recognise the hand from the earlier ransom demand. My question is this – why send it to you and not to Sir Marcus Burnhope?'

'That bothered me at first,' admitted Tunnadine, 'but I think I've worked out the answer. When Sir Marcus was given the opportunity to rescue his daughter, it was an abject failure. My suspicion is that, as a consequence, the kidnapper doesn't trust him. Aware of my relationship with Imogen, he's turned to me instead.'

'Why was the first exchange botched, sir?'

'I blame Colbeck for that. He insisted on impersonating Sir Marcus.'

'That's ever his way,' sneered Kee. 'He *has* to be in charge.'

'The exercise miscarried but at least the money was saved. Sir Marcus had been tricked. His daughter was never even there.'

'What makes you think that the kidnapper will stick to his promise this time?'

'It's the tone of his letter. He freely concedes that he tried to get too much for too little on the previous occasion. All he wants is what he calls a fair exchange.'

Kee's moustache twitched. 'It's still a fearsome amount of money, sir.'

'It will be found. I've already spoken to my bank. Besides,' said Tunnadine, 'I look to you to make sure that I don't part with a single penny.'

'I hope you'll part with a lot more than that if I do my job properly.'

'You'll be handsomely rewarded, Kee.'

'Thank you, sir.'

Tunnadine liked the man. He seemed alert, decisive and respectful. Years as a detective meant that he could remain calm under pressure. What Kee had not told him was that he was driven out of the Detective Department by Tallis because there were persistent rumours that he accepted bribes from criminals to let them go. It was Colbeck who'd first made the charge against Kee, hence the latter's undying hatred of him. The fact that Kee was guilty of the crime was irrelevant to him. He'd lost a position in which he could wield power and was now reduced to working on his own. Loss of status was compounded by a loss of income. This latest assignment gave him the chance to recoup some of those losses. A successful outcome would mean good publicity for the private detective. His name would replace that of Colbeck in the newspapers and the thought sweetened him.

'What's your advice?' asked Tunnadine.

'That depends on when the money is ready, sir.'

'My banker says that I can collect it in the morning.'

'Then while you're doing that, I'll take a train to Crewe. The letter is careful to give us no details of the actual exchange,' said Kee. 'It simply orders you to stay at a nominated hotel on a particular day so that instructions can be delivered to you there.'

'I'll check the railway timetable in *Bradshaw*.'

'Do you possess a weapon, sir?'

'I have several firearms and I'm a good shot.'

'Then we are two of a kind for I've been trained as a marksman. Between us, I feel sure that we can bring this fellow down – and his accomplice, for he will surely have one. Beware of more tricks, Mr Tunnadine. He's a guileful man.'

'I'll insist on seeing that Imogen is alive and unharmed before any exchange is made. We won't be palmed off with an ignorant country girl this time.'

In spite of the tiresome delays and the sudden changes of plan, Imogen Burnhope still retained complete faith in the man she loved. Terence Whiteside was everything that she had ever hoped for in a future husband. He was brave, handsome, kind, generous, unbelievably patient and filled with a spirit of adventure. Once she'd got to know Clive Tunnadine, the idea of marrying him was tinged with fear. His political career would always take

213

precedence and she would be compelled to lead the same empty existence as her mother, left at home and largely disregarded. Captain Whiteside was different. He'd offered her a vision of wedded bliss that had entranced her. They were to be secretly married in England before sailing off to France where, he told her, he owned an estate in the Dordogne. Far from discovery, they would create their own private Garden of Eden. The fact that the marriage still hadn't taken place dismayed her at first but Whiteside had persuaded her that it was only a matter of days before he took her as his wife.

Imogen might be lulled into a trance by his smooth tongue but Rhoda Wills was deeply troubled by the turn of events. There had been a definite excitement in the prospect of an escape to a foreign country, especially as it involved a degree of play-acting at Oxford station. Rhoda had willingly helped Imogen to put on an army uniform and had tied the bandage in place to conceal part of her face. She'd then expected to be driven to a remote church where the wedding ceremony would take place in private. In their exhilaration, neither she nor Imogen had stopped to question the validity of a marriage conducted in such a way. In the event, it never occurred. Instead of sailing off to the Continent with her newly-wed mistress, Rhoda was being kept in a hotel somewhere in Oxfordshire and fed on a sequence of what she now discerned as patent excuses.

It was, however, impossible to convince Imogen that anything was amiss.

'I'm very worried,' said Rhoda.

Imogen smiled. 'You're always worried.'

'Far too many things have gone wrong.'

'That's not true at all. The moment we stepped onto that train, everything went exactly as arranged. I changed into the uniform that Captain Whiteside had provided and I was whisked away from Oxford as the soldier.'

'I don't remember the train journey so fondly,' said Rhoda. 'You told me to put my head out of the window in the Mickleton Tunnel so that the smoke would darken my complexion and make it more difficult for your aunt to recognise me. All that happened was that my hat blew off and I ended up with a mouthful of dust and a stink of smoke in my nostrils.' Imogen laughed. Rhoda was aggrieved. 'It wasn't funny.'

'I'm sorry, Rhoda,' said the other. 'Without you, none of this would have happened. You helped to rescue me from Burnhope Manor. I'll always remember that.'

'Don't be grateful until you're quite sure that you *have* been rescued.'

Sharing a sofa in the bay window, they were in the larger and more well appointed of the adjoining rooms. It had the kind of lavishness to which Imogen was accustomed and proved to her that Whiteside really did possess the wealth of which he'd boasted. Rhoda gazed longingly through the window.

'It wouldn't be so bad if we were allowed to go outside.'

'We can't do that, Rhoda. We mustn't be *seen.*'

'But we've been cooped up for days, even eating our meals in here. We both need some exercise. Why can't we at least take a turn in the garden?'

'It's only a matter of time before we leave.'

'I wonder,' said the maid, doubtfully.

'You should read that favourite sonnet of mine. It was the one that Captain Whiteside quoted in his first letter to me. And have you forgotten the name of the locomotive that took us to Oxford?' asked Imogen, excitedly. 'It was *Will Shakspere*. That was a sign. The sonnet I've just mentioned was written by Shakespeare. The bit of it that I always call to mind helps me to ignore the minor inconveniences that have afflicted us. 'Love is not love which alters when it alteration finds . . .' That's how it is with me, Rhoda. Although our plans have altered slightly, my love has remained constant. *Will Shakspere* – I'll always remember the name of that locomotive and so, I trust, will you.'

'What I remember is losing my hat in that tunnel.'

'I gave you my own to wear when I changed into that uniform.' Rhoda fell silent but her expression spoke volumes. 'Why are you so sad?' asked Imogen. 'Don't you feel happy for me?'

'I wish that I could,' replied the maid. 'I didn't think that Mr Tunnadine would be a fit husband for you and I hated seeing the way your parents tried to bully you into marrying him. But are you really any better off now?'

'Of course I am. I've been blessed with a husband of my own choice.'

'But he's *not* your husband, Miss Imogen.'

'He soon will be. You and Sergeant Cullen will be the witnesses.'

'That's another thing I must mention,' said Rhoda, glancing over her shoulder. 'I've tried to keep my anxieties to myself because I don't wish to unsettle you in any way. However, I must speak out about the sergeant. He troubles me.'

'Why? He's been perfectly civil to both of us.'

'There's something about him I don't quite like.'

'He's Captain Whiteside's best friend. That in itself should be more than enough to commend him. Why this uncalled-for dislike of Sergeant Cullen? I find that lovely Irish lilt of his so musical.'

'It wasn't very musical this morning,' recalled Rhoda. 'He came into my room when I tried to open your trunk and he ordered me to leave it alone. He used a voice I'd never heard before and it shook me.'

'He was only repeating what the captain told us. Our luggage must be kept locked so that we can leave at a moment's notice. Besides, I don't need anything from the trunk, Rhoda. I'm comfortable in what I wear.'

'It upset me a great deal.'

'Then I'll ask the sergeant to apologise.'

'You might ask him something else at the same time.'

'What's that?'

'After he left the room,' said Rhoda, 'I wondered why he'd been so harsh with me. It was unkind of him. So I disobeyed his order. I unlocked the trunk and went through its contents. It's no wonder he didn't want me to look inside.'

'I don't understand what you're saying.'

'One of your dresses – the pretty red one you like so much – is missing. Either the sergeant or the captain must have taken it out.' Imogen blanched. 'Why do you think they did that?'

Before he caught a train back to Oxford, Colbeck made time for a fleeting visit to his house. When he heard that Madeleine was in her studio, he crept upstairs, opened the door quietly, then moved up behind her to put his hands gently over her eyes.

'Robert!' she cried in delight. 'You're home again.'

He took his hands away. 'How did you know it was me?'

'Nobody else would dare to interrupt me.' Turning to face him, she collected a kiss. 'Even my father would have the sense to keep clear of me when I'm painting. I went to see him yesterday evening, by the way.'

'How is he?'

'At the moment, he's mystified that you don't enrol him as a detective on your latest case. He thinks that he has special gifts when it comes to solving crimes on the railways. I'm too soft-hearted to tell him he'd be a terrible hindrance to you.' She put her paintbrush aside and wiped her hands on a cloth. 'How long can you stay?'

'No time at all, alas,' he replied. 'It will just be long enough for me to gather a few things and bring you up to date with what's been happening. As soon as I've done that, I'm taking Victor back to Oxford.'

'I envy him. I remember the time that you took me there for a day.'

'That was a nostalgic visit. This one has a more serious purpose.'

Madeleine followed him along the landing to their bedroom. While he collected a few items from the wardrobe, he gave her an outline of the latest developments. She was shocked to hear of the way that Tunnadine had shot the farm labourer and then been granted bail by a magistrate but her chief interest lay in what Colbeck had discovered about the plight of Imogen Burnhope.

'What an appalling situation to be in,' she said. 'I feel so sorry for her. This soldier you speak of seems to have got a hold over her that led her to make the most extraordinary decision. She'll have bitter regrets about leaving her family now.'

'The young lady may not have reached that point yet, Madeleine. When she does, the disenchantment is going to hurt her at a deep level. I do hope that we can get her safely back at the second attempt.'

'Do you think that Captain Whiteside will try to deceive you again?'

'I'm certain of it but he won't succeed this time.'

'What about Mr Tunnadine?'

'By rights,' said Colbeck, 'the man should be behind bars. In his heart, Sir Marcus knows that. It's the reason he agreed to my request that we say nothing to Tunnadine about the second ransom demand. If fortune favours us, we'll secure the release of Sir Marcus's daughter and her maid. While she's being consoled by her family, we can pursue the kidnapper and his accomplice.'

'She'll be in a very strange situation,' commented Madeleine. 'Having been cruelly misled by a man she loved, Imogen Burnhope will have to go back to one for whom she has no such affection. In a sense, she's caught between the devil and the deep, blue sea.'

'I dispute that, Madeleine. She could never go back to Tunnadine. If she had any real feelings for the fellow, she'd never have fled from him in the first place. This experience will have been sobering for her,' said Colbeck. 'She'll have suffered badly, yet she'll have learnt from her suffering. Put yourself in her position. If you'd been duped as she has obviously been, how would *you* feel?'

Face puckered, Madeleine took only a second to come to her decision.

'I'd feel as if I'd never trust another man as long as I lived,' she said.

'Does that include me?'

'You're an exception to the rule.'

'Tell me why.'

'Stop fishing for compliments, Inspector Colbeck.'

'I need something to sustain me during my night away from you.'

'Talk to Victor Leeming.'

'He has limited abilities when it comes to conversation, Madeleine, and he lacks your inimitable charm.' He kissed his fingers then touched her lips with them. 'Let me ask you one more question.'

'Who am I supposed to be – Madeleine Colbeck or Imogen Burnhope?'

'Pretend that you're the latter for a moment,' he said. 'Let me repeat my question. Suppose – for the sake of argument – that you're still under the spell of this clever individual. Suppose that you willingly deceive yourself until the point where the scales finally fall from your eyes.' He lifted her chin with his finger. 'What happens then?'

Imogen Burnhope was in such a state of anguish that she walked up and down the room before flinging herself into a chair then getting up to repeat the whole process again. Her maid's revelation had wounded her to the quick. Refusing to believe it at first, she'd stormed into the adjoining room and asked Rhoda to unlock the trunk. All of her dresses had been carefully placed in it. The moment the lid was lifted, she began to go through each garment, working her way at a frenetic pace to the very bottom. The evidence was undeniable. The red dress was missing. Imogen had seen it being folded into position so she knew that it had left Burnhope Manor with her. She could think of no reason why Captain Whiteside or Sergeant Cullen had removed it without even asking her permission. It was not merely a disconcerting incident. It was a first cruel jolt out of her beautiful dream.

A second jolt followed immediately. Her beloved captain was not at the hotel but she knew that Cullen was still there. Eager to confront him and demand the truth, she went to the door and discovered that a key had been turned in the lock from the outside. It was the same in her room. There was no way out. At a stroke, Imogen and her maid had turned from pampered guests into virtual prisoners. All the delays and adjustments to the original plan now took on a more sinister aspect. While she tried desperately hard to convince herself that Whiteside would never betray her, the truth at last began to dawn on her and it had a shattering impact. Insisting on being left alone, she moved restlessly around her room, pausing every now and then to stare through the window in the hope of seeing the return of the man who'd brought her there.

It was over an hour before she saw him ride up and hand his horse over to an ostler. As he walked towards the hotel, he saw her in the window and doffed his hat before making a low bow. It banished her fears for a few seconds but they soon came back to assail her. By the time he tapped on the door and turned the key in the lock, she was quivering with fright and bewilderment.

'What ails you, my love?' he said, seeing her distress and taking her in his arms. 'Is this the welcome that I get?'

She pushed him away. 'Please don't touch me.'

'But you like me to touch you, Imogen.'

'I want an explanation.'

'What sort of explanation?'

'To start with,' she said, 'I wish to know why Rhoda and I are locked into our rooms. That's never happened before.'

'Oh,' he said, grinning, 'is that all that's put that frown on your lovely face? It's my fault. I should have told you. While I was away, Sergeant Cullen had to step out of the hotel for a while. I told him to lock both doors so that nobody could disturb you. Your father has launched a search for you. Sir Marcus has offered a large reward for information leading to the discovery of your whereabouts. I didn't want some inquisitive underling to see the pair of you and tell tales. Don't you understand, my love?' he went on with a smile. 'You and your maid were not being locked in – other people were being locked *out*.'

It was a plausible explanation and she accepted it for a while. Imogen even allowed him to embrace her again but it was somehow different now. She no longer enjoyed the tender feel or the manly smell of him. The honeyed words he whispered in her ear had lost their potency. She stepped back.

'I want you to be honest with me, Terence,' she said.

'I've never been anything but honest,' he claimed.

'Where have you been?'

'I had people to call on and places to visit.'

'What people and which places?'

'Does it matter?'

'I have a right to know.'

'Then I can tell you that I had some dealings at a bank in Oxford and visited the man who's arranged our passages to France. It's taken him longer than expected to forge the passports. That accounts for the delay.'

'When do we leave?'

'We leave when everything is in order, my love. Don't fret about it.'

'You keep prevaricating, Terence. I'm bound to fret.'

He spread his arms. 'I thought you trusted me.'

Imogen studied him. She had never trusted anyone so completely in her life. She struggled to recapture that trust. Terence Whiteside was the same tall, dashing soldier she'd first met in Christ Church Meadow. He had a weather-beaten look that only added to his appeal. What she'd loved about him was that he was essentially a man of action. His years in the army had taught him to make decisions quickly. His life had often depended on these decisions. Imogen was impressed by that. When he started to court her, he did so with almost chivalric attention. Urbane and educated, he'd taught her to love Shakespeare's sonnets as much as he did, using quotations from them in his letters and drawing her ever closer to him.

She'd never seen him glower at her before but that was what he did now.

'What is going on?' he demanded.

'I asked for an explanation, that's all.'

'There's something behind your questions.' He looked towards the next room. 'Has that maid been whispering in your ear?'

'Rhoda is as anxious as I am.'

'She's a servant. I'll not have her upsetting my plans.'

'But your plans keep changing, Terence,' she said, emboldened by her anger. 'And you do things without warning us beforehand. When Rhoda tried to open the trunk, she was chided by Sergeant Cullen. She later discovered why.'

'Then she's an interfering bitch!'

Imogen was shaken. 'Don't speak like that about her.'

'I'll speak as I choose.'

'What did you do with my red dress?' she challenged.

'I've no idea what you're talking about.'

'Yes, you do. It was a favourite of mine and it was packed in the trunk. When Rhoda went through the contents, it was missing.'

'Then she must have forgotten to bring it,' he said, airily.

'I watched her putting it in the trunk. Where is it now?'

Her eyes were so full of accusation that he saw no point in maintaining the romantic fiction that they were runaway lovers. During his absence, Imogen had finally started to realise that she and her maid had been grossly misled. Her great adventure was no more than a sham

'From now on,' he said, sharply, 'you won't be treated with the same kindness and consideration. You are our prisoners. Your maid will move in here to share with you and Sergeant Cullen will occupy her room. If you attempt to escape or raise the alarm, he will have orders to shoot you down. In a day or two, we will move from here to Cheshire.'

Imogen felt faint. 'You told me that we'd be heading to Dover.'

'That's one of the many lies I had to use, my love. I have no estate in France nor do I have the wealth about which I spoke so grandiloquently. The second of those deficiencies is about to be repaired,' he told her with a smirk. 'You and your maid are no longer our travelling companions. You are the hostages who are set to earn me a veritable fortune from your father. Pray that he gives me what I ask,' he continued, moving to the door, 'or he'll never see his beautiful daughter alive again!'

He went out. Hearing the key turn in the lock, Imogen collapsed to the floor.

CHAPTER FOURTEEN

There was a limit to the amount of time that George Vaughan could comfortably spend at Burnhope Manor. In earlier years, when his cousin was there, he would play happily with Imogen for hours on end and not even notice the slightly forbidding atmosphere of the house. In her absence, his only companions were his ailing aunt, his judgmental mother and his sister. After the receipt of a second ransom demand, Colbeck had gone off to Oxford and Sir Marcus had headed for London to visit his bank, leaving the artist at the mercy of the two older women and with the fluctuating support from Emma. Lady Burnside was less of a problem because she was still confined to her bed but Cassandra Vaughan insisted on keeping her younger son there. Though not fully aware of the rumours about his alleged profligacy in Chelsea, she still compared him unfavourably with his brother. Her constant reprimands wore George down.

He was in the drawing room with Emma and their

mother. Torn between her love for her brother and her duty to obey her parents to the letter, his sister was in an awkward position. She watched the duel with growing unease.

'Why can't you be more like Percy?' asked Cassandra.

'I might ask why my brother can't be more like me.'

'You're being facetious.'

'No, I'm not, Mother,' he said. 'I'd be prepared to attend church on a more regular basis if Percy behaved less like a monk and more like a human being. If I take a step towards him, he should take one towards me. Wouldn't that bring us closer?'

'Yes, it would,' said Emma, tentatively.

'Of course it wouldn't,' said her mother. 'I'm not having Percy dragged down to your level, George. I want *you* to rise up to his standards of behaviour.'

He laughed. 'Holy orders are anathema to me. If I was hypocritical enough to climb into a pulpit, my London friends would storm the church and throw buns at me. I'm an artist, Mother,' he stressed. 'I follow my Muse.'

'That's arrant poppycock!'

'Mother!' exclaimed Emma.

'You've only yourself to blame for the way I've turned out,' he said.

Cassandra's eyes flashed. 'Don't be insulting!'

'Who taught me to draw when I was a child?'

'You did the same for me when I was little, Mother,' said Emma.

'Who sat me on her knee and guided my hand as I splashed watercolours onto the paper? It was *you*, Mother. You set my artistic career in motion. Emma could draw pretty pictures but Percy had no creative instincts,' he said. 'He hated being made to paint. All that my brother was interested in was the church because he loved the sound of the organ. It was like a siren call to him.'

There was a sizeable grain of truth in the charge and it silenced his mother long enough for him to urge her to accept his waywardness as an expression of his dedication to his art. Before she could return to the attack, he took his leave with elaborate courtesy. Emma did her best to persuade him to stay but he would not. Cassandra had one more shock to absorb. As she waved him off from the door, her son didn't climb into the landau to be driven to the railway station. Instead, with true egalitarian zeal, he clambered up beside the coachman. It was also an affirmation of friendship because he'd known and liked Vernon Tolley for many years. The coachman had only been a stable lad when George Vaughan and his siblings came to the house as children. Tolley let them feed the horses and play in the hayloft. They'd watched him grow to maturity and take on more important duties.

What the artist had wanted was the undemanding companionship of a decent man who'd done him favours over the years. Having at last escaped his mother's interrogation, however, he was now closely questioned again, albeit in a much more deferential manner. Tolley was desperate for any morsel of information. His passenger talked freely to the coachman. Tolley had been present at the bungled exchange of the ransom so there was no need to hold anything back. George Vaughan explained that a second demand had arrived.

'I gathered that, sir,' said the other. 'When I drove

Inspector Colbeck to the station, I sensed that something had happened. Later on, I took Sir Marcus to Shrub Hill and he was very short with me. That only happens when he's upset.'

'Now you know why.'

'So there's hope that the two of them are still alive?'

'The inspector was convinced of it, Tolley.'

'Does he have any idea where they can be?'

'He seems to think that they're somewhere in Oxfordshire,' said the artist. 'That's where the exchange will take place tomorrow and that's where the detectives will be conducting their search.'

Annoyed to leave the capital yet again, Victor Leeming was at least contented with their mode of transport. He held the reins of the trap they'd hired and controlled the horse with relative ease. It allowed him to explore his fantasy of being a cab driver, moving at an unhurried speed and listening to the rhythmical sound of hooves. He was shaken out of his daydream when one of the wheels went over a large stone and the whole trap tilted briefly before righting itself with a jolt.

'Where are we?' he asked, looking around.

'We're still a couple of miles from the area chosen,' said Colbeck, scrutinising the map across his thighs. 'We need to locate this vale, Victor.'

'How precise were the instructions?'

'They were carefully imprecise so that we could not find the exact spot of the exchange beforehand. In the guise of Sir Marcus, I am to go to a bridge and await further orders. Captain Whiteside – if it is indeed he – will want to make certain that I have not brought an impetuous accomplice with me this time.'

'Mr Tunnadine is a lunatic.'

'That's why he must know nothing of this second demand.'

'Being kept in the dark will make him very angry.'

'I don't care about that,' said Colbeck. 'By rights, he should be under lock and key. The superintendent has taken up the matter with the commissioner who will, in turn, refer it to the higher reaches of the judiciary. That fawning Worcestershire magistrate Tallis told me about should be rapped hard over the knuckles.'

'I think he should be in the same cell as Mr Tunnadine.'

'I'm inclined to agree.'

'The superintendent said that he was bowing and scraping to Sir Marcus.'

'Sycophancy is never pleasant to behold, Victor. It's one of the inevitable consequences of having a landed aristocracy. Incidentally,' Colbeck went on, 'I owe you an apology.'

'Why is that, sir?'

'I sent you to that artist's studio when George Vaughan wasn't there.'

'Somebody else was.'

'Oh?'

'It was the young lady with an arm missing in the painting.'

Try as he might, Leeming had been unable to forget his confrontation with Dolly Wrenson. It had been too harrowing to put behind him. In the hope of getting it off his chest, he confided in Colbeck. The inspector had to hide his amusement.

'You should have accepted it as a compliment, Victor.'

'I'm not used to compliments from ladies – not that she's really a lady, mind you.'

'Something about you clearly prompted her interest.'

'That's what disturbs me, sir,' said Leeming. 'What sort of man did she think that I was? All that she seemed to be wearing was a dressing gown.'

'The young lady obviously felt safe in the presence of a policeman.'

'Well, I didn't feel safe in *her* presence, I can tell you that.'

Colbeck grinned. 'I can't believe you were so bashful,' he said. 'Marriage to Estelle should have armoured you against any blandishments like that. You've been able to brush aside improper advances in the past without letting them trouble you.'

'It was different with this young lady, sir. She was no common streetwalker. Dolly was beautiful and – God help me – I'd been forced to look at that . . .'

'At that nude portrait of her – is that what you mean?'

'Yes, it is. Besides,' said Leeming, 'I have a mirror in my house. I know I have an ugly face. What woman would choose me because of my appearance?'

'Estelle did.'

'I know and I've been grateful ever since, sir. But this young lady would never have looked at me twice if she hadn't been eager to punish young Mr Vaughan. That was why she made improper suggestions to me. I was to be used as a weapon against him,' said Leeming, flicking the reins to increase the speed of the horse. 'It made me feel dreadful.'

'You have my sympathy,' said Colbeck, patting his knee. 'If we need to contact young Mr Vaughan at his studio again, I'll go in your stead.'

'Thank you, sir.'

'Console yourself with this thought. Had his brother, Percy, been accosted by this young lady, he'd have been even more scandalised than you. Religion has so far sheltered him from the world of feminine wiles, whereas George revels in it.'

'It's a closed book to me,' admitted Leeming, 'and I want it to stay closed.' They rode on for a few minutes before he spoke again. 'How can two brothers be so different in every way? Percy Vaughan is a curate who, according to you, believes in clean living and self-denial, while George shares a bed with . . . with a woman like Dolly. You wouldn't believe that they had the same parents.'

'Percy is the more interesting of the two, in my opinion. He's sombre and self-possessed with depths that nobody could plumb. George, on the other hand, is a true extrovert. He loves to cause outrage by his behaviour,' said Colbeck, 'but he's only playing at being an artist, I fancy. I found him engaging but a trifle superficial. Percy is the thinker in the family. I don't believe that his brother ever has a serious thought. George just does what appeals to him at any point in time.'

When he climbed the steps to the studio, George Vaughan was not at all sure what kind of reception he'd get. While Dolly was a voluptuous young lady, she was also very capricious. The threat she'd issued when he'd last seen her was worrying. He'd become so used to her companionship and her ready passion that he'd rather taken her for granted. The idea that he may have lost both was unnerving. He would never find a model as compliant as her or a lover as skilful and satisfying. Together, they could enhance his career; apart, he'd be working in a void without inspiration.

When he reached the door of the studio, he paused to listen. There was no sound from within. He was unsure whether to knock or simply to let himself in with his key. After much cogitation, he did both, tapping on the door then unlocking it. His heart sank. The room was empty and the bed unmade. When he looked around for a letter, he found none. Dolly appeared to have washed her hands of him and fled. He sat down on the edge of the bed with his head in his hands. It was minutes before he heard the floorboard creak.

She was there, after all. Dolly was hiding behind the screen where she used to undress before posing for him. Leaping up, he ran across the room and moved the screen aside. He was overcome with contrition.

'I thought I'd lost you, my darling.'

'That issue is still in the balance,' she warned.

'You gave me such a fright, Dolly.'

'It's the least you deserve for running out on me like that.'

'It was an emergency,' he said. 'I explained that to you.'

'Deeds mean more than words, George Vaughan. I pleaded with you to stay and you still went rushing off to Oxford. If you hadn't come back today, I was going to pack my things and leave. Artists are all the same,' she complained. 'They promise you the earth then drop you like a stone.'

'That isn't what happened.'

'It's what I *felt* happened and it hurt. It was the same with Sebastian when I was *his* model. He filled my ears with wonderful promises but never delivered them. That's why I ran away to you in the end. I've done with artists,' she announced, stamping a petulant foot. 'You're the third who's let me down.'

'I'll make amends,' he vowed. 'I love you, Dolly. I can't work without you.'

'Next time I'll choose a politician, like my friend. She says that they're much more reliable, especially if they're married. They're more grateful and they're far more generous.'

'I'll be generous when I become rich and famous.'

'We may both be old and grey by the time that happens.'

'No, we won't,' he said, taking her by the arms. 'You know that I have talent. You've told me a dozen times that I'm a better artist than Sebastian or the one before him. Success is only a year or two away – perhaps even a month or two. Stay with me, Dolly. We belong together.'

She broke away and walked to the window to look out across the houses.

'London is full of men who'd appreciate my worth,' she said. 'They'd keep me in the sort of luxury that my friend enjoys. I wouldn't have to put up with bare floorboards and that awful bed and the constant stink of oil paint.'

'Then you must go,' he told her, changing his tack. 'If I disappoint you so much, Dolly, then you're better off with some mealy-mouthed politician or some wealthy banker who can only see you when his wife is away. What I tried to do was to share everything with you – my time, my work, my money and my love. I didn't just fit you in between my marital commitments. Go to this friend of yours,' he urged, pointing to the door. 'Ask her how she reeled in her Member of Parliament. Find out exactly what she has to do to maintain his interest. Off you go, Dolly.'

She was stunned. 'Are you serious, George?'

'I don't want to hold you against your will.'

'But a moment ago, you said you couldn't work without me.'

'There are lots of Dolly Wrensons in the world. I'll find another one.'

'You're not . . . throwing me out, are you?'

'No,' he explained. 'I simply want you to make up your mind. First, I want you to understand why I had to leave so suddenly. Hear me out, please, that's all I ask. If, at the end of it, you still think I betrayed you, then we're better off apart. Is that acceptable to you?' She nodded. 'Then, come here.'

Leading her to a chair, he sat her down and gave her a full account of where he'd been and what he'd done while he was away. Dolly listened intently. When she heard that his cousin was in mortal danger, she let out a gasp. When he told her about the man being shot dead, she was overwhelmed with shame. Imogen Burnhope was in the most appalling predicament yet all that Dolly had done was to chide her lover for running off to see if he could in some way help her. By the time he'd finished, the tears were running down her cheeks.

He indicated the door again. 'Do you still intend to leave?'

'No, George,' she said, getting up and moving to the bed. 'Come here.'

'You told me that bed was awful.'

'It is when I have to sleep in it alone.'

'What about the stink of oil paint?'

She giggled. 'I'll hold my nose.' When he crossed over to her, she raised a finger. 'There is one condition, mind you.'

'What's that, Dolly?'

'When it's all over, please – *please* – give me another arm in the portrait.'

The change in their situation was so sudden and dramatic that it left both of them dazed. Imogen and Rhoda sat side by side in the room that they now shared and bewailed their fate. They were gullible victims of a plot. The man whom Imogen had trusted implicitly was no more than an unscrupulous fraudster with designs on her father's wealth. As a result of his flattering letters with their well-chosen quotations from Shakespeare's sonnets, she had been ensnared. She felt sick with grief. Rhoda, too, was wallowing in recriminations. It was her fault, she kept telling herself. Put in the privileged position of looking after her mistress, she'd instead helped to lead her astray. Rhoda was shocked at her own naivety. She was older, wiser and infinitely more mature than Imogen. The maid should never have allowed herself to be caught up in the fairy tale. Something else jabbed at her mind. Imogen was in flight from the tyranny of her parents and the horror of having to marry Clive Tunnadine. Rhoda, however, had regrets when she left. Vernon Tolley's admiration of her was requited in her breast. In putting her mistress's needs first, she'd had to forego her own interests. When she might have been encouraging the coachman, she was instead entombed in a hotel room with an armed man next door.

'There must be some way out,' she said, rising to her feet.

'We're trapped, Rhoda. There's no escape.'

'Why don't I try to distract Sergeant Cullen while you get away?'

'How can I go anywhere when the door is locked?' whined Imogen.

'Bang on it until a member of staff comes,' urged the maid. 'I'll keep the sergeant talking in the other room.'

'It's far too dangerous, Rhoda. In any case, where would I go? I have no money and I have no idea where we are. They'd come after me.'

'Complain to the hotel manager. Ask him to call the police.'

'You saw how far we drove from Oxford,' said Imogen. 'This place couldn't be more isolated. Besides, I couldn't endanger the manager by getting him involved. The captain and the sergeant both have weapons.'

'At least we can *try*,' insisted Rhoda.

Crossing to the door, she turned the handle and pulled as hard as she could. The door was firmly locked. She tugged away for a long time. All that she did was to produce a loud rattle and to tire herself. There was another consequence. The other door swung open and Sergeant Cullen stepped into the room.

'What do you think you're doing?' he demanded. 'You were ordered to leave that door alone. Captain Whiteside will hear of this.'

'Please don't tell him,' said Imogen. 'We meant no harm.'

'I know exactly what you meant. I'm on guard.'

'We won't touch the door again, I promise.'

'I'm taking no chances. I'll stay here with you.'

'Give us some privacy, at least,' said Rhoda, indignantly.

'You don't deserve it. If it was left to me, I'd stay in here all night with you.' He smirked at Rhoda. 'Wouldn't you like that?'

Recoiling from his taunt, she went back to the sofa. Cullen sat on the edge of the bed and regarded them. He was a solid man of medium height with livid battle scars decorating a craggy face. The lilting Irish voice that had appealed to Imogen now grated on her ear. His earlier courtesy had shaded into a military brusqueness.

'What's to become of us?' asked Rhoda.

'Wait and see – it will be a nice surprise for you.'

'You can't hold us against our will.'

'We didn't need to at first,' he said with a grin. 'The captain tricked you into coming along of your own volition, so you did. Now wasn't that a clever ruse of his? I didn't have to guard you at all. You *liked* being here with us.'

'Let us go,' implored Imogen. 'I'll give you money.'

'We can get far more from your father. You're his only child. That puts a high price on your head. If he doesn't pay up, of course . . .'

He had a smile like a gash in a ripe melon. They drew back as they realised the full implications of the threat that hung over them. Rhoda was frightened of the Irishman. Imogen tried to grasp at a final straw.

'This is no way to treat someone in my position,' she said with dignity. 'We should be released forthwith. When the captain returns, I shall appeal to him as an officer and a gentleman.' Cullen went off into peals of laughter. She was deflated. 'What is so amusing?'

'It's your description of Captain Whiteside,' he replied. 'First, he's no longer an officer and second, he was never a gentleman. The both of you will find that out very soon.'

Their reconnaissance was thorough and it gave the detectives some idea of what was in store for them. From a vantage point on one of the hills, the kidnapper would have an excellent view of the dale and be able to see if anyone was trying to creep up on him. Fringed with trees and dappled by the sun, the location favoured someone who wanted to control the exchange of hostages for money before making a swift departure. On the train journey back to London, they had a compartment to themselves and could therefore consider their options.

'I could get there early and hide in the trees,' volunteered Leeming.

'You don't know in which part of the wooded areas he'd be lurking.'

'I could use the telescope to find out, sir.'

'Captain Whiteside will be using a telescope on you, Victor. He'll scan the whole dale before he makes his move. There's nothing else for it,' said Colbeck. 'We have to follow his instructions. The safety of the hostages is paramount. Once they've been returned, we go after Whiteside and this Sergeant Cullen.'

Leeming blenched. 'Do we follow them on horseback?'

'Can you think of a quicker way?'

'They're from a cavalry regiment, sir. They know how to ride.'

'We can't expect to overtake them, Victor. We just need to pick up their trail and follow them. When they're well clear, they'll think that their mission was a great success and they'll relax. They won't expect us to be so close behind them.'

'Where will they go?'

'Oh, they'll have an escape plan worked out,' Colbeck told him. 'The chances are that the horses are hired from somewhere near a railway station, enabling them to hop onto a train and – as they think – make off with the ransom money.'

'I'm still not happy about riding a horse, sir.'

'We'll find you a quiet mount this time.'

'Where do you think they are at the moment?'

'Well, as I told you, my feeling is that they've been somewhere in Oxfordshire all the time. The further they travelled with the two ladies, the more chance they had of being seen. They'd have prepared a hiding place well in advance,' said Colbeck. 'They needed to keep Sir Marcus's daughter and her maid completely out of sight.'

The discussion continued all the way back to London and it distracted Leeming from the incessant din of the train and the rocking of their carriage. Though the evening was drawing on, they caught a cab and went straight to Scotland Yard. Tallis had departed but he'd left a message for them. It was waiting on Colbeck's desk. Picking it up, the inspector read the letter with an approving smile.

'The superintendent has been as good as his word,' he said. 'He made enquiries about our two suspects. Captain Terence Whiteside and Sergeant Manus Cullen did both serve in a cavalry regiment but neither of them has been anywhere near the Crimea. The heroics with which the captain left Mrs Greenfield spellbound were pure invention. No doubt he told the same stirring tales to Sir Marcus's daughter.' He folded the letter to put in his pocket. 'I thought it was Irishmen who were supposed to have the gift of the gab.'

'Perhaps the captain has Irish blood, sir.'

'He has the cheek of the devil, I know that.'

'Women are so easily taken in.'

'Don't tell that to your wife or she'll box your ears,' said Colbeck. 'In my experience, women have far more intuition than we do. Madeleine senses things that completely elude me. How easy is it to bamboozle Estelle?'

'It's near impossible, sir,' replied Leeming with pride. 'She'd have seen through all the nonsense that he fed to Sir Marcus's daughter.'

'Your wife doesn't have the slightest intention of running away from home to some phantom paradise. Estelle is very happy with her husband and children. Imogen Burnhope, by contrast,' said Colbeck, pointedly, 'was not happy with her lot. She *wanted* to believe there was something better for her and that made her credulous. When she learns the truth, it will be a heart-rending moment.'

'That's all the more reason to catch this lying cavalry officer and his friend.'

'They'll be caught and roundly punished, Victor.'

'Did the letter give you any idea where they've been living, sir?'

'No – but if you find out, please inform the army.'

'Why is that?'

'They're both deserters.'

* * *

Edward Tallis accompanied him to the bank then travelled back to Worcestershire with him in order to act as a bodyguard. Sir Marcus was carrying an immense amount of money in his bag and it never left his side throughout the two train journeys. In case of trouble, the superintendent had an old army pistol concealed in his valise. The other reason he went back to Burnhope Manor was to remind himself that he was still theoretically in charge of the investigation. Having telegraphed ahead to Shrub Hill, they arrived to find that a message had been taken out to the house. Vernon Tolley was waiting to drive them there.

The coachman did not have to guess what had happened this time. Sir Marcus and Tallis talked openly about the latest development in the case. All that Tolley did was to keep his ears pricked.

'What if they don't hand Imogen over?' asked Sir Marcus, beset by anxiety. 'What if she's no longer alive?'

'I feel certain that she is,' said Tallis, confidently. 'Without a live hostage, he has no bargaining tool. If we don't see your daughter, no money will be given.'

'He and his accomplice can live in luxury for the rest of their lives on the amount in this bag. Are you sure that Colbeck will be able to retrieve it?'

'I am, Sir Marcus.'

'It's galling to be compelled to buy my own daughter back like this.'

'Look at it another way,' advised Tallis. 'We've had hostages killed before now because their parents were either unable to afford the ransom or because they couldn't pay it in time. Captain Whiteside will get his money on time.'

'I look forward to his getting his just desserts.'

'So do I, Sir Marcus. As an army man, I'm horrified that this whole affair is the work of two deserters. They were a disgrace to the uniforms they wore. If they'd been under my command,' said Tallis, 'I'd have had them tied securely to a cannon and given two hundred lashes apiece.' He gave a grunt of satisfaction. 'It was a punishment that had a tendency to discourage others from similar disobedience.'

Though they talked freely about the treatment that Whiteside and Cullen should receive, they never once introduced Tunnadine into the conversation because they'd agreed to differ on the subject of his punishment. Each man had his own position and neither would be shifted from it. Where they did side with each other was on the decision to keep him unaware of the second ransom demand. If he was not at the exchange, he couldn't make another disastrous intervention.

When they reached Burnhope Manor, they waited until the coachman had put down the step and they alighted. Sir Marcus hugged the bag protectively as if it were a baby rescued from a house fire. The butler admitted them and they entered the hall to be welcomed by Cassandra and Emma Vaughan. A third member of the family had joined them. He darted forward to shake Sir Marcus's hand.

'Good evening, Uncle,' said the curate.

'What, in God's name, are you doing here, Percy?'

'I'm doing exactly what you just said. I'm here in God's name.'

'Percy wanted to offer his assistance,' explained

Cassandra. 'I wish that I could say the same of my other son but he disappeared off to London.'

'George *would* have helped,' said Emma, loyally. 'He's very brave.'

'I'd prefer to put my trust in Percy.'

'Why?' asked Sir Marcus. 'What does he intend to do?'

'I intend to appeal to the kidnapper,' said the curate. 'When he sees that I'm a man of the cloth, he'll know I pose no threat to him. I'll reason with him. I'll remind him of Christian teaching. I'll talk to him so persuasively that he'll hand over Imogen and her maid without asking for anything in return.'

Cassandra beamed. 'Isn't that a splendid idea?'

'No, Mother,' said Emma. 'It isn't. Percy will be in great jeopardy.'

'He won't be allowed anywhere near the kidnapper,' said Tallis. 'As soon as he sees that his instructions have been defied, the man will probably turn tail and run, taking the hostages with him. All that you'll have done, Reverend, is to imperil your cousin and her maid. I can't let you do that.'

'Neither can I,' said Sir Marcus.

'But I'm the ideal person,' argued Percy.

'You heard the superintendent. You will not be involved.'

'The exchange must be left in the hands of Inspector Colbeck,' said Tallis. 'He became Sir Marcus on the first occasion and will do so again.'

'No, he will not,' asserted Sir Marcus. 'The kidnapper specified that I should reclaim my daughter and that's exactly what I'm going to do. Inspector Colbeck will not be required this time. I will take the responsibility myself.'

Tallis quailed at the prospect but his authority had been overridden.

Clive Tunnadine congratulated himself on making two wise decisions. He'd hired Alban Kee and he'd told nobody else about the ransom demand. There had been some difficulty in raising the money at such short notice but he'd browbeaten the bank manager and eventually got his way. The politician had declined Kee's offer to act as a bodyguard, feeling that he could look after the money quite well on his own. He therefore dispatched the private detective to Crewe to get the lie of the land, intending to join him on the morrow. Tunnadine still felt vestigial guilt over the way that he'd assaulted Lucinda Graham. The flowers had acted as a balm and his apology had been accepted by her. Yet he knew it was not enough. Lucinda deserved to be wooed and cosseted. It would be the perfect way to take his mind off the tricky negotiations with the kidnapper that lay ahead.

Though she was pleased to see him, her wariness was evident. He called for a decanter of wine. When the servant had poured two glasses, Tunnadine and his mistress were left alone to drink, relax and enjoy each other's company. The bruises on her arms had been covered by her dress but, in spite of the cosmetics, he could see the telltale marks on her face. The main thing was that he'd now been forgiven.

Lucinda was even beginning to tantalise him a little. The compact had been made. He would spend the night in her bed and drive away the hideous memories of his earlier visit. Lucinda needed to be indulged.

'Did you mean what you said when you brought those flowers?' she asked.

'I'm a man of honour, Lucinda. Of course, I meant it.' He sipped his wine. 'What exactly was it that I said?'

'To be honest, you didn't exactly put it into words. You hinted.'

'And what was the import of my hint?'

She waved an arm. 'I could look to remain here for a while.'

'You can stay for longer than that, Lucinda. You've earned this house. My visits may be less regular in future but you won't be ignored, I guarantee. I think you know by now that I'm a man who enjoys the pleasures of life.'

'It's a joy to share them with you,' she said, nestling against his shoulder. 'You've taught me so much.'

'And you, conversely, have been an excellent tutor to me.'

'I am always at your command.'

'That's what I like to hear.'

They emptied their glasses, refilled them and got steadily more excited about the night of abandon that beckoned them. Tunnadine slipped an arm around her shoulders and took a first, lingering kiss. Lucinda stroked his thigh gently. When he put his glass aside, he stood up so that she could remove his frock coat for him. As she hung it carefully over a chair, she gave a teasing smile.

'Are you going to be nice to me tonight?' she asked.

'I'm going to be extremely nice and extravagantly attentive.'

'Make sure that you are, Clive.'

'Why do you say that?'

'Because you've given me a power over you,' she taunted.

'When a man gets married, he puts a dangerous weapon into the hands of his mistress.' She plucked at his cravat. 'If you don't behave exactly as I want you to, then I'll turn blackmailer and threaten to tell your wife.'

It was a disastrous comment to make. Blind rage seized Tunnadine and he lashed out violently. His first punch knocked her against the wall where he continued to belabour her with both fists. Blood gushed from her nose. He knocked out her two front teeth with a fearsome blow. When she fell to the floor in agony, he kicked her in the stomach then grabbed his coat.

'Get out of this house!' he shouted. 'If you dare to approach my wife, I swear that I'll kill you with my bare hands.'

It was over.

CHAPTER FIFTEEN

Early departures were a feature of the Colbeck household and Madeleine had learnt to accept them. A criminal investigation had an irregular timetable. Detectives had to respond to the turn of events and fit any domestic arrangements around them. Because he'd had the pleasure of spending another night at home, Colbeck did not complain when he had to leave shortly after dawn. Madeleine helped him on with his coat, then inspected him. He was as immaculate as ever.

'When you left Oxford all those years ago,' she said, 'I'll wager that you never thought you'd return there one day to investigate a crime.'

'That's true, Madeleine. In my undergraduate days, my vision of the future centred on prosecuting dangerous felons in a court of law. Now, I simply catch them.'

'Do you expect to catch this Captain Whiteside and his accomplice?'

'I have every hope of doing so.'

'He sounds like a worthy adversary.'

'Having been a soldier,' he said, 'he knows about strategy. It was the same with one of those men we apprehended in Scotland earlier this year. His military experience taught him to plan carefully ahead.'

'What will happen to the two ladies?' she asked.

'With luck, they'll be returned safely to Burnhope Manor.'

'It will be a fraught homecoming.'

'Our task is to take some of the anguish out of it.'

'The fact is that they ran away from the house and all that it represented. Imogen Burnhope's parents will have been horrified to learn that. There could be some serious repercussions.'

'Only if the parents are told the truth,' he pointed out, 'and I've done my best to disguise it from them. You're right, Madeleine. The two of them will chafe at being held as hostages but they will also dread the reception they'll get when they're released. Rhoda Wills, I daresay, will expect to be summarily dismissed for her part in the escapade. I want to save her reputation and that of her mistress. The only way to do that is to deceive their parents.'

Madeleine smiled. 'I didn't know you were a master of deception, Robert.'

'I have more than one string to my bow.'

'Yes,' she agreed. 'There are so many, I've lost count of them.'

Reaching for his hat, he was about to leave when a thought detained him.

'I wish that I could take you with me, Madeleine,' he said.

'Wouldn't I be a distraction?'

'You'd be a godsend to Imogen Burnhope and her maid. For days now, they've been in the hands of two heartless men whom they must have suspected by now of misleading them. What sort of ill-treatment have they had to endure? What kind of despair are they feeling?'

'It's impossible to imagine,' she said with a sigh of sympathy.

'If indeed they *are* released, what they will see are three detectives and Sir Marcus Burnhope. What they really need at that moment, however, is not a quartet of men but an understanding woman who can console and reassure them.' He stroked her cheek. 'You'd fit that role perfectly.'

'Thank you, Robert.'

'It would make things much easier for them.'

'What would Superintendent Tallis say?'

Colbeck laughed. 'His cry of rage would echo across six counties.'

'One day, he'll have to accept the value of women in law enforcement.'

'That day is centuries away,' he said, bestowing a farewell kiss. 'We've yet to convince our dear superintendent to accept the value of women.'

Ironically, the locomotive that took them to Oxford was *Will Shakspere*. When they boarded the train at Shrub Hill, Edward Tallis and Sir Marcus Burnhope didn't realise that it was the same engine that had taken the two fugitives on the first stage of their flight. In the comfort of their first-class compartment, both men complained when wisps of acrid smoke seeped in as they went through the Mickleton Tunnel. It never occurred to them that the driver and the fireman would be enshrouded in the billowing smoke because they had no protection whatsoever from it or from the elements. Concern for his fellow men was not something that Sir Marcus ever felt, especially when he was helping to pilot punitive legislation through the House of Commons.

'What if they attempt some subterfuge?' he asked.

'I think it unlikely, Sir Marcus. The kidnappers will realise that they can't get away with deception again.'

'These loathsome wretches are as slippery as eels.'

'Eels can be caught with the right net,' said Tallis, complacently. 'The name of that net is Inspector Colbeck.'

'I hope that he'll be at Oxford station to greet us.'

'He'll not only be there, he'll have hired transport to take us to the location of the exchange. You may expect a protest from him.'

'Why?'

'Colbeck won't be at all happy that you are planning to hand over the money yourself.'

'Imogen is my daughter!' bellowed Sir Marcus.

'It's your personal safety that we have to consider.'

'I don't give a fig for that, man. In order to get her back, I'll face any kind of danger. Well,' he went on, 'wouldn't you do the same if it was a daughter of yours?'

'I'm not married, Sir Marcus.'

'You should be. It would make you less stuffy.'

Tallis was dumbfounded. Nobody had ever dared to say such a thing to him. He felt insulted, particularly as the criticism came for a man whose commitments as a senior politician left him with almost no time to forge a bond with his only child. It took the superintendent fifteen minutes before he was able to speak again.

'Why not let Colbeck *accompany* you at the exchange, Sir Marcus?'

'The ransom demand stipulated that I should be there alone.'

'You could feign weakness and in need of someone to support you.'

'I'm not *that* decrepit yet, Tallis.'

'It was only an idea.'

'Please refrain from having another one.'

'I'll do as you wish, Sir Marcus.'

Tallis retreated into silence. Travelling with a member of the aristocracy meant a reversal of roles for him. Instead of being in charge and above contradiction, he was forced to do as he was told. It made him think of his days as a schoolboy when he was under the thumb of a despotic headmaster who liked to enforce his edicts with the swish of a cane. Sir Marcus had not actually struck him but Tallis felt that the remark about his bachelorhood was akin to the punishment he'd received at school. Both had left a lasting sting and a burning resentment.

The train steamed noisily into Oxford station and Tallis was pleased to see his detectives waiting on the platform. He now had allies. Sir Marcus stepped onto the platform first with the superintendent just behind him. Colbeck and Leeming came across to greet them.

'Is everything ready?' asked Sir Marcus.

'Yes,' replied Colbeck. 'The two of you will travel in the trap while the sergeant and I follow on horseback.'

Leeming was dubious. 'Is that really such a good idea, sir? I still think we should have hired a second trap.'

'Use your head, man,' said Tallis, putting steel into his voice now that he had someone of inferior rank to bully. 'How can you go in pursuit of these villains in a trap when they may be riding swift horses? Your proposal is inane.'

'Not to me, it isn't,' said Leeming under his breath.

'There's been a change of plan, Inspector,' Tallis went on, hoping to enlist Colbeck's aid. 'Sir Marcus has suggested that he should hand over the money.'

'It's not a suggestion,' said Sir Marcus, 'it's a decision.'

'Then it's one that I applaud,' said Colbeck.

Tallis was deeply hurt. 'I expected you to support *me*.'

'I fear that I'm not able to do that, sir.'

'Why ever not? You were the one who insisted on handling the exchange on the first occasion and you were right to do so.'

'This time is very different,' explained Colbeck. 'When I disguised myself as Sir Marcus, I was too far away from the kidnapper to be identified properly. As it happened, neither of the hostages was present. With luck, they will be there today. What will happen if Sir Marcus's daughter sees me posing as her father? She and her maid are bound to be startled and give me away. They will both suffer as a result. Is that what you wish to achieve? No,' he added, 'only Sir Marcus will suffice today, Superintendent. I will remain hiding in the trees with you and the sergeant.'

Tallis felt injured. Sir Marcus applied plenty of salt to the wounds.

'There you are,' he said, breezily. 'Listen to the inspector.

He thinks more clearly than you, acts more sensibly and puts the fate of my daughter first. You should learn from Colbeck. He could teach you a lot.'

Sergeant Cullen didn't actually carry out his threat to sleep in the same room as them but he left the door open between the adjoining rooms so that he could hear everything they said. Imogen and her maid passed a sleepless night. They felt horribly exposed and maltreated. Breakfast was served early in their room and Cullen stood over them while they ate it. He then put the tray outside the room for a servant to collect it. When Captain Whiteside came into the room, he was in a buoyant mood.

'Right,' he said, pointing to Rhoda, 'you're coming with us.'

'Where are we going?' she asked.

'We have a rendezvous with Sir Marcus Burnhope.'

Imogen stood up. 'Why can't I come?'

'Because I don't need you,' he replied. 'Rhoda will be enough to convince him that I'm in earnest.'

'But I want to see my father.'

'You've changed your tune, haven't you?' jeered Cullen. 'The reason you ended up here is that you couldn't wait to run away from him. One minute you hate your father; the next, you're dying to go back to him.'

'Imogen is going nowhere,' said Whiteside. He glanced at Cullen. 'You still haven't recognised Manus, have you?'

'It's because they never really look at me, Terence. They've only had eyes for their gallant saviour, Captain Whiteside, who came to their rescue when they needed him.' Leering at the women, he lowered his voice to emit a loud growl. 'Arrrrrrgh!'

Realisation dawning, Imogen and Rhoda drew back in alarm.

'It's him,' gibbered Rhoda. 'It's that terrible man who leapt out at us in Christ Church Meadow. He wasn't a vagabond at all. He was hiding there on purpose.'

'Yes,' confirmed Whiteside, 'and he'd also grown a beard and blacked his face for the purpose. Manus is a good actor. He even frightened me.'

While the men shared a guffaw, Imogen was horrified at how easily she and Rhoda had been tricked by the ruse. Whiteside had first won her gratitude, then proceeded to win her love and trust. The truth was humiliating. It made her feel both reckless and embarrassingly immature.

'It's time to go,' said Whiteside.

'I demand that you take me,' declared Imogen, leaping to her feet.

He sniggered. 'You're not exactly in a position to make demands, are you?'

'I need to see my father.'

'Rhoda can give him your regards.'

'If you leave me here alone,' she warned, 'I'll bang on that door and scream aloud until somebody lets me out.'

'Unfortunately, you won't be in a position to do so.'

'What do you mean?'

'Manus,' he ordered. 'Fetch the rope.'

As the Irishman went off into the next room, Rhoda challenged the captain.

'You can't tie her up,' she insisted. 'It's indecent.'

'It's practical. With a gag in her mouth, she won't be able

to call for help.' Taking Imogen by the shoulders, he forced her to sit down on an upright chair. Cullen returned with two lengths of rope. 'Truss her up like a turkey, Manus. I want her to sit there quietly until we come back for her.'

'Leave it to me, Terence,' said Cullen, standing behind Imogen.

'No,' she said with more anger than fear. 'It's inhuman.'

'And I won't let you do it,' vowed Rhoda, dashing forward to snatch the ropes from the sergeant's hands. 'I'll stop you somehow.'

Whiteside reacted at speed. Grabbing the maid from behind, he spun her round then slapped both of her cheeks with such force that she fell backwards onto the bed. Cullen retrieved the ropes.

'I did warn you that Captain Whiteside wasn't a gentleman,' he said, grinning.

They got there well in advance of the time stated and took up a position in the trees. As he surveyed the scene below, Colbeck noticed that there was now a significant difference to what they'd seen earlier. Running through the heart of the vale was a busy stream, glistening in the sunshine. The only visible place to cross was over a stone bridge. When they'd driven down to it on the previous day, he and Leeming had seen that it was just wide enough for a trap to go across. Larger vehicles would have to use a much bigger bridge over a mile away or ride even further afield to cross by means of a ford. Even a trap could not cross the stone bridge now. A massive rock had been rolled into place so that it restricted the width by almost two feet. There was no way that Sir Marcus would be able to move the obstruction on his own, so he'd be quite unable to cross the stream. The kidnappers wanted no pursuit when they made their escape.

The telescope picked up something else of interest as well. On top of the rock and held in place by a small stone was a piece of white paper, flapping in the breeze. Colbeck believed that the paper contained the instructions for Sir Marcus. It meant that the kidnappers were already there, concealed in the copse on the other side of the vale. Their own telescope would undoubtedly be in use. Taking his watch out, he checked the time, then turned to Sir Marcus.

'There's the best part of twenty minutes to wait,' he said.

'I'm not sitting up here that long,' answered Sir Marcus, impatiently. 'I want my daughter back.'

'You'll find a letter waiting for you on the bridge.'

Sir Marcus climbed back into the trap and lifted up the leather bag containing the ransom. Loath to part with it, he accepted that he had no choice if he wished to see his daughter alive again. He put the bag between his feet, snatched up the reins and flicked them. The horse trotted forward and the trap soon came into full view of anyone overlooking the vale. Colbeck saw something glinting among the trees.

'It's a telescope,' he said.

Tallis was rueful. '*You* should be driving that trap.'

'Sir Marcus has to go this time, sir.'

'Why did you have to agree with him? In situations like this, I expect you to support me without equivocation.'

'You gave the wrong advice.'

'I feel the same,' said Leeming. 'We had to do as the kidnapper ordered.'

'Sergeant,' hissed Tallis, making him draw back into the undergrowth, 'next time you wish to rid yourself of your mindless opinion, think twice before you open that disastrous orifice known as your mouth. I've heard more than enough nonsense coming out of it for one day.'

'Then the same stricture applies to me, sir,' said Colbeck, siding with his friend. 'The sergeant is only endorsing what I said. Why don't we all maintain a companionable silence and concentrate on the exchange? That's what brought us here, after all.'

Sir Marcus Burnhope was not enjoying the ride across the vale. To start with, he was unused to driving a trap. When he was at home in Worcestershire, his coachman satisfied all his travel requirements. Cabs served him well in London. He was now thrust into a novel situation, bumping over uneven ground and trying to control a horse that seemed to have a strange obsession with lurching to the left instead of following the commands of its driver. Sir Marcus had to tug hard on the reins to keep the animal heading towards the bridge.

There was a secondary problem. He became nervous. When he'd insisted on being involved in the exchange, he'd done so with complete confidence. There'd been no whiff of fear to trouble him. Now that he was on his way to the fateful encounter, doubts and anxieties emerged. Without any weapon at his disposal, he was on his way to meet two deserters from the army, hardened men who'd routinely borne arms and been taught to use them. All of a sudden, Sir Marcus realised how brave Colbeck had been in impersonating him at the first exchange. Making light of the fact that a gun was probably trained on him, the inspector had walked imperturbably into an open field. Sir Marcus, on the other hand, was deeply perturbed. His hands began to shake. The only thing which kept him going was the prospect of securing his daughter's freedom. Between his feet, the leather bag with the money in it seemed hot against his ankles. Sweat broke out on his brow and under his arms.

It was a long ride to the bridge but he eventually reached it, bringing the horse to a halt nearby. He saw the piece of paper fluttering in the wind and alighted from the trap. When he moved the stone and read the message, it was blunt.

PUT THE MONEY ON THE ROCK

Sir Marcus raised his eyes to scan the wooded ridge above him but saw no sign of life. There was not even a bird in the sky. He walked back to the trap and picked up the bag. It felt vastly heavier now and he had to cradle it in his arms. Taking it halfway across the bridge, he lowered it onto the rock with misgivings.

Then he waited.

Crouched among the trees, Colbeck was also waiting. Through the telescope, he watched with great interest and gave a commentary to Leeming and Tallis. The superintendent soon tired of hearing everything second-hand and he reached out.

'Let me have the telescope,' he said.

'You have to adjust it very carefully,' warned Colbeck.

'Just give it here.'

Taking the instrument, he tried to peer through it but

he seemed to be looking through a milky circle of glass. Everything was indistinct. He became tetchy.

'I can't see what's happening,' he complained.

'Nothing is happening, sir,' said Colbeck. 'Even the sergeant and I can see that. Nothing whatsoever is happening at all down there.'

In fact, a great deal was happening to Sir Marcus Burnhope. He was, by turns, worried, frightened, appalled, sickened, hopeful, depressed, cold enough to shiver and hot enough to sweat freely. It was deliberate, he told himself. They were deliberately making him wait while they checked that he was absolutely alone. The longer it went on, the more uneasy he became. He began to wonder if the kidnappers were simply playing games with him. It was almost a quarter of an hour before he saw the trap rolling out of the trees on the other side of the stream. Sir Marcus envied the skill with which the man was driving, zigzagging at speed down the incline, then getting increased pace out of the horse once they'd reached more level ground.

Beside the driver was a woman and Sir Marcus first thought that it was his daughter. He stretched out his arms to welcome her, only to drop them by his sides again when the trap got close enough for him to recognise Rhoda Wills. He rallied. Her appearance was at least a positive sign that the kidnapper was prepared to honour his commitment. Turning his attention to the man, he studied him with an amalgam of interest and loathing. This was the kidnapper who'd seized Imogen and held her captive. Sir Marcus had an overpowering urge to kill the man but he had neither the weapon to do it nor the strength even to move. The sheer enormity of what was involved in the confrontation had paralysed him.

When the trap skidded to a halt on the bridge, he could barely speak.

'Where's my daughter?' he asked, hoarsely.

'She's waiting up in the trees with my friend,' said Whiteside, jerking a thumb over his shoulder. 'When I'm satisfied that you've brought the ransom, Imogen will be released.'

'If you've laid a hand on her . . .'

The words died on his lips. He was in no position to make threats and he felt ridiculous for doing so. His gaze switched to Rhoda Wills.

'Is my daughter unharmed?' he asked.

'Yes, Sir Marcus,' she replied, uncertainly.

'Where is she being kept?'

'I'll ask the questions,' said Whiteside, jumping down and walking towards him. 'You've had ocular proof that the two ladies are at my mercy. Let's see if you've brought what I asked, shall we?'

When the man opened the bag, Sir Marcus went dizzy. He could barely see Whiteside counting his spoils. It was an effort simply to stay upright. Rhoda looked on in silence, desperate to yell out a warning but all too aware of the consequences both to her and to Imogen. The kidnapper smiled at Sir Marcus.

'You've obeyed your orders this time,' he said with approval. 'You also came in person. Last time, another man came in your stead. That annoyed me.'

'I want my daughter back.'

'Be patient, Sir Marcus. I'll bring her to you.'

'Why isn't she here now?' he turned to Rhoda. 'Answer me, woman.'

'She has more sense,' said Whiteside, tossing the bag into the trap and picking up the stone that had held the message in place on the rock. 'You will see Imogen in due course.' He climbed up beside Rhoda. 'Meanwhile, you have an important task, Sir Marcus.'

'What's that?'

'You have some chasing to do.'

Standing up, Whiteside threw the stone at Sir Marcus's horse and caught it on the flank. The animal neighed in protest then bolted alongside the stream. Sir Marcus had been tricked. He'd parted with an immense amount of money and got nothing in return. Shaking with impotent fury, he didn't know whether to go after his horse or to run towards the other trap. Whiteside removed the second option in a flash. Cracking his whip, he sent the animal in a semicircle before it set off at a gallop across the vale. Bouncing about beside him, Rhoda looked over her shoulder in mute apology at the part she'd been compelled to play in the deception.

Shocked, hurt and in despair, Sir Marcus slumped down on the stone bridge.

Colbeck hadn't needed the telescope to see what had happened. Even from that distance, he could recognise skulduggery. Leaping into the saddle, he kicked his horse into action and raced down the gradient to the vale itself. While he wanted to go after the other trap, he felt the need to restore Sir Marcus's means of transport or both he and Tallis would be completely stranded. To that end, he galloped across the grass at an angle to cut off the fleeing horse. It took him a long time to get within reach of the trap and even longer to bring it under control because the horse pulling it kept veering off at acute angles. When it eventually straightened, Colbeck eased up alongside it, leant over to grab the reins and gradually slowed its furious pace until he could drag it in a wide arc and bring it to a halt. Dismounting, he tied his own horse to the back of the trap, then clambered aboard again to begin the return journey. Colbeck was both sad and angry. The second meeting with the kidnapper had been a calamity.

In the distance, he could see the poignant sight of Sir Marcus Burnhope, sitting on the bridge in a state of bereavement. His heart went out to the man. When he looked far across to the right, Colbeck saw something else that provoked his immediate sympathy.

Victor Leeming was leading his horse by the reins and trotting across the grass with patent difficulty. It was a vivid depiction of master and servant. Secure in the saddle, Edward Tallis was clearly taking advantage of his superior rank.

Bound tight to a chair, Imogen Burnside was mortified. While the rope bit into her wrists and her ankles, it was the handkerchief stuffed into her mouth that troubled her most. Held in place by a gag, it made her feel as if she was being smothered to death. Yet her physical pain was mild compared to the mental torture she was undergoing. It was excruciating. She'd betrayed her family in order to be with the man she loved, only to find that he was using her as a passport to a fortune extracted from her father. There seemed to be no limit to the wickedness of Terence Whiteside and his accomplice. It made her wonder what would happen when they came back. Tied up and unable to defend herself, she could easily be molested. Now that he no longer had to wear a mask of politeness, Cullen had already started to ogle both her and her maid.

Where had they taken Rhoda? That was the question burrowing into Imogen's brain. What had they done to her and would her maid ever be able to forgive her for leading them into a continuous ordeal? Since the true situation had been revealed, neither man showed the slightest respect for their captives. Imogen and Rhoda had been kept in line with fulsome promises and luxurious accommodation. They were unnecessary now. Dire threats and lengths of rope were the order of the day. She and her maid could expect more of the same in the days that lay ahead. As the hours rolled by, Imogen felt as if she could hardly breathe and her bonds were cutting off the circulation of her blood. When she thought of her family, remorse was like molten lava inside her head. Her mother, already in poor health, would be laid low by her disappearance. Her father would also be suffering intensely.

Then there were her relatives in Oxford. Her uncle and aunt were God-fearing people who would never understand the irresistible urge she'd had to end one life and begin a new and supposedly better one. She'd acted in defiance of everything she'd been brought up to believe. In retrospect, she couldn't understand it herself and would never convince anyone that her impulse was a laudable one. George Vaughan was the only person who might appreciate her desire for freedom because he'd felt that urge himself. His sister, Emma, would be aghast at what her cousin had done. In her eyes, it would be wholly reprehensible. What of Percy, a deacon of the church, devoting his life to the fulfilment of a sacred purpose? He was the one she most regretted having to shock and betray. It was unfair on him. Percy Vaughan had always been kind, patient and clumsily tender with her. Imogen would hate to lose his undemanding love, yet even he would have no time for her now.

She was still mourning the total loss of respect from her family when the door opened and Rhoda Wills was hustled into the room by Whiteside and Cullen. The men were in good humour but the maid's only concern was for her mistress. Rushing across to her, she removed the gag then began to untie the ropes.

'What happened?' gasped Imogen.

'Your father did as he was told,' replied Whiteside, holding up the leather bag. 'He just paid a small fortune and got absolutely nothing in return.'

'I watched him through a telescope,' said Cullen with a ripe chuckle. 'He gave us all that money for a daughter who was trussed up in a hotel room miles away. Praise the Lord for stupid fathers!'

'He's not stupid,' said Imogen, defensively. 'My father's a good man.'

'Then why did you desert him?'

The gibe was like the stab of a dagger and it was unanswerable.

'You've got what you wanted,' Rhoda pleaded, 'why not let us go?'

'We got what we wanted from Sir Marcus,' said

265

Whiteside, 'but we still need the pair of you. There's no point in settling for one ransom when we can have two. Next time, it will be Mr Tunnadine who hands over the money. Yes,' he went on as he saw the look of amazement on Imogen's face. 'He doesn't realise that you were so eager to marry him that you were ready to sail off to France. The poor fool will be trying to get back a bride who can't bear the sight of him.'

Sir Marcus Burnhope was inconsolable. The ease with which he'd lost the ransom was breathtaking. To the loss of a vast sum could be added the horror of not even being allowed to see his daughter, let alone be reunited with her. When Colbeck reached him, he was still sitting dejectedly on the bridge.

'They tricked me,' he admitted, close to tears.

'We were watching, Sir Marcus.'

'Because he brought my daughter's maid, I was unguarded enough to part with the money. I've been fleeced, Inspector.'

'Did the maid say anything?'

'She told me that my daughter was unharmed but that was all. Now that I think of it, she was obviously under orders to tell me nothing else.' He glanced at the trap. 'Thank you for retrieving it for me, though, in truth, I've been so gullible that I deserve to walk all the way back to Oxford.'

'You'll be able to get there in a measure of comfort,' said Colbeck. 'My advice is that you should return to London with the superintendent. We can make contact with you at your club.'

Tallis and Leeming eventually reached them. While the

former dismounted, the latter sank down onto the wall beside Sir Marcus. Glistening with sweat, Leeming was seriously short of breath. Colbeck gave him no time to rest. There had already been a lengthy delay but pursuit was necessary. The trap was left for the two older men while the detectives rode off across the bridge at a canter. They followed a track that led them across the vale and up the hill to the copse at the top. They paused to take stock of the situation.

'This is where they were hiding,' said Colbeck. 'Which way did they go?'

'Does it matter, sir? They'll be miles away by now.'

'A trap won't travel as fast as a horse.'

'Do we have to gallop?' cried Leeming. 'I'm already saddle-sore.'

'Think of the two ladies, Victor. Their plight is more important than our discomfort. Let's see if we can pick up their scent.'

Digging in his heels, he rode off with Leeming several yards behind. It was only a matter of minutes before they came out of the copse into open country. A problem faced them and drew them to a halt once more. The track split into two. One meandered off to the left while the other went arrow-straight towards a wood in the middle distance. Colbeck chose the latter and set off again at a gallop. Leeming followed in his wake, more concerned with staying in the saddle than riding hell for leather. It was a mile or more before Colbeck raised a hand. Both horses were reined in. Leeming eased his mount up beside the inspector.

'What's wrong, Inspector?'

'We should have taken the other road.'

'How do you know?'

'I just sense it,' said Colbeck. 'Let's go back and start again.'

'Do we have to?'

'Yes, we do. We'll ride all day and all night, if we have to.'

Leeming rubbed his buttocks. 'I feel as if we've already done that, sir.'

Turning around, they followed the track until they reached the point where the two paths diverged. There was a serpentine quality to the second one. It wound its way past clumps of bushes and the occasional outcrop of rock, making it difficult to see what was ahead. They goaded their horses on until they came to a hill. Colbeck paused at the top to let Leeming catch up with him again. The sergeant was in pain.

'How much farther is it, sir?'

'About a mile, I'd say. There's our destination.'

'Where?' asked Leeming, gazing ahead. He saw the building that stood in its own extensive grounds. 'What's that?'

'It looks like a country hotel.'

'Is that where they've been staying?'

'There's only one way to find out, Victor.'

Now that they had a destination, Leeming was relieved. The ride was no longer as painful or – to his eyes – quite as pointless. Ignoring the thud of the saddle against his body, he tried to think of the two hostages. They were in the hands of men who seemed intent on keeping them. Unimaginable horrors might await them.

Colbeck rode so hard that he reached the hotel minutes

before his companion. Rushing into the building, he demanded to see the manager then gave a description of the four people he was pursuing.

'Yes,' confirmed the manager. 'They did stay here but you've missed them, I'm afraid. They left an hour or so ago.'

The train set off with the usual tumult and quickly gathered speed. Seated in a compartment with their captors, Imogen Burnhope and Rhoda Wills wondered how much longer their torment would last.

CHAPTER SIXTEEN

In spite of the pleasure of reconciliation, Dolly Wrenson felt the persistent nibble of remorse. She realised now that her anger at George Vaughan had been both unjust and unkind. It was wrong to characterise his disappearance as a desertion of her and to assert her claims over the needs of his cousin. Now that she understood what had actually happened, she was almost hangdog. Imogen Burnhope and her maid were caught up in a crisis that could easily end in their death yet Dolly had put her own selfish desires before them. She could not stop apologising to the artist.

'My behaviour was unforgivable, George.'

'You didn't know the full facts – nor more did I when I left here.'

'I should have been more understanding.'

'That would not have come amiss.'

'I should have trusted you.'

'That's certainly true, my angel,' he said, reaching out to embrace her. 'You should have remembered the vows we'd made to each other. I would never dream of walking out on the creature of pure loveliness that is Dolly Wrenson.'

'I was the one about to leave,' she said, sheepishly. 'I could kick myself for having such a ridiculous tantrum.'

'I like your tantrums. They put colour in your cheeks.'

Dolly giggled. 'You have a much nicer way of doing that, George!'

They were in the studio and an overcast sky meant that the light was too poor for him to work properly. He'd experimented with candles and an oil lamp but they cast only a fitful glow over his model. Yet they had, in fact, given him an idea of another portrait of Dolly, surrounded by flickering flames and dancing shadows, but it was a project for the future. The priority now was to finish the existing work and for that he needed good light.

'I need to buy some more paints,' he said, examining his stock. 'Would you like to come with me or will you let me go alone?'

'I'm not your keeper, George.'

'You tried to be when I last left this house.'

'It was very childish of me. I've grown up now.'

'I won't be long, Dolly. With luck, the light may have improved by the time I get back.' He could not resist a grin. 'Will you still be here?'

'I won't move an inch.'

'Thank you, my dove. Losing you would be like losing a limb.'

'Then you'll know how I feel,' she said, crossing to the easel and throwing back the cloth that covered it. 'Give me my left arm, George Vaughan.'

'I'll do more than that,' he promised. 'You can have one

arm of your own and two of mine to wrap around you all night. Will that satisfy you?'

'You know it will – now away with you, kind sir.'

After putting on his coat and hat, he gave her a kiss before leaving the room. She could hear his footsteps clacking down the infinity of steps to the ground floor. When the sound faded, she went to the window and watched him come out of the front door and walk jauntily down the street. Dolly chided herself once again for ever doubting him. George Vaughan had been the most handsome, selfless, tender, loving, indulgent man she'd ever met. His resources were limited at the moment yet he never stinted her. Though she'd lived in more comfortable quarters with another artist, she never used that fact as a stick with which to hit her lover. Luxury was irrelevant. Simply being with him was enough to fill her with contentment.

Dolly was seized by the urge to do something by way of contrition to give him visible proof of the way that she felt. Her first instinct was to tidy the studio, so she made the bed, moved the few sticks of furniture and began to pick up the various things scattered on the floor. All of a sudden, she stopped and burst out laughing. This was not the way to please George Vaughan. He loved the friendly chaos of his studio. It was his natural habitat. Order was inimical to him. He'd fled from the controlled environment of life at an Oxford college and gone in search of a world without rules and without conventional boundaries. Having gathered up a pile of items to set on the table, she grabbed them again and scattered the whole lot over the floor. Dolly even rumpled the bed again.

It was then that she heard the footsteps on the stairs. She

was surprised. It could not be her lover returning so soon. The shop that sold artists' supplies was some distance away. Even someone as young and athletic as George Vaughan could not get there and back at such speed. Dolly moved to the door and listened. The footsteps were slow and weary. She could almost sense the effort that it was taking out of her visitor. The sounds finally stopped and there was a faint knock on the door.

She opened it and saw the stooping figure of a young woman. Her face was a mass of bruises, her lips swollen and one eye was closed. Dolly did not even see the expensive attire her visitor wore. She was mesmerised by the injuries.

'Hello,' said the woman with relief. 'I found you at last.'

'What do you want?'

'You're the one friend who won't turn me away.'

'I'm sorry,' said Dolly, drawing back. 'Who exactly are you?'

'Don't you recognise my voice?'

'No, I'm afraid that I don't.'

'It's Lucinda,' said the other. 'Lucinda Graham.'

The thrill of the chase was a positive boon to Victor Leeming's buttocks. They no longer ached and his thighs no longer burnt. Having established the direction in which their quarry had gone, they were able to track them and that bred excitement in the sergeant. Country people tended to be observant. Because so few strangers passed them in the course of a normal day, they usually noticed those who did. Four people had galloped past. A man and two women occupied a trap loaded with luggage. They were accompanied by a horseman who sat high in the saddle and led the way. Colbeck and Leeming were painstaking in their search. By stopping at every farm and village, they found someone each time who could tell them whether the fugitives had passed that way or not. The route eventually became clear.

'They're heading for the railway,' said Colbeck.

'Are they going back to Oxford station?'

'No, Victor, it might be too much of a risk. They could be seen and recognised there.' He smiled. 'Wouldn't it be wonderful if they did go to Oxford and stood on the platform at the same time as Sir Marcus and the superintendent? That would be a very interesting reunion.'

'Where does this road take us?' asked Leeming, cantering beside him.

'According to the map, it will take us about three miles north-west to another stop on the OWWR. They headed for Handborough, I suspect.'

'That would mean going back over the line on which the two women travelled in the first place.'

'So?'

'The kidnappers are surely not taking them to Burnhope Manor, are they?'

'The train goes on well beyond Shrub Hill station – over thirty miles to be precise. They could get off anywhere along the line.'

'In that case, we've lost them.'

'Not necessarily,' said Colbeck. 'We will at least divine their escape strategy. That's a vital first stage to apprehending them.'

'Captain Whiteside is like a will-o'-the-wisp. No sooner do you see him than he vanishes again. This time, he's vanished with all that money.'

'He's clever and resourceful, Victor. He's kept his hostages in order to wrest even more by way of ransom. While the two ladies are highly valuable, however, they are also a threat to him. Imogen Burnhope, by all accounts, is exceptionally beautiful. She's bound to be noticed.'

Colbeck was proved right. They got to Handborough station and learnt that Imogen had been one of four passengers who boarded a train there and who travelled with a lot of luggage. The stationmaster remembered them well.

'It was odd,' he recalled. 'The tall man did all the talking and the two ladies never uttered a word. They clung together and didn't even acknowledge my greeting. It was almost as if they'd had their tongues cut out.'

'What about the trap and the horse?' asked Leeming.

'They'd been hired from stables near Oxford, sir. The tall man asked me to arrange their return and gave me a generous reward for doing so.'

'Where were they going?'

'They bought four tickets to Wolverhampton, sir.'

'Then we'll buy two to the same destination,' said Colbeck, instantly, 'and prevail upon you to return our hired horses as well.' He pressed some coins into the man's hands. 'Meanwhile, we'd appreciate a description of these four travellers.'

'Then I have to start with the younger lady,' said the stationmaster with a respectful chuckle. 'She was a real beauty, sir. I've seen none to match her, even though she seemed so very sad . . .'

Dolly sensed the needs of her friend at a glance. The first thing that Lucinda Graham sought was kindness and compassion. Taking her gently by the hand, Dolly led her across to the bed and lowered her down, sitting beside her with a gentle arm around her shoulder. They sat quietly for several reassuring minutes. It was only when Lucinda thanked her that Dolly went across to the jug of water, poured some into a bowl and then came back to her. She used a wet cloth to bathe her visitor's face, wincing as she saw the full extent of the injuries and wondering who could possibly have inflicted them. Her friend eventually spoke.'

'I tried two other friends before you, Dolly,' she said. 'One of them turned me away and the other showed no pity at all. In this state, of course, I couldn't possibly go home to my parents. They washed their hands of me years ago and would hardly take me back now. As a last resort, I came looking for you.'

Dolly squeezed her hands. 'And I'm glad you found me, Lucinda. You're always welcome here.' She looked around. 'I know that you're accustomed to much finer accommodation but this suits George and me.'

Lucinda's head dropped. 'I don't have any accommodation now.'

'Why not?'

'He threw me out.'

'Are you talking about your politician?'

'Yes, Dolly, I am.'

'I thought that he spent lavishly on you.'

'He did.'

'What made him turn on you like this?'

'I spoke out of turn.'

'I do that all the time, Lucinda,' said Dolly, 'but I don't get attacked for it. George loves the way I blurt out things

276

in company and cause embarrassment. He says that I'm incorrigible.' She appraised her friend. 'You're in agony, aren't you? I can see it in your eyes.'

'I'm aching all over,' admitted Lucinda, putting a hand to her stomach, 'but the worst pain is here. He kicked me, Dolly. When he knocked me to the floor, he kicked me as if I was a disobedient dog.'

'Have you reported him to the police?'

'There's no point.'

'It's a case of assault and battery.'

'Let it pass.'

Dolly was enraged. 'Let it pass?' she repeated. 'My dear friend is beaten black and blue and you want me to pretend that it never happened? I can't do that, Lucinda. The evidence is right in front of me. This brute needs to be punished.'

'It was my own fault.'

'Of course it wasn't – you're the victim. Have him arrested.'

'He's too important.'

'Nobody should be allowed to get away with savagery like this.'

'I can see that you've had no dealings with the police,' said Lucinda, dully. 'They'd never show me the sympathy that you have. Some men beat their wives all the time and the police never interfere. They're even less likely to take my part when they learn that I was attacked by the man who kept me. They're far more likely to laugh and tell me I deserved it. Policemen don't bother about people like me, Dolly.'

'Well, I bother.'

'Thank goodness that someone does.'

'And if you need somewhere to stay for a while, we'll help you.'

'You're so kind.'

Lucinda burst into tears and plucked a handkerchief from her sleeve. Dolly found a simple way to stop her crying. Leading her across to the easel, she tossed back the cloth to reveal the portrait. Her visitor goggled in wonder.

'Is that really you?'

Dolly laughed. 'It's not only me – it's *all* of me.'

'You look lovely . . . like a queen.'

'I don't think Her Majesty would pose for a portrait like that. It would be undignified for a real queen. George wanted to show me off to the world. Don't you think he's clever? Yes, it *is* little Dolly Wrenson,' she said, proudly, 'but the artist's skill has transformed me.'

Neither of them heard the feet approaching up the stairs. The first they knew of George Vaughan's return was when he walked through the door. Like Dolly, he was shaken by the visitor's appearance at first but he quickly rallied and pulled out a bottle of brandy from under the bed. After pouring a glass for Lucinda, he led her to the chair. Dolly, meanwhile, was giving him a breathless account of what had befallen her friend. He exuded sympathy.

'Someone must be called to account for this, Lucinda,' he said.

Dolly nodded in assent. 'That's what I told her.'

'Who is this rogue?'

'Oh, I couldn't possibly tell you that,' said Lucinda, anxiously.

'He needs a good thrashing. What's his name?'

'I swore that I'd never divulge it to anyone, George.'

'When did you do that?'

'It was when I first moved into the house.'

'And I daresay that you kept your promise, didn't you?'

'I did. Nobody else knows his name and nobody will.'

'But the rules have changed now,' Dolly pointed out. 'It was all very well protecting him when you were being kept by him but that's not the case now. He threw you out. He punched and kicked you, Lucinda. Do you really think it's your bounden duty to hide the name of a thug like that? If it'd been me that he attacked, I'd be shouting his name from the rooftops.'

'Dolly is right,' said the artist. 'This man may be a Member of Parliament but that doesn't entitle him to do what he did to you. He's no better than an animal. You owe him no loyalty, Lucinda. Tell us who he is.'

Clive Tunnadine arrived at Crewe station to be met by Alban Kee. The private detective had booked rooms at the hotel mentioned in the ransom note. Taking charge of the politician's luggage, he summoned a cab and they drove off. Tunnadine wasted no time looking at the surroundings. Crewe was a railway town with a station built in the Elizabethan style. They went past rows of identical houses where those employed at the thriving railway works lived. An element of neatness and symmetry had been imposed on a small community that had grown in size until its population was well past eight thousand. The hotel was just outside the town. As soon as Tunnadine had been assigned a room, he sat down in it with Kee to discuss the situation.

'Well,' he said, 'what have you decided?'

'The kidnappers have chosen well,' replied Kee. 'This junction allows them to travel in almost any direction. They could ride off overland, of course, but the railway will be much quicker. Before they meet you to collect the ransom, they'll already have bought tickets to their next destination.'

'They'll never get there.'

'That's my hope, Mr Tunnadine.'

'It's not a hope, man, it's a necessity. We must rescue the hostages and kill the scheming devils who had the gall to abduct them.'

'Shooting them must only be an option if all else fails, sir.'

'I want them dead.'

'I appreciate the sentiments,' said Kee, 'but you might get more satisfaction in handing them over to suffer the full force of the law. Besides, didn't you tell me that Sir Marcus Burnhope was offering a large reward for their capture?' He gave an oily grin. 'You'd be in a position to claim that.'

The thought appealed to Tunnadine. He stroked his chin pensively.

'No,' he said at length. 'I'd be in a position to claim it *and* to turn it down. That would redound to my credit. I have no need for the money and it would put me in my father-in-law's good books. More to the point,' he added, 'it would impress the dear lady I am to marry.'

'You will do that simply by coming to her rescue, sir.'

'That's true.'

'If we have to draw our weapons,' suggested Kee, 'let's shoot to disable them rather than to kill. A bullet in the knee will cripple them and cause agony.'

'It's good advice. We'll aim for the legs. But when we've

got them squirming on the ground,' said Tunnadine, 'I'll kick them hard until they beg for mercy.'

'You'd not do that in front of the ladies, surely?'

'I'll rely on you to divert them.'

'We are, of course, assuming that the hostages will actually be there,' said Kee, cautiously. 'At the first exchange, there was no sign of them. They used a decoy.'

'They won't try the same trick twice.'

'Perhaps not, sir, but they're wily enough to invent a new one.'

'Then we must be on our guard.'

Tunnadine was glad to concentrate all his thoughts on Imogen's rescue. It saved him from thinking about the way that he'd treated Lucinda Graham. She'd committed the cardinal sin of joking about blackmail. He felt that he'd been right to attack her and to drive her out of his life forever. She belonged to his past now and his future would be built around his wife. Once the marriage had settled into a rhythm, he decided, he could search for someone to replace Lucinda Graham. A mistress served a purpose that a wife simply could not. The notion of flitting between the two appealed to him greatly. At the moment, however, he had neither mistress nor wife. It was a thought that kept his brain simmering.

Alban Kee spread out an ordnance survey map on the table.

'The ransom will not be handed over in the town,' he concluded. 'They'll want to draw you out into the open so that they can ensure you are on your own. I've been looking at possible choices.'

'Good work!'

'I've marked them on the map.' He indicated some crosses. 'They'll pick a spot where they can be hidden while you are exposed to their scrutiny. It won't be far away from the town because they'll need to get back quickly in order to catch a train. The first thing I did when I got here yesterday,' said Kee, 'was to hire a horse and ride out on reconnaissance.'

'They will doubtless have got the lie of the land themselves,' said Tunnadine, looking at the areas marked by crosses. 'Which would *you* choose?'

Kee jabbed a finger at the map. 'This one, sir – it answers all their needs.'

'What about *our* needs?'

'I've not neglected those. They'll expect you to come in a trap so that you can drive the hostages away. I've hired one that will allow me to lie concealed beneath a rug. Even with a telescope, they won't be able to spot that there are two of us in it. You can hand over the ransom,' said Kee, 'in the knowledge that I won't be far away. Once the ladies are safe, I can come out of hiding.'

'I like the device,' said Tunnadine.

'All that I've done is to think ahead, sir.'

'You've given us the advantage of surprise and that's crucial.'

'What will happen afterwards, sir?' asked Kee.

'I'll be hailed as a hero and you'll be richly rewarded.'

'That's not what I meant, Mr Tunnadine. The point is that you chose not to apprise Sir Marcus of the fact that you received the ransom note. How will he react when he realises that you acted on your own without consulting him?'

'He'll be too overjoyed to offer any criticism of what I did.'

'Might he not at least be a little piqued?'

'There's only one thing that will annoy him.'

'What's that, sir?'

'He picked the wrong detective,' said Tunnadine, smugly. 'While I chose Alban Kee, he made the mistake of putting his faith in Inspector Colbeck. And where, may I ask, is the celebrated Railway Detective now?' His tone was contemptuous. 'He's chasing moonbeams in another part of the country.'

Wolverhampton was familiar to them. One of their most complex investigations had started there. A prisoner being transferred to Birmingham had escaped with the help of an accomplice and killed the two policemen guarding him. Like all people involved in law enforcement, Colbeck and Leeming had been deeply upset by the gruesome death of two fellow officers. It had made them redouble their efforts to catch those responsible. Their earlier visit to Wolverhampton had sent them off on a labyrinthine hunt that eventually proved successful. This time, however, they met with failure. They questioned almost everyone at the station. None of them could remember four passengers – two men and two women – purchasing tickets to another destination. One of the porters recalled seeing a beautiful young lady but he'd been too busy to take much notice of her. Evidently, the quartet had merged into the crowd to avoid arousing attention.

Leeming was dismayed. 'They've got away,' he said.

'So it would appear.'

'They may not even have taken another train.'

'Oh, I think they did,' said Colbeck, thoughtfully. 'It's the obvious thing to do. Travelling by horse and trap would be far slower. They'll have luggage, remember. We'll check the nearest stables but I fancy that they'll not have hired from any of them. They simply caught a train.'

'Then why did nobody see the four of them together?'

'A party of four people might be distinctive, but who would look twice at two couples? They could have travelled in separate compartments. Neither of the two ladies would dare to raise the alarm because they'd know that their respective captors were armed.'

'In which direction did they go, Inspector?'

'Your guess is as good as mine.'

'Well, my guess is that we've lost them for good,' said Leeming.

'No, Victor, they'll be back again, I assure you. Don't forget that they still have two priceless assets.'

'What will they do with the two ladies?'

'I'm certain that they'll attempt to extort even more ransom money somehow and overplay their hand. That's when we can step in.'

The sergeant was glum. 'So we did all that dashing around for nothing.'

'Put it down as healthy exercise.'

'The superintendent will call it a bad mistake.'

'He ought to applaud our enterprise,' said Colbeck, 'but I agree that he's more likely to blame us for our incompetence. Let's find out where the stables are and pay them a visit. At least we can be sure then that they haven't fled by means of horse and trap.'

'They could always have *stayed* here, sir.'

'I think not, Victor. This is an industrial town with few hotels that offer outstanding facilities. Captain Whiteside has expensive tastes and he now has the money to pay for them. An isolated hotel is what he'll want. There are not many of those near Wolverhampton. As you saw from all those smoking chimneys we passed on the way here, the Black Country is well named.'

'It's no worse than parts of London, sir,' Leeming conceded. 'There's the same stink, deafening noise and grime.'

After taking advice from the stationmaster, they went off to visit the nearest places where horses could be hired. Now that the chase had ended, Leeming's aches and pains returned. The prospects seemed bleak to him.

'I'm not looking forward to seeing Superintendent Tallis again,' he said.

'But he's going to welcome you with open arms,' teased Colbeck.

'We failed, sir.'

'We had a setback, that's all. The superintendent will appreciate that. He's not such an ogre. He has enough experience to know that we'll succeed in the end.'

While he wanted to admonish his detectives for their lack of success, Edward Tallis was forced into a position of defending them. He was seated behind his desk with an irate Sir Marcus Burnhope seated opposite him. Forgetting that he'd insisted on handing over the ransom in person, the visitor was acerbic in his denunciation of Colbeck and Leeming. Eyes protruding and voice rising, he slapped his thigh.

'They let me down badly, Superintendent,' he said.

'I'd have to take issue with you there.'

'Why didn't they arrest that man when they had the chance?'

'It's rather difficult to put handcuffs on someone when you're almost half a mile away,' said Tallis, drily. 'You took the initiative, Sir Marcus. Indeed, you made a point of doing so. As a result, you lost the money and left empty-handed.'

'The fellow was wholly without honour!'

'He's a criminal. They operate by different standards. You should have expected that. As for Colbeck, please remember that it was he who retrieved the horse and trap for you. It was a feat well beyond me and the sergeant is no horseman. But for the inspector,' Tallis emphasised, 'you might have had a long and tiring walk back to the railway station.'

Sir Marcus reluctantly accepted that he had been at fault but he still nursed resentment against the detectives. To mollify his visitor, Tallis opened his box of cigars and offered it to Sir Marcus. The two of them were soon puffing away and filling the room with cigar smoke. There was a noticeable release of tension. Sir Marcus contemplated his fate.

'It's dreadful,' he said, mournfully. 'Losing my daughter was the first shattering blow. Surrendering all that money was the second. But the worst of it is that there may well be a third.'

'I fail to see it, Sir Marcus.'

'Publicity, man – think of the newspapers.'

'To be honest, I try not to do so. They've never treated me kindly.'

'Imagine what they'd do to me if this story ever got out. Sir Marcus Burnhope, Secretary of State for India, has been robbed of his daughter and deprived of a veritable fortune. How my enemies would love that!' he cried. 'I'd never hear the end of their taunts and howls of derision. You must protect me from that, Tallis.'

'The best way to do that is to rescue the hostages, capture the men who abducted them and restore your money to the bank. Nobody else need ever know what happened at the two earlier meetings with the kidnapper.'

'The press will be sniffing around, Superintendent. They know that Imogen is missing because I've offered a reward. What if they learn the full truth?'

'It will not come from my lips, Sir Marcus, nor from those of my men.'

'Do I have your word on that?'

'In a case like this,' said Tallis, seriously, 'discretion is vital and that is what I can guarantee. I'll tell the press nothing. They have an unfortunate habit of getting hold of the wrong end of the stick – as I know to my cost.'

The two of them continued to draw on their cigars and create a fug. When there was a knock on the door, Tallis invited the caller to enter. He was a fresh-faced young detective who'd recently joined the department. Plainly in awe of the superintendent, he delivered his message in something close to a whisper.

'Speak up!' ordered Tallis. 'I can't hear a word.'

'There's someone asking to see you, Superintendent.'

'They'll have to wait. I'm in the middle of an important meeting.'

'The gentleman was most insistent.'

'Then he'll need to be taught the value of patience.'

'He said that, if I gave you his name, you'd admit him immediately.'

'I very much doubt that. Who is the fellow?'

'His name is George Vaughan.'

'Heavens!' exclaimed Sir Marcus. 'It's one of my nephews. What on earth is George doing here?'

'We'll find out. Send him in,' said Tallis, dismissing the young detective. The man went out. 'George Vaughan is an artist. Why should he be so desperate to see me?'

Sir Marcus was droll. 'Perhaps he has come to confess to some terrible crime,' he said. 'Even his mother has begun to despair of him.' He got to his feet as George Vaughan came into the room. They shook hands. 'How are you, young man?'

'I didn't expect to find you here, Uncle Marcus,' said the other, 'but I'm very glad that I did so. You should hear what I have to say.'

'I understood that you wished to speak to me,' said Tallis, stiffly.

'That's right, Superintendent. I have to report a heinous crime.'

'Of what nature is it?'

'A young woman has been brutally assaulted by a man.'

'Report that to the nearest police station, Mr Vaughan. It's not the sort of crime that we deal with, as a rule. I take it that the two people involved were well known to each other?'

'Yes, they were.'

'Then it's a domestic matter in which we don't usually get involved.'

'I've seen her,' said the artist, earnestly. 'He beat her to a pulp and threw her out of the house. Doesn't that arouse at least a scintilla of compassion in you?'

'Go back to your earlier remark,' said Sir Marcus, interested. 'Why were you glad to find me in here with the superintendent?'

'You know the man, Uncle. He's a friend of yours.'

Puffing on his cigar, Sir Marcus fell back on pomposity. 'My friends do not assault defenceless young women.'

'This one does,' insisted George Vaughan. 'If he can batter his mistress like that, imagine what he might do to his wife.'

'What are you babbling about?'

'Who is this person to whom you refer?' asked Tallis.

'His name is Clive Tunnadine,' said the artist, spitting out the name, 'and he is destined to marry my cousin, Imogen.'

'That's a preposterous allegation,' roared Sir Marcus, 'and you ought to know better than to make it. Really, George, I'm ashamed of you. Withdraw that charge at once, then leave us to deal with more important matters.'

'What I have to tell you has a direct bearing on these so-called more important matters, Uncle Marcus. Imogen has been kidnapped and we all wish her to be released very soon. But what is the point of liberating her,' he went on, gesticulating, 'if you're going to chain her in marriage to a monster who resorts to violence?'

'Leave the room at once. I'll hear no more of this.'

'No, wait,' said Tallis, intervening. 'Since your nephew is moved to come here, we must listen to his complaint in full. Like you, Sir Marcus, I do not believe that Mr Tunnadine is capable of the assault described to us, but then, I doubt if your nephew would take the trouble of coming here unless he has incontrovertible evidence to the contrary. Do you have such evidence, Mr Vaughan?'

'I do,' replied the artist, trying to compose himself. 'I apologise for bursting in like this but I implore you to hear me out. It's high time that both of you became aware of the true character of Clive Tunnadine.'

The letter was slipped under the door of the hotel room. By the time that Alban Kee had flung the door open, the messenger had gone. He picked up the missive and handed it to Tunnadine then he shut the door and locked it. Kee watched as the other man opened the letter and read it.

'It's from the kidnappers,' said Tunnadine. 'They've specified the time and place.'

CHAPTER SEVENTEEN

It was remarkable. Lady Paulina Burnhope began to improve. Weakened by illness and racked by grief at the disappearance of her daughter, she somehow found the strength to rally. The key to her recovery was the presence of Percy Vaughan. His mother had done her best to comfort her sister but Cassandra's gifts did not run to tenderness and the long bedside vigil tested her patience to, and almost beyond, the limit. Her elder son, on the other hand, had an inexhaustible supply of sympathy and understanding. When he talked, he knew exactly what to say and he also sensed when silence was the best medicine. Cassandra had brought a kind of subdued truculence to bear on her sister's condition. The Reverend Percy Vaughan was altogether more serene, sensitive and practical.

'I can't thank you enough,' said Paulina with a first smile in days. 'I feel so much better.'

'That's good to hear, Aunt.'

'You have a skill that your mother lacks – and, I must add, your brother.'

'George has other skills,' he said.

'None that can rival yours – you are curate, doctor and magician rolled into one. Your parishioners were blessed when you came among them.'

'It's true, Aunt Paulina, but not for the reasons that you've just given. I am praised in North Cerney simply for being there. The rector has an extraordinary capacity for being elsewhere on Sunday. Baptisms and burial services are always left to me. When I'm ordained as a priest, services of holy matrimony will also be solely mine. Oh, I'm not complaining,' he said, raising a palm. 'In fact, I enjoy being so fully involved in the care of the parish. It's a labour of love.'

He was sitting beside the bed in which she was resting on large pillows. A Bible stood on the table nearby but he'd had no need of it because his favourite passages were engraved on his memory and could be produced whole whenever they were required.

'You always were such a thoughtful boy,' she said, admiringly. 'All that George ever thought about was running around and playing pranks. Yet, for some reason, he was the undoubted favourite of your father.'

'It was right that he should be, Aunt,' said her nephew, hiding the sting he felt at the reminder. 'George was the younger and smaller son. He needed more attention.'

'God decided that we had only one child, alas, and I fear that we gave Imogen far too much attention. Well – to be candid – *I* certainly did. It's taken this terrible situation to make me fully aware of it,' she went on. 'I kept her on a leash, Percy. I controlled everything she did and everywhere she went.'

'You were only doing your duty as a mother.'

'I wonder. My sister gave her children more licence and more freedom to grow. You, George and Emma have blossomed into maturity whereas Imogen is still a child at heart. The fault lies with me.'

Percy Vaughan made no reply. His aunt had finally recognised something that had been abundantly clear to him for years. She'd penned her daughter in and now felt guilty that Imogen was so unprepared to face the real world and cope with the ordeal in which she now found herself.

She grabbed his arm. 'Imogen will come through this, won't she?'

'I've prayed for her continuously.'

'What are they *doing* to her?'

'One can only guess, Aunt Paulina.'

'I'm so frightened.'

'I understand your fears.'

'How can I still them, Percy?'

'Have faith in God's mercy and trust in Inspector Colbeck.'

Releasing his arm, she eased herself back and closed her eyes. The curate thought that she'd dozed off and he waited quietly at the bedside for several minutes. When he felt certain that he was no longer needed, he rose to steal away. Instantly, she opened her eyes.

'May I ask you something, Percy?'

'You may ask anything you wish.'

'Do you think that Imogen should marry Mr Tunnadine?'

He was taken by surprise. 'My opinion is immaterial,'

he said. 'The only person who can answer that question is Imogen herself. I assumed that she was very happy with her choice.'

'The engagement owed much to my husband. There's nothing amiss in that, of course,' she added, defensively. 'Parents have a perfect right to shape their daughter's destiny. We felt that it would be an advantageous marriage to both parties.'

'When it takes place,' he said, masking his displeasure, 'I'm sure that it will be everything that you and Uncle Marcus wished for.'

'But I've been having second thoughts, Percy.'

'Indeed?'

'I haven't simply been wringing my hands and listening to your mother,' she explained. 'I've been regretting all the mistakes I made in bringing up Imogen in the way that I did. I promised myself that, once this nightmare is over, I'll do all I can to show her more love and allow her more scope. And I'll be quite frank with her.'

'I've always thought of you as a very forthright person, Aunt Paulina,' he said. 'In that respect, you resemble Mother.'

'No woman could be as blatantly forthright as my sister, Percy,' she said with a pained expression. 'I've often been the victim of her forthrightness. On this subject, however, I have come to agree with her.'

'And what subject is that?'

'It's the man I was just asking you about.'

'Mr Tunnadine?'

'The awful truth is that . . . I don't think I like him.'

* * *

Clive Tunnadine and Alban Kee took all the precautions they felt necessary. Both carried concealed weapons and, in the privacy of a hotel room, they practised bringing them out at a moment's notice. It took only seconds for them to have a pistol in their hands. Kee had a second, smaller firearm hidden in his top hat. That, too, could be brought out in a flash. The two men were satisfied with their rehearsal. After checking his pocket watch, Tunnadine nodded.

'Let's go and surprise them,' he said, picking up the thick, leather bag containing the ransom.

'Don't hand anything over until you've actually seen the two hostages.'

'There's only one hostage that interests me.'

'We need both of them, sir.'

'Why?'

'After we've rescued her, Sir Marcus's daughter will need her maid to look after her. They'll have been through a lot together. Adversity binds people.'

'I'm the best person to look after her.'

'She needs female company.'

'That's for me to decide.'

Kee stepped back from an argument. 'Yes, of course, sir.'

'If we have to sacrifice her maid in order to secure her release, so be it. As far as I'm concerned, Rhoda Wills is expendable. She can go to hell, for all I care.'

Kee was startled by the heartless remark. He appreciated single-mindedness in his clients but he was less impressed by the cold-blooded streak that had just manifested itself. Even though he'd be well paid by Tunnadine, the detective was having doubts about working for him. He was beginning to see him in a new light that was exposing unpleasant aspects of his character.

'Are you sure that there'll only be two of them?' asked Tunnadine.

'That's my belief, sir. The kidnapper will need an accomplice to keep an eye on the hostages when he's not there. They're greedy men. That's obvious. They know that the more people involved, the less each individual would get of the ransom. Two people are all that it will take. One of them will bring the two ladies and the other will watch the exchange from a concealed position.' Kee patted the gun under his coat. 'That's the man I'll shoot and disable.'

'I'd still prefer to put a bullet through both men's skulls.'

'By doing that, you'd only be helping them to escape justice.'

'You think too much like a policeman, Kee.'

'That's how I was trained.'

Tunnadine regarded him shrewdly. 'Why did you and Colbeck quarrel?'

'He thought he was a better detective than me, sir.'

'And was he?'

'You've met him, Mr Tunnadine. What do you think?'

'I found him too arrogant.'

'That was the least of his faults. Pose yourself another question, sir.'

'What do you mean?'

'Where is Inspector Colbeck now?' asked Kee, triumphantly. 'He's nowhere to be seen. While he's cooling his heels in London with Victor Leeming, we're about to bring this whole business to a proper conclusion.'

'This case means a great deal to you, doesn't it?'

'Yes, Mr Tunnadine – I have a personal stake in it.'

'Why is that?'

'It could be my redemption, sir.'

'Really? In what sense?'

'I left Scotland Yard because I was not valued properly,' said Kee, bitterly. 'My skills were disregarded. What you've given me is the perfect opportunity to show everyone there that I can compete with Inspector Colbeck on equal terms and surpass him. I have a point to prove to the superintendent. When Tallis sees what I've done – what *we've* done together, that is – he'll be begging me to return to the fold.'

They were wrong. Expecting to be traduced by Tallis when they returned to Scotland Yard, they were instead confronted with some astonishing information. Colbeck and Leeming were told about the visit of George Vaughan.

'Can this be true, sir?' asked Leeming, agog.

'I don't know. I need you to verify the allegations.'

'How can we do that?'

'You must call at Mr Vaughan's studio immediately.'

Leeming was unsettled. 'Do I have to, Superintendent?'

'Don't worry, Sergeant,' said Colbeck, reassuringly. 'I'll be there with you. I'd like to hear from the young lady herself.' He turned to Tallis. 'How did Sir Marcus react to the news?'

'He refused to believe a word of it,' replied the other.

'Yet the evidence sounds very convincing.'

'Mr Tunnadine is a close friend and a future son-in-law. That puts him above reproach in Sir Marcus's eyes.'

'We've had experience of that attitude already,' said Colbeck, ruefully. 'Instead of being remanded in custody for shooting someone dead, he was set free by the magistrate on the advice of Sir Marcus.'

'That matter is still unresolved,' said Tallis, curtly. 'Nobody is above the law. Mr Tunnadine will be taught that in the fullness of time. Meanwhile, we have this lesser charge of assault on a young woman with whom he supposedly had a liaison.'

'But he is betrothed to Sir Marcus's daughter,' said Leeming, deeply shocked. 'Would any man sink so low as to dally with another woman when he's already made such a commitment?'

'Unhappily, it appears so.'

'What do you believe, sir?'

'I want the facts corroborated before I make a judgement.'

'That's very sensible of you, sir,' said Colbeck. 'Come on, Sergeant. It's time to find out a little more about the private life of Mr Clive Tunnadine.'

A few minutes later, they were sharing a cab that took them in the direction of Chelsea. Leeming's mind was filled with anxieties about meeting Dolly Wrenson once again. Colbeck, however, was thinking of the implications of what they'd heard.

'Would you call George Vaughan an honest man, Victor?'

'Yes, sir – he's very straightforward.'

'Why should he invent such a tale?'

'I'm not sure that he did.'

'Neither am I,' said Colbeck. 'It had the ring of authenticity somehow. I'm wondering which of the allegations Sir Marcus found more unpalatable – that Tunnadine kept a mistress or that he beat the poor woman senseless.'

'Either is enough to damn him, sir.'

'I agree.'

'No matter how close they are, even Sir Marcus would draw back from letting his daughter marry such a man.'

'Imogen Burnhope has already fled from him. That's how she ended up in jeopardy. Whatever happens, the wedding will never take place.'

'The lady is in no position to marry anyone at the moment.'

'Let's put her aside,' said Colbeck. 'Our first task is to speak to Miss Lucinda Graham. That's the only way to get the full measure of Tunnadine.'

Their disillusionment had come full circle. From the moment they boarded the train at Shrub Hill station, Imogen Burnhope and Rhoda Wills had been in a kind of dream. Met at Oxford station, they evaded attention by means of a stratagem they'd both loved. They'd been taken to a hotel with every luxury imaginable and treated with the utmost care and attention by the two former soldiers. Imogen had been floating on a cloud of romance. It was her maid who'd remained a little closer to reality. They had now come down to earth. The hotel in which they were being kept was cheap, shoddy and totally lacking in any refinement.

'Will they never let us go?' wailed Imogen.

'Not as long as they can use us,' said Rhoda, sadly. 'We've already earned them a lot of money by the sound of it, and they want more.'

'Father will surely have contacted the police.'

'Then where are they?'

'Detectives must be looking for us by now.'

'That's why Captain Whiteside and the sergeant have taken such trouble to cover our tracks. We've been rushed here, there and everywhere. Nobody will find us in Crewe.'

'It's a beastly place, Rhoda, full of noise and stench.'

'We were spoilt, living in the solitude of the countryside.'

'I realise that now. Why did I ever run away?'

Rhoda said nothing. Both of them had been asking themselves exactly the same question many times a day. Neither of them relished the replies they had. They had lost everything and were now in limbo. While their immediate future was black, even the prospect of escape could not cheer them. The joyous welcome that Imogen would receive from her family would turn to hostility when the truth was revealed. Then there would be a searing confrontation with Clive Tunnadine. Wherever she looked, there was more pain and anguish.

The sound of a key in the lock made both of them jump to their feet. When the door opened, Whiteside and Cullen marched into the room.

'Put on your hats, ladies,' said Whiteside, briskly. 'We're leaving.'

'Where are we going?' asked Imogen.

'I need to put you on display.'

'Why did you take our luggage away from us?'

'It's waiting at the station.'

'Are we going on another journey?'

'Stop badgering me and do as you're told,' said Whiteside. 'Remember the rules or there'll be trouble.'

'Both the captain and I are armed,' Cullen reminded them, 'and we'll not hesitate to shoot if we have to. Don't give us the excuse.'

Rhoda attempted defiance. 'What if we refuse to go with you?'

'Then you'll regret it for the rest of your life.'

'She won't *have* any life, Manus,' said Whiteside, taking a pistol from beneath his coat and holding the barrel against Rhoda's temple. 'Do you still want to refuse?'

With the cold metal pressed against her head, Rhoda's courage failed her.

'No, no – I'll do as you tell me,' she promised.

'That's what I like to hear.'

Imogen was horrified. 'Would you really shoot a woman?'

'I'll shoot anyone who gets in my way,' he said, replacing the weapon. 'That's what the sergeant and I did when we decided that the army no longer had anything to offer us. We had to shoot our way out.'

'Are you saying that you're *deserters*?'

'We are soldiers of fortune, Imogen, riding on the horseback of Fate.'

'All your stories about the Crimea were barefaced lies, then?'

'Not at all,' he said with a grin. 'They were all true. It just happens that I wasn't the person who experienced those adventures. They were recounted to us by someone who really had served in a cavalry regiment in the Crimean War. We borrowed his tales because they served our purpose.'

'So you're a deserter, a liar and a coward.'

'Cowardice is the one thing you can't accuse us of, Imogen. It takes courage to kill people, especially when they're trained soldiers. Do you know what they do to deserters? They execute them,' said Whiteside with a graphic gesture. 'Cowards would be too scared to flee. We had the courage to do so.'

'Yes,' added Cullen. 'We were brave enough to desert and clever enough to stay out of sight afterwards. Then we spotted you in Oxford one day.'

Whiteside laughed. 'And the long courtship began.'

'I'll never forgive you for what you did,' warned Imogen.

'With the rewards you've helped us to acquire, I can live quite happily without your forgiveness.' His voice deepened menacingly. 'All I demand is your obedience. That goes for you as well, Rhoda.'

'What did you mean when you said we'd be on display?' asked Rhoda.

'Imogen is going to meet the man she agreed to marry,' explained Whiteside.

'Why are we going to see Mr Tunnadine?'

He sniggered. 'The generous fellow is about to give us a great deal of money.'

Within minutes of meeting her, Colbeck and Leeming knew that Lucinda Graham was telling the truth. Her injuries were grotesquely obvious and her memories too detailed and poignantly recounted to be pure invention. Encouraged by Dolly, she poured out her heart. The detectives were saddened to hear that she had been kept as a mistress by Tunnadine for the whole period during which he'd wooed and won Imogen Burnhope. Leeming was outraged when told that the politician had intended her to remain in the house provided by him so that he could pay clandestine visits after he was married. Whatever charms Lucinda had were now hidden beneath the bruises and the swellings. The loss of her front teeth had robbed her of her alluring smile.

'Mr Tunnadine should be arrested, Inspector,' said Dolly.

'He already has been,' replied Colbeck, 'but this assault merits another arrest. He treated Miss Graham appallingly.'

'He thinks he's too important to be prosecuted.'

'We will have to disabuse him of that notion.'

'She was afraid to complain,' said George Vaughan, 'in case Tunnadine sought revenge against her. It's exactly the sort of thing he'd do.'

'I fancy that it is.'

'It will be a pleasure to put him under arrest,' said Leeming.

'Thank you, Sergeant!' gushed Dolly, touching his shoulder and making him pull back as if her fingers were red-hot. 'Lucinda needs someone on her side.'

'The law is on her side.'

'Every decent human being would support her case,' said Colbeck.

He had won Lucinda's confidence and given her a modicum of hope that her suffering would not go unacknowledged in a court of law. She found the fact that he'd once been a barrister very comforting and she was relieved to see that there was no hint of disapproval in him. Victor Leeming had been troubled by her immorality at first but came to see her as an unfortunate victim rather than as a young woman who'd willingly prostituted herself. His fears about Dolly Wrenson had been groundless. She was extremely pleasant to him and, like Leeming, clearly preferred to forget what had occurred at their last meeting. Now that she and the artist had settled back in together, she had no interest in other men.

'What will happen now, Inspector?' asked George Vaughan.

'We'll accost Mr Tunnadine and confront him with the allegations,' replied Colbeck. 'I'm certain that he'll deny any assault and claim that it's a case of his word against that of Miss Graham.'

'I'd choose Lucinda's version over his any day.'

'So would I,' said Dolly.

'Go and arrest the villain right now.'

'It's not as simple as that,' said Colbeck. 'We are, as you doubtless know, engaged in a much more serious investigation. Not that that eclipses what happened to Miss Graham,' he pointed out, 'but it means we may not be able to get immediate access to Mr Tunnadine. Our main concern is the kidnap and this latest incident is closely related to it, of course, but it can't be given priority. What I can promise you is that Mr Tunnadine will not evade punishment.'

'Men who attack women like that should be locked up in perpetuity,' argued the artist, bunching his fists. 'If you won't go after him, then I will.'

'Steer well clear of him, Mr Vaughan. I appreciate your feelings but I'd hate to see you being sued for assault, as you surely would. We have reasons of our own for wanting Mr Tunnadine behind bars. It's only a matter of time before we finally put him there.'

They had studied the map closely. Having been there before, Alban Kee had recognised the area to which they were being sent. He remembered the open field to which Clive Tunnadine had been directed by the letter from the kidnappers. It had a deep ditch running down one side of it and the other side was screened by a thick hedge. When they approached the field in the trap, only Tunnadine was visible. Kee was on his hands and knees under a rug at the driver's feet. He stayed there until they came to a stand of sycamore trees. Taking advantage of the brief cover, he hopped out of the trap and crept towards the hedge so that he could work his way along the field out of sight. Tunnadine, meanwhile, drove on until he reached the middle of the field. As instructed, he pulled the horse to a halt and waited.

There was no sign of life but that was exactly what he'd expected. He'd been dragged to an isolated spot less than a mile outside the town and was probably under surveillance. Someone had a telescope trained on him to make sure that he'd obeyed his instructions. He picked up the leather bag and set it on his knees. As he did so, his elbow brushed against the weapon holstered under his coat. The sensation gave him both reassurance and bravado. Tunnadine wanted to rescue Imogen but he wanted to punish her abductors even more.

It seemed like an age before anyone appeared. Just as he was beginning to think that he'd been tricked, he saw a trap emerging from the trees on the other side of the field. A man was driving it with Imogen and Rhoda squeezed in either side of him. As soon as they came within range, Tunnadine wanted to leap up and shoot the man but he knew that there'd be an accomplice somewhere and couldn't risk firing when the three figures in the trap were so close together. The newcomers stopped some twenty yards or more away. Whiteside stood up in the vehicle.

'Good day to you, Mr Tunnadine!' he called.

'Who the devil are you?'

'I'm the man who's come to trade with you.'

'Then hand over the two ladies at once,' barked Tunnadine.

'I'll give the orders, if you don't mind, sir.'

'I do mind.' He looked at Imogen. 'Has he harmed you in any way?'

'No, Clive,' she replied, nervously.

'Tell me the truth.'

'We are . . . as well as can be expected.'

'Where did they hold you?'

'You can talk to her after I've had what I came for,' said Whiteside, cutting short their brief conversation. 'Now, this is what you must do.'

'Don't presume to order me about,' said Tunnadine, belligerently. 'I'm not afraid of you.'

'Do as he says,' pleaded Imogen.

Whiteside smirked. 'Do what your beloved tells you.'

'Release her now or your life is forfeit.'

Tunnadine tried to pull out his weapon but, before he could do so, a gun had appeared miraculously in the other man's hand. Imogen and Rhoda shrunk back. Whiteside used the barrel of the weapon to indicate what he wanted.

'Get out of the trap,' he ordered. 'Walk forward ten yards and put the ransom down on the ground. Then you can go back again.'

'What will you be doing?'

'Oh, I'll be counting the money, sir. Once I've seen that you've paid me the prescribed amount, I'll set the ladies free.'

The politician hesitated. He'd been told by Kee to keep

the kidnapper talking for as long as he could so that the detective could get into position. He picked up the bag and climbed out of the trap.

'I despise you for what you've done,' he said with utter contempt.

'I can live without your good opinion, sir.'

'You'll be hunted down, you know.'

Whiteside laughed. 'Nobody's caught up with me so far.'

'How do I know that you'll do as you promised?'

'You don't.'

'Put that weapon away.'

'I rather like holding it, if you don't mind.'

'Where have you been keeping them?'

'They've been kept safe and sound, as you can see,' said Whiteside with a quiet chuckle. 'Now stop asking questions. You're worse than Sir Marcus.'

Tunnadine was shaken. 'You've seen Sir Marcus?'

'Yes, sir, he was kind enough to make a generous donation to me. Look at it from my point of view. Why send one ransom note when two will bring in twice as much? Now walk forward ten paces and put it on the ground.'

Tunnadine's brain was whirring. If Sir Marcus had paid a ransom, he'd clearly been tricked because the two ladies were still being held. Not only was the kidnapper untrustworthy, he was holding a gun. The politician needed help.

Staying low, Alban Kee had crept along the margin of the field. He'd removed his hat so that it didn't protrude above the hedge. He also removed the weapon inside it so that it was ready for instant use. As far as he could see, there was nobody about. By the time that the kidnapper appeared,

Kee was on his knees, peering through a gap in the bushes and able to see the confrontation between the two men. He put his hat down and took out the gun from inside his coat. With a weapon in each hand, he felt almost invincible. His overconfidence was mistaken. He was concentrating so hard on the scene in front of him that he didn't hear Cullen drop down silently from a tree some twenty yards behind him. The Irishman approached stealthily. At the very moment that Kee stood up to shoot, the butt of a gun struck him hard on the back of the skull.

'How kind of you to remove your hat for me, sir!' said Cullen as the body fell to the ground in front of him. 'Now, if you'll be so good as to let me have those dangerous weapons of yours, I'll put them where they can do no harm.'

Imogen Burnhope could not bear to look. Standing not far away was the man she had agreed to marry yet from whom she'd fled. Beside her was the person she'd been led to accept as a devoted lover, only to find out that he'd betrayed her for monetary gain. Neither of them had any appeal whatsoever to her. Forced into a choice, she'd have to pick Tunnadine because he'd never threaten to kill her as Whiteside had done. On the other hand, he'd revile her when he realised what she'd done to him. Imogen was in agonies. She was held fast between two millstones.

'Come forward and put the money down,' said Whiteside, sharply, 'or I'll shoot you where you stand and leave you for the birds to feed on.'

Tunnadine looked around hopefully but Alban Kee was nowhere in sight. He walked forward ten paces, put the bag on the ground then stood there with his hands on his hips and glared.

'Meet me face to face, if you dare,' he challenged. 'I want to look you in the eye.'

'Very well,' replied Whiteside, jumping down from the trap. 'I will. You're a lucky man, Mr Tunnadine. You picked well. Imogen will make a lusty wife for you.'

'Shut your filthy mouth!'

Whiteside waved the gun. 'Remember which one of us is armed, sir.'

'I'm not afraid of you.'

The kidnapper strode towards him, then stopped when he was a couple of yards away. He met the politician's withering stare without flinching. He raised the gun.

'Tip the money onto the ground and count it for me.'

'It's all there.'

'For Imogen's sake, do as you're told. Don't make me shoot. She hates the sight of blood.' He moved forward and kicked the bag over. 'Count it!'

Tunnadine was forced to obey. Having hoped for intervention from Kee, he'd concluded that the detective was not able to offer him assistance. He was on his own but at least he had a chance against the kidnapper. It was clear that the man could not be cowed into submission by the sustained glower that Tunnadine had used so successfully against political opponents. Force was the only answer.

When he bent down, he unlocked the bag, opened it out and tipped the contents onto the grass. Thick wads of banknotes tumbled out. Whiteside was gleeful.

'Don't worry, sir,' he said. 'The lady is worth every penny of it.'

'You've got your money – set her free.'

'Count it first. I want to be certain that it's all there.'

'Oh, it is,' said Tunnadine, removing the band from the first wad. 'If you're so keen to have the money, take it.'

He flung the banknotes at Whiteside's face and distracted him long enough to get hold of the gun and turn the barrel away from him. They grappled violently. The politician was not accustomed to a brawl, however, and Whiteside slowly got the better of him. He swung his adversary around so that Tunnadine's back was to the hedge along one side of the field. An ear-splitting shot rang out and the fight was over. The politician stiffened, let out a muffled cry then dropped to the ground where he lay squirming. Rhoda screamed and Imogen almost fainted. Whiteside calmly bent down and swept the money into the leather bag.

Cullen's head popped up from behind the hedge.

'I told you I wouldn't miss from that distance,' he shouted.

CHAPTER EIGHTEEN

When they left the studio, the detectives felt that they'd been able to offer some hope and succour to Lucinda Graham. She was still in obvious pain but there had been a spectre of pleasure in her one visible eye when she was assured that her dreadful injuries would lead to the prosecution of her attacker. As Colbeck and Leeming clattered down the long staircase, the sergeant was still bemused.

'How can an educated man like Mr Tunnadine do such a thing?'

'I suspect he'll claim that he was provoked,' replied Colbeck. 'It may be that he was, of course, but no amount of provocation justifies what he did to her. Miss Graham was no match for someone much bigger and stronger than her.'

'I feel as if I want to give him a good hiding, sir.'

'I feel the same, Victor, but it's not our task to administer punishment. That must be left to those empowered to do so. All that we can do is to report what we've learnt then try to find Tunnadine.' He glanced over his shoulder. 'The main thing is that she's being well looked after now. Dolly will be a good nurse.'

'George Vaughan deserves thanks as well. He's the one who reported the assault.' Leeming was puzzled. 'Why couldn't Sir Marcus believe the word of his own nephew?'

'It was because he couldn't admit to himself that he'd made such a disastrous error when he selected Tunnadine as his future son-in-law. He took him at face value.'

'What will he do when he learns the truth?'

'It will be interesting to find out when we put it to him.'

Leaving the house, they walked to a nearby cab rank and hired their transport. On the journey back to Scotland Yard, they turned their attention to the disappearance of Imogen Burnhope, Rhoda Wills and the two men holding them.

'Will the ladies ever be released?' asked Leeming.

'I don't know. Whiteside and his friend will not keep them long. They'll become a hindrance. My guess is that they may not be the first victims to fall into their hands or, indeed, the last. Having gained so much money from this abduction,' said Colbeck, 'they might well look for a new target. There are, alas, many unworldly and unsuspecting young ladies in wealthy households in this country. Kidnap is a profitable trade.'

'That's only if they can keep one step ahead of us, sir.'

'We'll have to take longer strides, Victor.'

Arriving at their destination, they went straight to Tallis's office to deliver their report. He was patently uneasy.

'This could be awkward,' he said, fingering his moustache.

'I don't see why it should be, sir,' said Leeming. 'The facts are clear. There's no doubt that Mr Tunnadine beat her.'

'Her injuries are consistent with the assault she described,' added Colbeck.

'All that may be true,' said Tallis, uncertainly, 'but Miss Graham, it seems, is a kept woman. She admitted quite openly that she was Mr Tunnadine's mistress.'

'What difference should that make, sir?'

'You, of all people, shouldn't need to ask me that, Colbeck. Courts of law take a very dim view of the allegations made by ladies of easy virtue and they're probably right to do so. Such women know the dangers before they enter these entanglements. In the eyes of some judges – and I'm not saying that I agree with them – the word of someone like Miss Graham carries less weight than that of a Member of Parliament.'

'There's no law that sanctions brutality,' said Colbeck.

'He knocked her teeth out,' said Leeming, pointing to his mouth. 'How much more proof of a crime do you need?'

'Don't you dare to hector me, Sergeant,' warned Tallis.

'All that the young lady wants is justice, sir.'

'Then let's set the process in motion.' He picked up a document from his desk and handed it to Colbeck. 'This is a warrant for the arrest of Clive Tunnadine on a charge of wilful murder. I've gone above Sir Marcus's head this time, so there'll be no friendly magistrate who'll simply wag a finger at the prisoner then set him free. Take the gentleman into custody.'

'He's no gentleman,' said Leeming, spikily.

'Do you have Mr Tunnadine's address, sir?' asked Colbeck.

'Yes, I do,' replied Tallis, 'but the best place to find him is at his club in Pall Mall. He and Sir Marcus are often there together.'

'Sir Marcus needs to be told the truth about his prospective son-in-law.'

'Yes, he does – but don't expect him to believe it.'

Thanks to the loving care offered by the Reverend Percy Vaughan, his aunt was able to shake off her fatigue, get dressed and come downstairs. Though she was still extremely anxious about the fate of her daughter, she was no longer prone to attacks of black dejection. Sitting in a high-backed chair in the drawing room, Paulina felt comforted by the presence of her sister and the two children. Cassandra could still carp and fizz when roused but Emma was a soothing guest and her brother even more so. Paulina was flabbergasted when yet another member of the Vaughan family arrived at Burnside Manor. Dominic Vaughan walked into the room to be greeted with contrasting reactions.

'Father!' cried Emma, leaping up to embrace him. 'It's so lovely to see you!'

'You're a welcome sight,' said her brother, equally pleased.

'Why do you have to butt in, Dominic?' asked his wife, almost peevishly. 'We were managing quite well without you.'

'Don't be so inhospitable,' chided Paulina, accepting a kiss from her brother-in-law. 'We're delighted to see you, Dominic.'

'Thank you,' he said. 'I felt that my place was here.'

'You couldn't be more welcome.'

'That depends on what he does,' muttered Cassandra.

Emma heard the comment. 'Mother – that's unkind!'

'As you see, Father,' said his elder son, 'Aunt Paulina has made a recovery of sorts. She hated being left upstairs and cut off from the latest news. Not that there's been a great deal of that, however, I fear. Superintendent Tallis from Scotland Yard stayed here overnight, then went off early with Uncle Marcus. We haven't seen either of them since.'

'What happened to Inspector Colbeck and the sergeant?' wondered Vaughan.

'They travelled separately from London. All four of them were due to meet at Oxford but we don't really know why.'

'Oh dear!' said Vaughan with a laugh. 'We're all at sixes and sevens, aren't we? Virtually, my entire family has come here while almost everyone else has gone to Oxford. If the situation were not so fraught, this would have great comic potential. You could get a diverting sermon out of it, Percy.'

The curate disagreed. 'I don't think the good people of North Cerney need to be given insights into our trials and tribulations, Father,' he said. 'In public, I prefer to draw a veil of privacy over the whole thing.'

'Percy preaches wonderful sermons,' said Emma, smiling in approbation.

'He has a rare gift,' said Paulina.

Cassandra was impatient. 'Come on then, Dominic. Why are you here?'

'It was because I fondly imagined that you might be missing me, my dear.' He kissed her on the cheek. 'I certainly missed *your* company. What really prompted this visit, however,' Vaughan went on, 'is that I had twinges of guilt.'

'Why – what have you been up to?'

'It was nothing that would arouse your disapproval,

Cassandra. I suppose what I felt was a sense of failure. If, as it seems, Imogen and her maid were abducted by a soldier who selected her as a target some time ago, then I am partly to blame. I should have been more aware of her attraction to such a scheming individual. Conceive of my horror,' he said, 'when I learnt that one of the most trusted scouts at the college had supplied information about my niece to this rogue.'

'If *you* feel guilty, Father,' said Emma, 'you can imagine how I feel. I was there when Imogen met this man. I had no idea that he had set up the encounter so that he could get to know her name.'

'You are not to blame, Emma.'

'I'm bound to bear some responsibility. My eyes were blinkered.'

'That's no bad thing in a young lady of your age,' said Cassandra.

'Yes, it is, Mother. Imogen and I were altogether too innocent.'

'Loss of innocence can be both painful and sobering,' said the curate. 'I've seen it happen too many times. Sadly, it's the fate that's befallen Imogen.'

'Where is she now?' asked Paulina, dolefully. 'That's all I wish to know. What is happening to my daughter?'

Imogen Burnside and Rhoda Wills sat in the waiting room at Crewe station in a state of paralysis. Neither of them could speak. They had both witnessed something so horrendous that it had left their brains numb. A man had been shot dead right in front of them. They knew from experience that Whiteside and Cullen were quite merciless but they were shocked to see just how uncompromisingly ruthless they could be. A wave of despair had washed over Imogen. While she had no real love for Clive Tunnadine, she admired the way that he'd stood up to Whiteside and actually fought with him, only to be killed by a bullet in his back. It was an unjust reward for his bravery and the fault lay partly with her. If Imogen had not foolishly been drawn into a romance that had never really existed, Tunnadine would still be alive and her father would not have been compelled to part with a vast sum of money. As she recalled the sight of the dead body on the ground, she felt as if she had blood on her hands.

Rhoda was equally powerless to move or speak. While she had never liked Tunnadine, she was rocked by the way that he'd been murdered and overwhelmed with pity for him. In order to rescue Imogen, he was not only ready to part with a great deal of money. He was also prepared to take the risk of facing the kidnappers in person. Not having been present at the first attempted exchange, she was unaware that Tunnadine had himself done exactly what Cullen had done and shot someone from a concealed position. The irony of the situation therefore eluded her. All that she saw was a man being cut down for a courageous act. Rhoda could not excuse herself. When the doomed romance first started, she had colluded with Imogen and believed all the glib promises Whiteside made to her. The dazzling prospects had blinded her to the pleasures she may have enjoyed at home. Vernon Tolley would have been a most suitable husband for her and she regretted blocking him out entirely from her considerations. The coachman deserved better.

The other reason that kept both women seated in silence was that Whiteside and Cullen sat either side of them like a pair of human bookends. While Imogen and Rhoda had lost their tongues, the two men chatted away inconsequentially as if they didn't have a care in the world. Nobody seeing them so relaxed and untroubled would guess that they were accomplices in kidnap, extortion and murder. The porter whom they'd hired to look after their luggage put his head round the door. It was the signal that their train was on its way. Taking Imogen by the elbow, Whiteside helped her up. Cullen did the same for Rhoda. The two women were eased out onto the platform.

Imogen at last recovered her voice. 'Where are we going?'

'I'm about to honour my promise to you,' said Whiteside with a mock bow.

'Do you *dare* to speak of honour, sir?'

'The sergeant and I obey a strict code.'

'Does it have to involve intimidating me and my maid?'

'Nobody forced you to come, Imogen. You were a volunteer.'

'That was because I didn't realise what I was volunteering for,' she said.

'You came because I offered to take you off across the sea,' he recalled. 'And that's exactly what I'm about to do. So you may have to take back your sneers and your suspicions. I really am going to . . .'

The rest of the sentence was smothered beneath the train's uproar.

Evening shadows were darkening the streets of the capital when they ran Sir Marcus Burnhope to ground at his club.

Throbbing with frustration at the way that his money and his daughter had been snatched away from him, he'd been drinking heavily but bore himself up well. He and the two detectives adjourned to a private room.

'Do you have any news for me?' he demanded.

'We have no news about the whereabouts of the kidnappers and their victims,' replied Colbeck. 'Enquiries are still continuing.'

'Then why have you bothered to come here?'

'We need to speak on a related matter, Sir Marcus.'

'It had better be an important one. I'll not listen to tittle-tattle.'

'You've already made your feelings known on this subject,' said Colbeck, 'but there have been developments since you heard what your nephew, George Vaughan, had to say.'

'If you've come to repeat those gross allegations,' warned Sir Marcus, 'you can save your breath. Mr Tunnadine is being unfairly maligned. I've known him for years and will vouch for his good character.'

'We *saw* what he did, Sir Marcus,' said Leeming, unable to forget the injuries to Lucinda Graham. 'We have the name of the young lady in question and the address at which Mr Tunnadine visited her on a regular basis.'

'And,' Colbeck put in, 'we also have the names of the servants who were, in effect, witnesses to the assault because they heard their master's raised voice clearly and they went to Miss Graham's aid after he'd gone out of the house and slammed the door after him.'

'It's a conspiracy,' asserted Sir Marcus. 'They're all in this together.'

'You wouldn't say that if you met the victim.'

'I've no intention of doing so.'

'Well, Mr Tunnadine will meet her in a court of law,' said Leeming.

'Don't be ridiculous, man.'

'He has to answer for his mistakes, Sir Marcus.'

'And so do you, Sergeant,' blustered the other. 'You can't come bothering me at my club on a trumped-up charge against a senior politician who is set to do great things for this country. Get out, the pair of you!' He rose to his feet and pointed to the door. 'I shall inform Superintendent Tallis of your disgraceful behaviour.'

'It was the superintendent who sent us,' explained Colbeck, taking a document from his pocket. 'He gave me this warrant for the arrest of Mr Tunnadine on charges of murder and assault. We'd hoped to find the gentleman here with you but it seems that we've drawn a blank there.'

Sir Marcus wobbled slightly before dropping back into his chair. All the bluster he could manage would not outweigh the authority of an arrest warrant. If the superintendent had been convinced of Tunnadine's guilt with regard to the assault on the young lady, it could not be dismissed so easily. He looked for another way out.

'Listen,' he began, his tone more emollient, 'I'm sure that you needn't go to the lengths of an arrest. I was there when Mr Tunnadine's gun went off. It could have done so accidentally. It was certainly not murder in any shape or form. You saw him open his wallet and offer compensation. Was that the action of a killer?'

'It was the action of someone who wanted to buy off the

family of the victim,' said Leeming. 'He didn't do it as if he was actually sorry.'

'Well, he was – deep down.'

'We never got to explore the depths of Mr Tunnadine's soul,' said Colbeck, archly. 'It's a fabled territory I'd hesitate to survey. What concerns me is that he shot a man who was struggling with me at the time.'

'Yes, he shot him in order to assist *you*, Inspector.'

'I don't remember calling for help.'

'Nor would you have needed it,' said Leeming. 'I've never met the man yet who could get the better of you in a brawl, sir – not if the fight was on equal terms.'

'In this case, they were very unequal, Sergeant. I had an unwanted marksman prowling along the side of the field. His finger was too quick on the trigger.'

'The charge will never stick in court,' warned Sir Marcus.

'Which charge – the murder or the assault?'

'You can drop the second one right now, Inspector. I'm sure that there's been a misunderstanding. When my nephew first made the accusation, I wanted to dismiss it as a piece of frivolous invention. You, however,' he went on, 'have convinced me that this young woman might have sustained a few injuries but they would surely be the result of an unfortunate accident. Mr Tunnadine will make amends.'

'The lady will not be bought off,' said Leeming, staunchly.

'All I'm suggesting is that she receives adequate compensation.'

'How can you compensate a woman who has been robbed of her beauty?' asked Colbeck. 'Her front teeth were knocked out and she may never be able to see properly through one eye again. That's not what I would call an unfortunate accident, Sir Marcus. Lucinda Graham has been deprived of her living.'

'And what kind of living was that?'

'She was Mr Tunnadine's mistress.'

'That's a foul calumny, sir!' roared Sir Marcus. 'Do you think I'd let any man of doubtful character marry my daughter? Clive Tunnadine is a man of high moral standards – in fact, his father was a bishop. If some woman of questionable virtue tried to lead him astray,' he said, 'then I'm not surprised that he lashed out.'

'We have an address, Sir Marcus. He is the registered owner of the house.'

'He owns a large number of houses. It's a major source of his wealth.'

'This house has particular significance.'

'Yes,' retorted the other, 'it contains a conniving young woman who probably sought to extract money from him and was – quite rightly – slapped down.'

'I can see that you'll hear no criticism of Mr Tunnadine,' said Colbeck, levelly. 'I admire your loyalty, Sir Marcus, but I'm bound to bewail your judgement. We'll trouble you no further. All that we ask is that you tell us where we can find the gentleman so that we can make an arrest.'

Sir Marcus folded his arms and looked away as if refusing to cooperate with them. The detectives waited patiently. Realising that he could put himself in trouble, the old man eventually yielded up an answer.'

'I can give you an address, Inspector, but he's not at home.'

'How do you know that, Sir Marcus?'

'I sent a courier there not an hour ago because I was desperate to see him. One of the servants said that Tunnadine had left London and that the date of his return was uncertain.' He gave a thin smile. 'I'm sorry to rob you of the pleasure of what I'd describe as an unnecessary arrest. It appears that Mr Tunnadine is unavailable.'

Clive Tunnadine lay on a slab in the dank room that served as a temporary morgue at the police station in Crewe. Tiny pieces of white plaster had started to peel off the ceiling and drop down like unseasonal snowflakes. The windowpane was cracked. The smell of damp was pervasive. There were steep undulations in the paved surface of the floor. Beneath his shroud, Tunnadine was happily unaware of the shortcomings of his accommodation.

Twenty yards away, in another room, Alban Kee was giving his report of the incident that led to his employer's death. The details were taken down laboriously by Sergeant Dean, a policeman in his late thirties with an ill-fitting uniform and a husky voice.

'What happened then, sir?' he asked.

'The fellow got back into the trap and drove off.'

'What about the man who fired the shot?'

'He had a horse nearby,' said Kee.

'Are you able to describe him?'

'He was too far away for me to get a good look at him.'

In fact, Cullen had been close enough to the private detective to knock him unconscious but Kee was not going to admit that he'd been taken by surprise. In his version of events, he'd been hiding in the ditch on the other side of the field, waiting to leap to Tunnadine's assistance.

Unpropitious circumstances, he claimed, prevented him from doing anything more than firing a shot after the departing kidnappers.

'Why didn't you pursue them?' asked the sergeant.

'What chance would I have against the two of them?'

'You told me that you were armed.'

'I felt that my first duty was to Mr Tunnadine,' said Kee, piously. 'I ran across to him in the hope that I could stem the blood and get him to a doctor but it was in vain. The shot was fatal. The bullet was lodged in his heart.'

He paused as if expecting a compliment for the way he'd behaved. Kee was also troubled by the persistent ache at the back of his skull. A large lump marked the spot where he was struck but he didn't want to draw attention by putting a hand to it. The sergeant went through his notes and corrected a few spelling mistakes before looking up.

'You've given a concise and accurate report, sir,' he said, 'and that very rarely happens when people have witnessed a murder. They tend to be far too upset to remember all the details.'

'Nothing upsets me, Sergeant. I was in the Metropolitan Police for many years. I always keep my senses about me. In your position,' boasted Kee, 'I wouldn't just sit around and question a witness. I'd be out looking for the killer.'

'My men have already done that, sir.'

'Oh – I didn't realise.'

'As soon as you arrived with the body,' recalled the sergeant, 'and gave me a brief account of what had occurred, I sent four of my constables to the railway station. As you so rightly pointed out, the fastest way to leave Crewe was by train.'

'After what happened, they certainly wouldn't stay here.'

'You were preoccupied for a while with moving the corpse and talking to the undertaker so you were unaware that one of my men returned from the station. It's not far away.'

Kee was on his feet. 'What did they find out?'

'They found what they always find – that Crewe is a busy junction with masses of people swirling around on the different platforms. Further to what you told me, I had them searching for two men in the company of two young women, one of whom was . . . very comely.'

'Did they see anyone matching the description I gave you?'

'No, sir,' replied the sergeant with a melancholy smile. 'They looked high and low but it was all to no avail. What we will be able to establish in due course is where they hired the horse and the trap, but that's of little help. Like you, I've no doubt that the four of them fled by train. Unfortunately,' he concluded, 'we have no idea which direction they took.'

Lucinda Graham was overwhelmed by the kindness they'd shown to her. While others had turned her away, Dolly Wrenson had taken her in and George Vaughan had shown the same concern for her. The two women had been friends for years but saw each other infrequently. When they did so, they always compared the situations in which they found themselves. Dolly talked about the promising young artist with whom she'd fallen in love and made light of their relatively straitened living quarters. Yet she never envied Lucinda when she heard about the rich politician who kept her in luxury. Dolly could enjoy the company of her lover all day and all night. Lucinda was at the beck and call of a man who would arrive at the house without warning and expect her to meet his needs instantly. No amount of money would coax Dolly into such an arrangement, especially as she'd now learnt of Tunnadine's fits of rage.

'Why did you stay so long with a fiend like that?' asked Dolly.

'I suppose that I enjoyed the benefits too much.'

'He treated you like a—'

'Yes, yes,' said Lucinda, interrupting her. 'There's no need to put it into words. Some men are like that. You always have to make allowances for something and with Mr Tunnadine there were a lot of allowances to make.'

'Did you never think of leaving?'

'Yes, I did, but I was too lazy to strike out on my own.'

'Well,' said Dolly, sitting back, 'I thought that George had a few faults but compared to Mr Tunnadine, he's a saint.' She laughed. 'That's perhaps overstating it. Given our life together, I don't think he'd qualify for sainthood.'

'He's a good man, Dolly, and he's *yours*. Hold on to him.'

'I intend to, Lucinda.'

They were in the studio. Dolly was seated on a chair while her friend occupied the bed. Lucinda lay there fully clothed. When they'd first encouraged her to lie down, she fell asleep from sheer exhaustion and awoke to find Dolly smiling down at her. The warmth of the friendship she'd received took some of the sting out of her injuries. She and her friend looked up as they heard footsteps on the staircase outside. It was not long before George Vaughan entered with an armful of food collected from other tenants in the house.

'They all owed me favours,' he said, cheerily. 'We've enough to keep us going for days.'

'Oh, I couldn't eat a thing, George,' said Lucinda, sitting up.

'But you must be starving.'

'It's agony to put anything in my mouth.'

'Surely, it won't stop you drinking,' said Dolly, getting up to search for glasses. 'George has managed to scrounge some wine.'

'That was from Hadrian Speen on the ground floor,' explained the artist. 'He was so grateful when I told him that he has exceptional talent as a painter.'

'Does he?' asked Lucinda.

'Yes, he does. He mixes the most remarkable colours.'

Dolly was still searching. 'Where did we put those glasses, George?'

'Stop just for a moment,' requested Lucinda. 'I need to speak to you.'

'But you can do that while we're drinking the wine.'

'Come and sit beside me, Dolly – please.'

Dolly obeyed the summons and George Vaughan squatted on a stool. As they waited for Lucinda to speak, she glanced nervously at them as if expecting criticism.

'I've reached a decision,' she declared.

'There was no decision to reach,' said Dolly. 'You're staying here tonight and there's an end to it. The bed is all yours, Lucinda.'

'This is nothing to do with your kind offer.'

'Oh, I see.'

'My decision concerns Mr Tunnadine,' said Lucinda, gabbling. 'I know that you'll think I'm stupid but I'm not going to institute proceedings against him.'

'But you *must*,' insisted the artist. 'He could have killed you.'

'I just can't face him in court, George.'

'You heard what the detectives said to you. He must be prosecuted.'

'I'll refuse to give evidence.'

'We've *seen* the evidence,' said Dolly. 'We're looking at it right now. Inspector Colbeck and the sergeant have seen it as well, not to mention the servants at the house. We'll all bear witness against this vile man.'

'It's no use, Dolly. You and George can keep on at me as much as you like. I won't change my mind. Yes,' said Lucinda, 'it may seem weak and stupid on my part but it's what I want. Besides, it's not as if Mr Tunnadine will go scot-free. Inspector Colbeck told us that he has a murder charge hanging over him. I just want him out of my life forever,' she emphasised. 'Clive Tunnadine no longer exists for me.'

After returning to Scotland Yard to report back to the superintendent, Colbeck took Victor Leeming across to the Lamb and Flag and bought him a drink. They enjoyed a convivial break then they went off to their respective homes. Both were perturbed at the way that the investigation had stalled. They had no clue as to the whereabouts of the kidnappers or, indeed, of Clive Tunnadine. At every turn, they were baulked. Arriving home by cab, Colbeck did his best to suppress his disappointment but Madeleine was too familiar with his moods to be misled. After giving him a welcome, she took him into the drawing room and sat him down.

'You've just missed my father,' she said. 'He spent the evening here.'

'How is he?'

'He's remarkably well for his age. He sends his regards.'

'That was kind of him.'

'He kept pressing for details of this case,' said Madeleine, 'so it's as well he isn't here now. I can see that you've not made much progress.'

Colbeck smiled. 'Am I so transparent?'

'I guessed the moment that I saw you. Am I right, Robert?'

'Unhappily, you are,' he told her.

He gave her a swift account of the events of the day and she listened with sympathy. Madeleine was particularly upset to hear of the beating that Lucinda Graham had taken from Tunnadine.

'He's supposed to be a Member of Parliament,' she said, angrily. 'Is that the kind of man you want helping to run this country?'

'Well, I'd never vote for him, I can promise you that.'

'He should be sent to prison for what he did.'

'Let's not spoil our time together by talking about him. How is your work?'

'I've had a more rewarding time than you, by the sound of it, Robert. I've almost finished the latest painting. Would you like to see it?'

'I'd love to, Madeleine.'

He took her upstairs with an arm around her shoulders.

When they entered her studio, he lit an oil lamp and held it close to the easel so that it could shed the light. Madeleine lifted the cloth that covered her painting and a locomotive was revealed, hurtling towards them with dramatic effect. It seemed about to drive off from the canvas. Colbeck squeezed her in congratulation.

'It's wonderful,' he said, scrutinising every detail. 'You've improved so much over the years, Madeleine. The locomotives used to look so passive when you first took up painting. Now they race along. The sense of movement is quite breathtaking.'

'It's my idea of how *Cornwall* looked at top speed,' she said. 'The first time I painted her, she looked very static. Having driven her, Father insisted on giving me all the details. She was built at Crewe over ten years ago for the LNWR. Her weight was twenty-nine tons and her driving wheel was eight feet six inches. I was able to show the coal capacity, of course, but things like the boiler pressure and the traction power are mysteries that only people like Father know about. What do you think, Robert?'

Colbeck was highly complimentary and not only because Madeleine was his wife. She really had worked hard to hone her skills. As he looked with pride at the cosy surroundings of her studio, he found himself comparing it with the draughty attic inhabited by George Vaughan. He'd made obvious sacrifices in order to pursue his dreams of success. Colbeck was about to remark on the contrast when he heard the doorbell ring. A servant answered the door and the unexpected voice of Edward Tallis rose up from the hall. Colbeck and his wife descended the stairs to greet him. Madeleine offered him refreshment but Tallis declined the offer, and not simply because he was uncomfortable in the presence of women. Clearly, he'd come to speak to Colbeck as a matter of urgency. Madeleine therefore excused herself so that the two men could go into the drawing room.

'I apologise for calling at this late hour,' said Tallis, rotating the top hat he was holding by the brim, 'but I felt that you ought to know the news.'

'What's happened, sir?'

'I received a telegraph sent by Alban Kee. Doubtless, you remember him.'

'Yes,' said Colbeck, 'I do – though not with great fondness.'

'You may warm a little towards him when you hear what he's told us. It seems that he was employed by Mr Tunnadine and was present when the fellow was shot dead by one of the kidnappers. Needless to say, the telegraph is brief. Kee has promised to give us full details when he gets back tomorrow morning. I'd like you to be there when he turns up at Scotland Yard.'

'Oh, I'll be there,' said Colbeck, sensing that a new stage of the investigation had suddenly opened up, 'and I'll make sure that Victor Leeming is there as well.'

'It looks as if that arrest warrant for Tunnadine will not be needed.'

'Apparently not – Sir Marcus will be shocked to hear of his death.'

'He'll also wonder why the man didn't confide that he, too, had received a ransom demand. Kee may be able to explain that. He will supervise the return of the body to

London before coming on to us with the full story of what happened.'

'From where was his telegraph sent, sir?'

'It came from the railway station in Crewe.'

Colbeck thought about Madeleine's latest painting. It featured a locomotive that had been built at the railway works in the same town. A smile touched his lips.

'Why do you find that amusing?' asked Tallis, gruffly.

'I'm not so much amused as excited, sir,' replied Colbeck, 'and I'm bound to ask a teasing question.'

'What is it?'

'When does a coincidence become an omen?'

CHAPTER NINETEEN

Sir Marcus Burnhope was troubled. After the detectives left him at his club, he went up to his room and sat in a chair with a glass of whisky beside him. Sleep was out of the question. Too many unanswerable questions plagued him. While the fate of his daughter still dominated his mind, the figure of Clive Tunnadine kept popping up and his friend was now in a slightly different guise. The allegations that Colbeck and Leeming had presented to him only served to infuriate Sir Marcus and forced him back on the defensive. Now that he was alone, however, and able to review what they told him with a degree of dispassion, niggling doubts began to appear. He recalled some joking remarks made in the House of Commons about Tunnadine, the kind of silly banter in which he never indulged and, as a rule, studiously ignored. Then there were the knowing looks that Tunnadine sometimes attracted and the nudges he'd seen between other politicians when his friend approached them. The jokes, looks and nudges now took on some significance.

Yet he still couldn't believe that Tunnadine was capable of the violence his nephew had described and the detectives had confirmed. Nor could he entertain the thought that his friend had kept a mistress. Tunnadine had always seemed so fully committed to political affairs that he had no time for dalliances of any kind and no discernible inclination towards them. The two men had sat on committees together, prepared reports for the Prime Minister and even travelled abroad as colleagues. In all the years that Sir Marcus had known him, there was not the slightest hint that Tunnadine had a secret life involving deception, immorality and violent behaviour. As he downed his whisky, he veered back to his original belief. Lucinda Graham's accusation, he concluded, was the work of a devious woman who sought to wrest money out of a decent man by threatening to blacken his name. The arrest warrant carried by Colbeck should – in Sir Marcus's opinion – have borne the name of the supposed victim of the assault. She was the real criminal.

Satisfied that he had rationalised the situation, he was ready to retire to bed. It was then that the letter arrived from Superintendent Tallis. It was delivered by a member of the club staff who awaited his response. When Sir Marcus read the contents of the missive, his bleary eyes widened in absolute horror. He immediately gave the man orders that he should be awakened at dawn. In fact, he needed no call next day because he found it impossible to doze off during the night. When he set off from the club in a cab, fingers of light were poking through the gloom of the capital. The train from Paddington took him to Oxford where he changed platforms and caught an express to Shrub Hill.

As on a previous occasion, he'd arranged for a telegraph to be sent to the station, asking for someone to ride to Burnhope Manor to alert his coachman. Vernon Tolley was therefore waiting to open the door of the landau and lower the step.

'Welcome back, Sir Marcus!' he said, politely.

'Drive me home.'

'I hope that you had a good journey.'

'You heard me, Tolley,' snapped the other. 'Do as you're told and get me back to Burnhope Manor as soon as possible.'

Dominic Vaughan and his elder son were up far too early for breakfast. To work up an appetite and to pray for the release of the hostages, they walked the quarter of a mile to the village church and let themselves in. It was Percy Vaughan who became the senior figure now, shepherding his father to the altar rail and kneeling beside him to recite a long prayer that somehow brought them closer together than they had been for years. Little had been said on the journey there. On the way back, however, father and son were able to have a proper conversation.

'That was a very moving prayer, Percy.'

'The words just came to me.'

'They were both poignant and appropriate,' said Vaughan. 'I'm so grateful that you decided to come to Burnhope Manor.'

'I was a prey to the same impulse as you, Father. I felt I was needed here.'

'If truth be told, you've been far more use than your mother. There are times when her presence can be a little abrasive and your aunt needs a more tranquil personality at her bedside.'

'I've only done what I've been trained to do.'

'It's more a case of instinct than training. You have a knack that nobody else in the family possesses. Emma is too inexperienced, poor girl, and George is too skittish. Had he been trying to comfort your aunt, he'd have made her feel worse rather than better.'

'I'd absolve him of that charge,' said the curate. 'What's happened to Imogen and her maid seems to have calmed George down immeasurably and given him a sense of maturity. It's made a great impact on all of us, of course, but it's taught my brother a valuable lesson about family values.'

'You could be right, Percy.'

Listening to the birdsong, they strolled on down the country lane. Dominic Vaughan was aware of a natural togetherness absent for a very long time.

'Your aunt said a strange thing to me last evening,' he said.

'What was it, Father?'

'Perhaps it's best if I don't repeat it. You might feel embarrassment.'

His son was curious. 'Was it to do with Imogen's engagement, by any chance?' he asked. 'If it was, then Aunt Paulina has already confided in me that she was not entirely happy with their choice of husband.'

'When I spoke to her, she added a rider.'

'Oh?'

'Your aunt said in passing that *you'd* be a far more suitable candidate for your cousin's hand.' Vaughan saw his son's confusion and felt remorseful. 'There,' he went on, 'I told you that it might bring a blush to your cheek.'

'Aunt Paulina is unwell,' said the other, covering his unease with a smile. 'I shouldn't pay too much attention to what she says. When I sat with her yesterday, her mind wandered constantly.'

Pretending to treat his aunt's comment as unimportant, he was instead deeply touched by it. Percy Vaughan had always felt that nobody at Burnhope Manor had ever taken him seriously. They were more interested in his brother's antics or in his sister's latest news. The curate had been slightly peripheral. The fact that someone had now spoken up for him filled him with a joy that was clouded by apprehension. Until the release of his cousin, any hopes he might nurse were illusory.

The two of them had almost reached the house when the landau came down the drive at speed and scattered gravel everywhere as it slid to a halt. Sir Marcus was on his feet at once. The coachman opened the door, let down the step and stood out of the way. As Sir Marcus alighted, they rushed across to him.

'You seem to be in a devil of a hurry,' observed Vaughan.

'I've had the most alarming news, Dominic.'

'Is it about Imogen?' asked his nephew in concern.

'Indirectly, it is,' replied Sir Marcus. 'A letter from Superintendent Tallis was delivered to my club. It informed me that Clive Tunnadine had been shot dead by one of the kidnappers. The only logical explanation for his confronting them is that they'd demanded a ransom from him as well.'

'Tunnadine was murdered?' gasped Vaughan.

'God rest his soul!' said the curate.

'The superintendent advised me to return here. He

believes that they may contact me with yet another demand. Their greed knows no bounds,' wailed Sir Marcus. 'Not content with tricking money out of me, they did the same to Clive Tunnadine then killed him. The villains are playing games with us – and there's still no sign of Imogen.'

'What about Rhoda Wills?' murmured Tolley. 'She's there as well.'

The hotel room in Crewe had been cramped and uncomfortable but it was almost luxurious when compared to the one in which they'd spent the night. It was small, sparsely furnished, uncarpeted and flavoured by an odour faintly redolent of horse manure. Imogen had taken the single bed, leaving Rhoda to occupy the sagging armchair. Neither of them slept a wink. The proximity of their captors made them too afraid to remove any clothing so they wore the same crumpled dresses they'd had on for days. Tunnadine's murder preoccupied them.

'Are they going to do the same to us?' asked Imogen, trembling.

'I think they have other plans,' said her maid, worriedly.

'It's frightening.'

What frightened Rhoda was the hungry look that had come into Cullen's eyes whenever he gazed at her. Imogen had patently been reserved for Whiteside, leaving the maid to his accomplice and Rhoda was deeply disturbed. The women had been so far unmolested but it was only a matter of time before the kidnappers moved in to enjoy their spoils.

'Do you hate me very much?' asked Imogen.

'I don't hate you at all.'

'But I was the one who landed you in this torment.'

338

'I've told you before,' said Rhoda, firmly. 'I was beguiled just as much as you. I was ready to believe false promises. If anyone should take the blame, it's me for urging you to take such a bold step into the dark.'

'I thought I was stepping into bright light,' admitted Imogen, sadly. 'Its glare completely blinded me to potential dangers.' She embraced Rhoda. 'Will we ever get away from this hell?'

The maid was determined. 'I think we have to – before it's too late.'

Given the history that existed between them, the detectives were never going to be pleased to see Alban Kee. They regarded him as the bad apple that had to be thrown away before it spread its mould to the rest of the barrel. Tallis looked at him with disdain, Colbeck's manner was cold and Leeming's hostility to the private detective was plain. Nevertheless, the man had to be endured because he possessed information that was vital in the hunt for the kidnappers.

They were in the superintendent's office at Scotland Yard and Kee was enjoying his moment as the centre of attention. Looking tired, he sat between Colbeck and Leeming. Tallis opened the questioning.

'Why did Mr Tunnadine employ you?'

'He'd lost faith in the abilities of the Metropolitan Police,' replied Kee with a sly smile, 'and wanted someone who was not so fettered by official procedure.'

'Then he chose the right person,' said Colbeck, smoothly. 'When you were here in the Detective Department, you never let official procedure hinder you in your pursuit of illegal bribes.'

Kee struck back. 'I resent that comment, Inspector.'

'And I resent what you did in the name of Scotland Yard.'

'I was dismissed unfairly on hearsay evidence.'

'We were glad to provide it,' said Leeming. 'It came from a trusted source.'

'Let's move on,' said Tallis, asserting his authority. 'The mistakes of the past can stay there. I want Kee to explain exactly what happened from the moment that he was hired by Mr Tunnadine.'

Alban Kee had his story ready and he told it without digression. Putting their dislike of the man aside, they listened intently. Kee's account was reasonably accurate until he reached the moment when he and Tunnadine came to the place appointed for the exchange of money and hostages. The private detective claimed that he'd been hiding in the ditch when the fatal shot had been fired. He would never confess to his former colleagues that he'd been knocked unconscious because of his incompetence. Colbeck was interested in the report he gave to the local constabulary.

'With whom did you deal at Crewe police station?'

'Sergeant Dean,' said Kee, 'and he responded promptly. His men asked questions at the railway station but nobody could remember the four people described to them. The sergeant also sent constables to nearby stables. One of them recalled hiring a trap and a horse to a man he said had the bearing of a soldier. The animals and the vehicle were returned at the time promised. Where the man who'd hired them went, nobody knows but I'd wager anything you choose that he and the hostages travelled by train.'

'That's a fair supposition,' said Colbeck. 'Thank you,

Kee. Your report was admirably concise and lucid.' He turned to Tallis. 'We must go to Crewe at once.'

'I'll come with you,' said the superintendent.

'There's no need for that, sir. Your place is here. Apart from anything else, there's the possibility that the kidnappers will try to extort money from Sir Marcus for a third time. They're brazen enough to do it. You need to be here to advise him.'

'Well, yes,' conceded Tallis, 'there's some truth in that.'

'This is the hub of the investigation. Remain here in order to control it. The sergeant and I will make our way to Crewe to see if we can pick up any clues.'

'Take me with you,' said Kee.

'That wouldn't be appropriate.'

'I can't think of anyone who'd be more appropriate in the hunt for the killer, Inspector. I was there when it happened. I have a right to assist you. It's the least I can do for Mr Tunnadine.'

'You've already done enough by bringing his body back to London and giving us the information we required,' said Tallis. 'Colbeck is right. Your involvement in this case is over. I bid you good day.'

'But I might be useful,' stressed Kee.

'We exhausted your usefulness to this department years ago.'

'I deserve a chance to prove myself, Superintendent.'

'You had that chance when Mr Tunnadine hired you,' Colbeck pointed out, 'and you failed. There's nothing more to be said.'

Kee continued to protest but his entreaties were in vain. Tallis ordered him to leave. Leeming got up to show him out then closed the door firmly behind him. The prospect of leaving London sparked off his usual reluctance.

'What do we do when we reach Crewe?' he asked.

'We find out where the four of them went and go in pursuit,' said Colbeck.

'But they could have gone hundreds of miles away by now.'

'Then that's where we'll hunt them down. Gather your things together now, Sergeant. When I've dispatched an important letter, it will be time to leave.'

'What's this about an important letter?' said Tallis.

'I think that Lucinda Graham should be made aware of Mr Tunnadine's death,' said Colbeck. 'Any prosecution of him is impossible now, of course, but it will make her sleep more soundly if she knows that he is no longer a threat to her.'

Coming to the studio in Chelsea had been the salvation of Lucinda Graham. She was among friends who cared and who did not sit in judgement on her because of her way of life. She was treated solely as a victim in dire need of love and comfort. Lucinda now hurt far less and felt much better. Over a late breakfast with Dolly Wrenson and George Vaughan, she was even able to talk about something other than her ordeal at the hands of her lover.

'What made you become an artist, George?' she asked.

'I was called to it,' he replied. 'I didn't choose art – it chose me.'

'You make it sound like a vocation.'

'That's exactly what it is, Lucinda. It's what I was born to be. My brother, Percy, is a curate in a little church in

Gloucestershire. From the age of ten, he wanted to be a clergyman. In the same way that Percy answered his call, I answered mine.' He waved an arm. 'This is my church. Dolly is my congregation.'

Dolly shook with mirth. 'I hope that your brother's congregation doesn't behave the way that I do or he might be in serious trouble. I can't see the ladies in his parish posing in the nude, somehow.' She pointed to the easel. 'You've seen what George can do. He can bring me to life on canvas.'

'I captured your essence, that's all,' he said.

'It's so wonderful that you can work together,' said Lucinda. 'I envy you.'

'Artists are always looking for models.'

'How could I be a model with a face like this?'

'The bruises will go and the eye will heal,' said Dolly, encouragingly. 'Keep your mouth closed and you'll be as beautiful as ever.' She heard footsteps on the stairs. 'Who's that coming up here?' she wondered. 'You didn't forget to pay the rent, did you, George?'

'No, no,' he said, 'I gave the landlady a month in advance.'

'I'll see who it is.'

Dolly got up and crossed to the door, opening it at the precise moment when a young man was about to knock. He was a courier from Scotland Yard. When he'd delivered his letter, he bade farewell and trotted off down the stairs. Dolly closed the door behind him and crossed over to Lucinda.

'It's for you,' she said.

Her friend drew back. 'It's not from *him*, is it?' she said, fearfully. 'If it is, I don't even want to touch it. Open it for me, Dolly.'

'It has your name on it.'

'Just find out who sent it.'

Dolly opened the letter and saw Colbeck's name at the bottom. When she read what he'd written in his neat hand, she let out a whoop of surprise.

'What is it?' asked the artist.

'Inspector Colbeck has sent news that he felt Lucinda should hear.' She handed the letter to her friend. 'Take it, please. It will cheer you.'

When she read the letter, Lucinda shuttled between joy and disbelief, thrilled that the man she hated had been killed yet uncertain that such a miracle could really have occurred. George Vaughan was baffled. He looked to Dolly for enlightenment.

'Lucinda's prayers are answered,' she told him. 'Mr Tunnadine is dead.'

Euston station was filled with its customary pandemonium when the detectives arrived there. Victor Leeming had been bracing himself against the possibility of being away from home for days but he realised how selfish his concern was. The inspector was in the same position, leaving a wife behind him for an unspecified period. Colbeck would suffer the same pangs of separation.

'It's time I called you to mind, sir,' said Leeming.

Colbeck grinned. 'I flattered myself that I was always in your thoughts, Victor.'

'You'll feel sad to leave your wife behind you while we go to Crewe.'

344

'No, I won't.'

'You'll miss her, surely?'

'Not this time,' said Colbeck. 'Madeleine is coming with us.'

Leeming was taken aback. It was true. Madeleine had been waiting for them by the bookstall. When she saw them coming, she walked over to them to receive a kiss from her husband and a look of astonishment from Leeming. Colbeck bought the tickets, then led them to the appropriate platform. The train was already waiting for them so they found an empty compartment and climbed in. Having escaped the hullabaloo outside, Colbeck was able to justify the step he'd taken.

'The two ladies have been through a hideous experience,' he said. 'They've not only been abducted and used as pawns by these men. They witnessed the murder of someone they knew well. Such an event would unnerve anyone.'

'It would terrify me,' confessed Madeleine. 'You'll remember how upset I was in similar circumstances.'

'If and when we rescue them, they'll be distraught.'

'They'll be distraught and distracted, Robert.'

'With the best will in the world, Victor, you and I may not be the ideal comforters.'

'I see what you mean, sir,' said Leeming. 'They need another woman.'

'Fortunately, Madeleine was at hand.'

'I think you might have phrased that differently,' she complained. 'I'm not simply there like an umbrella that can be reached out of the stand on a rainy day. I'm grateful for the chance to help but I'll not be taken for granted.'

Colbeck was penitent. 'I take back what I said without hesitation.'

'I think you should.'

'You can offer a priceless service to us, Madeleine, far greater than any umbrella could manage. There's no doubting the fact that Imogen Burnhope and her maid will be relieved to see Victor and me, but I fancy that they'll be even more pleased to set eyes on you.'

Rhoda Wills wedged the chair against the door, then they shoved the bed against it to add more resistance. She opened the window, looked down, then signalled to Imogen.

'There's nobody about. You go first.'

'It's too dangerous, Rhoda.'

'It's far more dangerous to stay here. You saw what they did to Mr Tunnadine. Do you want to end up like that?' Imogen crossed to the window and looked out with trepidation. 'Yes, it may look difficult but think of the number of times you've ridden a horse and taken it over a fence. That needs a lot of courage. Show the same bravery now,' urged Rhoda. 'Lower yourself onto the roof below, work your way along it, then climb down the drainpipe to the ground.'

'I can't do it,' said Imogen, pulling back. 'It's impossible in this dress.'

'Lift it up and tuck it in. That's what I'll do.'

'What if we fall?'

'We won't fall if we take care. Please hurry. They'll be here any moment.'

Imogen was in two minds. Part of her wanted to follow her maid's bold plan of escape. Their room was on the first floor. The roof of an extension was only feet below. It would be relatively easy to climb onto it. Getting down to the ground from there would be more problematical. Rhoda was so eager to get away that she was even prepared to jump from the roof. Imogen's desire for escape was balanced by her fear of injury and retribution. Even if she got to the ground without tearing her dress or breaking an ankle, she couldn't expect to outrun the two men. They would catch the fugitives and punish them accordingly. Rhoda's scheme consisted of leaving the hotel and hiding nearby but they had no idea where they were or what cover was available.

'We must go now,' insisted Rhoda, trying to instil some confidence in her. 'What they have in mind for us may be far worse than what we've already suffered. They think they've broken our spirits, but they haven't.'

'No,' said Imogen, reviving. 'They haven't.'

'I'll help you out of the window.'

'You go first, Rhoda. I'll follow you.'

Clambering onto the roof with a dress to hamper her was not easy but Rhoda did it eventually. She turned to help Imogen, advising her not to look down and guiding her with both hands. They were now both on the roof of the extension, edging their way to the corner so that they could descend by means of a thick drainpipe. When they got to the second stage of their flight, they heard an ominous sound. Someone was trying to get into their room. Their fortifications were holding firm but the door was being rattled with ferocity. Suddenly, the noise stopped.

Terrified of being caught, Rhoda changed her plan. She lay face down on the roof and lowered herself slowly backwards until she was hanging from the guttering. She then let go and dropped heavily to the ground, jarring both legs as she did so but causing no real injury. She begged Imogen to do the same thing and the latter copied her maid, soiling her dress as she worked her way down the roof then dangling from the guttering. Rhoda reached up to steady her.

'Leave go now,' she said.

Imogen obeyed and dropped to the ground, falling over but so pleased to have got free that she almost shouted with joy. Rhoda helped her up and they hugged each other excitedly.

'We did it,' said Imogen. 'We did it, Rhoda.'

When they tried to run off, however, Whiteside was blocking their way.

'Where do you think *you're* going?' he asked, menacingly.

The return to Crewe brought memories rushing back for all three of them. Years before, it had been the scene of an incident that set the detectives off on one of their most challenging assignments. When a trunk was being unloaded from the roof of a railway carriage, it fell and landed on a large hat box, breaking the strap so that the lid flipped open. Out of the hatbox rolled a human head. It had taken Colbeck and Leeming a long time to match a dead body to it and to identify a killer. In the later stages of the investigation, Madeleine had more than proved her worth. The severed head at Crewe station had taken them all the way to that year's Derby at Epsom. The present case, they felt certain, would involve a different itinerary.

While he went off to the police station, Colbeck left Madeleine in the waiting room with Leeming. Sergeant

Dean was very helpful, especially when he realised to whom he was talking. He'd been a humble constable when Colbeck was in the town investigating the earlier murder and had been very impressed by the thoroughness of the Railway Detective. To be able to assist him now was in the nature of an honour. Dean told his visitor everything he'd already heard from Alban Kee with a few minor discrepancies. Colbeck was curious.

'What did you make of Mr Kee?'

'Is he a friend of yours?' asked Dean, cautiously.

'No, he's far from it, Sergeant.'

'Then my impression was that he didn't tell me the full truth, sir. Like you, I'm used to listening to people giving long accounts of crimes and I've learnt to pick out the wheat from the chaff. In fairness,' he went on, 'there wasn't much chaff with Mr Kee's story but I thought I detected some.'

'I think that you're about to confirm my own reservations,' said Colbeck. 'What seemed perverse to me was that he should try to hide in a ditch which was difficult to get out of when he would have had far better protection behind the hedge on the other side of the field.'

'That's exactly what I was about to say, Inspector. Mr Kee gave me the precise location so I rode out there to investigate the site. Nobody would choose the ditch over the hedge.'

'What did you infer from that?'

'Well,' said Dean, rubbing the side of his nose with a finger, 'I think he *was* behind that hedge but was somehow prevented from interfering. He lied to us.'

'You've sound instincts, Sergeant.'

'Thank you, sir. But I discovered something else that

may help you. When I drove back to the railway station, I timed the journey. The stables which they'd used are very close. Mr Kee gave me the exact time of the murder and the kidnappers would have gone immediately to the station. Allowing time for them to return what they'd hired,' said Dean, reaching for a sheet of paper on his desk, 'I had a rough idea of the first train they'd be able to catch.'

'They certainly wouldn't have wanted to linger in Crewe,' said Colbeck, 'because they'd know the murder would soon be reported by Kee.'

Dean handed over the paper. 'This is a list of trains that left here in the hour after they'd returned to the stables. My guess,' said Dean, 'is that, before they met up with Mr Tunnadine, they'd already booked tickets.' Colbeck scanned the list. 'Is that of any use to you, Inspector?'

'It's invaluable. I congratulate you.'

'Thank you, sir.'

'I think I know exactly the train that they took.'

'How did you work that out, sir?'

'It was my first thought,' said Colbeck, 'and you've given me the evidence to buttress it. The men we're after are former soldiers – Captain Whiteside and Sergeant Cullen. They've extracted a substantial amount of money out of two separate people, one of whom they shot dead. What they need now is a hiding place.'

'That's true.'

'They've chosen somewhere they think we're unlikely to find them.'

'Have you worked out where it might be?'

'I think so. Our superintendent searched army records to identify these two individuals. They're deserters who live on their wits. Manus Cullen was born in Dublin. This is the train they caught,' decided Colbeck, tapping the sheet of paper. 'It would have taken them to Holyhead. They were on their way to Ireland.'

Choppy water made the crossing very unpleasant. The one time that Imogen and Rhoda had been afloat before was on the placid surface of a lake where the pull of the oars caused the only ripples. The sea was altogether more aggressive, hurling its waves at the side of the vessel as if indignant that anyone should dare to ride upon its back. Both of them felt so sick that all they could think about was the heaving of their stomachs. Terence Whiteside, on the other hand, suffering no discomfort, was very much aware of their escape attempt and vowed that they wouldn't be given a second chance to get away. While they were on board, of course, there was no possibility of flight but he nevertheless separated them so that they could not devise a plot. He and Imogen sat side by side in a tiny cabin while Cullen and Rhoda were seated on deck together. As long as the women were kept apart, they'd never try to run away.

They were in sight of the Irish coast before Imogen's queasiness slowly abated. She finally found her voice again.

'Why did you have to kill Mr Tunnadine?' she asked.

'I didn't do so, Imogen,' he reminded her. 'It was the sergeant who fired the shot. Mr Tunnadine disobeyed his instructions, you see. He not only had a weapon on him, he brought an accomplice who hid behind the hedge ready to shoot at me. His name was Alban Kee. After he'd knocked the gentleman out, the sergeant relieved him of his business card as well as the two weapons he carried. In other words,' he argued, 'Tunnadine had planned to have us killed by his accomplice. We acted in self-defence.'

'What you did was appalling.'

'Your memory is letting you down, Imogen.'

'You both deserve to be hanged.'

'We've escaped the noose before,' he said with a laugh, 'and will no doubt do so many times more. But I obviously need to remind you of some of the things you said in your letters. You didn't love Tunnadine. In fact, you grew to dislike him intensely and feared being married to him. I was a far more acceptable bridegroom.'

'That was before I knew your true character.'

'Oh, you still have a lot to learn about me yet, Imogen,' he warned. 'We are going to live together in a fine house as man and wife – except that our union will not be blessed by the church. Don't let that trouble you. "Love is not love which alters when it alteration finds." You'll be a wife in reality if not in the eyes of God.'

'Never!' she said, recoiling from him. 'I hate you for what you did.'

He chuckled. 'Then I'll have to woo you all over again, won't I?'

'I'd die sooner than let you touch me.'

'That's not a practical alternative for you at the moment,' he said, seizing her arm. 'You'll do exactly what I want when I want it. At the same time, naturally, your maid will be obliging the sergeant. We were annoyed when you tried to escape from that hotel in Anglesey but we were also rather pleased.'

Imogen was astonished. 'Pleased?'

'Yes, it showed that the pair of you had more spirit than

we'd imagined. That was an interesting discovery. I like spirit in a woman. All my previous "wives" have had that, Imogen,' he told her with a grin. 'Take heart from the fact that you'll be keeping up a noble tradition.'

Madeleine Colbeck was not looking forward to the short voyage. While she was delighted to be working alongside her husband, the prospect of sailing across what looked like a turbulent sea was rather forbidding. Her anxieties were negligible compared to those of Victor Leeming. He was squirming in sheer terror. Even though he'd once sailed with Colbeck to New York and back, he was no experienced sailor. In fact, that voyage had made him resolve never to leave dry land again but he had no choice. His only hope was that a mistake had been made and that the fugitives had not, after all, fled to Ireland. He and Madeleine stood on the windswept quay and watched the waves pounding remorselessly away. Gulls wheeled and dipped in the air above them, their piercing cries making conversation difficult for Leeming and Madeleine. They were surrounded by scores of other passengers who'd made the journey to Holyhead.

It was a long time before Colbeck eventually returned. Madeleine was relieved to see him at last and Leeming was praying that he'd tell them their visit to Ireland was unnecessary. In fact, however, he was waving something in his hand.

'I've booked our passages,' he said. 'We'll be sailing within the hour.'

'The sea is far too rough, sir,' protested Leeming.

'You'll soon get used to that once we're aboard, Victor.'

'Are you sure that they went to Ireland?' asked Madeleine.

'Yes,' replied her husband. 'I've just spoken to the booking clerk. It looks as if they're travelling as two couples. The names of Mr and Mrs Terence Whiteside were in the book alongside those of Mr and Mrs Manus Cullen. From the point of view of the ladies, I fear, they're very much unholy alliances.'

The wind stiffened and the waves continued to lash the quayside, prompting the apprehensive Leeming into a whole series of protests. Madeleine's qualms were stilled now that she was holding her husband's arm. She began to see the voyage as an adventure. When their vessel finally arrived and unloaded its passengers, they joined the long queue that filed aboard. None of them looked over their shoulder to see the last passenger step out of the shadows in order to join the ship.

Alban Kee was determined not to miss out on the chase.

CHAPTER TWENTY

Win Eagleton knew how to choose her moment. She busied herself in the kitchen until all her chores had been done, then she went in search of him. Vernon Tolley was leaning against the carriage, pressing tobacco into his clay pipe before he lit it. He puffed hard for a few seconds. The horses stood between the shafts in readiness for instant departure, should they be called upon. Nobody else was about as Win padded across the courtyard. Wrapped up in thought, the coachman was completely unaware of her approach. It was only when she stood directly in front of him that he knew that she was there.

'I know what you're thinking,' she said with a sympathetic smile.

'Do you?'

'Yes, Vernon, you're thinking about that hat in the Mickleton Tunnel.'

'That wasn't on my mind at all, Win,' he said. 'I was just wondering when Sir Marcus would need me again. I was told to stand by.'

'Where is he going?'

'He may not be going anywhere. The situation seems to change by the hour.'

'You know about Mr Tunnadine, don't you?' she said in a whisper. 'They were overheard talking about it at breakfast. What an awful thing to happen to him! He was shot dead. The wedding will not take place now, but then,' she added, slyly, 'I don't suppose that it would ever have done so.'

'What do you mean?'

'Well, they're not coming back, are they?'

'Don't say that, Win!' he protested.

'It's no good pretending.'

'That's not what I'm doing.'

'Both of them disappear, Rhoda's hat is found in a tunnel and a man is murdered in cold blood. If that doesn't convince you, what will?'

'I'm busy,' he said, moving away. 'You'll have to excuse me.'

She followed him across the yard. 'But you're only waiting for Sir Marcus.'

'I'd prefer to do it alone.'

'Why are you always avoiding me?'

He stopped and faced her. 'I'm not avoiding you, Win. I just want to be left on my own. I have things to think about.'

'But that's why I came, Vernon. I hate to see you moping.'

'I'm not moping.'

'Yes, you are and you've been doing it for days. I simply want to help you.'

'You can do that best by letting me get on with my job.'

'Smoking a pipe and resting against the carriage – what kind of work is that?'

'I may be needed at any moment.'

'It's not only Sir Marcus who needs you,' she said, softly. 'We all do, Vernon. Everyone in the kitchen is worried about you. We know what Rhoda meant to you and we're so sorry that she'll never . . .' Feigning grief, she used the back of her hand to wipe away a tear. 'I loved her as well. That's why I'm in mourning, too.'

'Rhoda is not dead,' he insisted.

'No, no, of course not,' she said, hurriedly. 'She's still alive and so is Miss Imogen. They'll come back very soon and we'll all be happy. It's wrong to let the waiting get us down. We must be patient. However,' she added, 'we have to be ready just in case anything does go wrong.' She inhaled deeply. 'I've always loved the smell of your tobacco. Whenever you light that pipe, I like to be near you.'

After a last puff, he tapped the pipe against his heel and the tobacco spilt onto the ground. He put the pipe in his pocket and looked her in the eye.

'Yes,' he said with slow deliberation, 'there *is* a chance that Rhoda may never come back. There is a chance that something bad has happened to them. I accept that. If that's the way it is, then I know exactly what I'd do.'

'What's that, Vernon?'

'I'd leave Burnhope Manor and look for work elsewhere. I'd move far away, Win. There's nothing to keep me here.'

Stung by the rebuff, she turned on her heel and scuttled back to the kitchen.

Tolley was glad to have shaken her off. Alone at last, he sighed deeply.

'Where are you, Rhoda?' he pleaded. 'Where *are* you?'

* * *

357

Rhoda Wills took the warning seriously. She'd crossed the Irish Sea with a large number of passengers but she'd been told what would happen if she tried to shout for help. Cullen never left her side. When he sat beside her, she could feel the pistol beneath his coat. It had already accounted for Tunnadine. If she disobeyed orders, Rhoda knew that she could be the next victim. At any other time, a visit to Dublin would have excited her but she left the vessel with dread in her heart. What caused her most anxiety was that she and Imogen were kept apart. Cullen hustled her into a cab and they were taken to a nearby hotel with the luggage. When he booked two rooms, her hopes rose slightly. She was to be reunited with Imogen, after all. They could offer each other solace.

Instead, she was conducted to a room at the top of the hotel and pushed into it by Cullen. The first thing he did was to drag her across to the window.

'The most beautiful city in the world is out there, Rhoda,' he said, beaming, 'but don't even think of exploring it by trying to run away again. It's a very long way down to the ground, as you can see. You'd be dead as soon as you hit the pavement.'

'Where are the others?'

'You just worry about yourself.'

'I want to know where Miss Imogen is.'

'She disappeared the moment we boarded the vessel,' he said with a smile. 'She's Mrs Whiteside now and she'll soon be entertaining her husband in the room next door. You'll stay here until your own husband is ready for you.' He bared his teeth. 'Goodbye, Mrs Cullen.'

'Stay away from me,' she cried.

'Now that's not the way to start our honeymoon, is it?' he taunted.

After letting himself out, he locked the door behind him. Rhoda could hear his laughter echoing along the corridor. She went back to the window and looked down. Cullen was right. There was no escape. Rhoda was trapped.

Miraculously, the swell seemed to drop, the wind lost its bite and the vessel was able to sail on an even keel. Though the sea was by no means calm, it no longer rocked their steam packet so violently. Even someone as unsettled as Victor Leeming felt the urge to go up on deck and sample the fresh air. Colbeck and Madeleine were already there, standing in the stern and watching the posse of gulls that had trailed them from Holyhead. Momentarily, they felt as if they were setting off on a holiday but the sensation then vanished. They were in pursuit of two dangerous men and that ruled out any possibility of leisure or enjoyment.

'What are Irish railways like?' she asked.

'You may well have the chance to find out, Madeleine.'

'You travelled on them before, didn't you?'

'Yes,' he said. 'The system is nowhere near as complex as the one we know but, then again, it's not so absurdly cluttered. While we have far too many railway companies, Ireland has too few, but that will change in time.'

'Father thinks that one company should have a complete monopoly.'

'And would that company happen to be the LNWR?'

Madeleine laughed. 'How ever did you guess that?'

'And I daresay that a standard gauge would be compulsory

and your father would have Brunel exiled to the most distant part of the British Empire.'

Chatting happily, they walked arm in arm beside the bulwark until Colbeck saw something out of the corner of his eye. He kept up the same unvarying pace as they walked past the saloon.

'Wait here,' he said, drawing her aside.

'Where are you going, Robert?'

'I'll tell you in a moment.'

Doubling back, he used the crowded deck as a means of moving unseen towards the stern, ducking and dodging as he moved along. Dozens of people were standing at the bulwark, gazing out to sea. Leeming was one of them but Colbeck left him where he was. The person who interested him was sauntering along with a cigar in his mouth. When he drew level, Colbeck clamped a hand on his shoulder.

'I thought I recognised you, Kee.'

'Good day to you, Inspector,' said the other, amiably.

'You followed us.'

'That's not true at all. I've always wanted to visit Ireland.'

'Don't lie to me,' said Colbeck. 'You'd never have tracked them on your own so you sneaked after us. You're not part of this investigation.'

'I ought to be,' argued Kee. 'Tunnadine was not the most pleasant man to work for but he paid me handsomely. I owe it to him to catch his killer.'

'You owed it to us to give an honest account of his death.'

'That's what I gave you, Inspector.'

'Not quite,' said Colbeck. 'I felt that the facts had been doctored slightly and so did Sergeant Dean. If you followed us to Crewe, you'll know that I went off to the police station. The sergeant was an astute man. Because you told him exactly where Mr Tunnadine had been shot, he rode out there to examine the site and he noticed a lacuna in your story.'

'I gave you both a truthful report.'

'Then you are a poor strategist. You obviously learnt nothing from your time at Scotland Yard. Why hide in a ditch when the hedge on the other side of the field would have served your purpose far better?'

Alban Kee was about to rely on bluff but he knew that it would have no effect.

'Very well,' he admitted, 'perhaps I did make one slight change to the story. I was hiding behind the hedge when someone clubbed me from behind.' He removed his hat. 'I had a lump the size of an egg. You can still see it.'

'Yes, I can,' said Colbeck. 'It serves you right for not looking over your shoulder. Count yourself lucky that your attacker didn't finish you off there and then. Tunnadine didn't pay you to tell lies.'

'He paid me to protect him and I failed.' Kee replaced his hat gingerly. 'Use me, Inspector. Every investigation needs another pair of hands.'

'Yours are tainted, Kee. They've taken too many bribes.'

'Never listen to false rumours.'

'Never defy Superintendent Tallis,' warned Colbeck. 'He said categorically that you were not involved in this case. When we reach port, I'm putting you on the first vessel back to North Wales. If you resist, I'll report you to the superintendent on my return.'

Kee smirked. 'Two can play at that game.'

'What do you mean?'

'If you report me for interfering in an investigation,' said the other, 'then I'll report you for recruiting your wife as a detective. That *is* Mrs Colbeck, isn't it? You and she seem very close.' He chortled. 'What is it to be? Do I stay and help you or does Tallis hear that you've dared to employ a woman?'

Colbeck was cornered. He knew only too well what the superintendent would say if he found out the truth. Colbeck's own position at Scotland Yard would be in doubt. The very notion of a female detective was an abomination to Tallis.

Kee smirked again. 'It looks as if you have another assistant,' he said, chirpily. 'Why don't you introduce me to Mrs Colbeck? She and I are two of a kind. Officially, neither of us actually exists.'

Imogen Burnhope was panic-stricken. In crossing the Irish Sea, she'd been taken further and further away from the possibility of rescue. She'd also been deprived of the company of her maid. Yet protest had no effect on her captor. Whiteside had her completely under his control and she could do nothing. She was horrified when they reached the hotel and she was taken off to the bedroom booked by Cullen for them. Whiteside had stolen her heart, betrayed her, kidnapped her and tricked her father out of an immense sum of money. Even more alarming was the fact that he'd let Cullen shoot the man to whom she'd been engaged. Imogen had lost almost everything – her freedom, her family, her maid, her friends and her trust in human nature. All that she had left to forfeit was her virginity and the thought petrified her.

The irony was that she'd been more than ready to yield it up in the marriage bed to the man who now led her into the hotel room. But there was no wedding and the person she'd adored was now both hated and feared. Hands on hips, Whiteside studied her with a proprietorial smile.

'You're all mine now, Mrs Whiteside.'

'I'm not your wife and never will be,' she retorted.

'That's not what you said in your letters,' he reminded her. 'You wanted to be Juliet to my Romeo, a passionate woman who defies her family to run off with the man she loves and marry in secret. Well, here I am, and unlike Romeo, I won't be taking poison to give the impression that I'm dead. I'm very much alive, Imogen, as you'll soon find out.'

'I want to see Rhoda.'

'She's rather preoccupied with Manus.'

'What's he doing with her?'

'I daresay that he's thinking about consummating the marriage – not that he and your maid are actually married, of course, but he'll overlook that. Manus is very accommodating in such situations.' When he stroked her hair, she backed away at once. 'There's nowhere to run. Why not surrender graciously?'

'I don't want you anywhere near me, Terence.'

'Your letters told a different story.'

'That was because I was beguiled. You used Shakespeare to ensnare me.'

'Yes,' he said, happily, 'the Bard was a very useful accomplice. I've long admired his work, you see. Before I joined the army, I worked as an actor for a while and took part in some of Shakespeare's plays. It was an education.

Once you've learnt the lines, you never forget them. Once you fall under the spell of the sonnets, you want to pass on their magic, as I did to you.'

'That was cruel and despicable of you.'

'It may seem so at the moment, Imogen. When you get to know me properly, you realise that I'm the charming and devoted swain that you took me for at the start. I courted you and conquered you, remember.' He opened the door. 'By the time I come back, I expect you to have accepted that.'

Victor Leeming was angry that Kee had followed them and manipulated himself into the investigation. The situation was irremediable, however, so he agreed to work with the private detective. Earlier in their careers, the two men had got on well. It was only when Kee was corrupted that the two fell out. There was professional rivalry at stake. Having been on the track of the kidnappers from the very start, Leeming expected Colbeck and himself to be instrumental in the arrest. They had put in the long, taxing days of pursuit. He didn't want Kee to steal their thunder.

Madeleine disliked their new assistant from the outset. He seemed too glib and devious for her taste. It was evident that he wanted to be the one to catch the fugitives and claim the credit. Colbeck decided to forget their past differences and exploit the man's skills. By working for Tunnadine, he'd earned a place in the investigation and was eager. The blow delivered by Cullen had wounded Kee's head and his pride. He wanted revenge, always a powerful incentive.

When the ship docked, they were among the first to disembark. Colbeck had already given them their orders.

Having spoken to the captain of the vessel, he'd learnt the names of the best hotels in Dublin and deployed his men accordingly. Leeming was sent off in one direction with a shortlist of names while Kee went to check out hotels in the opposite direction. Colbeck and Madeleine would work their way through a third list. He stressed that nobody was to tackle the kidnappers on his own. If they were discovered, he was to alert the others when they met at an agreed location at the heart of the city.

Leeming went off with resolute strides but Kee fairly scampered away.

'I don't like him, Robert,' said Madeleine. 'He's too sly.'

'Since I'm landed with him, I have to use him.'

'I'm glad you didn't send them off together. Victor obviously detests him.'

'Yes, Kee is an unprepossessing individual,' said Colbeck, sighing. 'He's also a potential weakness, which is why I hope we find the kidnappers first.'

'I don't understand,' she said.

'Captain Whiteside and his accomplice have never seen us. We have the advantage of surprise. Alban Kee doesn't. He was knocked unconscious by Sergeant Cullen. If he turns up at their hotel, he might be recognised.'

Sir Marcus Burnhope was under immense strain. Expecting to be contacted by the kidnappers yet again, he kept going to the window in the library and peering out. The rest of them were there but, in the tense atmosphere, nobody dared to speak. Percy Vaughan was seated beside his aunt so that she could draw strength from his presence. A nervous Emma was on the sofa, flanked by her parents. Vaughan was looking enviously around the shelves and Cassandra, for once, was silent, her effervescence sapped by the seriousness of the situation. When Sir Marcus was at rest, the only sound in the room was the methodical ticking of the ormolu clock on the marble mantelpiece. When it chimed on the hour, they were all startled.

Without any of the detectives, Sir Marcus felt bereft. Tallis was in London but the whereabouts of Colbeck and Leeming were unknown. It left Sir Marcus feeling isolated. If a ransom demand did come, he wanted someone there to advise him. It irked him to think he might have to pay the kidnappers twice yet he'd do so if it would ensure his daughter's release. Hands behind his back, he did a circuit of the library, impervious to the others. He was about to return to his seat when he heard hoof beats approaching the house at speed. As he darted to the window, he found Dominic Vaughan beside him, equally anxious to see who the newcomer was. A figure in uniform galloped up to the front of the house and reined in his horse before dismounting.

'Stay here,' said Sir Marcus, heading for the door.

The others waited for several minutes before he returned. Desperate for news, they were all on their feet at once. He waved a piece of paper in the air.

'This was sent to the telegraph station at Shrub Hill,' he announced. 'It's a message from Superintendent Tallis.'

'What does it say?' croaked his wife.

'Inspector Colbeck has gone to Ireland.'

Cassandra voiced the general dismay. 'What is Imogen doing *there*?'

* * *

366

The loss of Rhoda Wills was a devastating blow to Imogen. The woman had been both friend and fellow prisoner, sharing the same privations and doing her best to keep their morale high. It was thanks to Rhoda that they'd attempted to escape and, even though they'd failed, they had the satisfaction of knowing that they'd done something positive instead of just meekly waiting to see what would happen to them. Their punishment had been separation. Together, they could support each other; apart, they were powerless. When she stood at the window of her hotel room, Imogen looked down on pretty rows of Georgian houses with a pleasing symmetry. People were hurrying to and fro on foot or by cab. While they were enjoying the precious gift of freedom, Imogen was locked away, dreading the moment when Terence Whiteside would return to claim his prize. She was in purgatory.

Whiteside was in the hotel bar, savouring a celebratory drink with Cullen. They sat in a quiet corner and congratulated themselves on their achievement. Their haul was big enough to keep both of them in a state of prosperity for the rest of their lives, with the added bonus – at least in the short term – of an attractive mistress for each of them. Cullen was practical.

'How long do we keep them?'

'They can stay until we tire of them, Manus.'

'Then what happens? We can hardly let them go now.'

'Don't worry about that,' said Whiteside. 'Enjoy what we have to the full before we think of getting rid of it. Before that, of course, we can divide the spoils.'

'What about the jewellery?'

'That belongs to Imogen.'

'I think we should have half each.'

'Then you're very much mistaken.'

'I've seen it,' said Cullen. 'It's worth a fortune. I'm not going to miss out on my share of that. All right,' he went on, sensing his friend's hostility, 'let her keep it as long as she's with us but, when we dispose of her, it's a different story.'

'Don't get too greedy,' said Whiteside.

'And don't you get too forgetful. Fifty-fifty was the split we agreed and you've already reneged on that, Terence.'

'No, I haven't.'

'Then take a look at the ladies side by side. You get the real beauty and I have to make do with the other one. That's not fifty-fifty,' he joked. 'By rights, we ought to take it in turns with Sir Marcus's daughter.'

'She's all mine,' warned Whiteside, picking up his glass, 'and so is her jewellery for the time being. Bear that in mind, Manus.'

While they discussed their plans and enjoyed their drink, they were both thinking about what awaited them upstairs. Whiteside was patient but Cullen's mind kept drifting. In the end, he excused himself and sauntered out of the bar on his way to an enforced tryst with Rhoda Wills. Seconds later, he was back.

'Terence,' he said, sitting beside him, 'he's out there.'

'Who is?'

'It's that detective I knocked out in Crewe. He's *followed* us. We haven't escaped, after all.'

'Calm down, calm down,' said Whiteside. 'Is the fellow alone?'

'He seemed to be.'

'Then there's nothing to worry about. If he was hiding behind that hedge, he may have seen me but not you.'

'That's true. He won't know me from Adam.'

Whiteside stood up. 'What was he doing?'

'He was talking to the manager.'

'Get out there and keep an eye on him,' said the other, easing him towards the door. 'I'll sneak off upstairs. Let me know what he does and how you think we should react. Remind me of his name.'

'Alban Kee.'

Kee had done it so many times before that he was an old hand. When he'd asked for information about hotel guests, managers had invariably become indignant and told him that it was against their policy to disclose details of any kind to strangers. All that Kee had to do was to slip some banknotes into the manager's palm and the hotel register was suddenly open to him. He felt a glow of triumph when he saw the name of Terence Whiteside, ostensibly travelling with his wife. In the next room, Manus Cullen was staying with Mrs Cullen. Kee was thrilled. Those were the names given to him by Colbeck. He'd found the kidnappers.

His orders were to go to the meeting place and await the others. Since the guests were booked in, they would not be going anywhere. Kee could come back with reinforcements and the arrests could be made. On the other hand, if he caught both men himself, he could bask in the glory. After seeing such a display of courage and enterprise, Tallis was bound to have him back in Scotland Yard. Kee would not only have proved his mettle, he would have outshone

Robert Colbeck at last. There would be a substantial reward from Sir Marcus Burnhope and the kind of lavish praise in the newspapers that he had always sought.

The decision was made. They were his.

Colbeck was getting both restive and annoyed with himself. He and Madeleine had been waiting for some time in Sackville Street, the grand thoroughfare that ran through the middle of Dublin, lending a grace and elegance that was reminiscent of towns like Bath and Cheltenham. The street was wide enough to allow a carriage and four horses to turn in a circle and there was a bright cleanliness about the city that would put most of the districts of London to shame. Leeming had been to the four hotels on his list without success. Colbeck and Madeleine had visited the same number.

'Where is he?' asked Leeming, irritably. 'He only had three on his list.'

'Well, it's not because he was slow,' said Madeleine. 'When he left here, he went off like a greyhound.'

'I blame myself,' said Colbeck, looking in vain down the street. 'I shouldn't have left him alone. I thought we could cover the hotels more quickly if we split up.'

'Do you remember the places where he went?'

'Yes, Madeleine.'

'What was the last one on the list?'

He took out a sheet of paper and checked it. 'The Belvedere,' he said.

Alban Kee was careful. He familiarised himself with the geography of the hotel so that he knew where all the exits were. His first target was Manus Cullen. According to Colbeck, it was Terence Whiteside who'd been there on two occasions to take the ransom from Sir Marcus. It was reasonable to expect that he'd done the same with Tunnadine. Because he was lying unconscious behind a hedge, Kee never had the opportunity to take a long look at Whiteside but if the latter did confront Tunnadine, then the man who clubbed the detective to the ground had to be Cullen. As he recalled the blow, Kee's whole skull throbbed. It was time for retribution.

He ducked into a space beneath the main staircase so that he could check and load his gun before thrusting it into the holster under his coat. Hat in hand, he went up the stairs to the room where Cullen and his wife were apparently staying. First, he listened at the door but could hear neither voices nor movement inside. When he tried knocking, he got no response yet sensed that somebody was in the room. He knocked harder and stood back. Someone came up the stairs and saw him.

'Good day to you, sir,' said Cullen, genially. 'May I help you?'

'I was just calling on a friend but he doesn't seem to be there.'

'Is he a good friend of yours, sir?'

'As a matter of fact, he is.'

'Then I daresay you'd like to give him a pleasant surprise. My name is Peter O'Malley and I'm the deputy manager. If you can guarantee that you are what you say you are, then I'll be happy to use my pass key to let you in.'

Reassured by the sound of an Irish voice, Kee invented a plausible tale about his putative friendship with the very man standing next to him. By way of showing his credentials, he added all kinds of details.

'Hold on, sir,' said Cullen, laughing. 'That's enough. I'm convinced that you're the gentleman's friend. In we go.' Producing the key, he inserted it in the lock and turned it. He opened the door and stood back to let Kee enter the room first, going in after him. 'There you are, sir. Your friend will be delighted to see you.'

Kee was staring at the woman who'd jumped up from her chair in alarm.

'Who are you?' he asked.

'My name is Rhoda Wills, sir.'

'I've been looking for you.'

'Then you've found her at last,' said Cullen.

Kee hadn't realised that the man was standing directly behind him. Hand on his gun, he swung round but he was no match for the Irishman. Cullen had already taken out a long-bladed knife and he thrust it between Kee's ribs with shuddering force. When the detective fell against him, Cullen lowered him gently to the ground and watched the blood staining his victim's shirt and waistcoat. Rhoda drew back against the wall in horror with a hand over her eyes. Cullen put an arm round her and held the blade close to her face.

'One word out of you and it will be *your* blood on this knife next.' Tearing the coverlet off the bed, he threw it over the dead body and grinned. 'He'd only himself to blame,' he said. 'He was a private detective hired by Tunnadine and he'd never learnt to watch his back. This is the result.'

Cullen went out again and locked the door behind him.

He walked over to Whiteside's room and banged on the door with a fist. It was opened instantly.

'What's happened?' asked Whiteside.

'I had to kill him. We need to leave.'

When they reached the Belvedere Hotel, Colbeck went inside with Madeleine and left Victor Leeming outside. The sergeant found a position from which he could watch the front and side exits. He kept his back against a brick wall so that he could not be surprised from behind. The hotel was popular. Cabs arrived at regular intervals to drop off or pick up customers at the main door. Leeming felt certain that Alban Kee had found out something and decided to keep it to himself. Unlike the sergeant, he had no loyalty to Colbeck. Indeed, he would seek any opportunity presented to him to get his own back against a man involved in his dismissal from Scotland Yard. Bringing Kee into the investigation had been a mistake in Leeming's opinion. Lives were at risk. In a case as dangerous as this one, absolute trust between the detectives was required.

As soon as he revealed his identity, Colbeck gained the manager's trust. He was told that Whiteside and Cullen had checked into the hotel with their respective wives. The manager also mentioned that someone else had shown great interest in the guests. His description of the man confirmed that it was Alban Kee. After taking note of the relevant room numbers, Colbeck sent Madeleine outside to warn Leeming that their quarry was in the hotel. Colbeck went upstairs. It was a long climb but he ran up the steps as fast as he could, stopping when he reached the top landing so that he could catch his breath. He then went to the room occupied by Whiteside. There was no need to knock because the door was slightly ajar. Inside the room was evidence of a swift departure with a few items of abandoned clothing and a small, empty valise on the floor. Rushing to the window, he looked out but all he could see was Leeming maintaining his patient vigil with Madeleine at his side.

Colbeck went to the adjacent door, only to find it locked. When he looked through the keyhole, however, he saw something that riveted him fleetingly to the spot. The coverlet was on the floor hiding something beneath it. One foot protruded. Colbeck had the eerie sensation that he was looking at Alban Kee's shoe. His first instinct was to alert the manager to what had happened but there was a more pressing need. The kidnappers were making a run for it. Pursuit was a priority. Having come up the main staircase, he knew that they hadn't descended that way. He searched the corridors until he found the backstairs then shot down them three at a time.

Imogen and Rhoda had taken the same route at a much slower pace. Holding their skirts up with one hand, they clattered down the uncarpeted stairs. Whiteside and Cullen were behind them, struggling with the luggage because they didn't wish to let the hotel staff know that they were quitting the building. It meant that the two women had a chance for a whispered conversation.

'He was stabbed to death right in front of me,' said Rhoda, still shaking.

'Who was he?'

'He was hired by Mr Tunnadine, apparently.'

Hopes flickered. 'You mean that he was a detective?'

'Yes, he came searching for us.'

'Then others may also be hunting for us, Rhoda.'

When they reached the bottom of the stairs, Whiteside barked an order.

'Open that door for us and stand aside!'

Leeming was the first to see them. Having left by the rear exit, they came round the side of the building where he and Madeleine were standing. Cullen led the way, bent double by the weight of the trunk on his shoulder. Whiteside was next with the lighter luggage while Imogen and Rhoda were close behind him. Since they were carrying nothing, it would have been easy for the two women to dash away but the look of terror in their eyes explained why they didn't dare to do so. When he reached the front of the hotel, Cullen lowered the trunk to the ground and hailed a cab. As it rolled into position, Leeming made his move, hiding behind the cab as he crept towards them. It was Cullen who failed to watch his back this time. Turning to pick up the trunk, he was suddenly tackled by Leeming and brought to the ground with a thud. Before he could grab his gun or his knife, Cullen was pounded with heavy punches then lifted by the scruff of the neck and hurled against the wall of the hotel with such force that he was dazed. Leeming already had his handcuffs out.

Whiteside had been taken by surprise but reacted quickly. He pulled out his pistol and aimed it at the sergeant, only to have his arm knocked sharply upwards by Colbeck who'd come hurtling around the corner. There was a deafening report as the gun went off but the bullet went harmlessly in the air. Madeleine didn't wish to be left out of the action. During the commotion, she rushed forward and grabbed Imogen by the wrist, pulling her away and beckoning for Rhoda to follow. The two women were only too glad to get away from the violent struggle. They cowered in a doorway on the other side of the road and watched the drama unfold.

Leeming had handcuffed Cullen and disarmed him, earning a mouthful of abuse for his trouble. Blood dripping down his face, the Irishman was kicking out wildly. Dodging his foot, Leeming caught hold of it and pulled hard so that Cullen pitched forward onto the pavement, banging his head yet again. Whiteside, however, was more difficult to overpower. Though his gun had been ripped away from him, he had teak-hard fists. He grappled with Colbeck, trying everything he could to shake him off, punching, stamping, lifting, using his knees and spitting into the inspector's face. Colbeck clung on until he was bitten hard on the neck. The pain made him release his hold and Whiteside ran off, snatching up a valise and using it to knock Leeming backwards with a vicious swing when the latter tried to intercept him. The kidnapper hared across the road and ran towards the cab rank further down the street.

Colbeck was after him like a beagle sighting a fox. The bite on the neck had drawn blood that was staining his cravat. It infuriated him. Sprinting across the road, he lengthened his stride and began to make ground on his adversary. When he realised that he was going to be caught, Whiteside turned to face him. He was panting heavily and sensed that he'd met his match. Trying a different tactic, he patted the valise.

'I've got thousands of pounds in here, my friend,' he

said, opening it and taking out a handful of banknotes. 'Let me go and you get a decent share of it.'

'That money belongs to Sir Marcus Burnhope and Clive Tunnadine. I'm here to retrieve it and to rescue the hostages.'

'What kind of man turns down an offer like that?'

'One who's come to arrest you for all manner of crimes,' said Colbeck, stoutly. 'The army would love to have you but we have first claim on you now.'

When he moved forward, Colbeck had to duck beneath the flailing valise. Whiteside made another wild attempt to get to the cab rank but he soon had some additional baggage to hamper him. Colbeck had jumped on his back and got an arm around his neck, applying so much pressure that the man could hardly breathe. The valise was heavy but Whiteside was loath to part with the huge ransom he'd collected from two sources. He staggered on a few more yards before his legs buckled. Colbeck gave him no chance to bite this time. As Whiteside pitched forward onto the ground, Colbeck grabbed his hair and banged his head repeatedly on the pavement. All the strength drained out of him and his grip was eventually so weak that he had to let go of the fortune he'd amassed.

Madeleine had watched it all from the other side of the road with the two hostages. Imogen was both elated and worried, delighted to be free at last, yet fearing that the architect of their misery would get away. Though the violence turned her stomach, she had nothing but praise for the determined way in which Whiteside had been caught, subdued and handcuffed.

'That was wonderful,' she said. 'Who is that man?'

'It's my husband,' replied Madeleine, proudly. 'He's Inspector Colbeck of Scotland Yard. We've come to take you home.'

When the two prisoners had been installed in separate cells in Dublin police station, Colbeck was able to visit a doctor to have his wound examined. He was less worried about his neck than he was about the damage to one of his favourite cravats. After medical treatment, he returned to the Belvedere hotel where he informed the manager that there was a corpse in one of his rooms on the top floor. He remained until an undertaker was summoned and the body of Alban Kee was taken away, then he joined the others. Since it was necessary to stay the night in Dublin, he'd suggested another hotel because the Belvedere held too many grisly memories for the hostages.

Throwing her arms around him, Madeleine gave him a warm welcome.

'How are you feeling now, Robert?'

'I've collected a few bruises,' he said, 'but they'll soon fade. What about the ladies? Have they settled in?'

'Yes, they have. After being kept apart by the kidnappers, they chose to share a room. They've been able to wash and change out of the clothing they've worn for days. Rhoda said it was the first time she felt really clean.'

'What about all that money?'

'Victor had it put in the hotel safe,' she said. 'He counted it out so that he could get a receipt for the amount and said there was enough in that valise to buy this hotel and several others. It was very brave of him to take on Cullen.'

'He had the sense to know that I'd be able to come to his aid very soon. I'm afraid that Alban Kee didn't have the advantage of a partner. He sought to arrest both men on his own and it was a fatal decision.'

'At least he won't be able to tell the superintendent about me.'

'I'd much rather have had Kee alive and keeping to his promise of saying nothing. There'll be a wife and family back in London who'll have to cope with some tragic news.' He brightened. 'You've really come into your own now that the hostages are liberated. They warmed to you immediately,' he said with a smile, 'and I remember doing exactly the same when we first met. However, I'll postpone my thanks until a more fitting time. We must concentrate on the two ladies now. They need care and compassion.'

The evening began slowly. Rhoda Wills was embarrassed to be dining at the same table as the others and Imogen Burnhope was still adjusting to the notion that the nightmare was finally over. As the meal progressed, however, they both relaxed. It was Leeming who chose the moment to shift the conversation to their kidnap.

'What exactly happened?' he asked.

'We're too ashamed to tell you,' said Imogen. 'It was our own fault, really.'

'The inspector thought that Captain Whiteside had persuaded you to leave the train in disguise at Oxford station.'

'It's true. We were coaxed into a trap.'

'They were so nice to us at first,' recalled Rhoda, 'but

they soon changed. Once we became their prisoners, it was terrifying.'

'You don't have to tell us the full story,' said Colbeck. 'Some of it is best forgotten, I fancy. We're just grateful that you're both safe and well. You can go back to Burnhope Manor and return to your old lives.'

Imogen was distressed. 'But we can't do that, Inspector,' she said, forlornly. 'What will they think of us when they learn that we actually ran away? I can see that it was madness now but the fact remains that I fled my entire family.'

'Why spoil the homecoming by telling them that? They'll be so overjoyed to see you again that they will doubtless spoil you. Let them do just that,' urged Colbeck. 'Say nothing about why you left and simply celebrate the joy of being back.'

'Are you advising us to tell lies?' asked Rhoda, shocked.

'I'm suggesting that you hold back some of the truth.'

'It's the kindest thing you can do in the circumstances,' said Madeleine. 'Why cause so much hurt when it's in your power not to do so? Why punish yourselves by reliving every moment when you can be spared some of the agony? You made a mistake and you've suffered dreadfully as a result. Do you really want to add to that suffering?'

'Well, no,' said Imogen, thoughtfully. 'We don't.'

'There you are, then,' said Leeming. 'It's all settled.'

'I was brought up to tell the truth,' Rhoda put in.

'Did you tell the truth when you left Burnhope Manor?'

She was cowed. 'No, Sergeant – I didn't.'

'Remember that.'

'None of us can imagine what you endured,' said Madeleine with sympathy. 'It must have been horrendous.

That's all that your parents need to know. They only want their daughter back home again. They don't wish to be told that she ran away. And they'll welcome Rhoda back as well because she helped you through your appalling trial. There's only one question you need to ask.' She put a gentle hand on Imogen's arm. 'Do you *want* to go back to Burnhope Manor?'

'Yes, I do,' said Imogen, smiling.

'And so do I,' added Rhoda.

Edward Tallis was almost jubilant when the telegraph arrived. It had been sent from Holyhead station. By the time that it reached Scotland Yard, his detectives were on their way back to London with two hostages, two prisoners and a coffin containing the body of Alban Kee. Tallis spared his former colleague the tribute of a sigh but his pity was drowned beneath his pleasure. He arranged for a telegraph to Burnhope Manor via Shrub Hill station. It was important for the family to be told the good news as soon as possible.

He was about to reach for a cigar by way of celebration when he remembered another member of the family who'd be waiting for news. After writing a short letter, he sent it off by hand to an artist's studio in Chelsea. George Vaughan had as much right as the others to know that all was well at last.

Uniformed policemen were waiting at Euston station to take the prisoners away and a porter wheeled in the long box used for transporting a coffin without attracting too much attention from travellers milling around. After bidding the hostages a fond farewell, Madeleine left the train to return home. Colbeck and Leeming escorted the others to Paddington where they caught a train to Oxford and changed to the OWWR. Being back on a line that was their escape route was a chastening experience for Imogen and Rhoda. Having left with high hopes, they were going back with shattered dreams. When they got to Shrub Hill, the landau was waiting with Sir Marcus standing beside it. Imogen ran to his arms and he embraced her warmly but the detectives were touched by another reunion. Rhoda Wills took one look at Vernon Tolley then flung herself gratefully into the coachman's arms. He was her future now. She would not imperil it by admitting that she'd once run away from him.

Sir Marcus insisted on taking Colbeck and Leeming back to the house so that everyone could congratulate them. The welcome was extraordinary. The entire staff was waiting outside the front door. As the hostages walked between the two lines, they were given enthusiastic applause. The only person not clapping was Win Eagleton. She had lost Tolley for good now.

As the front door opened, they saw everyone was standing in the hall. Paulina needed to use Cassandra for support but it was not to her mother that Imogen instinctively ran. It was the Reverend Percy Vaughan who found her inexplicably in his arms. Colbeck and Leeming were amused at his expression of mingled perplexity and sheer delight.

Everyone wanted to shake the hands of the detectives and tell them what a remarkable job they'd done. Colbeck and Leeming let the praise ooze all over them. It was Sir Marcus who sidled up to them for a quiet word.

'You did manage to retrieve *all* my money, didn't you?' he asked.

* * *

On their return to London, they had to deliver their report to the superintendent. As soon as that was done, Leeming went home to his wife and family while Colbeck caught a cab to the house in John Islip Street. Madeleine wanted to hear all about the reception they'd had in Worcestershire and was surprised to learn of the way Imogen had first turned to her cousin.

'He's a curate,' she said. 'You told me that he was intense and scholarly. He's the complete opposite of an intrepid soldier like Captain Whiteside. A man who wears a cassock can hardly compete with one in a bright-red uniform.'

'Oh, I think he'll compete very well, Madeleine. Besides, Whiteside was no soldier. He was a deserter who exploited an impressionable young lady. Percy Vaughan will never do that. That's why his cousin turned to him. There's no doubt in my mind that she made the right choice this time.' He cocked his head to one side. 'Which would you prefer – soldier or curate?'

'I'd like someone with the courage of one and the compassion of the other.'

'Do you think that such a man exists?'

'I know he does,' she said with a smile. 'I married him.'

The rest of the conversation took place elsewhere.